Never Look Back

Susan Lewis is the internationally bestselling author of over fifty sensational novels across the genres of family drama, thriller, suspense, crime and romance – including the Richard and Judy picks *One Minute Later*, *I Have Something to Tell You* and *Don't Believe A Word*. She is also the author of *Just One More Day* and *One Day at a Time*, the moving memoirs of her childhood in Bristol during the 1960s. Following periods of living in Los Angeles, the South of France and the Cotswolds, she currently lives in Somerset with her husband, James, and their beloved, naughty little dog, Mimi.

To find out more about Susan Lewis:

www.susanlewis.com
/SusanLewisBooks
@susanlewisbooks
@susanlewisbooks
@susanlewisbooks

Also by Susan Lewis

SUSAN
LEWIS

NEVER
LOOK BACK

HarperCollins*Publishers*

HarperCollins*Publishers* Ltd
1 London Bridge Street,
London SE1 9GF

www.harpercollins.co.uk

HarperCollins*Publishers*
Macken House, 39/40 Mayor Street Upper
Dublin 1, D01 C9W8, Ireland

First published by HarperCollins*Publishers* Ltd 2025
1

A catalogue record for this book is available from the British Library.

ISBN: 978-0-00-873420-6 (HB)
ISBN: 978-0-00-873421-3 (TPB)

This novel is entirely a work of fiction. The names, characters and incidents portrayed in it are the work of the author's imagination. Any resemblance to actual persons, living or dead, events or localities is entirely coincidental.

Set in Sabon LT Std by HarperCollins*Publishers* India

Printed and bound in the UK using 100%
Renewable Electricity at CPI Group (UK) Ltd

MIX
Paper | Supporting
responsible forestry
FSC
www.fsc.org
FSC™ C007454

This book contains FSC™ certified paper and other controlled sources to ensure responsible forest management.

For more information visit: www.harpercollins.co.uk/green

To my dear Cotswolds friends,
Charles and Emma Howeson
Sue and David Wethey

Prologue

'I think, my love, that I might have come up with a way out of the unfortunate situation we're in.'

Rudi Kaplan had uttered the words softly, rhythmically, making them sound like part of a song. His wife, Romy Kaplan, looked up from the notebook she was writing in, and her heart skipped a beat as she watched him leave the piano. He'd spent the past half an hour there, playing some of the gently haunting tunes he'd composed in recent times. They were meant to soothe him, as her writings were meant to soothe her, and they did in their way, but the spectre of what was happening to them never truly went away, not even for a minute.

As their eyes met, Romy's were already shining with hope and trust. She had so much faith in him that she sometimes feared it might be more of a burden to him than a blessing. He would insist, of course, that everything about her was a blessing, that the best thing he'd ever done in his life was marry her, over forty years ago, but she couldn't help fearing that the terrible events that had taken them over were weighing more heavily on him because of her.

Casting a quick glance over her shoulder to where his eyes were now directed, she saw that he was staring at their portraits, hanging side-by-side over the dining table. In their elaborate gilt frames, they were too large for this tiny cottage, but there they were, and his, to her mind, was a true work of art. Whenever she assessed them as a pair, she felt that his had been created by a superior hand to the one that had created her own, but it hadn't. The same artist had done both, taking a lot of time to get to know them first, encouraging them to share stories of their lives together, their dreams for the future. In the end, the capturing of Rudi's charm and irony, the soulfulness in his deep-brown eyes, the enlivening hints of him as a younger man, made Romy love the painting almost as much as its subject.

Hers was – different. Like her, and yet not, as though the artist hadn't quite seen her, or had maybe tried to turn her into someone else. The woman depicted certainly had Romy's naturally high cheekbones, full-lipped smile and silver-blonde hair styled in a wispy sort of bob, but even Rudi, who professed to adore the painting, agreed that the playful light in her luminous violet eyes wasn't quite there. Nor was the infectious energy she exuded, or the natural vivacity that drew people to her; the crafted contours of her slender face made it appear more oval than heart-shaped, even a little harder than she was in reality.

'My love,' he murmured softly, looking at her now as he reached for her hand.

She smiled and put aside her notebook and pen. Even after all these years, the romance in him could cause her heartbeat to quicken, and his voice, at least to her ears, remained as hypnotically melodic as it had ever been. Everyone had always loved it when he sang – folk, jazz, even opera – but he hadn't done much public singing lately.

'The idea came to me a couple of weeks ago,' he told her softly, as though afraid of being overheard. 'I've been thinking it through, and now I feel ready to share.'

Knowing how protective he was of her, how hard he tried never to trouble her with something until he'd worked out a way to handle it, she said, gently, 'Would you like a brandy to sip while you tell me?'

Clearly loving how easily she read him, he said, 'Yes, and perhaps we'll take it outside, over to the lake?'

It was something they often did: enjoy a twilight pick-me-up at the water's edge, no more than a dozen steps from their front gate. With the sun shimmering its last rays over the surrounding valley slopes before disappearing behind the hill, it always felt the perfect place to end the day. Sometimes, they'd put on music and dance, cheek-to-cheek, Rudi crooning softly in her ear. Neighbours from the smattering of nearby cottages would occasionally join them, bringing their own cocktails, music and chitchat. A truly lovely group of new, dear friends who'd made this tucked-away lakeside enclave their home. Some were their age, others younger. No children, which was a shame; Romy had always loved children and was sad never to have had any of her own.

Rudi took himself off to 'their bench', almost hidden amongst a cluster of yellow irises and milfoil, carrying jumpers and blankets in case it turned cold. It was still early March, after all. As Romy watched him from the kitchen window, she reflected, as she often did, on how fortunate they were to have found this place at the heart of a meandering and leafy vale with no one to bother them much or to ask too many questions. It was very different to what they'd had before, of course, but it didn't matter; what really counted was that they had one another and were no longer in danger of doing harm to anyone.

'You two are so much fun,' their new neighbours often told them. 'You really know how to enjoy life. We didn't get together much before you came, hardly even knew one another. And you're a fabulous cook, Romy. All your exotic recipes, and Rudi's stories . . . As farfetched as fairy tales, but no less fascinating for that. The places you've visited. The things you've done.'

Feeling a wave of nostalgia approaching, a current of memories bent on carrying her away from the moment,

Romy stepped out of the tide and waved cheerily to Nula Higgins, their neighbour from two doors down, as she went chugging past in her old VW Polo. Romy often walked with Nula and her dog, climbing stiles and wooded hillsides up to the common where cattle had priority over traffic and winds blew in from afar.

She knew she should head outside, but she was nervous about what Rudi might have to say. She mustn't let herself hope that there was any real way out of their situation, however hope was hard to suppress.

Satisfied that Rudi was settled, his wispy hair being gently tossed by a wayward breeze, she turned to survey the room behind her, taking a moment to remember what she was supposed to be doing. This little home of theirs was so quaint and old, with its wooden beams criss-crossing the sloping ceiling, a red-brick fireplace in the sitting area and awkwardly fitting French doors that opened onto a back patio and lawn. There were dozens of photographs and books around the place, along with special mementoes from all over the world and plenty more still in boxes in the spare bedroom. Squashed in under the stairs was Rudi's mother's roll-top desk that served as their office, while the treasured piano sat wedged into a small alcove at the far end of the dining table. Two antiquated chintz sofas flanked the hearth, where Rudi's daily fire was turning to ash. He liked it to remain lit, no matter the weather, so she went to stoke things up with a poker and dropped on a log.

Ah yes, drinks – and she'd take out some nibbles as well.

As she stooped to open a kitchen cabinet, she found herself falling into the trap of paranoia that so often dogged them these days. It was as though they were being sucked back into a dark and distant past, to a time when they'd known beyond doubt that they were being watched and listened to. It was a time when the world had been a very different place to what it was now. And they had been different people.

Today, when the feeling and fear of another presence came over them, they escaped by going to their bench, especially when they had something important to say about 'the situation'.

After filling a tray with glasses and small bowls of nuts and olives, she spotted Rudi's mobile on the windowsill and decided to leave her own next to it. They wouldn't need them this evening. If anyone called, they could always leave a message. Much better that they had the time to themselves, without interruption.

A few minutes later, with everything set out between them, Rudi tapped his glass to hers and said quietly, 'Here's what I think we should do.'

Romy was hardly daring to breathe. Was there really a way out of the dreadful position they were in?

'I think we should contact Cristy Ward,' he told her.

She blinked in surprise, several times. She knew the name, of course; everyone did – more than that, she'd once known Cristy's mother, someone she'd thought about often over the years, but never as much as these past few months. Had they ever actually met Cristy? They'd come across so many people in their lives, but Romy couldn't immediately recall ever having been introduced to the well-known podcaster.

'Layla could probably put us in touch,' he said, seeming to pick up on her concern.

Her eyes widened slightly as she realized this was true. Her goddaughter, Layla, had worked with Cristy Ward a few years ago when they were both in TV.

'I think Cristy Ward will help us,' Rudi declared decisively.

It didn't take Romy long to see why he thought that, or to agree that he could be right. There was no need for her to consider it more thoroughly; he'd already done that, or he wouldn't have mentioned it.

'But would she want to?' she countered cautiously.

'We won't know unless we ask.'

This was true: they wouldn't, and Romy would be all for it were she not now thinking of the risk involved. They were only enduring this to protect those they loved, and what had already been done to them and others could also be done to Cristy Ward.

'We don't want her to get hurt,' Romy said worriedly. 'And she'd have to . . . How much do you think we can tell her?'

'I'm not sure about that,' he admitted, 'but maybe we should talk to her, without going into *all* the detail, and let her decide if she wants to get involved. If she doesn't, or if we think we've made the wrong decision . . . well, we can just leave the meeting and come home again.'

Romy nodded slowly. Cristy did seem like a good choice of person to go to, for all sorts of reasons, mostly to do with her mother.

'Do you think Layla would set something up?' Rudi asked.

Certain Layla would, if she asked, Romy said, 'She's in Dubai, remember, but that doesn't matter. The question is, how do we stop her mentioning it to her mother when they're next in touch? Beth's already worried enough about us; I don't want to add to it.'

Beth was Romy's best friend of almost sixty years; they were as close as sisters, maybe even closer than that.

Rudi sipped his drink and stared thoughtfully out at the water, where shadows of fish skittered about in the darkness and tiny bubbles of air broke the surface. They seemed to Romy to embody all their memories, their fears, everything they needed to keep hidden that just kept rising up again.

'How was Beth when you spoke to her earlier?' Rudi asked.

'Actually, she sounded quite good. The effects of the last chemo have started to wear off. She's looking forward to our trip.'

He smiled. 'It'll do you some good to get away for a few days too,' he said. 'Is Johnny planning on joining you?'

6

'I don't think he can, but you know we'd love it if you came.'

'No, no, this is for you and Beth, some time together in your happy place while she recuperates and recharges. I'll stay here and keep thinking.'

'Good idea,' she whispered, leaning over to kiss him. 'I'll miss you while I'm gone.'

'I'll miss you too,' he said and kissed her back.

CHAPTER ONE

'Wait! What?' Cristy exclaimed, having to stop Layla to make sure she'd heard right. 'They're dead? Both of them?' She really hadn't seen that coming, or had she just not been paying proper attention? A quick glance at her podcast cohost, Connor Church, told her that he'd been equally as blindsided.

'No, no, Rudi's dead,' Layla Cates hastily corrected, 'but Romy . . . Well, that's why I'm here. We've no idea where she is.'

'So he died, and she disappeared?' Cristy said. 'At the same time?'

'No, he died back in March, the 21st to be precise, and the last time anyone saw her was six weeks later, on 7th May, so just about a month ago.'

As she took this in, Cristy regarded Layla intently, trying to remember how long it had been since she'd last seen her. It surely had to be six or seven years when Layla had briefly worked as an intern at the TV studios where Cristy had been a senior-editor with Connor leading her research team. These days, following Cristy's break up with her husband who continued to exec-produce and present the news, she and Connor ran a successful true crime podcast.

So, Layla, must surely be around thirty by now, and was, according to the email she'd sent out of the blue last week, based in Dubai. However, she was here today, at the

Hindsight production office on Bristol's Harbourside, lovelier than ever with her flame-red hair and topaz-blue eyes, and seeming to exude an air of confidence that had to be admired considering her not-so-well-hidden distress.

Responding to the clear sense of urgency in Layla's tone, Cristy said, 'Maybe let's slow things down for a moment. When you say that Rudi Kaplan, your godfather, is dead. How exactly did he die?'

'Actually, Rudi's not my godparent,' Layla corrected, grief clearly etched across her face, 'but he – he drowned in the bath.'

Cristy blinked. 'An accident?'

'Maybe. The post-mortem showed that he'd had quite a bit to drink, which wasn't unusual for him, but . . . well, it wasn't straightforward. There were some marks around his neck and on his arms that could have been consistent with some kind of a struggle.'

'Is that what the autopsy said?' Connor asked.

'I think so, but the coroner's ruling was accidental death.'

'Where was Romy when it happened?' Cristy asked.

'In Portugal with my mum,' Layla said. 'They've always been best friends, you see, and we own a townhouse there. Rudi was alone in the cottage, and when he didn't answer his phone for a couple of days, Mum and Romy flew back to make sure he was all right. Romy found him . . . You can probably imagine how awful it was for her. They think he'd been in the bath for four days by then.'

Shying from the thought of it, Cristy asked, 'Was anyone with her when she went in?'

'My mother was downstairs. She'd driven them both from the airport. I was in Dubai but I flew back as soon as I could arrange time off. Poor Romy was in a dreadful state. They were very close, her and Rudi, true soul mates, and the fact that there were a few days when the police were saying it might not have been an accident only made things worse.'

9

'And you think her disappearance now has something to do with his death?'

Layla frowned. 'I suppose so. It's all so complicated.'

'Did Romy believe the death was an accident?' Connor asked.

Layla pulled a face. 'It's hard to say for certain. Sometimes she seemed to, other times not. My mother could tell you more about that, because she was there at the time. All I know is that they decided in the end that the injuries had been caused earlier by him getting caught up in something while swimming in the lake opposite their house. According to the neighbours, he'd swum that day.'

'And this was back in March?' Cristy asked.

Layla nodded.

Connor said, 'And now, almost two months later, Romy has vanished?'

'That's it. As I said, they were very close. We couldn't imagine how she was going to cope without him, but she seemed to be managing, at least in the early weeks. Then . . . this. She left her home suddenly. No one's seen her in six weeks. She's been posting on Facebook, but it's all a bit weird, not really like her. Mum and I are so worried. We've tried getting in touch, but Romy's phone is always switched off. I flew in a couple of days ago and went straight to her cottage to try and find out what was going on, but there was no sign of her or her car. I asked her neighbours if they'd seen her, but they haven't, and they're worried too.' Her voice cracked. 'I just don't know what to think . . .'

Pushing his dark framed glasses higher on his nose, Connor said, 'And now you're hoping we'll help you to find her?'

Layla's troubled eyes left his and moved back to Cristy. 'And maybe some answers about Rudi?' she dared to venture.

'When did your mother last see her?' Cristy asked.

Layla sighed. 'She thinks it was a couple of weeks after Rudi's funeral. My mum hasn't been well, so . . . Anyway, she'd been trying to spend time with her before the cancer returned, but Romy kept insisting she was all right, that she could cope on her own. As Dad says, they're as bad as one another when it comes to not wanting to be a burden, so they end up not seeing one another when there's probably no one they want to lean on more. I just don't understand why she hasn't been in touch . . . I know it's been a difficult past year for Romy, with Mum's illness, Rudi's death – and even before that, when they lost the big house and moved to where they are now.' Her voice trembled. 'Or were until recently.'

As there was a lot to unpack there, Cristy asked, 'Have you spoken to the police about Romy's disappearance?'

Layla swallowed hard. 'They're not interested. As far as they see it, Romy is a perfectly healthy woman of sound mind and body who has a history of impulsive travelling – but that was when Rudi was alive . . .'

'So what do you think might have happened to her?' Connor prompted.

Layla shook her head helplessly, and reaching into her bag, she pulled out a single sheet of paper. 'I wanted to show you this. . . '

Taking it, Cristy read the printed email and looked at Layla again.

'"*Can you give me a number for Cristy Ward?*"' Layla quoted aloud. '"*There is something R and I would like to discuss with her. Let's keep it as our secret for now.*"'

'When did she send it?' Cristy asked, searching for the date.

'That's the thing,' Layla replied, looking pained. 'It must've gone into my junk folder. I found this printout at the cottage, dated 11th March. Ten days before Rudi died.'

Cristy was frowning hard now. This really wasn't making much sense. 'You said she's still posting on Facebook?'

Layla nodded quickly. 'She's posted a couple of little videos of herself in the past few weeks – since she disappeared from her cottage – saying she's having the best time and no one should worry about her, that she'll be back soon.'

Cristy's eyes widened. No wonder the police wouldn't engage. 'But if she's telling you she's all right . . .'

'That's the trouble: she might be saying she is, but why isn't she answering her phone? Where is she? And *when* is she intending to come back?'

Cristy glanced at Connor, hoping he might have something useful to say.

'It's a mystery,' he confirmed uselessly.

Repressing an eyeroll, Cristy said, 'I'm afraid we're not private detectives; we're podcasters reporting on the facts of *crimes* . . .'

'I appreciate that,' Layla interrupted hastily, 'but I thought, given she wanted to contact you . . .'

Stepping in, Connor said, 'Do you have a particular reason to think that something . . . *unusual* might have happened to her?'

Layla gave an uneasy laugh. 'There was a time when almost everything about Romy's life was unusual . . . She and Rudi were truly free spirits, and a bit . . . unconventional, I suppose. Not in a bad way – they were the sweetest, kindest, most fun people you could ever wish to meet. My parents always described them as innocents abroad, and I think that sums them up perfectly. Everyone loved being around them, and their house – when they were at the manor – was always full of friends from far and wide . . . They probably didn't even know half of them, or had met them on some trip or another . . . Talk about welcoming . . . No one ever got turned away, or not that I knew of, and my mother can't remember it either. She and Romy have been best friends since school, so they've known one another a very long time.'

'Maybe she's just decided to take some space for a while,' Connor said gently. 'People do, sometimes, when they're grieving. And if her videos are telling you she's OK . . .'

Layla almost groaned. 'That's more or less what the police said, but Romy's not like that. Honestly. She's always so considerate of other people's feelings. She really isn't someone who'd just ignore our messages when we're saying we're worried about her.'

'So there are no responses at all?' Cristy asked.

Layla shook her head. She looked close to tears by now. 'Only to say she's fine and having a good time and we must stop worrying because there's really no need to.'

'When was the last time you saw her?' Connor asked gently.

'I came back for a few days at Easter.'

'How did she seem then?' Cristy asked.

'Calmer than she'd been after the funeral, on the surface, at least. She wouldn't have wanted anyone to know she was grieving, but of course she was. How could she not be, when so little time had passed?'

'Can I ask how old she is?' Cristy said.

'Sixty-six, same as my mother, and she's never had any health issues, unlike Mum, which is what also makes her disappearance concerning. For her not to even ask how Mum is when she knows the cancer came back . . . Well, I don't care what she's saying on Facebook – it just doesn't make any sense.'

'Maybe we should take a look at the posts?' Connor suggested.

Layla nodded quickly, took out her iPad and clicked through to Romy's page. 'Here's the first,' she said, and turned the screen so Cristy and Connor could view the playback.

Cristy watched closely as the static image of an attractive older woman with silvery fair hair and an exquisite heart-shaped face came to life. 'Hello, my lovely friends,' she said, her voice soft and warm, 'just wanted to let you know that I'm fine. Actually, I'm feeling better than I have in quite a while. It's good to be away, no reminders here, so please

13

don't worry about me. I'll keep in touch and be sure to let you know as soon as I'm coming back.'

As the reel ended, Layla clicked on to the next. This time, Romy's hair was twisted into a messy knot at the top of her head, and she was wearing sunglasses. She began by saluting the camera with a glass of white wine. 'Bottoms up, everyone. Hope you're all lovely and well. I'm missing you and wish you were here living *la dolce vita* with me, but I'll be back before you know it and we can raise a glass or two together.' She blew a kiss, and the image froze on her pursed lips.

Connor looked up at Layla. 'Any thoughts on who could have been holding the camera?'

'I've wondered that, but it could be anyone, a waiter, someone in her tour group, if she's on a tour, one of her many friends we know nothing about . . .'

'Do you recognize either of the locations?' Cristy wanted to know.

'I don't think so. The backgrounds aren't very clear . . .'

Connor exchanged a glance with Cristy. 'We could get Jacks to take a look? He's *Hindsight's* resident tech genius,' he explained to Layla, 'but he's hiking in Peru at the moment, not due in again until the week after next.'

'I realize,' Layla said, 'that if we had more to go on, something concrete to say she's . . . not in a good place, or someone suspicious was seen the day Rudi drowned, it would be easier to run with. But we're still left with the question of where she is now, and why she just up and left without telling anyone where she was going, or when she'd be back. Or why she and Rudi wanted to talk to you.' Layla took a deep breath, clearly trying to hold back her emotions. 'Look, I'm not expecting you to make a decision right away. I understand you're going to need some time to discuss it, and maybe there's nothing you can do but . . .'

Cristy's eyes found Connor's, and she could see he was

already on board for this, in spite of the many other projects they were currently reviewing for the next series.

She turned to Layla. 'OK, why don't you send us over the details, what you know, who you've spoken to and anything else you think might be important? You have my email address.'

'Thank you so much,' said Layla. There were tears in her eyes now, threatening to spill out. 'I'm so grateful. It's just, we've all been so worried, and—' Her voice cracked.

As Layla turned away to hide her tears, Cristy said gently, 'Why don't we go for a coffee before you go – on the waterfront? Help you calm down a bit?'

Layla nodded miserably, and after a glance back at Connor, Cristy led Layla to the door.

CHAPTER TWO

Ten minutes later, Cristy was carrying two drinks to a table outside the Harbourside Kitchen.

It was a lovely early June day with dazzling patches of sunlight reflecting on the water and the welcome scent of summer in the air. Although it was not weekend-busy, there were still plenty of tourists queuing up to visit the SS *Great Britain*, grandly contained in its exclusive dry-dock right behind the café, and many more waiting to board the cross-harbour ferry. It was always enjoyable being here on a sunny day, watching the world float or stroll past, while the sounds of seagulls, laughter and nearby construction work created its own kind of symphony. Bristol was Cristy's home, and this small, cobbled square only steps away from Quinn Studios where *Hindsight* was based, was as familiar to her as the leafy courtyard outside her apartment complex at the other end of the harbour.

'Thank you,' said Layla, as Cristy set the coffees down. 'Sorry for getting upset before. It's just, between Mum's cancer, Rudi's death and Romy disappearing like this . . . I'm on furlough from work for the next few months, to help look after Mum, so there's not much distraction and I'm just . . . struggling a bit.'

'I'm sorry you've been having a tough time,' said Cristy gently.

'Thanks.' Layla shook her head, as though to push away

the difficult thoughts. 'It's lovely here, isn't it?' She sighed, raising her faintly freckled face towards the sun. 'My parents used to bring us here a lot when we were young. Not that it was like this then, no cafés or brand-new apartment blocks with waterfront views, but Brunel's masterpiece has always been a big draw.' She blushed slightly as she looked at Cristy. 'Of course, you know that; you're from Bristol too, aren't you?'

'That's right. My parents used to bring me here too.' Of course, it would have been quite a lot longer ago than Layla was referring to. 'Where does your family live?'

'Just outside of Pensford, which I think isn't too far from where you grew up?'

Cristy said, 'We were in Chew Stoke.'

Layla smiled. 'It's strange, seeing you again after all these years,' she said. 'How have you been? How are the children? I was sorry to hear you and Matthew had split up.'

Cristy shrugged. Although it had been one of the most devastating times of her life, it mercifully felt like a long time ago now. Her ex-husband had married again – although with his wife Marley and their baby son in the US, and Matthew still in the UK, Cristy didn't think the marriage would necessarily last. Not that it was any of her business. Although they were good friends these days, they'd both moved on. 'The children are well,' she said, smiling. 'Aiden's doing his GCSEs now, and Hayley's away at university.'

'And I heard you met someone else?'

Cristy crooked an eyebrow.

'I read about it,' Layla explained. 'It was in all the papers and online when you and David first got together.'

Cristy couldn't deny that it had been, but thankfully the world had found other things to get excited about since she and David Gaudion, the suspected killer featured in *Nothing to See Here – Hindsight's* deep dive into a triple-murder just over a year ago – had become an item. This meant they were no longer the object of lurid and crazy scrutiny, were simply enjoying a relationship that was coming to mean more and more to her as time went on. Not that it was without its complications with Cristy being firmly based in Bristol, while David was over in Guernsey, but when they were together, none of that mattered.

Taking a sip of her drink, Layla said, 'I understand why you might not be keen to help me get to the bottom of whatever's happened to Romy. Why would you even care about her when, according to her, she's having the time of her life somewhere and doesn't want to come home? But if you knew her like I do . . .'

'Then tell me more about her,' Cristy said.

Layla's smile filled with fondness, as if she were about to embark on one of her favourite subjects. 'Well, she's one of those people that everyone immediately loves. You know the type: she never has a bad word to say about anyone and always looks on the bright side even when there really isn't one. Rudi was the same; it's how come they had so many friends. Hangers on, some might call them, but they'd never have thought it themselves. They just loved life and people, and nothing ever seemed to faze them. Apart from Rudi dying so suddenly – that was really hard for Romy.'

'And you couldn't be sure whether she accepted it was an accident?'

'To be honest, I don't think she did believe it, but being the way she is, she didn't want to make a fuss or upset anyone . . .'

'Who would she have upset?'

Layla shrugged and shook her head. 'The police? She wouldn't want to take up their time when they had so many more important things to be dealing with. That's how she'd have seen it. She'd also have been worried about Mum. And there were the neighbours – these days they live somewhere called Bellbrook, a secluded and close-knit little hamlet a few miles from Tetbury, and Romy was afraid the press and lots more police might descend on them and ruin their peace and quiet, never mind their gardens. I know it probably sounds bonkers to you, that she'd put everyone else first when Rudi had died, but that's a perfect example of who she is. She's always been overly concerned about everyone else, to a degree that can make you quite . . . impatient with her at times.'

Knowing the type, Cristy took a sip of coffee as she said, 'So let's start with Rudi. Do you have any theories on who might have wanted to harm him?'

'I'm afraid none of us do. I'm including my parents and brother in that, because we've discussed it at length. We just feel that something's not right – not so much about Rudi's death; we'd have probably accepted it was an accident if it weren't for the way Romy reacted to it. One day, she was certain Rudi would never have been so careless as to fall asleep drunk in the bath; the next, she was saying it had happened before so it was an accident that had found its time. It ended up with her telling us to let things alone and say prayers for him.'

As Cristy assessed this, she turned to gaze across the harbour, where a wedding couple was being photographed on the bow of a highly decorated barge.

'I've sent everything to the police,' Layla told her, 'but so far no one's got back to me.'

'That'll be because she's making a point of telling you that she's absolutely fine and she'll be in touch when she's ready to come home,' Cristy pointed out.

Layla seemed to deflate as she stared down at her coffee.

'Look,' Cristy said, 'I'm sure you know the statistics, but just in case: someone is reported missing every ninety seconds here in the UK. A hundred and seventy thousand people disappear every year—'

'And a good proportion of them don't want to be found,' Layla interjected. 'I got all that on day one when I went to the police, and I understand their reluctance to take it any further – I really do. Who in their right minds is going to believe that what she's actually doing in those posts is calling out for help?'

Cristy's eyes widened with interest. 'How do you come to that conclusion?'

'Mum is certain of it.'

Cristy waited. There had to be more than that.

Layla shrugged. 'OK, I realize you can't see or hear it when you watch the reels, but that's how we're reading them. Incidentally, Mum would be here now if she could, but she's undergoing more chemo at the moment and today isn't a good day.' Before Cristy could respond, she continued, 'If you're going to turn me down, then please recommend a good private detective. I'm sure you must know someone . . .'

Cristy raised a hand. 'As a matter of fact, I don't,' she said, 'but I can tell you this: it's clear to me that Connor wants to help you, and as we still haven't committed to a new series for the autumn yet, it's possible we could look into it for you.'

Layla gasped as her eyes flooded with tears. 'Do you mean it?' she cried, clutching her hands to her face. 'I mean, I know you wouldn't say it if you didn't . . .'

'Remind me how long she's been gone?'

'A month.'

'Definitely not long enough to overexcite the authorities, even without the videos, but leave it with me, and either Connor or I will get back to you as soon as we've gone through your notes and discussed them with the rest of the team.'

CHAPTER THREE

'Has anyone got hold of Rudi Kaplan's autopsy report yet?'
Harry Quinn asked, making himself comfortable on the
production office sofa next to his wife, Meena, who shifted
along to make room.

Meena was as proud of her Indian heritage as she was
dismissive of her beauty, and as good a friend to Cristy as
Cristy had ever needed. As co-owners of the podcast studios –
also ex-colleagues of Cristy's and Connor's from back in their
TV days – the Quinns regularly attended *Hindsight* meetings,
especially when something new was on the horizon. Not that
a decision had been taken about this particular case yet, but
as the business and finance brains behind operations, their
input was always valued, even if they weren't members of the
core investigative team.

'I emailed the coroner's office this morning,' Connor told
him, attaching blow-ups of Rudi and Romy's headshots
(provided by Layla) to the whiteboard they used for their
projects.

In hers, Romy was laughing into the camera, appearing
delighted about something, and came across as the kind of
woman who would be a lot of fun to know. Rudi's shot
was arresting and, in a way, intriguing, given his intensely
watchful expression and barely suppressed amusement.
Yes, Cristy thought, she'd probably like to know him too –

although she had to admit her judgement was probably currently being influenced by what she'd heard about them from Layla, who clearly adored them. She only had to consider how she'd viewed David Gaudion, the subject of *Hindsight's* first major podcast, when she'd first seen him – as the brutal killer of three - then she'd probably be more mindful of how misleading looks, and other people's opinions, could be once the complexities of truth were revealed.

'Haven't heard back yet,' Connor added. 'It could be that the request will have to come from a relative. We'll see.'

As he stood back to assess the photographs, Cristy felt the poignancy of the board's stark emptiness beneath the childless couple, making them seem, at this early stage, as if they were . . . adrift? Was that what she was thinking?

'Did Rudi have any other family besides Romy?' Clover asked, apparently sharing Cristy's thoughts. With her colourful character and equally as colourful beaded hair, Clover St Jean was one of the series' senior researchers, alongside Jackson Caine, their tech expert.

'Layla's pretty certain there isn't anyone,' Cristy told her. 'The problem we're up against, if we go ahead with this, is twofold: first, Romy could walk back through the door at any minute and we'll have wasted our time; secondly, if she doesn't, we've got absolutely no way of tracking her. Her phone is permanently switched off, apart from when she's posting apparently, and no banks, phone companies or internet providers are going to share anything with us.'

'So how will you take things forward?' Harry wanted to know.

'It's highly likely we won't be able to, but for some reason, that's making me even more determined to test what we do know. Without Jacks digging into the tech side of things, we're still limited, but Clove's been studying the responses to Romy's Facebook videos and . . .' She gestured for Clove to take over.

'It's clear,' Clove began, bunching her hair behind her head as she read from her screen, 'that Layla and her parents aren't the only ones who are worried about Romy. There are quite a few responses to her posts. Here's one from a friend called Jenny who, according to her profile, lives in Lyon: *"Salut, chérie, looking good as ever. Glad you're having a great time, but really need to talk. Please call me back."* I sent a direct message to Jenny,' Clove continued, 'and to others who've posted similar comments, and every reply I've had so far has echoed what Layla told us, that it just isn't like Romy to go off without a word and not to call back when someone asks her to.'

'What about texts or WhatsApps, that sort of thing?' Harry asked. 'Or the comments on Facebook – is she responding to any of them?'

'Yes, occasionally, there are messages where she follows up with things like, *lots to tell when I'm back,* or *do you remember when we were in Greece together,* or *thanks for the book recommendation, loving it.* Nothing specific about where she is or what she's doing, apart from, as she says, having a good time.'

'Is she on any other social media?' Meena asked.

'She had an Insta account for a while, but it hasn't been used for a couple of years. Layla says she's always been more comfortable with Facebook – same goes for a lot of people her age.'

'Does *anyone* have any theories as to where she might be, or what could have happened to her?' Meena persisted. 'I mean, if something has.'

'They're all mystified,' Clove replied, 'and worried. Have a listen to this voice note I got in response to one of my messages.'

She hit play on her computer and sat back as the recording began.

CALLER: 'It's Theo Crush here, old friend of Rudi and Romy. I got your message asking if I've seen or heard from Romy since I posted on her Facebook page. I haven't, and it's been a while now. This is quite out of character for her, and considering what she's been through, I am becoming increasingly afraid – yes, afraid – for her well-being.'

Frowning, Harry said, 'Have you spoken to this guy?'

'We've been trying to get hold of him since yesterday,' Cristy assured him, 'but he's either not picking up or he just hasn't got our voicemails yet.'

'According to his Facebook profile,' Clove continued, 'he deals in eighteenth- and nineteenth-century musical instruments and is based in Vienna.' She shrugged. 'Just thought I'd throw that in. Not sure how, or if, it's relevant.'

'Any details about his friendship with Rudi and Romy?' Cristy asked. 'Photos of them together, that sort of thing?'

'Yes, a couple that look as though they were taken at his shop on Stallburggasse – guess that's the street – and one of them with Crush and his wife – presume it's his wife – at a concert, but I haven't gone very deep yet. Here's another "old friend" who rang me back. She's someone I did have a chat with, and she agreed to me recording the call, so here goes. Her name's Hester McInlay, by the way.'

HESTER: 'Please don't let anyone try to tell you that dear Romy has gone doolally or has tried to harm herself. It's true she was devastated by Rudi's passing, and maybe even a little unhinged by it, but who wouldn't be considering how close they were and everything that's happened to her. She never believed his death was an accident, no matter what she told everyone else, and if you ask me, she knows who did it. Maybe they've come for her now.'

Meena's eyes widened as she turned them to Cristy. Cristy nodded for her to continue listening.

CLOVER: 'Can you be more explicit about who "they" might be?'

HESTER: 'I can't name names, if that's what you're asking, but I do know that something . . . *sinister* went on around the time they left the manor. Romy told me so herself . . . "We have to do this, Hestie," she said, "it's the only way to stop them going after everyone else."'

CLOVER: 'Did she explain that?'

HESTER: 'No. She didn't want to talk about it again, and if I tried, she kept insisting I'd misunderstood what she'd said.'

CLOVER: 'Did Rudi ever mention anything similar?'

HESTER: 'No, but I wasn't quite as close with him as I was with her. Dear man. My husband, Richard, performed with him a few times, you know. Everyone adored Rudi. He was good enough to be a professional; everyone said so. I think he considered it once in a while – he did so enjoy being on stage – but in the end, he couldn't be bothered with the routine and discipline of it all. They didn't like constraints, him and Romy. It's what set them apart from the rest of us. Singing and dancing – that's what made their world go round. Of course, having a lot of money helped.

'Anyway, if you're interested in finding out where Romy

is – and I hope you are, because someone should be – you might want to look into what really happened to Rudi. As I said, I don't know anything for certain, but it could give you some clues.'

'And that,' Connor said, as Clove stopped the recording, 'is when I contacted the coroner's office.'

'So you're already putting a podcast together on this?' Meena said. 'Given the recordings?'

'We're just gathering material at the moment,' Cristy replied. 'We're not sure there's a series in it – how can we be when she could turn up at any time? Anyway, I rang Hester McInlay back myself, and she told me that she and her husband felt sure it was some bad investments on Rudi's part that resulted in them having to leave the manor.'

'Which was when?' Harry asked.

Clove checked Layla's notes. 'September last year.'

'Any detail about the investments?'

'We don't even know if they were a thing,' Cristy pointed out. 'But something else Hester said, which both she and Layla's mother appear to agree on, is that Romy and Rudi weren't themselves over the summer before leaving the manor. Apparently, they always threw at least three or four parties – July Fourth, Bastille Day, Rudi's birthday – but last year, there was only Romy's birthday celebration at the beginning of May. Nothing after that.'

'According to Hester,' Clove continued, 'they didn't go on holiday anywhere, they were at the manor the whole time until the end of September, and on the one occasion when Hester and her husband did go over, they got the impression Rudi and Romy were eager for them to leave. It was really strange, Hester said – Rudi kept putting a finger to his lips, kind of shushing them, and Romy was constantly looking over her shoulder as if she thought someone was following her.'

'I'm hoping to talk to Layla's mother, Beth, in the next couple of days,' Cristy picked up. 'She and Romy have known one another forever, and apparently Beth's keen to talk to me as soon as she's up to it. She's having a bad reaction to her latest bout of chemo.'

'Poor thing,' Meena murmured. 'Having been there, my heart goes out to her.'

Reaching out to squeeze Meena's hand, Harry looked at Cristy as he said, 'It's your decision, obviously, but if you want my thoughts on this . . . You'll be as aware as anyone that if you end up uncovering something . . . "sinister" or actually criminal, the police will take it straight off your hands. So where's that going to leave you if you're mid-series by then?'

'If we get to a point,' Connor answered, 'where we think Romy could be in danger, or has even gone past that point – and I think we all know what I mean by that – obviously we'll take it straight to the police. Until then, I don't see any harm in helping Layla and her family get to the bottom of what's really going on.'

Meena was looking worried. 'So it could be a live investigation as opposed to the retelling of a cold case? Is that really how you want to proceed?'

'The last two series have had really strong elements of breaking news about them,' Connor reminded her defensively, 'so, if there is anything to this, it could fit right in.'

Clearly sensing the kickback, Harry said, 'Just think about it before you fully commit.' He clocked the way Cristy and Connor exchanged glances and added, 'Unless there's something you haven't yet told us about?'

'You have sponsors,' Meena pointed out, when neither of them answered. 'I know you don't welcome any sort of outside interference, but if you want a decent budget, they matter.'

Cutting Connor off before he got annoyed, Cristy said, a

little too sweetly, 'Thanks for the reminder, Meena. We both realize that it would be hard to produce anything the way we do without the sponsors. And equally as important to us is the support we know we can always rely on from you and Harry.'

CHAPTER FOUR

A few days later, Connor and Cristy left the M4 at junction eighteen and headed towards the sleepy little hamlet of Bellbrook, buried deep in the hallowed Cotswolds. Connor was driving, so Cristy took a moment to absorb the glorious spectacle of sun-drenched fields stretching all the way out to far horizons, with the occasional glimpse of farms and livestock breaking into the patchwork. There was a reason why this part of the country was so desirable; it was simply and quietly stunning.

Several minutes later, after turning off at a quaint market town to continue the journey, she began recording.

CRISTY: 'OK, we left the main road a while ago, and we're now in a wooded valley with a river running alongside us . . . It's gorgeous, shady and peaceful, dappled sunlight, tangles of wildflowers . . . Every now and then, we pass a sign to a farm, or the gated entry to a private estate . . . There was a time when some very wealthy merchants had their homes around here – think textiles, grain, metals. No idea who lives in these properties now. More likely hedge fund managers or rock stars . . . And royalty, of course.'

CONNOR: 'Ah, here's the humpback bridge Layla mentioned, and just past it, parked in a lay-by, we find an Amazon delivery truck trying to blend with nature.'

Laughing, Cristy turned off the recorder and sighed luxuriously. 'This really does feel like the middle of nowhere,' she commented, loving the towering avenue of old oaks they were passing along, with silvery bands of sunlight streaming through the branches like magical touches. 'And yet it can't be more than six or seven minutes since we left the main road. Ah, I've just spotted a lake – over there, through the trees. Layla said to look out for it and then we should take the next turning right.'

Changing down a gear, Connor stifled another yawn as he said, 'Sorry, up half the night with the baby.'

'Well, you do want her to have teeth, don't you?' Cristy responded dryly.

With a groan, he drove slowly along a narrow, hedge-lined road, until they shuddered over a cattle-grid and found themselves at the edge of a truly dreamy rural idyll. The lake, glittering blackly and enticingly in the late morning sun, was to their right, while a smattering of picture-book cottages, a couple of converted barns and an old water mill basked in the lee of the wooded hill to their left. On the opposite bank were more woods climbing densely and steeply to the skyline.

'You have to photograph it for the website,' Cristy told him. 'I know we're not posting anything yet, but this just has to be seen to be believed. It's utter paradise.' She thought about that and added, 'Or it could be spooky as hell when the mist is down and night's drawing in.'

'Well, it's definitely the right place,' Connor told her and nodded towards Layla as she came out of the closest cottage to wave them forward.

'You found it!' she cried, rushing to open Cristy's door and looking, for a moment, as though she might hug her.

'Are you OK?' Cristy asked, noticing Layla's bloodshot eyes.

Layla laughed awkwardly and pushed back her hair. 'Yes, I'm fine,' she said. 'Just relieved you're here, and, as you can see, a bit emotional . . . Idiot that I am, I was hoping to find her inside when I let myself in just now. I was even gearing myself up to apologize for wasting your time, but . . . there's still no sign of her.'

'Or of anyone having been inside since you last came?'

Layla shook her head. 'Everything's still as it was when she left. Or I presume it is – nothing looks out of place, and I haven't moved anything myself.'

Putting a comforting hand on her arm, Cristy said, 'Let's go take a look. Maybe we'll find something . . . helpful.'

Accepting Connor's friendly hug as he joined them, Layla said, 'I've been through everything, but by all means look again.'

'Any obvious things missing?' Cristy asked, taking her bag from the car. 'Such as clothes, toothbrush, toiletries?'

'It's impossible to tell with the clothes,' Layla replied. 'The wardrobes seem quite full. Rudi's stuff is still there, and hers . . . I'm not sure anyone would know if I'd taken a few things out of my closet, and I'm not familiar enough with Romy's to make a call. Two toothbrushes in the bathroom, assorted toiletries.

'Anyway, I've put some coffee on, and I brought milk with me, just in case.' Pushing open the small front gate she added, 'I've asked Nula, one of the neighbours, if she'll pop in when she gets back from her walk. As far as we know, she was the last one to see Romy here.'

Cristy's phone rang and seeing it was David, on Facetime, she said, 'Sorry, I need to take this. Shouldn't be long,' and clicking on, she turned towards the lake shore, where a cluster of drooping irises, hairy willowherb and milfoil seemed to be protecting an old wooden bench.

'Hi,' she said tenderly when he appeared on the screen. With his penetrating blue eyes and easy smile, not to mention the two-day stubble she didn't get to see that often . . . Actually, the last time was only a week ago, when he'd popped over to Bristol to spend a couple of nights with her, but it hadn't been long enough, and now here she was, experiencing butterflies as if they were still a brand-new romance when they were a good six months down the line. 'I'm hoping you have good news?' she prompted.

'She's home,' he confirmed. His eldest daughter Rosaria had spent the past couple of days in hospital, being nursed through a horrible bout of flu. Having Down's and an autoimmune condition meant she was particularly vulnerable when it came to viruses, and being so deeply loved by her family and everyone who knew her meant it had been an extremely worrying time. 'We picked her up about an hour ago. Mum's upstairs with her now, trying to coax her into bed – she's having none of it, of course, but my money's on Mum winning, if only because Rosie's still pretty weak.' His mother, Cynthia, had played an invaluable part in helping him to raise his three children, and she continued to run the house with Anna, twenty-seven, coming and going from her flat in St Peter Port, and the girls' half-brother, Laurent, aged twelve, at school on the island.

Sinking down on the bench, Cristy said, 'Please give Rosie my love, and as soon as she's up for it, I'd love to hear from her.'

Dryly, he said, 'I won't tell her that yet, or she'll be straight on the phone. Where are you? I don't think I recognize that background.'

'We've just arrived in the hamlet I told you about . . .'

'Ah, the missing woman who's been posting on Facebook.'

Accepting the irony with a grimace, she said, 'Something like that. It's possible, of course, that she doesn't want to be found, but for the moment, we're going with the chance that something might have happened to her.'

32

'Do you have time to talk me through your theories?'

'As yet, we don't really have any, but we're about to take a look around the house.'

'Then I should let you go. I just wanted to update you on Rosie's progress. And to say that I'm missing you.'

'I'm missing you too.' It was true, she was, and she couldn't actually see how it would change with him living in Guernsey and her based in Bristol. Their time together was too often limited, although maybe made all the more precious by the absences. 'Remind me when you're off to Denmark?'

'Flights are booked for the middle of next week. Laurent's coming.'

'You're taking him out of school?'

'Just this once. I've told him it can't happen again.'

'So it could be a while before I next see you?'

'A couple of weeks, for certain, but I kind of have to do this . . .'

'It's OK,' she laughed, 'I get that it's an annual thing with old friends, salmon fishing and sailing, and it's great that Laurent's going with you.'

'You know I wanted to invite Aiden?'

'I do, and it was wonderful of you to think of my crazy son, but with him being right in the middle of GCSEs I'm truly glad you didn't mention it, or he'd have been there like a shot.'

With a laugh, he said, 'Maybe next year. Anyway, I'll ring off now. Let's catch up again later.'

After the call ended, Cristy sat for a moment, gazing absently out at the lake, feeling her and David's closeness as if it were a tangible presence, right here with her, watching the rippling water, tracking a moorhen with three chicks darting in and out of the ragwort, a pair of swans gliding aimlessly through vivid green patches of weed. What was to become of their relationship, she wondered to herself, taking a moment to glance along the bank to where a magnificent weeping willow was trailing in the shallows. Could they carry on like this, with him firmly entrenched in his beautiful island home, and her not willing to leave Bristol? Why was she even asking herself the question, when the subject of them making a more permanent commitment hadn't even been raised?

Getting to her feet, she was about to turn towards Romy's cottage when she spotted someone getting into a boat on the opposite shore. They were too distant for her to make out anything about them, but when it became apparent they were rowing this way, she gave a friendly wave.

No response.

Assuming she hadn't been seen, Cristy shrugged and turned to go into the cottage.

CHAPTER FIVE

'Everything OK in Guernsey?' Connor asked, glancing over his shoulder as Cristy entered the kitchen. He was standing beside Layla, studying something on a desk in front of them.

'Rosie's home now. Thank goodness.' Cristy immediately noticed the portrait of Rudi hanging behind the dining table. 'This is quite impressive.'

Layla smiled as she saw where Cristy was looking. 'Romy told me she actually swooned when she first saw it,' she said, 'and who can blame her? He was a good-looking man.'

He was indeed. Real film star looks.

'I remember them declaring the artist a genius find,' Layla continued. 'Expensive, but money was never an issue for them. Until, I guess, Rudi made some bad investments and everything changed.'

'Can you tell us any more about that yet?' Cristy asked.

Layla shook her head. 'Only that he always ran his own portfolio, and according to Dad, there were definitely some clangers over the years. Rudi used to tell stories about them, making himself the butt of the joke. The losses never seemed to faze him. I suppose he always thought he could make the money back again. They were super-extravagant, actually insanely generous, so we've been wondering if they just ran out of funds. Whatever the reality, they ended up having to leave the home that had been in Rudi's family for generations.'

'And that was around nine months ago,' Cristy stated, still assessing the painting as if the incredible likeness could somehow provide the answers. 'Isn't there one of Romy?' she asked, looking around the room.

'It's upstairs in the spare bedroom. She never really liked it, so after he'd gone, she moved it.' After pouring a coffee, Layla handed the mug to Cristy, saying, 'Please help yourself to one of the pastries. I picked them up from the bakery in town. They're always very good.'

Deciding she did quite fancy a Danish, Cristy selected the smallest and bit into it as she took a good look round. The place was very homey, full of olde-worlde charm and cosy furniture, with the smoky scent of a long-dead fire hanging lightly in the mote-speckled air. Beams criss-crossed the ceiling, and a small red-brick fireplace was tucked behind a fender. A set of French doors stood open to the back garden, where big, blousy roses climbed over the perimeter wall.

Noting an assortment of photographs along the mantelpiece, Cristy took another sip of coffee and went to study them. She smiled when she found several of Layla from over the years, many with Romy and another woman, presumably Beth, Layla's mother. There were plenty of Rudi and Romy together, either laughing or hugging or standing side-by-side in front of various landmarks from around the world. And on closer inspection, to her surprise, there were some recognizable faces in quite a few.

'They obviously moved in elevated circles,' she remarked, picking up one of the Kaplans with the ex-leader of a French political party, his wife and three other suited men.

Glancing round, Layla smiled as she said, 'There was a time when they got invited just about everywhere from Budapest to Bangkok, Cairo to Canberra. I could continue with the alphabet, but I'm sure you get the drift.'

'How did they know all these people?'

'I guess they started out as friends of friends, meeting at

parties – Rudi was a brilliant networker, and he spoke quite a few languages, so it was never difficult for them to mix. Or to host eclectically interesting dinners. Which they did, often, right up until last May . . . If there was anything after that, we don't know anything about it.'

Cristy moved on to a collage on the wall and stood back to admire the shots of Romy striking various dance poses. Those that were full length showed her to be a slender, graceful woman with a ballerina's poise, while in some, she exuded a very definite ballroom energy. Amusingly, right in the centre, was a shot of Rudi apparently singing his heart out.

Turning back to his portrait, Cristy studied it more closely. There was no mistaking the cultured, urbane sort of air he emanated, while seeming not to take himself too seriously. And yet, as hypnotic as the painting was, she wasn't sure she'd be able to live with an image that was so lifelike and . . . domineering, after he'd gone. Did she mean domineering? She wasn't entirely sure, but there was something about it that seemed to go past the charm to a place she couldn't quite define.

'I don't think we should try again,' Connor declared, stepping back from the desk in the corner. 'We'll just screw things up if we do.'

'What's that?' Cristy asked.

'Romy's laptop,' Layla explained. 'It's password protected, and my two guesses haven't got us anywhere.'

'She didn't take her laptop with her?' Cristy remarked in surprise.

'Jacks could probably get into it,' Connor said, 'if he was around, but maybe we should take it to the office anyway. Clove's pretty savvy when it comes to tech.'

'Does Romy normally leave her laptop behind when she travels?' Cristy asked Layla.

'I'm not sure. I'll text Mum. She'll probably know the answer to that.'

As she sent the message, Cristy continued looking around, not entirely sure what she was hoping to find apart from signs of a hasty exit, maybe, or some kind of struggle, or an orderliness that could suggest a planned departure.

'I haven't come across anything I think might be useful yet,' Layla told her, putting aside her phone, 'but as you can see, there's a lot to go through.'

There certainly was. So much clutter. 'How did you get in the first time you came here to check on her?' Cristy asked, going to sift through a pile of magazines on the coffee table.

'I used Mum's front door key, but it turned out I could have got in the back, because the French doors were open.'

As Cristy's eyebrows rose, Connor said, 'She'd left them open?'

Layla shrugged. 'The lock isn't very reliable. Sometimes they seem closed, but then they just come apart again.' She laughed uneasily. 'It can be a bit scary actually, if you're here alone.'

After going to check for any signs of forced entry and finding none, Cristy said, 'What about post? Presumably there's been some since she left?'

Layla opened up a sideboard drawer and pulled out a bunch of flyers. 'Just these,' she said, passing them over. 'I pick them up each time I come. Actually, I've only been twice, this is the third time . . . Nothing today, and no idea why I've kept those.'

'What about actual letters?' Cristy asked, taking a quick look through. 'I'm thinking bank statements, utility bills, that sort of thing.'

Layla frowned. 'I haven't seen any. Maybe she's gone paperless?'

'There still ought to be something,' Connor commented, looking over Cristy's shoulder. 'And have the bills been paid, I wonder?'

'How would we know if they're on direct debit?' Layla asked.

'We need to take the laptop back to the office with us,' Connor decided, 'see if we can get into it. Even so, we could find ourselves having to call a whole slew of energy suppliers to try and pay a bill for this property. If the address is on their records, we'll know if anything's outstanding or if it's all up to date. It still won't tell us where she is, obviously, but it might give us something.'

Putting the flyers down, Cristy said, 'Is there an answerphone anywhere?'

'Upstairs, next to the bed,' Layla replied. 'I've checked it, and the only messages are either cold calls or friends trying to find out where she is and asking why she isn't getting back to them.'

Cristy said, 'You should make a list of who's been in touch in case we need to contact them. Have you checked the fireplace to see if she might have burned something before she left?'

Connor went to check and as he pulled a charred chocolate wrapper from the ash, Layla gave an anguished sort of laugh.

'She's always loved Snickers,' she said. 'We had a cake made out of them for her sixtieth, and she kept telling us she wasn't going to share it with anyone. She did, of course, and I wouldn't be surprised if she ended up having none of it herself.'

'Hello! Hello!'

They all turned as a stout, late-middle-aged woman with neat grey hair and a waggy-tailed scruff of a dog came into the kitchen.

'Ah, Nula.' Layla smiled, going to her. 'Thanks for coming. This is Cristy and Connor, who I told you about.'

Nula treated them to a frank up and down before holding out a hand to shake. 'I've listened to your podcasts,' she told them brusquely. 'Very good. Yes, very good. Glad you've decided to get on board for this. You are on board, aren't you?'

Connor glanced at Cristy as he said, 'Life vests already fastened . . .'

'We want to help if we can,' Cristy broke in. 'It's nice to meet you, Nula.'

'You can call me Mrs Higgins until we know one another better. Are you going to record this?'

Surprised and amused, Cristy said, 'Would you like us to?'

'It's what you do, isn't it? Why else would you be here?'

Barely disguising a smile, Cristy said, 'Do you have something to tell us you think might be helpful?'

'Well, that's for me to know and you to find out.'

As Connor snorted a laugh, Layla quickly said, 'Will you have a coffee, Nula?'

'Don't mind if I do. And one of them pastries. Did you get them at Hobbs House?'

'I did,' Layla confirmed, and offered her the plate.

'I won't have one then,' and blinking rapidly, Nula plonked herself down at the table, waiting to be served.

'What's wrong with Hobbs House?' Cristy dared to ask.

'Nothing,' Nula replied stiffly.

Choking back a laugh, Cristy said to Connor, 'Why don't you get the gear? I'm sure Mrs Higgins will enjoy being our first interviewee.'

As he went, Nula began blinking again. 'Haven't you recorded Layla yet?' she asked. 'I'd have thought she'd be the first on your list.'

'Actually, she was,' Cristy confirmed. 'We sat down with her yesterday, but you'll be the first witness, so to speak.'

With a harrumph, Nula said, 'I'm not one to push myself forward,' and digging in her bag, she passed the dog a treat. 'Good boy, Busty.'

'Busty?' Cristy echoed.

40

'Short for Buster. I hope you like dogs. Can't be doing with people who don't.'

'They're my favourite,' Cristy assured her, and to Layla, she added, 'While we're waiting for Connor, do you mind if I look in the fridge?'

'Of course not, but there's nothing in it,' Layla told her.

'It was all going off,' Nula informed them, 'so I threw it away. What's the point in keeping rotten food?'

'None,' Cristy assured her, making a mental note of Nula's apparent ease-of-access to the cottage. 'It just might have given us an insight into when she was last here or when she was planning to come back . . .'

'How?'

'Well, without seeing it, it's not easy to say, but if there were long shelf-life items—'

'Have you watered the roses?' Nula asked Layla.

'Not yet, but I will,' Layla promised.

'Don't worry, I can do it. She'll be very upset if no one takes care of them. She was very helpful with my garden when I went to stay with my nephew for a few days in May.'

Exchanging a look with Layla, Cristy said, 'Maybe I can have a quick look round upstairs?'

'She's not up there,' Nula told her. 'I've already checked.'

Cristy wondered how they were going to control this woman and felt the relief of Connor's return. Before Nula could get distracted by anything else, she said, 'Why don't we do your interview now, Mrs Higgins? I'm sure you have other things you need to be getting on with . . .'

'Free all day,' Nula told her, 'but happy to record when you are.' She shot a scowl at Connor that clearly startled him and made Cristy want to laugh.

After running a quick sound check, Connor gave the thumbs-up to begin.

CRISTY: 'If you could start by telling us who you are . . .'

NULA: 'I'm Nula Higgins, Romy's neighbour two doors down, and her friend. We're all friends around here, and that's mostly thanks to Romy and Rudi. They are very sociable people, and I don't mind admitting, hurtful though it is, no one really spoke to me before they came last autumn. I know I have my ways and they don't always suit everyone, but Romy, she *saw* me. That's how they say it now, isn't it? Romy *saw* me.'

CRISTY: 'And would you say that you *saw* her?'

NULA: 'Oh yes, I saw her all right – most days in fact. We walked together with Busty here, and sometimes, if the weather was nice, we'd have a little picnic next to the lake. She always had time for everyone, did Romy, and now, here I am, talking about her in the past tense as if something has happened to her . . .

'Well, I think something has. It must have, because I'm sure she wouldn't just go off without telling me. There's her roses to think of, and she'd promised to do the newsletter for our community mag. She wouldn't let us down over that, not after saying she was happy to take it on. Oh, and there's her job at the giftshop in town. She loves helping out on Fridays and Saturdays. People go in specially to say hello to her. You ask Olivia if I'm not right. She owns the place.'

Turning to Layla, Cristy said, 'Did you know Romy had a job?'

Layla shook her head. 'The first I've heard of it.'

'Well, she did,' Nula informed them tartly. 'And in case you're interested, Olivia at the shop loves dogs.'

Avoiding Connor's eyes, Cristy returned to the recording.

CRISTY: 'Maybe you can talk us through the last time you saw Romy.'

NULA: 'You haven't asked me yet if I thought she had any secrets.'

CRISTY: 'Do you think that?'

NULA: 'No.'

CRISTY: 'So why bring it up?'

NULA: 'Because I never used to, but now I've changed my mind. I think she must have, but whatever they were, they're none of my business.'

CRISTY: 'Did something happen specifically to make you change your mind?'

NULA: 'She disappeared, didn't she? That's when I got to thinking that we never knew all that much about her and Rudi really. I mean, they were newcomers, compared to the rest of us, although they never really felt like that. Right from the get-go, they blended in, making it seem like they'd been here forever. They'd talk about the places they'd been, the adventures they'd had, even some of the people they knew, but apart from Layla here, and her mother, they never seemed to have any friends. Or none who came to visit, anyway. It was like . . . like their past hadn't moved here with them, if you know what I mean, and there's never any escaping it, is there? No matter who you are, or what you might have done.'

CRISTY: 'So you think Rudi and Romy might have been, what . . . ? Running from something?'

NULA: 'I've got no idea. All I can tell you is the last time I saw Rudi, he was getting out of the lake after a swim. And the last time I saw Romy was the day after the King's coronation.'

CRISTY: 'But that was over a year ago.'

NULA: 'True, but the first anniversary was five weeks ago, on the first May bank holiday. We had a little party out front to celebrate. Quentin from next door brought the champagne – he's part-owner of a wine shop in Tetbury – and the rest of us did all the cooking. Romy made scones. I whisked up some vol-au-vents, a speciality of mine. Anyway, I saw her the next morning as I was going past with the dog, she was in the window and gave me a wave. After that she was gone.'

CRISTY: 'So she left later on Tuesday?'

NULA: 'I think so. I noticed her car wasn't there on the Wednesday morning, and it's never come back. So, she could have gone any time on Tuesday evening or Wednesday before I realized the car wasn't in its usual spot.'

CRISTY: 'What kind of car does she drive?'

NULA: 'She's got one of them Smarts, you know, with two seats. She and Rudi loved bombing about the countryside in it. Gave them a proper thrill it did, like a couple of kids in a go-kart. It made me feel a bit sad to see her driving it on her own after he went. She didn't go quite so far or so fast any more.'

Sensing Connor had something to ask, Cristy gestured for him to step in.

CONNOR: 'Did you see anyone coming or going from the house in the days leading up to Romy's disappearance?'

Nula puffed out her cheeks as she thought. Eventually, she shook her head.

44

NULA: 'No one I didn't recognize, no. Strangers stand out a bit around here, so I'd have noticed if there was someone who hadn't been around before. That's if I was looking, of course. I don't see everything that goes on in our little bit of the world. I've got a life, you know.'

CONNOR: 'So someone could have visited her?'

NULA: 'I can't say yes or no to that. I can only say I didn't see anyone.'

After signalling to Connor to stop recording, Cristy said to Layla, 'There must be some documentation around for the car. If nothing else, it'll give us a registration number that we can try to have tracked.'

'There's a ton of boxes and a couple of filing cabinets upstairs,' Layla said. 'Also, Mum was insured to drive it, so she might have the details if I can't find anything here.'

'I think it's a disgrace,' Nula declared, 'that the police aren't getting involved in this. They should be taking fingerprints and checking for blood and hairs and stuff. And they'd have tracked her phone down by now, I'm sure of it. They do something with triangles that tells you where someone is when they're making a call, and she's obviously using the phone if she's posting on Facebook and sending messages.'

Cristy said, 'Do you have keys to this house, Mrs Higgins?'

Nula nodded. 'And she has keys to mine. It's what neighbours do.'

'How often have you been in here since she disappeared?' Cristy asked.

Nula shrugged. 'Two or three times, just to check if she'd turned up and left her car somewhere else. Usually, I just go straight round the back to take care of the roses.'

'Did you ever notice while you were doing the watering that the French doors were open?'

Nula turned to look over her shoulder. 'Can't say I did, but there's a bit of a problem with them. Always has been. Luckily, there's no history of break-ins around here, but that's no reason to be lax. I kept telling her she ought to get the lock fixed, especially after Rudi went and she was here on her own.'

'Did she ever seem nervous of someone getting in?'

'If she was, she'd have done the repair, wouldn't she? She kept saying she meant to get round to it, but doesn't look like she did. But I can tell you this: she was forever checking for bugs. They had a real thing about them, her and Rudi. It's why, she told me, they spent so much time over on the bench, even in bad weather. They didn't feel as creeped out over there, was how she put it.'

Cristy looked at Layla, who appeared both surprised and baffled.

'I never knew they had that sort of problem or phobia,' Layla stated.

'Well, they did,' Nula told her. 'You can ask the bloke who comes every now and then to clean the place. I don't think he ever finds anything that isn't in all our homes, but some objectionables are easier to live with than others, aren't they? Personally, I can't abide snakes, but luckily, we don't get too many of them around here. Or not of the reptile variety, anyway.'

CHAPTER SIX

A few hours later, Cristy and Connor were back at the office, with the tall sash window wide open and fans at full speed to try to cool the stuffy air.

'I know it sounds crazy,' Cristy declared, as she turned from the whiteboard where she'd just added Nula's contact details, 'but Connor and I both leapt to the same conclusion – if you can call it a conclusion, and actually you can't. It's just where our heads went. But honestly, *bugs*! The place regularly being *cleaned*, as in "swept" clean? Nula clearly thought they meant insects, but what does it say to you?'

Harry Quinn dabbed a trickle of sweat from his receding hairline. 'I guess the same as it said to you,' he concurred.

'And when you add to that Hester McInlay's comments about being shushed the last time they were with Rudi and Romy,' Cristy continued, 'and Romy constantly looking over her shoulder. Tell me where that's supposed to take us.'

Clove quickly jumped in. 'Please say someone was spying on them. It'll make things so much more exciting!'

With a raised eyebrow, Cristy sat back down at her desk. She was glad Harry and Meena had dropped in for an update – hopefully it was a white flag after the tense meeting a couple of days ago, and as they hadn't mentioned it, nor had she and Connor.

'So, is there any more of this Nula's interview than you've just played us?' Meena wanted to know.

'No, we ended it there,' Cristy replied, 'and then somehow managed to persuade her to leave before getting Layla's reaction to what had been said.'

'And it turns out,' Connor ran on, 'that Layla heard the comments the same way we did. Not that she had any idea *who* might want to eavesdrop on her godmother, or why there seemed to be a regular check on the place, but we decided it was time to start a "sweep" of our own. And . . . guess what we found.'

'*No!*' Clove gasped, clasping her hands to her cheeks. Then, 'Sorry. Getting ahead of myself.'

'It was in a rummage drawer,' Connor said, holding up a business card. 'I guess we all have one of those, don't we?'

Harry and Meena didn't look certain.

'It's somewhere you chuck stuff you don't know what to do with,' Clove explained. 'So what is it?'

Taking the card, Harry read out loud. '"Sherman Security Services".'

'The address is Wotton-Under-Edge,' Cristy told him, 'so we made a detour on our way back, but the shop was all shuttered up – as in closed, not out of business. We left a message on the answering service for someone to get back to us. Meanwhile, the website is quite impressive, offering everything from tracing agents to data recovery, from counter surveillance to . . . bug sweeping services.'

'They can even apparently carry out lie-detection tests, should we ever require one,' Connor added for good measure. 'Anyway, the possession of this card throws an intriguing light on things, wouldn't you say?'

'Almost as intriguing,' Cristy said, 'as the photos of them with various world dignitaries.'

'Oh my God,' Clove murmured, looking like she might swoon.

'So what does Layla have to say about it all?' Meena wanted to know.

'Clearly, it was no surprise to her that the Kaplans were well connected,' Cristy replied. 'As for them using a security service to check their home . . . She was certainly thrown by that, and so was her mother after Layla told her. The call was on speaker, so we used Connor's phone to record it.'

Taking out his mobile, Connor scrolled to recording and hit play.

BETH: 'But it doesn't make any sense. Why would anyone . . . I mean, Rudi and Romy knew a lot of people, yes, and I admit some were at quite a high level . . . But they've never been involved in anything like this . . . whatever *this* is.'

CRISTY: 'So Romy never mentioned anything to you about fearing she was being monitored in some way?'

BETH: 'No. I mean . . . Well, I should probably tell you that Rudi used to come up with some very tall tales at times, so this card you've found could be no more than a prop he used for entertaining his neighbours. I'm not saying it is . . . I don't actually know what I'm saying, but I'll talk to Johnny, my husband, when he gets back, see what he thinks about it.'

CRISTY: 'Thank you. And the reason the Kaplans left their previous home . . ?'

BETH: 'I'm afraid we don't know the details, but Johnny has always said that Rudi, as an angel investor, was quite a soft touch. In fact, both he and Romy were forever getting caught up in other people's dreams and all too often found themselves throwing good money after bad. And, of course, they were impossible spendthrifts.'

CRISTY: 'Well, the spendthrift part of that might answer why they had to give up their home, but it doesn't explain why they were using the services of a security company at the cottage.'

As Connor tapped to end the recording, Meena said, 'Where's Layla now?'

'We left her going through the contents of a filing cabinet in the spare bedroom,' Cristy replied. 'Connor had to force it open, but first glance didn't yield much more than old credit card statements, a wadge of handwritten letters from over the years, and various documents to do with the property. Seems they owned it outright. Bought for cash last September. Layla's going to see if she can find any bills, so we can check if they're still being paid.'

'The fact the cabinet was locked,' Connor continued, 'could mean there's something inside worth finding.'

'I'm not sure I'd want to stay in that cottage on my own,' Clove said, grimacing, 'not if they thought they were being spied on.' She shuddered. 'Imagine someone watching your home or listening to everything you say. It's like being stalked, only worse.'

This reminded Cristy of the person she'd spotted getting into a boat on the opposite shore. They'd been in the middle of the lake by the time she and Connor had left Bellbrook, just idling there.

She scrolled to Layla's number.

'Hi,' Layla cried when she answered, the sound of air rushing past almost drowning her voice. 'You must be back at the office by now.'

'We are. Where are you?'

'On the M4, and I'm bringing a couple of things to show you. Not sure they'll make us any the wiser, but I thought I'd let you guys make the call.'

'OK. Did you see or speak to anyone else before you left?'

'No more Nula, thank goodness, just the postman, who didn't have anything for Romy. Oh, and the landline rang a

50

couple of times. No one there when I picked up, so I tried 1471. The number was blocked, and it kind of creeped me out after the second time, so that's when I decided to call it a day.'

'Did you see anyone in a boat on the lake as you left?'

'Can't say I noticed. Why?'

Dismissing the question for now, Cristy said, 'Any idea what's on the opposite shore, apart from a lot of trees?'

'To be honest, I've never been over there, but as far as I'm aware, that's it. I think it's private property, actually. It could even belong to the Gatcombe Estate. What are you thinking?'

'Just getting a lay of the land,' Cristy replied. 'Are you coming straight here?'

'That's the plan, so I should see you in about fifteen or twenty, depending on traffic.'

As Cristy rang off, Connor said, 'What was all that about a boat on the lake?'

'Did you notice someone was there, about thirty metres out?'

He shrugged. 'I guess, kind of. Why?'

'He caught my attention getting into the boat on the opposite bank just after we arrived – and he was still floating around when we left. It probably doesn't mean anything, but if, as Layla says, there's nothing over the other side apart from trees . . . Well, I'm not sure where I'm going with it, so let's move on.'

'I have a question,' Harry said. 'Didn't you do an interview with Layla yesterday?'

'We did,' Connor confirmed, 'in which she basically outlines most of what's in her notes . . .'

'So there's more background on Rudi and Romy?' Harry interrupted. 'I don't think Meena and I have heard that yet.'

'Then let me put that right straight away,' Connor responded, and turned to his keyboard to call up the audio file. 'OK, popcorn at the ready . . . I'll skip through the self-intro and . . . Here we go . . .'

CRISTY: 'Can you tell us about Haylesford Manor, where Romy and Rudi lived before moving to Bellbrook?'

LAYLA: 'Sure. It's an amazing place about five miles north of Cirencester, at the end of a beautiful tree-lined driveway. It was in Rudi's family for generations – his great-great grandfather was an East-India merchant whose son became some kind of industrialist, and *his* son invested big in oil at just the right time . . .

'Actually, you'll have to get the full story from Dad, but regarding the house itself . . . It's early Georgian in style, quite grand, but not vast like some from that period. It has six or seven bedrooms, plus the top floor servants' quarters where us kids used to sleep whenever we went to stay. There's a super-elegant drawing room, a dining room that could seat twenty or more, a fabulous library and four or five acres of lovely grounds – think streams, orchards, wildflower gardens and views to die for.

'I remember spending hours staring out of the windows, imagining horse-drawn carriages coming up the drive with elegant ladies on board – a bit *Bridgerton*, I suppose, although this was long before the series, obvs. Sometimes, I didn't have to imagine, because Rudi and Romy loved themed parties – Regency, Roman, Bohemian . . . You name it. Romy was such a romantic – actually, they both were, and they were seriously into dressing up. Oh, and if they had guests from overseas, they used to get them to wear their traditional costumes, if they had one. That was always great fun, trying to guess where they were from. My brother was quite good at that.'

CRISTY: 'Do you know how Rudi came to inherit the manor and family fortune?'

LAYLA: 'He was the only surviving relative when his uncle died, but they had a great relationship, so I don't think he got it by default or anything like that. He was pretty young when it all fell into his lap, still in his thirties, I think. It obviously gave them a wonderful life for years and years, but in the end . . . Well, maybe they never had as much as appearances suggested.'

CRISTY: 'It must have been really difficult for them when they were forced to sell Haylesford Manor?'

LAYLA: 'I'm sure it just about broke their hearts, but they wouldn't ever talk about it. We didn't even know it was happening until Romy emailed Mum one day with her new address. Of course, Mum and Dad drove straight there to find out what was going on, but they were told not to worry about anything; they were happy to be in their "delightful new cottage".

'It was the same when I went to see them a month or so later . . . That must have been late October. By then, they actually did seem quite settled. It was always typical of them to make the best of a situation, and if their other friends stopped coming, which most of them did . . . Well, they weren't in a position to host anyone the way they used to, and to quote Romy, "you can't blame people for getting on with their lives". Which is what they were doing themselves until . . . Well, until all this came along.'

When Connor stopped the recording, Harry said, 'What I'd like to know is who was advising Rudi Kaplan financially.'

'According to Layla, he ran his own portfolio,' Cristy replied.

53

'But surely someone was brokering – you know, acting on his behalf.'

'Good question,' Connor responded. 'We haven't found any details of a broker or adviser yet – or a lawyer, come to that – but they must exist.'

'What about Romy?' Meena asked. 'Is she also from a wealthy background?'

'She grew up as an only child in Somerset,' Cristy told her, 'went to the same school as Layla's mother, and mine, actually, though she was a fair bit older - and dropped out of uni during her first year after meeting Rudi. He'd already graduated from Cambridge by then and wanted to go travelling, so she went with him. They got married a year later, which was around the time he joined the Foreign Office.'

'Doing what?' Harry asked.

'At the beginning, I don't know, but apparently he was posted to Moscow at some point – Layla thinks around '84, '85 . . . Romy went with him, and was given a job at the British Embassy, probably as a typist or a secretary, and they were there for four or five years before Rudi was expelled, along with half a dozen other diplomats.'

'So about the time the wall came down?' Harry put in.

Cristy nodded. 'After that, they lived in the States for a while, and then Rudi inherited from his uncle in '96 and they returned to England.'

Meena said, 'So officially, they haven't worked for almost thirty years?'

'I don't think so, at least not in any sort of conventional sense – until more recently, apparently. Nula tells us Romy was part-time in a local giftshop – which reminds me, Clove: I've got the owner's details, so maybe you could make contact.'

'On it,' Clove responded, making a note. 'Meantime, Cambridge, Foreign Office, Moscow?'

'In the 1980s,' Meena added. 'Philby, Blunt, Maclean?'

Cristy cocked an eyebrow. 'Their time was a bit before Rudi's, but even his was forty odd years ago, and on the face of it, at least, there's nothing to connect him to the intelligence services, apart from the Moscow expulsion.'

'Isn't everyone who works at the British Embassy in Moscow involved in espionage one way or another?' Clove asked, appearing to work on two laptops at once. 'Back then, and now.'

Regarding her curiously, Cristy said, 'What are you doing there?'

'This is Romy's laptop,' Clove explained, turning it around. 'I'm not at all sure about being able to get in. Jacks is our man, so why don't I try to track him down in Peru, see if he can talk me through it, or suggest someone we can give it to?'

'I'll leave that with you,' Cristy told her, and looked up as a car pulled into the small parking lot outside their window. Seeing it was Layla, she said to Harry and Meena, 'Do you guys want to sit in for this? Or have you had enough for now?'

'I've got a meeting in five,' Harry responded, checking his watch, 'and aren't you supposed to be voicing a pod for Kelly Gates's show?' he said to Meena.

'That's tomorrow,' she responded, 'but I do have some calls to make.'

As they got up to leave, Harry hesitated for a moment, then said, 'Remind me, when did Rudi and Romy move into their cottage?'

'Last September,' Cristy replied. 'Why?'

He shrugged. 'I'm just thinking, if his death and her disappearance have anything to do with the loss of his estate . . . Well, I guess I'm just trying to figure it out.'

'As are we all,' Cristy commented wryly, glad that it had apparently captured his attention.

'What if Rudi was a Russian agent?' Clove blurted

hopefully, 'and the high-living and great wealth was just a front? His inheritance, the manor . . . everything could have been a legend. I think that's what they call it.'

Clearly amused, Harry and Meena went on their way, and moments later, Layla came in, all freshness and glorious hair in spite of the heat.

'God, it's humid today,' she declared, sinking down on a sofa in front of the open window, while fanning herself with a notebook.

'Let's have a drink,' Cristy suggested and got up to inspect the fridge in their corner kitchenette. 'Seems we have lemonade, water, wine or beer.'

'I'd love a beer,' Layla sighed.

'Same here,' Connor piped up.

When Clove didn't say anything, Cristy turned to her.

'Wow,' Clove muttered, staring at her screen, 'definitely didn't see this coming.'

'What is it?' Cristy asked.

Clove sat back. 'Better take a look.'

CHAPTER SEVEN

Cristy went to peer over Clove's shoulder as Connor wheeled in his chair and Layla joined them. Romy's laptop was still on the log-in page, on Clove's a frozen image of Romy looking smiley and tanned was filling the screen.

'Oh my God!' Layla gasped. 'Is that a new video?'

Clove hit play, and Romy gave a breezy, breathy laugh, then said, 'Hello, my darling ones. You'll never guess where I am. It's bringing back so many memories, all of them happy. I wish I could stay forever, but I'm missing you all so much. Not to worry – I'll be home soon.' Leaning in closer, she whispered, 'Everything's cool and coming up roses,' and with a little giggle, she turned away from the camera.

A moment later, the screen went dark.

Cristy glanced at Layla, who looked stunned.

'She seems . . . kind of cheerful,' Layla remarked uncertainly. 'I mean, that's natural for her – she's always upbeat – but given where we are . . . I don't understand how she can act as if everything's normal?'

'She could be in denial,' Connor pointed out. 'My mother was like that after my dad passed; she kept talking to him as if he was still there, even answering and laughing as if he was talking back.'

Layla nodded slowly. 'A kind of self-protection thing,' she murmured. 'I guess better that than think of her tearing herself apart in grief or going into the darkest depression. Can you play it again?' she asked Clove.

Clove did, and as they listened and watched, Cristy noticed the shadow of someone falling lightly across the table Romy was seated at. 'Stop,' she said, 'do you see that?'

They all did now it had been pointed out.

'The person holding the phone or camera,' Clove mused.

'Could just be a waiter,' Connor said.

Accepting he was probably right, Cristy said, 'When was this posted?'

Clove checked. 'At 4.38, so just over twenty minutes ago. I'll set up an alert, so we'll know the instant something drops from now on.'

'Try calling her,' Cristy said to Layla. 'Her phone could still be on, presuming it was her phone she used. Can we check that, Clove?'

Clove grimaced helplessly. 'Maybe Jacks could, but beyond my skillset, I'm afraid.'

'Straight to voicemail,' Layla told them. 'Romy! It's me. Where are you? We really need to speak to you. Call me back as soon as you get this.'

Connor was still studying the reel. 'Wherever she is,' he said, 'it seems to be somewhere hot.'

'Well, that narrows it down,' Cristy responded dryly.

'OK, it doesn't look like this country . . .'

'The oleander bushes and church square suggest somewhere Mediterranean,' Cristy conceded, 'but it could equally be South America or Sydney . . . Is that some kind of statue or fountain there, to the right?'

Clove tried zooming in, but everything just dissolved into pixels.

As Romy's face filled the screen again, Layla said, 'The more she's telling us not to worry, the more worried I feel.'

'What I'd like to know,' Cristy stated, returning to her desk, 'is what made her post this video now, today, when we've just been at the cottage? Is it a coincidence? Or . . . what else could it be?'

'Let's check the dates she uploaded the others,' Connor said, scrolling to them, 'see if there's any kind of pattern.'

It didn't take long.

'Random days,' he said, 'but kind of a week apart. I guess it tells us that she's keen to keep in touch, even if she doesn't want to speak to anyone directly.'

Layla said, 'If you're thinking we should respect her space and back off, I might agree if only she was in touch with Mum. There's no one closer to her now that Rudi's gone, so it just doesn't make any sense for her to do this on Facebook and not make a call.'

Bothered by the omission herself, Cristy said, 'Why don't you let your mother know about this latest video. Maybe she'll recognize the background or see something we're missing?'

'Is it possible,' Clove ventured as Layla sent a text, 'that there's a hidden message in what she's saying?'

Looking doubtful, Connor signalled for her to play it again.

'Not getting one myself,' he said when it finished.

'Maybe because it's not meant for you?' Clove countered.

'Are there any responses to the video yet?' Cristy asked.

Checking, Clove said, 'Two so far. Ursula Schneider: *"We're having a party on 25th July. Hope you can make it."* Barber Seviglia: *"Left a message on your mobile, still waiting for you to call."* Another's just popped up . . .' She stopped, pulled a face and glanced awkwardly at Layla.

'What?' Layla asked, and went to look over Clove's shoulder. Her eyes widened as she read the post. 'Oh my God,' she murmured. 'Who is that?'

Having it up on her own screen now, Cristy read it out. 'AV: *"We know where you are, Romy, and we know what you did. Easy to run, not so easy to hide. Give our best to Rudi."*'

'What the fuck?' Connor muttered, as Layla stared at the screen in shock.

'Does AV mean anything to you?' Cristy asked her.

Layla shook her head. 'I don't understand it. Running and hiding, giving best to Rudi . . .'

'I'll try making contact,' Clove said, and got straight to work.

'It's so . . . sinister,' Layla protested, clearly still struggling to take it in. 'Who would say something like that when everyone knows Rudi's dead?'

'Maybe this person doesn't,' Cristy countered.

'And if he or she knows where Romy is,' Connor put in, 'why are they having to point it out?'

'That's why it's sinister,' Layla cried. 'It sounds like a threat.'

'No details on their profile,' Clove declared. 'Whoever posted could have created one specially.' She grimaced apologetically. 'Sorry, it's the best I can do. Jacks would probably be able to find out more.'

Cristy turned to Layla. 'I know you probably don't want to hear this,' she said, 'but we can't be certain that Romy's actually posting anything herself. I get that it appears to be her, but the videos could have been shot at any time and uploaded by someone else. Is there a way to find out whose phone or computer was used?'

Clove shook her head defeatedly. 'Once again, Jacks is your man,' she replied.

Cristy looked at Layla. 'If it isn't her posting the videos, any thoughts on who it could be?'

Layla shook her head worriedly.

'OK,' Cristy declared. 'I'm just posing the question – we've nothing to say that it isn't her, so all we can do for now is wait to see if she responds to this anonymous post, and in the meantime, why don't I add something from me?'

'Great idea!' Connor declared. 'Saying what?'

Cristy shrugged. 'I could ask her if she still wants to get in touch and if she does, why not private message me?'

'Yes, yes,' Layla urged. 'It'll be really interesting to see how she reacts.'

As Cristy got started, another response popped up. 'Your mother's just commented on the post,' she told Layla. 'She's saying . . . Oh God . . .'

Seeing Cristy's expression, Layla quickly read it herself and frowned deeply, closing her eyes.

'I'm sorry, she does this sometimes,' she said shakily. 'She thinks playing the death's-door card might guilt-trip Romy into calling. I don't know why she thinks it'll work this time when it hasn't before. I guess she just feels she has to do something.'

Understanding Beth's frustration, while feeling for Layla, Cristy began composing her own post, reading the words aloud as she typed. '"*Hi Romy, would love to chat. You can contact me via messenger or use the* Hindsight *links on our website. Would be good to hear from you.*"'

Getting the thumbs-up from Layla, Cristy logged off and sat back in her chair. Time to move things on, she decided. 'So, spoils from the cottage,' she prompted, as Layla returned to the sofa.

Opening her bag, Layla said, 'OK, the car's registration document was in the filing cabinet, so we have the registration number now. I can also tell you that her mobile phone server is Vodafone, and she's with Octopus energy. I found a photocopy of her passport – no sign of the actual one, or of her driver's licence, but – wait for this – there's a copy of a contract with Sherman Security Services dated from October last year, which appears still to be current.'

Clearly intrigued, Connor took it from her.

Layla continued, 'There were two thousand euros in her bedside cabinet, and this notebook full of her scribblings.'

'That's a lot of ready money to have left behind,' Clove commented. 'And why euros, not pounds?'

Layla shrugged.

'Anything interesting in the notebook?' Cristy asked.

'I've only flicked through, but from what I can tell, it's filled with extracts from her favourite classics. It's something she's always done when she's stressed or worried, or if she just wants to distract herself for some reason. She copies out passages from various books – *Jane Eyre*, *Wuthering Heights*, *The Mill on the Floss* . . . I guess whatever she has to hand.' Seeing Cristy's surprise, she added, 'She finds it soothing,' and opening the notebook, she read the first handwritten lines aloud:

'"*All sorts of allowances are made for the illusions of youth; and none, or almost none, for the disenchantments of age.*" Robert Louis Stevenson,' she informed them.

Cristy and Connor exchanged glances. 'Is it all like that, right through the book?' he asked.

Flipping the rumpled pages, Layla said, 'It seems to be, yes. I've told Mum about it, and she'd like to see it, so I'll take it home with me, if that's OK?'

Realizing she could hardly say no, Cristy said, 'Of course.' As it wasn't a journal, or an account of the past few months, there was no reason to object. 'If she finds anything significant, then I'm sure she'll let us know.'

'Oh, she will,' Layla assured her.

Still eyeing the book, Clove said, 'I wonder if there are some hidden codes in there. You know, like the first word of every fourth line, or the last sentence of . . .' She trailed off as Layla treated her to a hostile stare. Clearly Layla wasn't keen on seeing her godmother as some sort of spy.

'Hey, Mum!'

Cristy turned round, and her heart swelled with pleasure to see her son Aiden practically filling the office doorway he'd grown so tall. He looked as chilled as he always did in scruffy T-shirt and denim shorts, although he'd clearly just come from the barber's given the number one cut to the sides and back and thickly tousled top.

Her spirits sank a little when Matthew appeared behind him, as insouciantly good-looking and pleased with himself as ever. She should have guessed he'd find a way to crash her and Aiden's plans for a meal out this evening; he was making a habit of it these days. She just wished it was David who'd turned up to surprise her, David who'd somehow find a way to spend the whole weekend with her as Matthew no doubt would.

'Is that you? Layla!' Matthew asked cheerfully. 'I heard you were around, but I wasn't expecting to see you here.'

'He was,' Aiden announced, earning himself a heavy tread on the foot as Matthew went to greet Layla. 'He saw your car.'

Laughing, Cristy said, 'How did the exams go today?'

Aiden shrugged and went to fist-bump Connor. 'Being your son, I probably aced them,' he replied.

'Don't forget who else played a part in your brilliance,' Matthew reminded him.

'Yeah, right,' Aiden retorted. His dark eyes shone with an irony that was so redolent of his father's, back in the early years, it made Cristy's heart skip.

'We're almost done here for the day,' she said, turning back to her computer.

'You'll join us for dinner, I hope?' Matthew said to Layla.

'Oh!' Layla exclaimed in surprise. 'Are you sure? I . . . My brother's with my parents tonight, so I probably could get away.'

'I'm free,' Connor told him. 'Jodi and Aurora are at Jodi's mum's until Sunday.'

'I can change my plans,' Clove piped up.

Matthew looked at Cristy, apparently expecting her to say something. When she only shrugged, he broke into a laugh and threw out his hands. 'OK, everyone's welcome,' he declared. 'We just need to find somewhere that can fit us all in.'

'You go on ahead,' Cristy instructed, 'and text to let me know where you are. I want to call David before I leave.'

Matthew's expression clouded. 'You're not still seeing him, are you?' he groaned. 'I thought you might be over it by now.'

Shooting him a look that she knew he'd understand perfectly – *nice try, but you willing it won't make it happen,* she waited for them all to leave and decided to write up some notes from the day before trying David.

A little while later, after failing to get hold of him and receiving a text from Aiden to let her know they were at The Olive Shed, she was packing up to leave when her mobile rang. Seeing it was Beth, Layla's mother, she quickly clicked on.

'Hi, it's Cristy,' she said. 'How are you?'

'Layla's not answering her phone,' Beth told her, 'so I hope you don't mind . . .'

'No, it's fine. She probably doesn't have a signal where she is. Is everything OK?'

'Well, I'm not sure that it is. I've just . . . Well, I think I've just had a call from Romy.'

CHAPTER EIGHT

'So it was definitely Romy?' Connor asked, as soon as Cristy had brought them up to speed. They were at a pavement table outside The Olive Shed with assorted platters of delicious tapas spread out for sharing, along with large glasses of chilled white wine, all going down a treat.

'The call was from her number,' Cristy replied. 'Beth could hear someone breathing, and she kept calling out, "Hello, Romy, is that you," but then the line went dead.'

'So she doesn't know for certain it actually was her?' Connor pressed.

Cristy shook her head. 'Beth tried ringing back, but was diverted to voicemail – not straight away, as has happened before. Interestingly, it was an international ring tone.'

Layla sat back in her chair, clearly more worried and perplexed than ever.

'I guess you've tried phone-tracking software?' Matthew ventured.

'We've never got anywhere with it,' Layla told him, 'because the phone's almost never on.'

'You should try finding out where she was when it was last in use,' Aiden told her.

'How do we do that?' Clove wanted to know.

'Well, I don't think *you* can, but her provider should be able to.'

'Good luck with that,' Connor grumbled. 'Data

protection. But I think it's worth you and your mum trying to get something out of them, Layla. I know you're not family, but they might be willing to help if they know you're concerned.'

Topping up everyone's glasses, Matthew said, 'You say she's not in this country?'

'Which chimes with her latest Facebook post,' Clove piped up. 'Not that we could identify the location, but it definitely looked foreign.'

'So that's narrowed it down,' Aiden remarked, helping himself to a chicken thigh dripping in harissa and honey. 'Can we load up on the patatas bravas?'

Matthew looked round for a server. 'Cristy, we saved the last calamari for you, but we can always get more. Actually, let's go for a second round of everything. Everyone OK with this Picpoul?'

'Bring it on,' Connor encouraged, raising his glass. 'So, what's our next move, apart from editing the interviews we have so far?'

'There are lots of people we're still waiting to hear back from,' Cristy replied. 'The giftshop owner who Romy worked for, for one. Otherwise I suggest we head over to the cottage tomorrow and see if we can find anything else there.'

'I can come too,' Layla said. 'There must be something in their papers about Rudi's finances.'

'Sounds more interesting than revising,' Aiden grumbled.

'Cristy, are you not going to have that calamari?' Matthew asked.

'Yes, I am,' she cried, slapping his hand away.

'Dad, are you ordering?' Aiden said, as a server hovered.

After doing the honours, Matthew turned back, picked up his wine and said, 'OK, no more shop. Cris, why don't you tell us how David was when you spoke to him?'

Managing not to roll her eyes, she said, 'Actually, I couldn't get hold of him.'

Matthew feigned surprise, before nodding knowingly. 'Probably means he's dumped you,' he said.

She sighed. 'Oh shut up.'

'You're such a dork, Dad,' Aiden told him.

With a grin, Matthew said to Layla, 'Why aren't you drinking?'

'I have to drive,' she reminded him. 'It's all right for those of you who live in walking distance of everything.'

'We don't,' Aiden reminded her. 'Or we do, when I'm at Mum's. Not at Dad's, though.'

'Are you still in Leigh Woods?' Layla asked Matthew.

Cristy said, 'He is, when he's not in LA with his wife.'

'Which is hardly ever,' Aiden told her.

'Doesn't she come here?' Layla wanted to know.

'No, but the baby did for two whole months,' Aiden replied. 'His name's Bear, and he's cute as hell. Dad was gutted when he had to take him back, weren't you?'

Matthew didn't deny it. 'We still miss him, don't we? Cris, you were amazing while he was here. I'd never have managed without you.'

'You had nannies,' she reminded him, annoyed that he was making her seem a part of his new family, 'and Hayley came to stay for two weeks. She's the one who was amazing.'

This was true, given their daughter was in her second year at Edinburgh and could have done without having to play stand-in mother to a child whose real mother was in Santa Fe making a movie. She'd only taken the time out because Cristy had been in Marrakech with David and she'd felt sorry for her father.

As the conversation moved on to Connor's baby, Aurora, Aiden's plans for the summer, and Layla's life in Dubai, Cristy checked her phone to see if David had tried to get hold of her. He hadn't yet, but it didn't matter; she'd call him when she got home – after she'd brained Matthew for suggesting she'd been dumped.

'I don't know why you have to do that,' she snapped at him as he and Aiden walked her back along the waterfront later. 'It's childish and makes you look like an idiot.'

'If I didn't know better, I might think I'd hit a nerve,' he responded dryly.

'And if I didn't know better, I might think you're trying it on with Layla.'

'She's pretty hot,' Aiden pointed out, 'if you're into older women, which she would be for me, but I thought you liked them young, Dad, given Marley's my age.'

'She's twenty-three,' Matthew protested, as Cristy snorted a laugh.

'But still a child in so many ways,' Cristy put in, and immediately felt mean for mocking Marley's arrested emotional development. 'Seriously,' she said, 'how's she settling back into life in LA with the baby?'

Sighing, Matthew said, 'OK, as far as I can tell.'

'Do you have any plans to go out there anytime soon?'

'I think I've had all the time off I can get away with for a while,' he replied. 'I guess there's a chance she might come here. Well, we know she would if you asked her to.'

Cristy stayed silent.

'It's weird that, isn't it?' Aiden commented. 'How she's ended up crazier about Mum than she is about you? I mean, I get it, I feel the same . . . Just kidding.' He laughed as Matthew cuffed him. 'She is though, isn't she? Totally into Mum?'

'Because she lost her own mother,' Cristy said, 'and for some unfathomable reason, she's trying to cast me as the replacement.'

'So she comes in, breaks up your marriage, marries your ex, has his kid, and now she wants to come live with you so you can help bring her and Bear up at the same time.'

'That's not how it is,' Matthew protested. 'As far as I know, she doesn't want to leave LA, but she'd definitely visit if Mum wanted her to.'

'The guilt-trips aren't working,' Cristy told him. 'She's your wife, he's your son – you deal with it.'

'Mum's moved on,' Aiden informed him. 'And now she's got David, that's where her focus is, and who can blame her? All respect, Dad, but you were the one who got yourself into all this, and you've got to admit, David's a great guy. I'd marry him if he asked me.'

Laughing, Cristy said, 'I don't think he's asking anyone, but he'll be glad to know you're keen.'

'Don't you have someone to call?' Matthew asked Aiden.

'Nah,' he replied. 'Loving chatting with you guys.'

They'd reached the Prince Street Bridge by now, time for Cristy to turn off towards the Redcliffe end of the harbourside, so she said, 'You know, you two really don't have to come any further. Where's your car, Matthew?'

'Actually, it's at yours,' he admitted. 'We needed to pick some things up for exam-man here, so we'll stick with you.'

Having no choice but to yield, Cristy crossed the cobbled road and said to Aiden, 'So what have you got tomorrow?'

'Uh, let me think . . . psychology? Geography? It might be chemistry.'

'You're not doing chemistry.'

'Thank God for that. I was just starting to worry.'

Cristy walked on quietly, knowing he was teasing her, while still not taking this crucial stage of his education any more seriously than he took anything else. He and Matthew talked cricket and some band they were both into, and more about Aiden's ever-changing plans for the summer.

When finally they reached the leafy courtyard in front of her apartment block, she searched for her keys and looked up again quickly as Aiden said, 'Hey! We weren't expecting to see you here. So cool.'

At the sight of David getting up from the wall next to the front door, Cristy's heart turned over. He was so impossibly good-looking with his shock of thick, fair hair and piercing blue eyes, and so relaxed in his manner that she still had problems believing she'd once seen him as a cold-blooded killer.

'Hey to you,' he said, taking Aiden's hand and pulling him into a loose hug. 'How're things?'

'Yeah, good,' Aiden replied. 'In parental hell, as uje, but have an escape plan hatching.'

Laughing, David turned to Matthew and greeted him equally as warmly. 'Good to see you,' he said. 'How're things in the news world?'

'Probably about the same as the money world,' Matthew responded, clearly torn between his instinctive liking of the man and an abiding wish to get him out of their lives. Cristy never knew whether to be annoyed or amused by Matthew's reaction to David. Well, whatever he thought, David wasn't going anywhere. 'What brings you here? Apart from the obvious, of course,' Matthew asked.

'That's about it,' David replied, his laughing eyes going to Cristy. 'I had a last-minute thing come up in London, so rather than fly back tonight, I took a train here.'

Wishing Matthew and Aiden would evaporate so she could give free rein to a welcome, she said, 'This is the kind of surprise I love, but if you're thinking of inviting these guys in for a coffee or nightcap—'

'Mine's a Bailey's,' Aiden jumped in.

'Are you serious?' Matthew snorted. 'That's a girl's drink.'

Aiden looked at his mother. 'He doesn't get it, does he?'

She shook her head.

'You're not supposed to say that sort of thing any more, Dad. It's sexist.'

Clearly baffled, Matthew turned to David.

'Count me out of that one.' David laughed. 'But, Aiden, if you want a Bailey's—'

'You can have one at Dad's,' Cristy said, pushing Aiden towards Matthew's car.

Looking injured, Matthew said. 'Sounds like it's time for us to go, son. If you're staying for the weekend, David, it would be great to catch up.'

'Always good to see you,' David assured him, and Cristy kind of melted, because she could tell he was as keen for them to be alone as she was.

CHAPTER NINE

The following morning, Cristy was in front of her laptop in the dining area of her open plan kitchen-sitting room when David wandered through from the main bedroom. He was unabashedly naked and in such great shape for a man his age – any age actually – that she felt an undeniable urge to walk him straight back to bed.

'Found you,' he murmured, stooping to kiss her upturned mouth. 'And coffee's already made.'

'Help yourself,' she said, as he went to do just that. She watched him for a moment, drinking in the splendid physicality of him until he turned and his ironically raised eyebrow made her laugh. 'What are your plans?' she asked, returning to her laptop. 'You know I'd love you to stay for the weekend . . .'

'I need to get the afternoon flight,' he broke in. 'It just didn't feel right to be on the mainland and not see you. Any chance you can come back to the island with me?'

She grimaced, wishing she could. 'Layla messaged earlier to say her mother could be up to seeing us tomorrow. Given how she's struggling with her chemo, we need to take the opportunity while we can.'

'Sure,' he said, checking his phone before coming to look over her shoulder. 'Is that your missing woman?'

Turning to the screen where Romy's Facebook video was lined up, Cristy said, 'It's her latest post from yesterday. I was trying to figure out where she is, but I'm afraid we need Jacks for that. And then there's this really creepy response . . .' She scrolled down so that he could read it. 'We've no idea who this AV is. He – or she – doesn't seem to have been active on Facebook beyond that one comment, so it could just be some troll at work. Interestingly though, Romy reacted to it overnight with a kiss-blowing emoji – read into that what you will – but she hasn't responded to me, or Layla's mother, Beth. Or anyone else as far as I can see.'

'So what's she actually saying in the video?' he asked.

She shrugged. 'Not to worry about her, she'll be in touch soon, and she's definitely not looking distressed or particularly lonely, or as if she's been coerced into making the reels. In fact, as you can see for yourself, she seems perfectly relaxed.'

'So apart from the sleazy post, remind me why everyone's worried?'

'Mostly because she's not talking to anyone on the phone, although she might have called Beth last night – still not sure about that because whoever it was didn't speak. And there's also the curious discovery that she and her husband were quite possibly using a security company to check their cottage for listening devices.'

'Really?' David sounded as incredulous as he did sceptical.

'There have been other indicators that they were – how shall I put it? – nervous of being overheard or watched, and we found a contract between them and said security company that proves something was going on.'

'OK, interesting. And now he's dead, and no one knows where she is . . . Why don't you send me the link, and I'll have my tech guy see if he can help with the location of this video?'

'Would you? That would be great,' she said, getting right to it.

A moment later, she looked down at his hand as he slipped it inside her robe, and a flare of heat shot through her. 'Are you trying to distract me, by any chance?' she murmured, and moaned softly as he cupped her breast.

'How am I doing?' he asked, and pulling her to her feet, he eased the robe down over her shoulders to make her as naked as him.

*

Much later, after dropping David at the airport, Cristy drove to the office to find that Clove and Connor had been joined by the Quinns and the podcast's sponsorship liaison executive, Isabel Penny – aka Iz - had apparently blown in like a whirlwind. With her indefatigable insouciance and borderline eccentric dress-sense, Iz was usually as effusively supportive of everything *Hindsight* as they could wish for.

Today, however, she was clearly not thrilled by the prospect of a live investigation for the next series – not that her editorial input was going to hold much sway with Cristy and Connor. However, as she was responsible for bringing in the money, and had also, apparently, been swayed by Meena and Harry's reservations, she had to be given a hearing.

'It's not that I consider it a bad idea,' Iz explained, her normally friendly face and slightly self-effacing manner overshadowed by concern. 'Obviously it's intriguing, but I'm not sure how to sell this to the sponsors.'

'Well, as I see it,' Connor responded tightly, 'that's *your* job. What we're focused on is a woman whose life could very well be in jeopardy . . .'

'What you need to tell them,' Cristy cut in swiftly, 'is that we're happy to do this without their backing, if that's what they want, but I don't think it is, so we'll leave it with you, Iz, to sort things out. I know you're more than capable . . .'

'That's unspeakably patronizing,' Meena scolded. 'She's just trying to point out that you're not even sure yourselves that you actually have a series here.'

74

'And say what you like about the sponsors,' Harry chipped in, 'you wouldn't be where you are today without them, so it's maybe a good idea to keep that in mind.'

Cristy glared at him, knowing he was right and hating him for it. 'I'm not going to get into an argument about this,' she told him. 'Connor and I have to be somewhere. FYI, it's to do with this case, and I'll make no apologies or excuses for it . . .'

'Please don't be like that,' Iz implored. 'I'm on your side, honestly. I'm just trying to get ahead of things in a way that'll please everyone and make sure that we end up with the right series.'

'And no one is doubting your investigative or journalistic skills,' Meena added, 'or your judgement when it comes to a good story—'

'That's exactly what you're doing,' Connor told her angrily, 'and frankly if there's no trust between us—'

'All right! All right!' Harry cried, holding up his hands. 'The last thing we need is to start falling out when, as Iz said, we're all on the same side.'

'Except she, and you, clearly want us to back off the search for Romy . . .'

'That's not what anyone's saying,' Meena protested.

'Funny, because that's what we're hearing,' Cristy shot back. 'So, if you want us to take this elsewhere or to go it alone . . .'

'No, please don't do that,' Iz implored. 'I'm sorry I've started this. It wasn't my intention, I swear. I just . . . Maybe I'm not seeing things clearly enough yet. Let me sit down and look at what you have so far, if you can spare the time to go through it with me . . .'

Cristy looked at Clove, who immediately said, 'Happy to do it.'

'So where are you and Connor going?' Harry wanted to know.

Still royally pissed at him for his part in the last few minutes – for all she knew, he and Meena had actually stoked it – Cristy said, 'Clove had word this morning from the owner of a giftshop where Romy worked part time.'

'Olivia Gibson,' Clove put in helpfully.

'Apparently she has something of potential significance to share,' Connor added, 'and we'd like to find out what it is.'

They were almost at the door when Iz said, 'Do you actually think Rudi Kaplan might have been murdered? It could change everything if you find out he was and the coroner missed it, or even covered it up.'

*

'No pressure there,' Cristy commented, as she and Connor drove away from the office to begin the journey to Gloucestershire. 'On any front.'

'I effing hate money,' he grumbled. 'It controls everything, and those who have it are always the biggest jerks.'

Unable to suppress a smile, Cristy said, 'I'll tell David you said that. Anyway, I think they'll come round, whatever their misgivings might be right now. Clove will do her bit, and hopefully we'll have more things to stack up by the end of the day.'

'Provided the giftshop owner comes through. Brave bluff by the way, about us walking and going elsewhere. I think it did the trick.'

'Maybe, for now. What really matters is that we believe we're doing the right thing.'

After a pause, Cristy added, 'We do, don't we?'

'Sure we do. No doubt about it.'

Enjoying the dryness of his tone, she checked a text from Aiden letting her know he was sure he'd nail chemistry - such a twit – and put in a quick call to Clove.

'Can you speak?' she asked when Clove answered.

76

'Oh, hi Cristy,' Clove sang out, her tone making it clear that she wasn't alone.

'Am I on speaker?' Cristy asked.

'No, no, that's fine.'

'OK, well, sorry to land you with everything, but I know we can trust you to sell—'

'Totally on it,' Clove assured her.

'Great. Anything else we need to know about the woman we're about to interview?'

'Nothing new since I gave you my original notes. She sounds pretty posh, kind of what you'd expect from someone in that neck of the woods. Friendly, concerned. Keen to help in any way she can. On a different matter, I got word just after you left that Jacks is expected to turn up at a base camp sometime today or tomorrow. They have satellite phones, so I might be able to speak to him.'

'OK, good. If you do make contact, best make sure you've got a list of what you need to ask, and files to send if he can receive them. Remind me when he's back?'

'Next Friday, due to be here the following Monday.'

'Good. In the meantime, David's asked one of his guys to take a look at the latest Facebook video to see if he can work out where it was shot. I'll keep you updated on that, and you know how to get hold of us if you need to.'

As she ended the call, Connor's phone rang.

'Hey, Layla,' he said, accelerating to join the M4. 'Are you at the cottage yet?'

'I arrived about five minutes ago,' she told him, 'and there's been a bit of a . . . development.'

Connor glanced at Cristy. 'Go on,' he prompted.

'Quentin is with me,' Layla said, 'Romy's immediate next-door neighbour. He heard someone moving about in here last night, actually early hours of the morning. He looked out to see if Romy's car was back, but the space was still empty and he—'

Cutting in, Cristy said, 'Is he going to be around for the next couple of hours? We'd like to come and talk to him after we've seen Olivia if he is.'

'He's saying yes, he's happy to wait until you get here,' Layla replied.

'That's great. I'll let you know when we're on our way.'

Forty minutes later, they were driving down the hill into Nailsworth, an appealing old mill town at the heart of one of the Stroud Valleys where craft- and bookshops, cafés, delis and galleries made it as welcoming a place as Cristy had ever visited.

'How far do you reckon this is from Rudi and Romy's?' she asked, as Connor found a place to park around the back of the high street, near Morrisons.

'Fifteen minutes?' he guessed. 'What's the name of the place we're looking for?'

Checking Clover's notes, Cristy said, 'Liv and Lavish.'

She looked up and saw they were right opposite the quaint little store, with its smart gold-and-navy awning over a bay window displaying all sorts of candles, jewellery, picture frames and ceramics entwined by fairy lights and soft white tissue paper.

A bell rang as they opened the door, and to Cristy's surprise, she saw that the place was much bigger than it had appeared from the outside. So many gifts, from toys to trailing plants, ornate boxes, racks of cards, earthenware pots, throw pillows, children's books, diffusers and soaps. It was the kind of emporium she knew she and her daughter, Hayley, could easily become lost in for several hours.

'You must be Cristy and Connor.' A tall, dark-haired woman with a large nose and friendly grey eyes was heading their way, already reaching out a hand to shake. 'I'm Olivia, or Liv, whichever you prefer. It's good of you to come all this way to see me. I'd have happily come to you. Such a strange thing about Romy, isn't it? We've been so worried. Alice, would you mind manning the till while I take our guests through to the back?'

A dainty young girl with feathery fair hair and crimson cheeks appeared from behind a display of hand-painted mugs, and said, 'Big fan of the pod – hope it's OK to say that. Good luck finding Romy. We're all onside for it.'

Cristy smiled. 'That's good to know,' she said, and followed Olivia and Connor through a door marked *Private* into an Aladdin's cave of an office, where two chairs had already been cleared for guests.

'Please, sit down,' Olivia said. There was too much merchandise stacked up around her desk for her to get to the other side, so she perched on an exercise ball, but bounced up again as she said, 'Refreshments before we begin? I can offer tea, coffee . . .'

'We're fine, thanks,' Cristy assured her. 'I take it you're OK with us recording what you say?'

'Oh, of course – I was expecting it. Not that I can tell you much, I'm afraid, although there was something . . .'

'Just give us a minute,' Connor interrupted, still setting up.

Olivia watched as he pinned a mic to her collar, tested it and gave the signal to go ahead.

OLIVIA: 'As I was saying, something unusual happened, here at the shop, less than a week before Romy disappeared. I take it we're dating her disappearance to the last time she was seen, the day after the Coronation bash over at Bellbrook?'

Cristy nodded.

OLIVIA: 'Yes, well, it was the Friday before that. During the afternoon. It's not unusual for people to drop in for a chat with Romy – she's acquired quite a fan club since joining us at the beginning of the year, so I didn't think anything of it when a young woman turned up that particular day. I presumed she was a tourist, not having seen her before – we get lots of them going through – but then I happened to spot her passing something to Romy. I think it was a note or a card. After she'd gone, I could see Romy was . . . not quite herself, upset, distracted, so I asked if she was all right. She said she was, but then she asked if I'd mind her leaving early. She wanted to get home.'

CRISTY: 'And this was the Friday before she disappeared? So 3rd May?'

OLIVIA: 'That's right. Of course, I didn't know until the following Friday when she didn't turn up for work that anything was wrong. I tried calling her, and in the end, I drove over to check on her. That's when her neighbour, Nula, told me that no one knew where she was.'

CRISTY: 'Can you describe the woman who gave the note to her?'

OLIVIA: 'I'd say she was probably early thirties, with short fair hair, around five feet six, quite slim . . . Oh, and she had an accent of some sort. I only heard her saying goodbye to Romy, something along the lines of, *see you soon*. She sounded Irish, or maybe it was Scottish. It was so fleeting I'm afraid I can't be sure, and I'm not very good with that sort of thing. Oh, and her eyes were incredibly blue. Really striking. I wondered if she had those special lenses in.'

Cristy glanced at Connor in case he had anything to add.

CONNOR: 'How did Romy come to be working here? Did you advertise . . . ?'

OLIVIA: 'No, nothing like that. We met quite by chance while I was walking my dog on the common and she was with her neighbour Nula, also walking the dog. We got chatting, and when Romy realized I owned one of the giftshops in town, she became quite excited. She said she'd always longed to own one herself, so I invited her to drop by anytime, and the next thing we knew, she was working little shifts on Friday afternoons and all day Saturday. She loved it. I sometimes thought she'd have done it for free if I'd allowed it, but of course I didn't. I couldn't pay much, but she was happy to have a little pin money, as she called it.'

Something off the books, Cristy reflected to herself, as Connor brought the recording to an end and started to pack up.

After thanking Olivia warmly and asking her to be in touch if she happened to see the woman again, or if she remembered anything else she thought might be helpful, they returned to the car. Minutes later, they were heading deeper into the countryside, while speaking to Layla on the phone.

'I can't say I've ever met anyone who fits the description,' Layla replied, after Cristy repeated Olivia's words. 'But obviously Romy knew a lot of people . . . I'll find out if it rings any bells for Mum. Where are you now?'

'On our way to you,' Connor told her. 'Is Quentin still there?'

'Still here and still very keen to tell you what happened last night.'

CHAPTER TEN

Quentin Maloney turned out to be as wonderfully dapper as any man of his generation could be, with his paisley smoking jacket and silk cravat. The big bushy eyebrows that seemed to blend with his mass of grey curly hair only added to the avuncular appeal of his cheery smile. He was waiting for them at his front gate with Layla and was as eager to tell them about himself, his dead wife, two sons, three granddaughters and his wine shop, as he was to help with the search for Romy.

'I don't mind admitting,' he said, as Connor began setting up to record, 'it gave me a bit of a scare in the night.'

They were seated around his small garden table now, sheltered from the sun by a rickety parasol and so close to an array of hanging bird feeders that Cristy could actually smell the nuts inside. There was no sign of anyone on the lake today, or in the other cottages, although the sound of a nearby lawnmower told of someone being at home.

'OK, keep going,' Connor said encouragingly, once the mics were set up.

QUENTIN: 'Well, I couldn't make out what the noise was at first. I was in that deep a sleep, I thought for a minute I was imagining it, but it soon became clear that I wasn't. My first thought was burglars, downstairs, but then I realized it was coming from next door. Obviously, I assumed Romy was back . . .'

CRISTY: 'What time was it?'

QUENTIN: 'Twenty past one when I checked the clock. I didn't mind being woken up – it was good to know she'd turned up at last – but when I went to the window to make sure it was her . . . Well, there was no sign of her Smart. Then I noticed this black car, half-parked on the verge the other side of the cattle-grid. Its headlights were off, but it looked like a Range Rover or similar, and someone was sitting in the driver's seat.'

CONNOR: 'Did you see anyone get in or out of it?'

QUENTIN: 'No. There was just this man . . . I presume it was a man, sitting behind the wheel, and the sounds from Romy's spare bedroom – the other side of the wall from where I was – as if things were being moved around.'

CRISTY: 'You mean, like furniture?'

QUENTIN: 'It could have been that, or boxes – there are a lot in there – but Layla and I have been up to take a look, and nothing seems out of place.'

LAYLA: 'Apart from a few empty coat hangers on the bed that I'm sure weren't there before.'

CRISTY: 'Suggesting that Romy, or someone else, came back for clothes?'

LAYLA: 'That was my assumption, but I've no way of telling if anything's been taken without knowing everything that was there before.'

CONNOR: 'According to her phone, she was overseas last night.'

LAYLA: 'You mean when she rang but didn't speak to my mother?'

CONNOR: 'Precisely. Quentin, did you see anyone leave the cottage, or the car driving away?'

QUENTIN: 'I heard it go, but I didn't see it. Nature called, I'm afraid, and by the time I got back to the window, there were just the tail-lights going off into the dark. It's most peculiar that nothing appears to have been disturbed upstairs, because I know what I heard. It was like something heavy was being shifted. I'd have gone to find out what was happening, but I'm not a young man and if it was burglars, there's no knowing what they might have done if I'd caught them in the act.'

CONNOR: 'You were right to be cautious, especially as Romy's car wasn't there.'

LAYLA: 'What was it all about, that's what I'd like to know. And was it her – or someone else?'

Though Cristy had a theory on what might have been happening, she didn't want to voice it while Quentin was there, so after signalling to Connor to end the recording, she said, 'If nothing's missing and no one's hurt, I guess we can only wait to see if they come back again.'

'I'll definitely be keeping my eyes and ears open,' Quentin assured her. 'Just don't depend on me for any heroics, that's all.'

After they'd thanked him again and gladly accepted his generous offer of two bottles of Chablis to take home with them, Cristy led the way over to Romy's cottage, where Layla had left the door ajar.

Once inside, Connor said, 'Are we seriously thinking that Romy stole into her own home in the dead of night to take a few clothes and shift around some furniture or boxes before just leaving again?'

'Obviously, if she's overseas, it wasn't her,' Cristy responded, 'or it *was* her and someone else has the phone.'

Clearly having no explanation for any of it, Connor said to Layla, 'I don't suppose you've found what you actually came here for?'

'You mean whatever there might be concerning Rudi's financial interests?' Layla replied. 'I haven't looked yet, but I'll make a start now.'

'Before you do that,' Cristy said, 'here's what I think could – I stress *could* – have been happening last night. I admit the coat hangers kind of skew this, but not necessarily. I'm wondering if someone came to remove whatever listening devices they'd planted.'

Layla's eyes rounded.

'The timing of the visit is interesting,' Cristy explained, 'coming right after we were here. So was someone listening in, or watching . . . ?'

'The man in the boat,' Connor broke in.

'Possibly,' she conceded. 'Any word from Sherman Security yet? It'll be good to know when their last visit was, presuming it wasn't the middle of last night.'

'I'll try them again,' Connor replied, 'but with it being Saturday . . .'

As he dialled the number, Layla took herself upstairs for another look round.

Cristy turned to stare at Rudi's portrait, feeling oddly as though it could tell her something if she only knew how to look at it in the right way.

'Hey, yes, it's Connor Church here,' he said into the phone. 'I left a message . . . Mr Grayling, that's right. Manager of Domestic Surveillance. Is he there by any chance? Oh, great. Thanks, yes, I'll hold.'

Cristy turned round in surprise and stepped in closer as Connor switched the call to speaker and pressed to record.

They'd sort out permissions later, once they knew what Grayling had to say.

GRAYLING: 'Sorry, Mr Church. I was going to call you back on Monday, but as I'm in the shop today and you're on the line . . . What can I do for you? You mentioned something about one of our residential clients. I'm sure you're aware we can't give out confidential information . . .'

CONNOR: 'Of course, I understand that, but I'd really appreciate it if you could confirm that you have a contract with the Kaplans at Number 1 Bellbrook? We have a copy of it – all we want to know is if it's still active.'

GRAYLING: 'Can't one of the Kaplans answer that for you?'

CONNOR: 'I'm afraid Mr Kaplan has passed away, and we don't know where Mrs Kaplan is at the moment, which is why we're in touch with you. It's a bit of a long story, but if you're able to tell us when you last visited her home . . . ?'

GRAYLING: 'As I've already said . . .'

CONNOR: 'I'm not asking you to reveal what was found – although happy to hear it if you can see your way to it. We'd just like to know if your visits were about listening devices or hidden cameras, anything like that.'

There was a lengthy silence from the other end as both Cristy and Connor held their breath and crossed their fingers.

GRAYLING: 'OK, I'm prepared to say this: none of our technicians' reports show a positive discovery in that location.'

CONNOR: 'Thank you. And when was the last inspection carried out?'

GRAYLING: 'You're going too far . . .'

CONNOR: 'A month ago? Before that? After? Just give me an idea.'

GRAYLING: 'I hope you realize this is off the record – the last sweep was 12th April, the next is due on 12th June.'

CONNOR: 'Thank you. Just one more thing: if anyone gets in touch to cancel or change the date or the service, please will you let us know?'

GRAYLING: 'Goodbye, Mr Church.'

The line went dead, and Connor rang off with a growl of frustration.

Cristy said, 'You did well to get that much out of him, and actually, it's all we need for now – confirmation that nothing's ever been found, and when the next visit is due. Which is, in fact, this coming Wednesday, so it could mean someone's planting and removing devices in between the security checks. Hence, the visit last night, to clear the place before the Sherman technician turns up to do his "sweep".'

Nodding thoughtfully, Connor said, 'I think one of us should be here when the technician comes. We might get more out of him or her than I've just managed out of Grayling.'

Agreeing, Cristy said, 'Let's put it in the diary, and now I think we'd better head back to the office. If you've been checking your messages, you'll know that Iz is waiting for us, and I'm starting to feel bad about the way we walked out on her.'

'Not having the same problem,' Connor assured her, 'and I guess I won't mind rubbing her nose in the two interviews we've just bagged. Three including Sherman Security. There's a series here, whether her bloody sponsors want to see it or not.'

'She'll make them see it,' Cristy declared confidently, and going to the foot of the stairs, she called up to Layla, 'Do you need any help?'

'Yes, unless you have somewhere else to be,' Layla shouted back. 'Some of these files go back years, so I'm thinking of packing them up and taking them home.' Coming out onto the landing, she said, 'I heard you talking to the security firm. So someone has been checking the place over for bugs?'

Cristy nodded.

Layla's expression was grim. 'I don't know whether to be scared, creeped out, or what I should be,' she said, 'but I do know I'm not keen to stay here on my own if you need to go.'

Understanding her reticence, Cristy said, 'We'll help you load up your car, and then we really should get back to the office.'

CHAPTER ELEVEN

It was mid-afternoon by the time Cristy and Connor walked through the door to find Iz and Clove working quietly at their desks, and Iz looked so pleased to see them that Cristy felt sure if she'd had a tail, she'd have wagged it.

'Things are definitely looking up,' Iz effusively assured them. 'I'm working on a strategy for the sponsors that is going to be much enhanced by the interviews you've just done.'

'You already know about them?' Cristy asked, puzzled.

'I forwarded the recordings to Clove,' Connor told her.

'Combined with everything else Clove has explained,' Iz continued, 'I foresee an extremely exciting woman-hunt unfolding, and calling the public to arms is a fantastic way to kick things off. Of course, we'll have all and sundry claiming sightings from Australia to Timbuktu, but as we know, audience engagement is as vital to ratings as it is to results. So, based on that, I think we need the supersleuths back on board to handle the social media onslaught I'm sure will come. We know from the last series that they're extremely good at sorting the meat from the gravy.'

Connor's eyes went to Cristy, who shrugged.

'We ran a team of four before,' Iz rattled on, opening up her laptop, 'so I think we should start with them and add more if the need arises.'

'And you're really thinking of moving them into the meeting room across the hall?' Clove asked dubiously.

Iz's round face shone with eagerness and the kind of simple sincerity that made her, in Cristy's view, almost impossible to dislike, in spite of how irritating she could be at times. 'Happy to make it happen if it works for you guys,' she declared, 'but just as easy for them to do it remotely, if that's what you'd prefer.'

Keen to avoid any attempt at sponsorship oversight, given the back up team was recruited by Iz, Cristy said, 'We don't need them that close, so remote is fine.'

Noting that down, Iz said, 'Now, I think we need to work on some contingencies, just in case Romy suddenly turns up asking what all the fuss is about—'

'You're not a producer,' Connor interrupted tightly.

'No! No, of course not. Sorry, not trying to overstep, just want to be prepared, make sure I've got your backs, so to speak, should you need it. Content is definitely down to you, but like I said earlier, if you can find out for certain that Rudi was murdered and the authorities have covered it up . . . Is that what you're thinking?'

'It's a possibility at this stage,' Cristy told her, 'based on no actual evidence, so we definitely don't want it going public.'

'No problem, sealed lips – just wanting to point out how great it'll be for ratings if you're right.'

'But not quite so great for him,' Connor pointed out dryly. 'Although, as he's dead, I don't suppose he's in a position to care much one way or the other now.'

Iz's answering smile was uncertain. She never did get Connor's humour, hard as Cristy knew she tried.

'OK,' Cristy said, turning on her computer, 'you've come all this way to see us, so let's get down to the business end of things. It'll be good to know more about the backers you're planning to bring in this time around and what they'll expect of us in a promotional sense.'

'Not editorial,' Connor reminded her darkly.

The next few hours passed swiftly, carried along by Iz's

indefatigable enthusiasm for everything and clear determination not to upset anyone again today. In the end, it was past six before anyone realized the time. In fact, they might have gone on even longer had Jodi, Connor's wife, not waltzed in, looking extremely glamorous in full make-up and a sleeveless cream silk jumpsuit.

'Oh Christ! I forgot,' Connor cried, slapping a hand to his head. 'Theatre? Right?'

Jodi nodded, her dark eyes laughing as she sank onto the visitor's sofa and propped her long legs up on one arm. 'I'm back from Mum's specially,' she reminded him, 'but don't worry – still plenty of time. If you've got any wine in that fridge . . .'

'Coming right up,' Clove assured her, 'but aren't you still breast-feeding?'

'I've expressed enough today to keep Aurora going for a month, so make it a large one. Hi, Iz, lovely to see you. Are you leaving already?'

'I've been here most of the day,' Iz replied, packing her bag. 'If I go now, I should make the seven o'clock train.'

After she'd gone, leaving an almost tangible exit-whizz in her wake, Cristy said to Jodi, 'So how is my beautiful goddaughter?'

'Loving being with her nana,' Jodi replied, 'almost as much as we're going to love having a night to ourselves.'

Connor was immediately alert. 'Just wondering why we're wasting it at the theatre when we could be at home, putting on a show of our own?'

Archly, Jodi said, 'We've bought the tickets now, and it's something I want to see. We'll have the rest of the night and all of tomorrow morning before Mum brings Aurora back. Is David still around?' she asked Cristy. 'Matthew said he was here last night.'

'He was; should be back in Guernsey by now. You've seen Matthew?'

'I spoke to him this morning about my weekly "good news" slot. I'm thinking I might be ready to start back in a few weeks.'

'Speak of the devil,' Cristy said, as David's name came up on her phone. 'Hey you, I guess you're back safely.'

'Hours ago, and I'm about to run out again, but before I do, I thought you'd like to know that my tech guy took a look at your Facebook video, and he's got some clarity on the background.'

Cristy's heartbeat quickened. 'Really? So can you tell where Romy is?'

'Yep. The statue is of Infante Dom Henrique.'

'Who?'

'Henry the Navigator. He's Portuguese, fifteenth century. The church in the background is Santa Maria, and there's an old slave market nearby, although it's not in shot . . .'

'Hang on, how do you know if it's not—'

'Google Maps. So, it's the main square in Lagos – spelled L-a-g-o-s but pronounced *La*-gosh – on the Algarve.'

Cristy blinked. 'He saw all that when we couldn't make out anything at all?'

'Seems these things can be done when you know how. Anyway, that's where she was when she made the video. All you have to do now is find out who she was with, and if she's still there.'

'As to who, there's only a shadow . . .'

'There's a reflection in her sunglasses. I'll send the enhancement now. I think it might surprise you – quite a lot.'

CHAPTER TWELVE

The following morning, Cristy was at Layla's family home on the outskirts of Pensford – an old, sandstone farmhouse with views across open fields to the long-disused viaduct that had been a source of great fascination for Cristy's father, back in the day. She'd just shown Beth Cates the video enhancement of Romy in Lagos, and though Cristy wasn't surprised by Beth's response, she was concerned by the distress it had clearly caused.

'But it can't be Rudi,' Beth protested, still studying the reflection in Romy's sunglasses. 'It just can't.' She looked beseechingly up at Cristy, her pale face blotched with sores, her naked eyes bloodshot and haunted. It wrenched at Cristy's heart to know how much she was suffering, while trying to hide it for her family's sake even more than her own.

Beth touched a skeletal hand to her turban, which had started to slip sideways, and Cristy felt her heart stir again when Layla tenderly straightened it. Being here, seeing mother and daughter like this, was bringing back too many memories of the care she'd taken of her own mother in the final months, and how hard it had been – still was, all these years later – to let her go.

But this was about Romy and the reflection in her sunglasses that appeared to be Rudi's.

'You have to admit it looks a lot like him,' Layla said,

going to lower a blind to protect her mother from a sudden stream of sunlight.

'But Rudi's dead,' Beth reminded her. 'So obviously it can't be him.'

'But are you sure about that?' Layla challenged gently.

Beth looked puzzled. 'About Rudi being dead? Of course I am . . .'

'But what if he isn't?'

The way Beth recoiled from the suggestion was hard to watch. 'What on earth are you saying?' she cried. 'Romy found him herself – you know that – so I don't understand what's going on here.' She looked at Cristy, clearly needing her to explain.

'I think we're looking at someone who's very similar to Rudi in appearance,' Cristy told her. 'I mean, we can't see the eyes – it's only the lower half of the face and neck . . .'

'But what if it *is* him?' Layla interrupted. 'Remember, that AV character on Facebook said, "give our best to Rudi".'

'Stop it, Layla,' her mother insisted. 'I grant you, it looks like Rudi, but we know it can't be, so I'll tell you what's most likely happening. She's met someone who reminds her of him, and this whole . . . escapade she's on . . . is some sort of crazy romance to try and distract herself from the terrible grief. You know how impulsive, even irrational she can be at times, and his death was such a horrible shock for her . . .'

'And the reason she's not calling you?' Layla asked. 'Apart from that one attempt on Friday evening when no one spoke, so we still don't know for certain it was her.'

'It was definitely her number,' Beth pointed out, 'and I'm sure the reason she's reluctant to speak to me is because she knows I'll try to talk sense into her and make her come home. Cristy, I hope you're not listening to any of this, thinking this person is Rudi. I couldn't bear it if you did.'

Feeling for her, Cristy said, 'It's possible this is an old

94

video that's been . . . repurposed, for want of a better word, in order to deflect—'

'Surely no one would do that,' Beth protested, clearly unwilling to follow what Cristy was suggesting, although Cristy could tell she wasn't entirely sure of what that was.

Cristy simply said, 'Why don't we set it aside for the moment and try to deal with why Rudi and Romy were having their home regularly inspected by a security company.'

'And what someone was doing there in the early hours of yesterday morning,' Layla added. 'By the way,' she said to Cristy, 'I asked Mum about the young woman the giftshop owner described, and she can't think who it might be.'

Worry had crept back into the shadows around Beth's eyes, and Cristy could almost feel her fragility. Even if Beth was feeling stronger today, she was too weak to deal with so many unanswered questions, especially of this importance.

'I'm afraid there isn't a good explanation for any of it,' Beth said softly, and reached for Layla's hand. After a moment, she looked at Cristy. 'What I'm about to tell you,' she said, 'well, it's hard to see how it has anything to do with what's going on now – it was so long ago, back in the Eighties . . . Anyway, I think you might already know that Rudi and Romy were both working for the British Embassy in Moscow. She was a shorthand typist; he was in a more senior position, something to do with defence, I think, and we used to tease him about spying on the Russians. Of course, they used to accuse everyone of that, especially in that particular Embassy; it just went with the territory.

'Johnny and I visited them once; we had a marvellous time, all of us. Of course our hotel room was bugged – everywhere was back then, including their apartment. They never seemed to take it very seriously, but when he was expelled, along with several others . . . Please understand, I'm not trying to say that we suddenly began to suspect that Rudi really was a spy; we were much more inclined to believe him when he said the net had been cast wide for expulsions and he'd just got caught up in it. He wasn't upset or particularly sorry to leave Moscow. Their time there was coming to an end anyway, and so off they went to America . . .' She stopped and swallowed. 'I'm sure Layla's told you all this.'

'She has,' Cristy confirmed, 'but it's good to hear it from you too.'

Beth nodded distractedly. 'I'm really not sure it's relevant – in fact I'm certain it isn't – but with all this talk of security . . .' She sighed and shook her head helplessly. 'What *is* going on?' she asked, almost of herself. 'She wanted to be in touch with you, Cristy, but now she isn't responding to your posts, or mine. And that ugly message someone sent . . .'

They turned as a stocky man of medium height and generous weight – presumably Layla's father – came into the kitchen with a very old cocker spaniel close on his heels. With them was a younger man Cristy realized must be Layla's brother, as he had the same vibrant red hair as his sister, cut short and blended with a close-shaved beard.

'You must be Cristy,' Johnny Cates said, holding out a hand to shake. 'Sorry I wasn't here when you arrived. Had to take the dog to the emergency vet.'

'Are you OK?' Beth asked, stooping to cup the dog's grizzled head in her hands.

'The vet says there's plenty of life in him yet,' Barry assured her, going to embrace her. 'How are you?' he asked tenderly.

'I'm OK,' she said, patting his hand.

He turned to Cristy, his eyes overly bright, it seemed, until she realized they were filled with tears and the latent, persistent fear of losing his mother. 'Thanks for trying to help with Romy,' he said. 'It's been quite a strain on Mum, not knowing where she is.'

Cristy smiled. 'I just wish it was proving easier to find her,' she said. 'Things aren't quite as . . . straightforward as we'd hoped.'

'Things rarely are with Romy,' he commented wryly and turned as his father pulled up a chair to sit at the table.

'So what have we missed?' Johnny asked, bunching his hands together.

Beth rotated Cristy's laptop so he could see the screen. 'Tell me who you think that is reflected in Romy's sunglasses,' she said.

Peering in closer, he started to frown. 'When was this taken?' he asked, glancing up at Cristy.

'Romy posted the video a couple of days ago,' Beth answered. 'We watched it together, remember? Cristy's had some work done on it, and this is what's come up.'

Barry took a look and sounded shocked, even offended when he said, 'I can see it looks like Rudi, but obvs it can't be him . . .'

'But what if it is?' Layla interrupted.

Her brother and father regarded her askance. 'What are you saying, sugar?' Johnny asked. 'We know Rudi's dead . . .'

'What we know is that Romy didn't want to make a fuss when it happened,' Layla reminded him. 'She wanted the whole thing over quickly. Even the police thought the circumstances were suspicious at first—'

'Layla, stop,' Beth broke in, clearly agitated.

'Yes, stop,' Barry told her, 'because what you're saying, or implying, Layla, is outrageous, insane even, and you can see how it's upsetting Mum.'

Flushing, though apparently not ready to let it go, Layla said, 'Did you see Rudi yourself, Mum, when Romy found him in the bath?'

Beth looked confused. 'No, I didn't,' she admitted, 'but I saw Romy and what a state she was in. Darling, this is a crazy way of thinking. Rudi's dead, and now we have to focus our efforts on finding Romy.'

'Too right,' Johnny said gruffly and got up to fill the kettle.

Barry said, 'What are you making of it all, Cristy? I mean, you're not thinking that's Rudi, are you? In the reflection.'

'I admit it threw me when I first saw it,' Cristy replied, 'and with everything being so . . . unpredictable . . .' She broke off, realizing she was heading down the wrong path. Starting again, she said, 'Beth was obviously there when Romy found him in the bath. Even if she didn't actually see him herself, she'd have witnessed them carrying the body out?' She looked at Beth for confirmation.

Beth nodded and swallowed. 'He was covered up, obviously,' she said, 'but yes, I saw it.'

'So, even if they'd wanted to,' Cristy said, 'and heaven only knows why they would, they'd never have got away with trying to pass someone else off as Rudi. And there would have to have been someone else involved if it wasn't Rudi in the bath.'

After allowing a moment for everyone to take that in, Layla said, 'What if they just took Romy's word for the fact that it was him, and all the time it *was* someone else?'

'Oh, come on, Lay,' Barry chided, while his mother groaned. 'That's just crazy.'

Layla's eyes flashed. 'You're the one who's always said there was more to them than the rest of us were seeing,' she snapped.

'Yeah, but not like that.'

'You actually called them dodgy!' she cried. 'Don't deny it – I was there when you said it.'

'I meant they had a dodgy past, because they did. All that stuff in Moscow . . .'

'Nearly forty years ago, so hardly relevant to bring it up now.'

'I didn't – you did. And you've got to admit some of their friends do come over as a bit suspect – not that there's anything wrong with that. We've all got dubious mates, even you; theirs are just richer or classier or smarter—'

'Stop!' Beth cut in fiercely. 'Both of you. This isn't getting us anywhere, and Cristy doesn't want to hear your bickering. I'm sorry,' she said to Cristy. 'We're all on edge over this, and stress often brings out the worst in people.'

Cristy looked at Layla and saw that although she had plenty more to say, she was holding back for her mother's sake. It reminded Cristy of the spats she used to have with her brother and how their mother would step between them. Oddly, it made her miss him and wonder how he was over in Canada. They should make an effort to be in touch more often. It wasn't as if they didn't care about one another, because they did; he was just getting on with his life in Toronto, much as she was getting on with hers here.

She almost winced when Layla said, 'If you didn't actually see the body, Mum . . .'

'It was Rudi,' Beth said forcefully. 'Now please, Layla, I don't want to hear any more.' She reached for a tissue and dabbed her eyes. 'For heaven's sake, do you realize what you're accusing your own godmother of? How could you even think such a terrible thing of her?'

As Layla glowered at her brother and he arched his eyebrows as though he'd scored a point, Cristy made a mental note to find out if further ID checks had been carried out after Rudi's body had been taken to the morgue. If they hadn't . . . well, they'd cross that when – *if* – they came to it.

For now, keen to settle things down, Cristy said, 'I think we should continue to assume that it was Rudi who died. The man in the reflection, while he bears a strong resemblance, could actually be anyone. Or maybe it is him and the video has been recycled in a way to—'

'Romy wouldn't know how to do that,' Barry protested. 'But even if she did, why would she?'

'Good question,' Cristy conceded, 'but maybe let's focus on where the video was shot for the moment and when it was posted. We know it was Lagos in the Algarve . . .'

'Why believe that if you're not believing anything else?' Barry countered.

'Actually, it does make sense that she'd be there,' Beth cut in. 'I mean, if anything makes sense in all this, and I'm not sure it does.' Her lashless eyes came to Cristy's. 'Johnny and I have a small townhouse a few miles from Lagos on a golf resort, nothing fancy, but Romy's always loved it there. She enjoys the simplicity of it, she says. We used to go quite regularly, just the two of us. We were there right before Rudi died . . .'

Cristy said, 'Would you mind if I started recording?'

Beth glanced at her husband, then at her son and daughter.

'I'm cool with it,' Barry told Layla. 'Just remember, I'm not the one trying to say it wasn't Rudi who drowned . . .'

'Enough!' his father barked. 'If you two are going to carry on, you need to leave the room.'

'I'm not going anywhere,' Layla retorted. 'I'm the only one who really cares where she is—'

'That's a stupid thing to say,' Johnny snapped. 'You know how important she is to your mother. To all of us.'

Immediately contrite, Layla said, 'I'm sorry, Mum. I didn't mean that. He just winds me up sometimes.'

'Maybe I should go,' Barry offered.

'No, no, we want you here,' Beth insisted, and reached for his hand. 'It's all going to be fine. We can do this. Just take deep breaths, and remember, this is about Romy, not any of us.'

Cristy managed not to smile as both Layla and Barry obeyed their mother's breathing instructions.

'We're happy for you to record,' Johnny said. 'Just please stop if we start embarrassing ourselves again.'

'I'll only use what you want me to,' she assured him.

He nodded his thanks and said, 'It's good for Beth to be doing this. She needs to feel . . . involved. She and Romy go back a long way, you know, right to their school days.'

'Which reminds me,' Beth said, watching Cristy reach into her bag for the recorder, 'there's something I have to tell you, but it can wait until we've done this.'

Though intrigued, Cristy decided not to press her, simply placed a mic on the table, and after identifying them all for the recording she said, 'I was going to start by asking you, Beth, about the time of Rudi's death, but maybe we should leave that for now?'

'No, I'll tell you what I can,' Beth insisted, 'but you two are not to interrupt,' she instructed her children. 'Especially not you with all that nonsense, Layla.'

Putting a finger to her lips, Layla signalled for Cristy to continue.

'OK, if you're sure,' Cristy said to Beth, 'maybe you can tell me if Romy seemed worried or agitated before you cut short your stay in Portugal.'

BETH: 'Yes, as a matter of fact she did. Not all of the time. When we were first there, she was OK, but as the days passed and she couldn't get hold of Rudi . . . Well, she became increasingly worried. Anyone would, especially when they usually spoke on the phone a few times a day.'

CRISTY: 'Did she say what she thought might have happened, why he wasn't answering the phone?'

BETH: 'Only things like it didn't make any sense; he should have been at home, or he always carried his mobile. And she couldn't understand why he wasn't trying to call her. Oh, and of course she hoped that he hadn't been hurt, you know, in some sort of accident.'

CRISTY: 'Did she contact anyone to find out if they'd seen him or knew where he might be?'

BETH: 'I'm sure she rang Nula, her neighbour, and

Johnny. She called you didn't she, to find out if you'd heard from him?'

JOHNNY: 'That's right, but I hadn't. I offered to drive up there to check on him, but . . .'

BETH: '. . . In the end, we decided to fly home. She kept saying she had a really bad feeling about things, and well . . . as it turned out . . .'

Cristy allowed a few moments to pass, realizing it would be insensitive, as well as distressing for Beth, to start asking for a minute-by-minute account of what happened when they got to the cottage and Romy found Rudi in the bath. They could always come back to it if necessary.

For the moment, she decided to move things on.

CRISTY: 'Can you tell us something about the police investigation that followed Rudi's death?'

JOHNNY: 'If you ask me, they didn't seem able to make up their minds what had happened from one minute to the next. First it was an accident; then it wasn't . . . Had someone broken in? Not that they could find evidence of. Were the injuries caused by someone holding him under or by him swimming into some tree branch or other? Then they wanted to know if we knew of anyone who'd want to harm him. Of course we didn't, and nor did Romy. They didn't have enemies, only friends – at least as far as we knew . . .'

BETH: 'Until that awful message on Facebook.'

JOHNNY: 'That was just a crank. Put it out of your mind.'

BETH: 'I keep trying to, but then I ask myself: why did she think someone was spying on them? She never

102

mentioned a word of that to me, and we always told one another everything.'

LAYLA: 'Except you don't know where she is now.'

BARRY: 'I thought you promised to stay quiet.'

BETH: 'I guess she might have held a few things back when I wasn't well; she wouldn't have wanted to worry me, but something like that . . .'

CRISTY: 'How about Rudi? Did he ever say anything to any of you about being monitored in some way?'

JOHNNY: 'Not a word, and believe me, I'd remember something like that. No, the only thing that really comes to mind about him over recent times is how he was able to hide what was happening to him – you know, running out of money and having to sell the house. I'm amazed by that, when he must have been in trouble for a while – those things don't happen overnight, do they? But the first we knew of it was when Romy gave Beth a change of address.'

BETH: 'You can probably imagine how shocked I was, but she didn't want to discuss it. She just said the manor had become a drain on them financially, so it was time to downsize.'

CRISTY: 'Was there anyone else living at the manor with them before they left? A housekeeper, for instance?'

BETH: 'Yes, yes, there was Inge. I can't recall her surname, and I'm not sure of her actual title, but I guess she was a kind of housekeeper-cum-PA. I know it made Romy sad to let her go; she was always very fond of Inge . . . I'd say they were quite close, but it's hard not to be close with Romy; she makes everyone feel so special.'

CRISTY: 'I know Layla talked to you about the woman who passed Romy a note in the giftshop. Could it have been Inge?'

BETH: 'Not from the description Layla gave me. Inge's much older, probably around sixty.'

CRISTY: 'OK. If you're able to remember Inge's full name, or anything else about her, it might be useful to talk to her anyway.'

BETH: 'Of course. I'll do my best.'

CRISTY: 'I know Romy stayed in touch with you after they moved, but what about her other friends?'

BETH: 'She had so many, and I can't be sure who she did or didn't stay in contact with. I only know that they more or less stopped entertaining. Of course, the cottage was too small to throw the kind of parties they used to, but they'd always been very social and welcoming before, and they loved putting people together. We used to call them the matchmakers, whether it was business or romance, or just people who came from the same part of the world . . .'

CRISTY: 'Layla mentioned they had a lot of foreign connections?'

BETH: 'Because they travelled so much, and with Rudi speaking so many languages . . .'

Beth stopped and turned to her husband. 'You know, the more I think about it, the more certain I feel that she's staying in the townhouse. She has keys, and she knows all the codes for the pool and gym and WiFi.' To Cristy, she said, 'She's always called it her happy place, and that's what she's saying in the videos, isn't it? That she's happy and we shouldn't worry.'

'We should call the complex managers to ask if someone's staying there,' Johnny suggested.

'Or,' Layla jumped in, 'we could go there and see for ourselves.'

As Cristy blinked, Beth said, 'Yes, maybe you and Cristy should do that. At least then you'd get to speak to her.'

Before Cristy could point out how bizarre it would be for Romy not to have told them she was using their house, Barry said, 'And if she isn't there, maybe you'll find something to tell us where she is now?'

*

Half an hour later, with a trip to Portugal already half-planned for the coming week, Beth reached for Cristy's hands to say goodbye. 'You know,' Beth said, 'there's a certain serendipity, or irony, or whatever it's called – maybe poetry – in you helping to find Romy.'

Surprised, Cristy tilted her head.

'We knew your mother, Romy and I. Many years ago. She was in the sixth form when we were a couple of giggly, starry-eyed thirteen-year-olds. We adored her. She was so glamorous and adventurous and kind. All the girls looked up to her; we all wanted to be her. Romy and I felt especially privileged that she had a private room at the end of our dorm. Along with the other girls, we used to listen outside her door as she played her records, and we'd dance . . . Romy and I always believed we were her favourites, but I daresay the others all thought the same.' Beth smiled reflectively. 'What I remember the most about her, apart from her lovely looks and having a boyfriend with a motorbike—'

'Probably my dad,' Cristy said, smiling over the lump

105

forming in her throat. Hearing about her mother as a girl in her late teens was like a balm she hadn't even known she needed.

Beth nodded. 'Yes, I know she married young, but what made her extra special in our eyes was how wonderful she was with Romy after Romy's mother died. She used to go out of her way to make Romy feel special and . . . safe, I suppose.' Her eyes came to Cristy's. 'She was the one who suggested Romy should try writing down passages from her favourite books to help her over the worst of her grief. It might be a helpful distraction, she said. She knew, of course, that Romy had a great love of literature, so it was the right thing to suggest, and it's advice that Romy has followed ever since, right up to the notebook Layla found a few days ago.' Beth smiled sadly. 'If that one tells us anything, it's that Romy was feeling the need to distract herself again, to lose herself in something that wouldn't hurt or frighten her.' She blinked slowly as she considered her last words. 'I have found no significance to the passages I've read so far,' she said, 'but I'll keep going, mostly because it soothes me to lose myself in her choices. I feel like I'm sharing something with her. Does that sound silly?'

'Not at all,' Cristy assured her.

Beth regarded her curiously. 'Doesn't it seem serendipitous to you that all these years later, Helen's daughter is coming to Romy's rescue?'

Cristy couldn't deny it, nor did she want to.

'You're a lot like her, you know.'

'Except a lot older than when you last saw her.'

Beth squeezed her hands. 'I can only begin to imagine how much you must miss her,' she said. 'You won't know this, but Romy and I came to the funeral. We stood at the back to pay our respects to the young girl we remembered and the lovely wife and mother she'd become.'

Having to swallow, Cristy whispered, 'Thank you. I know she would have appreciated that, and I certainly do.'

Beth smiled. 'Maybe she did know,' she said softly. 'We liked to think so anyway, and seeing you here today helps me to believe that in her way, through you, she's still looking out for dear Romy.'

CHAPTER THIRTEEN

Later in the day, with the distant thrum of a band playing on the Harbourside, Cristy was sitting in her small patio garden, going through her notes. Almost unconsciously she was inhaling the scents of jasmine and honeysuckle, a couple of early summer arrivals in her loosely curated tangle of wildflowers and budding succulents. It seemed that everything today was reminding her of her mother, from this colourful little haven in the centre of town to the chirrup and tweet of birdsong. She had a very real sense of her being close by. Ten years and she still missed her terribly, and hearing Beth Cates speak of her so warmly had left her feeling quietly reflective and not a little emotional.

'It was wonderful to get a tiny snapshot of her like that,' she told David when he rang, 'and oddly, it seemed to matter even more for it being so long ago, when she wasn't even as old as Hayley. We forget to see our parents as young people, don't we? We just take them for who they are today, oblivious to who they were and what mattered to them before we came along.'

Wryly, he said, 'I know my mother would wholeheartedly agree with that.'

She smiled. 'How is my favourite person?' she asked, picturing Cynthia, in her mid-eighties now and yet still seeming as young and lively as a woman half her age.

'She's doing just fine, thanks,' he responded. 'Missing

you, of course – we all are – and now, with you going off to Portugal next week, and me to Denmark, I'm starting to wonder when I'll next see you. Are you actually going to go to Portugal?'

'Layla wants to, and as it was clear Beth doesn't want her to take off alone, I ended up agreeing to go with her. I can't imagine we'll be there more than a couple of days, so it's you and your male-bonding commitment that's causing the delay in us getting together.'

Not without irony, he said, 'Of course it's my fault. Everything is. So when exactly will you leave?'

'Not before Wednesday. Aiden will have completed his final exam by then, so I'll feel more comfortable about abandoning him, as he likes to put it.'

'Not that he doesn't have a father close by, but OK, I get your need to be around until the important bits are over. Where are they this evening?'

Going inside to pour herself some wine, Cristy said, 'Aiden assures me he's revising, which probably means he's got some friends over to play video games, or he's at the concert you can probably hear over on the waterfront. Matthew, would you believe, is taking Layla out to dinner.'

'OK,' David said, drawing out the word. 'Why do I get the feeling you're not too thrilled about that?'

'I wouldn't mind in the slightest if I didn't think he had an ulterior motive. And that too would be fine if he weren't a married man.'

'So are you concerned about Marley? Or Layla?'

'Both, I guess.'

'Dare I say, neither are your problem?'

Sighing, she said, 'You're right, they aren't. I just hate the idea of someone getting hurt, and there's no doubt in my mind that someone will. Maybe I won't care so much if it's Matthew, although I'm not sure I mean that. As infuriating and self-absorbed as he is at times, he's still my children's father, and deep down I know he's as vulnerable as the rest of us.'

'He's a great guy, in a lot of ways. Not without his faults, I grant you, but at least you've never had to worry about him being a serial killer.'

Choking on a laugh, Cristy said, 'I stopped believing that about you almost from the day we met, so quit reminding me and tell me what you're doing this evening.'

'Well, I've got dinner with a couple of clients at Pier 17 . . .'

'One of my favourites.'

'I know, and tomorrow Laurent and I are getting some sailing in prior to Skagen. Now, talk me through what you're hoping to get out of Portugal. Is Connor going with you?'

'That's the plan. We're hoping to stay at Layla's parents' place, but that could prove awkward if Romy really is there, given it only has two bedrooms.'

'So what are you going to do if Romy *is* there?'

'That's hard to answer until we see her. I guess the most important thing is to know that she's safe and why she isn't making direct contact with anyone.'

'And if it turns out she's just trying to get some time to herself? You won't only be crashing her space; you won't have much of a podcast on your hands.'

Cristy sighed. He was right of course, because if Romy was OK – and obviously she hoped she was – she couldn't not be mindful of the fact that they might have wasted a lot of time and effort on a series that was going nowhere. In the end, she said, 'There's something odd going on here, I'm certain of it, but if she does turn up wondering what all the fuss is about it'll still be interesting to find out why she and Rudi felt the need to hire a security company.'

'What did Layla's parents have to say about that?'

'They didn't know anything about it, so couldn't throw any light on it, but now listen to this: Layla is starting to question whether or not it was actually Rudi who died in the bath.'

'Are you serious? Don't tell me this has come from the reflection in the sunglasses?'

'It has.'

'But it's just someone who looks like the guy,' David said. 'Surely?'

'That's the most obvious conclusion, or it's an old image reused. I don't suppose your guy had anything to say about that?'

'No, but I can always ask. Anyway, it's sounding as though you think Layla could be right?'

'Let's just say we need to find out what further identity checks are carried out in a situation like Rudi's, because if they accept the next-of-kin's word that it's their nearest and dearest . . . Well, that does open things up for more scrutiny, wouldn't you say?'

'I guess . . . but Beth was there, wasn't she?'

'Yes, but Romy was the only one who went into the bathroom before the emergency services arrived, so she's the only one who saw him who'd have *known* it was – or wasn't him.'

'Jesus,' he murmured, taking a moment to absorb this. 'And if it turns out not to have been him . . . ? Do you know if the body was cremated or buried?'

'Cremated.'

'Then how's anyone ever going to know for certain?'

'I've no idea, but maybe, if it was someone else, it answers why Romy was so keen to shut everything down and move on.'

With an incredulous laugh, David said, 'This could be one hell of a case you've got on your hands, because if Romy and Rudi have managed to fake his death, kill someone else and now disappear . . . Well, first of all it begs the question why they would even need to do something like that? And second, why on earth is she posting videos?'

'To stop people looking for her? If she keeps telling everyone she's all right, they'll eventually leave her alone and get on with their lives. I'm not saying that's what's happening, but it could be. The third question is one you've already asked: if it wasn't Rudi who died in the bath, then who the heck was it?'

CHAPTER FOURTEEN

Cristy wasn't sure if it was the wind or the heat that hit first as she and Connor emerged from the terminal building at Faro Airport. Both were so intense that it was no easier to walk with dignity than it was to stay cool.

'It's not usually as bad as this,' Layla shouted over her shoulder, fighting to hold onto her wheelie bag as they crossed the road to the concrete sprawl of a car park. On reaching a wooden platform in front of a ramshackle kiosk, she immediately climbed onto it and pressed herself into the unruly crowd waiting to pick up rental cars.

'I guess they don't do queuing here,' Connor commented, as he and Cristy waited, holding onto his glasses as his hair rose up for take-off.

'I came once, as a child,' she replied, totally mishearing him over the roar of wind and planes, and tucking her own hair into a band, she pointed to the side of the shack, where it appeared slightly more sheltered.

Her mobile buzzed in her bag. 'Who's this?' she muttered. After reading the text, she shouted in Connor's ear, 'Clove's at Romy's cottage, and apparently the technician from Sherman's has just turned up. She'll message again after she's spoken to him.'

Connor gave a thumbs-up to show he'd heard. Then yelled, 'What's the deal with the rental car? How come Layla's picking it up, not us?'

'She'd already booked it by the time I offered. She wants to be useful as our chauffeur, but I hope you brought your driver's licence anyway.'

'I did, and some printed head shots of Rudi and Romy just in case we need them. How far is it to where we're going?'

'About an hour, I think. I'm just going to text Aiden to remind him to water my garden tonight.'

'I'll let Jodi know we've arrived. Are we an hour ahead here?'

'No, same time zone.'

Finally, after a forty-minute wait in the gusting wind and blazing sun with no shade, followed by an hour's drive west, and a quick whirl around a supermarket to pick up supplies, Layla turned into the exclusive and almost tranquil splendour of the Santo António golf resort.

What had happened to the wind? It was as if they'd been magically transported from the heart of a maelstrom into an oasis of unruffled calm.

This place was certainly impressive, Cristy reflected, taking in the immaculate green courses, trailing bougainvillea and soaring palms as they drove further into the complex.

And then there was the light, so soft and surreal and unmistakably Mediterranean. It was like stepping into a dream.

'Sorry we're not going over there,' Layla said, directing them to look across a grassy valley to where dozens of whitewashed villas glistened resplendently on the hillside. 'We call them the WAG villas, all show and luxury lifestyle. We rent one sometimes, if more of the family come down, but today we just have our humble abode, which is right around the corner now. At least it has the good manners to be right opposite the main pool and spa.'

'Not that we've come for that,' Cristy pointed out, while wishing for nothing more than a dive straight into a perfectly chilled pool. 'God, it's hot,' she remarked, as they came to a stop and climbed out of the car into what felt like fifty degrees but was probably more like thirty. She almost wished for the wind to pick up again.

'Let's get the place opened up,' Layla said, and fishing out her keys, she went to unlock a pretty little townhouse with a bright blue front door, sand-coloured window frames and copious amounts of bougainvillea spilling over a shady side terrace.

Cristy held her breath. The resort manager had already told them that no one had been seen here recently. Nonetheless . . .

Layla pushed open the door, calling, 'Hello? Is anybody here?'

Silence.

She stepped inside, disappearing into darkness.

With a quick glance at one another Cristy and Connor followed, and blinked as Layla threw open the shutters to allow air and sunlight to flood the small sitting room.

Cristy looked around. 'It's lovely,' she declared, taking in the large couch, two armchairs, a small round dining table and pale wood sideboard. Definitely no sign of anyone living here and she felt a wave of disappointment mix with a growing determination to get to the bottom of this mystery.

'There's a bedroom and bathroom upstairs,' Layla told them, 'a second en suite through that door there, and over here is the kitchen.'

As she went through an arch next to a colourfully tiled fireplace, Connor dropped his bag on the sofa. 'I guess this is my bed,' he declared, testing out the cushions for comfort. 'I hope you're sorting drinks in there,' he called out to Layla.

'There's ice in the freezer,' she announced, coming back into the room, 'but before you wonder who filled the trays, I requested it when I was in touch this morning. The fridge is empty, and nothing else to suggest she's been here.'

Picking up on her dismay, Cristy said, 'Well, it's still possible she was in Lagos a few days ago, so let's head there once we've freshened up and changed into something cooler.'

'And had a drink,' Connor added firmly.

Ten minutes later, Layla carried three gin and tonics and a dish of pretzels onto the terrace, where Cristy and Connor were close to being hypnotized by the peaceful symphony of thwacked golf balls, pool splashing, erratic birdsong and breeze-rustled palms.

Smiling, Cristy reached for her drink and raised it to Layla. 'Here's to finding Romy,' she said.

'To finding Romy,' the others echoed, clinking glasses.

Putting his glass down, Connor said, 'So, I was making up the sofa for later, and here's what I found behind one of the cushions.' He put a small scrap of card on the table.

Reaching for it, Cristy's eyes widened as she realized what it was. 'An airline baggage receipt,' she declared, 'in the name of . . .'. Her eyes shot to Connor, then immediately went to Layla.

Layla took the card, and her mouth actually fell open. 'Oh my God! Kaplan. It's for a flight from Bristol on 6th June.' She looked from Cristy to Connor. 'So she was here last week?' she said incredulously. 'This is a day before the latest video was posted.'

Taking the label back, Connor said, 'It must have fallen off her passport.'

'Presuming it was on her passport and not his,' Cristy put in mildly.

Layla and Connor stared at her.

'It just says Kaplan,' Cristy pointed out. 'For all we know, it was attached to Rudi's passport.'

'But . . .' Layla protested. 'I mean . . . How?'

Cristy shrugged. 'You were the one who cast doubt on him dying in the bath,' she reminded her.

'So we're believing that now?' Connor put in sceptically.

'I think,' said Cristy, 'until we hear back from the coroner's office about identity checks, we should keep an open mind.'

As Layla's eyes closed in dismay, Cristy said to Connor, 'Did you check to see if there were any more tags?'

'I did,' he confirmed. 'This was the only one.'

Turning to Layla, Cristy said, 'Well, it seems we can safely conclude that Romy, or Rudi, or both of them, have been here in the past six days, without any officials at the resort being aware of it. Does that sound likely to you?'

Reaching for her phone, Layla said, 'I'll give reception another call.'

A few minutes later, having spoken with one of the site managers, she said, 'They're adamant no one's been staying here, but they're going to contact the cleaner and ask her to come and see us in the morning.'

'Lucky you speak Portuguese,' Connor commented.

'Hardly fluent,' Layla responded, and clearly still dazed by the unexpected discovery, she picked up her drink.

They sat quietly for a while, mulling everything over: the things that simply didn't fit together or even make sense on their own. Surely it was Romy who'd taken the flight and mislaid the baggage receipt, Romy who'd been here at the house, and Romy who'd posted the video. But had Rudi been with her? If so, where were they now?

Checking her mobile when it vibrated on the table, Cristy said, 'Clove!' and switched focus as she clicked the call to speaker. 'How are you? Are you still at Romy's cottage?' she said, as she answered. 'How did it go with the technician?'

'I'm great, thanks,' Clove told her cheerily, 'not at all bothered that I was left behind while you two go swanning off to the tropics.'

'Not quite the tropics,' Cristy said wryly, 'but I don't suppose it'll help if I say we wish you were here?'

'Nope, not one bit. Anyway, I'm back at the office now, and I've just emailed a link to the chat I had with the techie.

He was completely ripped, by the way – definitely my type; photo also attached.'

'So he was talkative?' Connor prompted. 'Anything interesting?'

'Check it out. See what you think.'

Once Connor had found the recording, Cristy ended the call and reached for her drink, ready to listen.

CLOVE: 'It's Wednesday 12th June, and this is a chat with Ricky Boulder from Sherman Security Services, taking place in the front garden of Romy Kaplan's home in Gloucestershire. Ricky, you were just telling me that you've been coming here regularly more or less since the Kaplans moved in around nine months ago. So obviously you've met them?'

RICKY: 'Sure. Great guys, always very friendly and interested to know if I found anything. I was very sorry when I heard Rudi had passed away.'

CLOVE: 'Have you ever found anything during your searches?'

RICKY: 'Nope.'

CLOVE: 'Not once?'

RICKY: 'Never.'

CLOVE: 'What exactly were you looking for?'

RICKY: 'The usual low-tech stuff: listening devices, mini-recorders, hidden cameras, that sort of thing.'

CLOVE: 'Where would you expect to find them, if there had been any here?'

RICKY: 'I guess in lamps, under tables, attached to routers or electrical gadgets . . .'

CLOVE: 'So all over the house, not just downstairs?'

RICKY: 'That's right.'

CLOVE: 'And how did the Kaplans seem when you told them the place was clear?'

RICKY: 'Relieved, I guess, but they still wanted me back every couple of months.'

CLOVE: 'Did they ever tell you who they thought might be spying on them?'

RICKY: 'No, and not my place to ask.'

CLOVE: 'Did they ever help you to look?'

RICKY: 'No. They either waited in the sitting room or on a bench over by the lake if the weather was good.'

CLOVE: 'The last time you were here, did Mrs Kaplan mention anything about going away, or maybe not being around the next time you came?'

RICKY: 'Not that I recall. It wasn't long after her husband had passed, and you could see how hard it had hit her. They always struck me as being very close.'

CLOVE: 'So, no plans that you know of to go travelling or to stay with a friend, maybe?'

RICKY: 'No, nothing like that, but listen, I was hardly her closest mate, so for all I know, she was planning something, just didn't want to discuss it with me.'

CLOVE: 'OK. Do you have keys to the place?'

RICKY: 'No, so if you hadn't been here today, I wouldn't have been able to do my job. Do you want me to, by the way? Happy to carry on if you say so.'

CLOVE: 'Yes, why not? I'm not expecting you to find anything, but as you're here . . .'

The recording dropped and moments later picked up again.

CLOVE: 'Ricky's gone now. Another all clear, but Nula, Romy's neighbour, went into the house with him, and she noticed something I guess no one else would have. Can you tell us what it was, Nula?'

NULA: 'It's not so much what I saw as what I didn't see. The portrait of Romy that she moved to the spare bedroom? It's gone. I've looked for it, and I shall again, but there's a space upstairs where it used to be leaning against the wall, face in. She never liked it much, you see. I can tell you it was definitely there the last time I looked because I dusted up there only last week, and I wouldn't have missed a big gap like that.'

When the playback stopped, Cristy turned to Layla, who appeared so deep in thought that it was a moment before she seemed aware of them waiting for her to speak.

'I'm trying to remember,' she said, 'if it was there the last time I went in. I know we talked about it, but do you recall seeing it when we went upstairs?'

'I guess we wouldn't have noticed if it was facing the wall,' Connor pointed out.

'But if it *has* gone,' Cristy said pensively. 'Do you think it's what Quentin, the neighbour, heard in the middle of the night – someone taking it?'

'How big is it?' Connor asked.

'I guess about three feet by two, and I wouldn't say it was heavy. Not that I ever picked it up, but it didn't appear to be. So not sure how much noise would be made moving it around.'

120

Cristy called Clove again and said, 'Did you and Nula try to find the painting after Mr Ripped had left?'

'We did,' Clove replied, 'and it's definitely not there.'

Bewildered, Cristy said, 'But who on earth would want to take it?'

Layla's eyes darkened with yet more confusion as she said, 'The only person I can think of is Rudi.'

'Are you kidding me?' Clove said from her end.

'I'm just saying,' Layla responded, 'he's the only one I know who had any real appreciation for the painting, and I can't think of anyone else who'd want it.'

'Apart from Romy?' Connor put in lamely.

'What are you guys on over there?' Clove demanded. 'Are we now actually thinking that he didn't die back in March? I thought we were waiting to hear from the coroner.'

'I'll call you back,' Cristy told her and quickly rang off.

Layla was shaking her head. 'I can't see why Romy would want it,' she said. 'She really didn't like it, and are you seriously suggesting that she entered her own house in the dead of night to pick up some clothes and steal her own portrait? Why on earth would she do that?'

'Why would Rudi?' Connor countered.

Cristy began scrolling through Facebook on her phone. 'OK, the baggage label is dated 6th June, Romy's last video was posted on 7th June, we think while she was here in Portugal. Quentin was woken up in the early hours of 8th June.' She looked up. 'Setting aside the total weirdness of why anyone would want the portrait, I guess it's possible Rudi and/or Romy flew back to . . . collect it?'

'Because?' Connor prompted.

Cristy shrugged. 'I've no idea. And it definitely doesn't tell us where they are now.'

'They could have paid someone to get it for them,' Layla suggested, 'or is that taking us too far down the rabbit hole?'

They sat quietly after that, each with their own thoughts

as the distant hum of golf carts circling and stopping on the nearby course floated in on the breeze.

In the end, Connor said, 'Here's a scenario for you, based on Clove's interview with the security tech guy: someone's been going into the cottage to plant their devices right after it's been swept, and leaving them in situ until just before the tech comes again? That could explain why nothing's ever been found.'

'I think I put that forward before,' Cristy reminded him dryly, 'but if it's right, then "they" – whoever they are – obviously know about the contract and when visits are scheduled.'

'Which could lead us to wonder if someone at Sherman Security is involved?' Connor mooted.

Sounding wretched, Layla said, 'We still don't have any actual proof that they were being spied on, and as for why anyone would be that interested in them . . . ? I just don't know where to go with that.'

Sighing, Cristy picked up her glass and finished her drink. 'We're clearly coming at things the wrong way,' she stated. 'We need some more radical, out-of-the-box thinking that fully accepts there's a lot more to the Kaplans than even you and your family know, Layla. So, could any of this date back forty-odd years to their time in the Foreign Office, which probably meant the intelligence services?'

'You're sounding like my brother now,' Layla protested.

'Does that mean he thinks there's a connection?'

'He definitely likes the idea of one, but that's him all over. Mum and Dad don't agree, and they're much more likely to know.' Sighing, Layla stared down at her drink. 'It's not looking good, is it?' she asked.

Considering the way their minds were working concerning Rudi's death, Cristy decided it best not to answer that – killing a third party in the bath before taking off to God only knew where both stretched credibility and raised the intrigue

122

to a level they couldn't handle right now. So she simply said, 'Why don't we take ourselves into Lagos to see what we can find out there? How well do you know the town?'

'Well enough to get us to the main square,' Layla replied, 'and to be able to suggest a couple of places to eat. Best bring a jacket or some sort of wrap in case you need it.'

CHAPTER FIFTEEN

An hour later, after parking close to the marina, where luxury yachts were jostling with fishing boats, rubber dinghies and leisure cruisers, they crossed a busy footbridge over to the town's seafront boulevard. Dozens of stalls selling everything from bikinis to flip-flops, kaftans to straw hats, cork accessories to daytrips, were spread out along the palm- and oleander-lined boardwalk where tourists were browsing and haggling, taking selfies and generally having a good time.

'It's going to be hard to spot anyone in these crowds,' Connor commented, as they reached a kids' carousel and merged into a street of music and general holiday chaos.

'Let's record some of this for atmos,' Cristy said, 'and I'll try a voiceover.'

Minutes later, she was half-shouting into a handheld mic.

CRISTY: 'We're making our way through the popular coastal town of Lagos, where you can hear as many English voices as Portuguese – maybe more. The bars and restaurants are rammed, entertainers in abundance. I'm sure you can hear the trombonist we're passing . . . How on earth we're going to spot Romy, if she's here, heaven only knows, but we're determined to give it a try.

'OK, we've just crossed a small plaza, piazza, whatever it's called here, with a fountain at its heart, and now we're heading along Rua Afonso de Almeida – not sure who he was, but more cafés and novelty shops – you can get a tattoo here, Connor, or maybe a hair wrap.'

CONNOR: 'Have you seen this tiny dog, perched on an accordion while its owner plays?'

CRISTY: 'Cute. OK, we can't be far from the main square now . . .'

LAYLA: 'This way, down to the left.'

They let the recording run, collecting up effects until finally they emerged into a comparative oasis of calm.

CRISTY: 'The church is on the opposite side of the square to where we are, looking quite lovely in the pastel shades of twilight. We're standing next to the old slave market . . . You know, it's actually making me shiver to think of all the suffering that went on here a couple of centuries ago. It's like the ghosts are still present, and if you listen hard enough, you might even hear them, the chains, the beatings . . .'

CONNOR: 'We're walking towards the statue now, and it is . . . Yes, it's Henry the Navigator, who, I believe, was responsible for kicking off this nation's slave trade back in the fifteenth century . . . I need to double-check that . . . Anyway, unlike Britain's Edward Colston, whose statue was famously torn down and dumped into Bristol harbour a few years ago, old Henry is definitely still standing.'

CRISTY: 'Let's get some shots of it and the square . . .'

Connor took out his phone and got to work. Layla did the same.

CRISTY: 'Everything's so quiet here, and white or sandstone . . . There are a couple of restaurants that have the same name – Dois Irmãos – so I'm guessing they're owned by brothers.'

CONNOR: 'Let's go check if anyone remembers seeing Romy – maybe even shooting a video for her. I'm guessing, from the angle it was taken, that she was on the terrace of that one there.'

CRISTY: 'He's pointing to the smaller of the two restaurants, which looks as though it might be more of a tapas bar.'

It didn't take long for them to establish that no one in either of the eateries recalled seeing Romy – or Rudi – in recent times. However, considering the number of tourists coming and going throughout the year, it was hardly surprising. And were they really expecting anyone to have seen Rudi lately when, no matter where their suspicions and imaginations were taking them, there was absolutely nothing to say he was still alive?

'Would you be willing to put up a couple of posters?' Connor asked one of the restaurant managers. 'Just in case someone recognizes them?'

'Claro, claro, this is not a problem, and I will contact you if there is any news. Now, you would like to eat? We have a table free, over here on the terrace.'

Eyeing the huge selection of fresh fish and live seafood inside a refrigerated display case, Connor said, 'I'm definitely up for some catch-of-the day. How about you guys?'

'Gambas for me,' Layla said eagerly.

'Me too.' Cristy smiled. 'And maybe on our way back to the car, we should try showing the headshots around a few more places in town.'

Once they'd given their food orders, Layla looked up from

her phone, saying, 'Mum's just sent me something she found in Romy's notebook. She found it written into a chapter from *The Woman in White*.'

Confused, Cristy asked what it said.

Opening up the email's attachment, Layla explained, 'Mum's typed it out to make it easier to read . . . Romy's handwriting is notoriously difficult. Anyway, apparently it starts off with text from the book, except I don't think it's accurate . . . I'll read it . . . *"It's the twenty-second day of February. The long cold winter is drawing to a close, and it's terrible the things that are happening to us – and what we are in danger of doing to others. Is there really only one way to escape it? I feel so frightened at times, and I know Rudi does too. We have been fools and we continue to be . . ."* Mum says that from there it reverts to Wilkie Collins's text, but on the next page . . .' Layla read from the email attachment again: 'Apparently, the following was worked into a chapter from *Jane Eyre*. *". . . it's like being haunted, surrounded by ghosts watching, waiting, controlling, never able to speak to them, hear them or even touch them. Will they ever leave us alone?"'*

Cristy shivered, and Connor muttered, 'What the actual f—?'

'Can you forward it to us?' Cristy asked.

Moments later, it was on her phone. After quickly scanning it, she said, 'OK, so we can assume that the *Woman in White* entry was written on 22nd Feb, a month before Rudi died. So what terrible things were happening to them? And what on earth does she mean about being in danger of doing something to others?'

Layla regarded her helplessly.

Reading from his own phone, Connor said, 'There's no date on the *Jane Eyre* piece, but she's asking, *"Will they ever leave us alone?"'* He looked up. 'Who on earth is she talking about?'

Layla was clearly still as mystified as they were.

'Has your mum said who she thinks it could be?' Cristy asked.

Layla shook her head as she quickly checked the covering email. 'All she's saying is: *"If there was something going on to frighten her this much, why on earth did she never say anything? I don't understand it."*'

Connor said thoughtfully, 'Do we show this to the police? I mean, it surely throws a whole new light on the fact she's missing?'

Cristy looked at Layla. Connor was right, of course: this could somewhat change things, although she had to wonder how seriously the police would take a couple of cryptic insertions into some literary text. 'Maybe Clove should go through the notebook from here,' she suggested, 'just in case there's more.'

Layla looked doubtful. 'I don't think Mum will be willing to give it up now she's found this,' she said. 'Not that she won't share if she finds anything – I'm sure she will – but she'll want to be the first to read it.'

Which was a no about giving it to the police, Cristy realized. A response she found intriguing, although perhaps not altogether surprising.

CHAPTER SIXTEEN

The following morning, Cristy and Connor were drinking coffee on the townhouse's small terrace while Layla busied herself in the kitchen.

'So, any further thoughts on the notebook entries?' he asked, biting into a *pastel de nata*.

Putting her mug down, Cristy said, 'Well, given how unspecific they are – sinister, yes, but definitely obscure – I think the only chance we have of working out what they mean is if Beth manages to find any more. And even then . . . I can't see the police being particularly interested at this stage.'

'I agree, but speaking for myself, I find them quite fascinating. I think we should get Layla to read them out for a recording. No idea where we can use them yet, but it'll be good to have them.' He looked up as the doorbell rang.

'It'll be them,' Layla called out. 'I'll go.'

By the time Cristy and Connor stepped into the sitting room, Layla was already showing in the visitors, two women – one old and quite portly, the other slim and sloe-eyed.

'This is Isa, who runs reception,' Layla explained, indicating the younger female.

'And this is Maria.' Isa smiled as she shook Cristy's hand. 'She was a little worried about coming alone – she does not speak English, you see – so I hope is not a problem that I am here too.'

'Welcome,' Cristy said warmly to Maria, hoping her tone would help put the older lady at ease. 'Thank you for coming.'

As Maria nodded, still clutching tightly to the strap of her shoulder bag, Layla gestured for everyone to sit down.

'Can you ask Maria if she's OK with us recording what she says?' Cristy said to Isa.

Cristy watched the older woman's wary face as she listened to the request and waited as she gave a verbose response.

'She says is not a problem,' Isa told them, 'and she hope she can help.'

'I guess you've already explained why we want to talk to her?' Cristy said, as Connor prepared to record.

'*Sim*, I have, and Layla explain to me on the phone that you find a baggage receipt in sofa?'

'That's right.'

'Maria will tell you what happen, and you will decide if she did the right thing.'

Intrigued, Cristy turned to Connor, and receiving the go ahead, she began by asking Maria, via Isa, when she'd last cleaned the house they were in.

Maria's reply was so lengthy and animated that Cristy started to wonder if they'd moved on to other things.

ISA: (TRANSLATING) 'She wants you to know that yesterday morning, while she is here, in this house, a woman comes to the door and ask if she can leave a note for Miss Cates. She has not seen this woman before, but she look very nice, so she let her come in and while she write the note, Maria clean in the kitchen. Then the woman leave, and later, when Maria also is leaving, she sees there is no note.'

Cristy and Connor exchanged glances and Cristy quickly brought out a photograph of Romy to show to Maria.

CRISTY: 'Is this the woman?'

Maria's reply was clear from the grave shake of her head.

ISA: (TRANSLATING) 'No, this is not her. The woman who come is very much younger, maybe thirty.'

CRISTY: 'Can Maria describe her?'

Maria spoke animatedly again, first pointing to her eyes, then to her mouth.

ISA: 'She says she is not tall and not short; she has very strong blue eyes, and when she smile, there is small gap between the front teeth.'

Cristy glanced at Connor again, then at Layla. It surely had to be the same young woman Olivia Gibson had seen pass Romy a note in the giftshop. So who was she?

Speaking to Maria in Portuguese, Layla asked a question that received another solemn shake of the head, followed by a short burst of words.

LAYLA: 'I wondered if anyone was with the woman, and Maria says she didn't see anyone.'

CONNOR: 'Ask her how long the woman stayed.'

ISA: (TRANSLATING) 'A few minutes, no more.'

CONNOR: 'Did she go anywhere else in the house besides this room?'

Maria's answer was clearly negative.

CRISTY: 'Is there anything else Maria can tell us?'

After Isa had translated, Maria's eyes came regretfully

to Cristy, and she splayed her hands to show she had no more.

Cristy smiled at her, and signalling for Connor to stop recording, she said to Isa, 'Please thank her for coming today. She's been very helpful, and perhaps she'll let us know right away if she sees the woman again.'

A few minutes later, with Isa and Maria gone, Cristy said, 'The most striking part of that, for me, apart from it almost certainly being the same woman Olivia Gibson described, was the fact that she, whoever she is, apparently knew Layla was coming here.'

'Yeah, that was a stand-out for me too,' Connor agreed. 'And the next question is why did she come in here, given she didn't leave a note?'

'OK, I know this is going to sound crazy,' Layla said, 'but maybe she planted the baggage receipt?'

Thinking it did sound crazy, while half-agreeing, Cristy said, 'Without knowing for certain if, or when it was "mislaid", we can't actually tie it to the woman. But OK, say that was why she came in here: how did she get it? And why did she plant it?'

They stared blankly at one another, having no logical explanation, only more questions without answers.

*

An hour or so later, Cristy was on the phone to David. 'Are you on your way to the airport yet?' she asked, feeling momentarily depressed by how separate their worlds were.

'Just arrived. Flight's delayed, and Laurent's gone to get drinks, so tell me how it's going over there? Any signs of Romy yet?'

Sighing, she sat back in her chair and stretched out her legs, then brought him up to speed. When she'd finished, he remained silent for a while, taking his time to assess what

132

he'd heard, and apparently finding it as perplexing and bizarre as she did.

'So,' he said, eventually, 'a woman, not Romy but could be the same one from the giftshop, blags her way into the house where you are, possibly plants a baggage receipt that belongs to Romy – or Rudi – and leaves again?'

'Sounds crazy, doesn't it?'

'And just as crazy, we have someone, maybe Romy or Rudi, stealing into their own Gloucestershire home in the dead of night, removing a portrait, and taking off again.'

'We don't know if it was them. It could have been anyone. Anyway, we know she was here, in Portugal, partly thanks to your guy's work on the video, and the date on the baggage receipt that tells us that she flew in on 6th June. Unless it was Rudi who got the flight. We'll have it scanned at the airport when we return to see if the barcode reveals more than just a surname.'

'I'm sure it will, and I'll be fascinated to hear which of them it was. So, what's it all adding up to at the moment?'

'I wish I had an answer for that. If they're hiding from something, or someone, we haven't come across anything yet to tell us who or what it could be, apart from a couple of strange notebook entries that don't actually make any sense. They simply tell us that she was scared of something or someone, and so was he.'

'Well, whatever's behind that, my best guess is that this whole thing is about money. Don't ask me how – it's just got to figure in there somewhere, because it always does.'

'You'll get no argument from me on that, but as we haven't yet been able to find any financial records, address books or calendars, how are we going to find anything out?'

Sounding amused, David said, 'I have an idea what might be coming.'

Cristy laughed. 'Given all your contacts in the financial world, would you be able to get some idea of how and when Rudi lost all his money?'

'I can always try, but if he ran his own show . . . Regardless, he has to have worked with someone, so send me what you do have – anything will help – and I'll make a few calls when I get to Denmark. We'll see where that takes us.'

*

A while later, Cristy was strolling barefoot along the shoreline of Salema, a quaint seaside village with cobbled streets and noisy cafés, nestled into the small arc of a cove, where locals' fishing boats were currently basking on the sands. She was relishing the warm breeze as much as the refreshing coolness of the lazily lapping tide over her feet, while mulling over her conversation with David and taking in the almost dreamlike cliffs, cast as they were in a haze of Mediterranean sunlight.

She'd left the others a few minutes ago, lounging in a beach cabana following their lunch of delicious tomato and garlicky sardines, crusty chunks of *broa de milho* to soak up the oils, and a couple of bottles of perfectly chilled Alvarinho. The talk had mostly been about the mysterious woman who'd dropped into the townhouse yesterday, but it was getting them nowhere to go over and over the same thing.

Beautiful as it was here, they were wasting their time, she felt sure, so all that was left to be done was to check in for their flights first thing tomorrow and return to England. It hadn't been a wasted trip, they had the baggage receipt and the reported second sighting of a mysterious blue-eyed woman. However, they still felt a long way from answering the most important question of all - where the heck was Romy?

CHAPTER SEVENTEEN

Less than twenty-four hours later, Cristy was at Bristol Airport, staring uncomprehendingly at the printed form in front of her. It wasn't making any sense, yet there was no mistaking what it said.

'Who the heck,' she demanded, looking at the lost-luggage clerk as though he, rather than the scanned barcode, had produced the information, 'is Casey Kaplan?'

The skinny young man glanced nervously at Connor as he shrugged and said, 'I shouldn't really be showing you that, it's only . . .'

'I'm sorry. I didn't expect you to know.' Cristy apologized. She turned to Connor, saw he was equally as confounded, and said to Layla, 'Do you know who it is?'

Layla shook her head helplessly. 'I've never heard of him,' she replied.

'It could be a woman,' Connor pointed out. 'Gender neutral name.'

Going with it, Cristy said, 'Are you thinking of the woman who might have left the receipt at the house? I guess that could make sense, at a stretch, but it still doesn't tell us who she is. You're sure there's no other family?' she asked Layla.

'As sure as I can be,' Layla responded, 'but I'll text Mum to see what she says.'

Taking out his own phone, Connor began a search for Casey Kaplan, while Cristy thanked the clerk and tucked the printout into her bag. Curiously, along with giving them the full name, the barcode had also produced Romy's address at the cottage and her mobile number, which another quick check told them was still switched off.

'Mum's not aware of any family,' Layla said, as Cristy drove them out of the airport a while later, 'but she's wondering if it could be Rudi's actual name, with Rudolph being a middle?'

'Casey Rudolph Kaplan,' Connor muttered, and started up a new search.

'We need his birth certificate or passport,' Cristy said, deciding not to ask if Beth's suggestion meant she was starting to wonder if it hadn't been Rudi in the bath.'

'Or driver's licence,' Layla added, 'but I haven't come across any of them yet. Do you keep that kind of stuff after someone's died?'

'I guess some people do,' Cristy said.

'Oh God, maybe it's another indicator that he *is* still alive,' Layla groaned. 'I haven't found any ID for Romy either, and it's not usual to take your birth certificate travelling, is it? You'd have thought that, at least, would be somewhere in the cottage.'

Finding it all just as odd as Layla clearly did, Cristy said to Connor, 'What time are we supposed to be seeing Iz today?'

'Not until four,' he replied, 'but I haven't looked at any of the promo scripts yet – have you?'

'Not a one, so we best make them a priority when we get back. Layla, are you coming with us, or can I drop you somewhere?'

'My car's outside your office,' Layla reminded her, 'and I was thinking I might take a drive up to the cottage to have another look round. Not that I'm doubting Nula, but that portrait has to be somewhere – it's too weird to think someone actually snuck into the house and took it. And while I'm there, I'll have another go at finding something official with Rudi's full name on it.'

136

'Maybe we should come with you,' Cristy suggested, and immediately realized that wasn't such a great idea. 'We can't let Iz down at such short notice,' she said. 'She's probably already on her way from London.'

'Iz can't make it,' Clove told them when they pulled up outside Quinn Studios to find her sitting under the copper beech with Meena, both of them sipping cold drinks. 'Problem with the trains,' Clove explained. 'If you check, you've probably had the email by now, and maybe don't bother going inside – we're in the middle of a power cut.'

'Since when?' Connor asked, looking up at the building as if it might be staging some sort of protest.

'About half an hour ago,' Meena replied. 'They're doing their best to fix it, but until they do, the whole area is an electricity free zone.'

'Iz wants to know if you're still intending to upload the Call to Arms next Tuesday,' Clove told them. 'That's what she's calling it, by the way.'

'I can live with that,' Connor responded, turning to Cristy.

She shrugged. 'Fine by me, but we should have a full production meeting on Monday about what's going into it.'

'Good to hear,' Clove declared, 'because before we went dark around here, I received a message from one of Romy's Facebook friends that we might want to use. Theo Crush? He's just remembered a letter he received from Rudi last summer and thought we might like to see it. There was an attachment to his email, but everything went down before I could open it and my phone's not happy with the format, so no idea what it says yet. Just thought I'd mention it in case it has any bearing on anything.'

'It'll be interesting to find out more,' Cristy responded, 'so let us know when you've seen it. In the meantime,' she said, to Layla, 'it looks like we can come to the cottage with you . . .'

'Hang on, hang on,' Connor interrupted hastily. 'Some

of us have wives and babies to go home to. In my case, only one of each, but I wouldn't mind seeing them today, so how about we go tomorrow?'

'And on second thoughts,' Layla said awkwardly, 'I probably ought to go and check on Mum before I do anything else. Barry went back to London yesterday, so Dad will be coping on his own. I'm sure he's doing fine, but I know Mum's keen to hear about our time in Portugal.'

Cristy turned to Clove.

Grimacing an apology, Clove said, 'I've kind of got plans for later. Happy to join you as early as you like in the morning.'

Cristy threw out her hands. 'Well, that's me royally dumped.' She laughed.

With an amused arch of her eyebrows, Meena said, 'So where's David? Maybe postpone your visit to the cottage and pop over to Guernsey for a couple of days?'

'I would if he was there, but he's in Skagen for the next two weeks. He's also,' she told Clove, 'going to try to get us some background on Rudi's finances, so let's add it to the board so we know who's doing what and when.' Turning to Connor, she said, 'Something else we ought to take a look at while we're in Gloucestershire tomorrow is Haylesford Manor. It might be interesting to find out who lives there now and whether they had any direct dealings with Rudi and Romy when they were taking the place over.'

'Sure,' he agreed, 'a bit of background could add some intriguing texture. Clove, have you made contact with Jacks yet, to find out if he's back?'

'I have, and he's spending the weekend getting up to speed with everything, so he'll be here first thing Monday to, I quote, "get the show on the right road".'

CHAPTER EIGHTEEN

Cristy had just arrived home and poured herself a drink when Clove rang to let her know that the power was back on at the office and she'd now managed to open Theo Crush's attachment.

'I'm just waiting for Connor to join the call,' Clove said, 'so he can hear . . . Ah, here he is.'

'What's up?' Connor asked.

After explaining why she was in touch, Clove said, 'Crush's covering message makes a bit more sense now . . . Actually, it doesn't make any sense at all, but you'll see what I mean when we get to it. First up, I'll read you the letter he received from Rudi.'

'Do we need to record it?' Connor asked.

'Maybe, but with a male voice, so we can do it later. OK, here goes: "*My dearest, dearest Theo, I know you'll never be able to forgive me for this. How could it be possible when I'll never be able to forgive myself? Please understand I did my utmost to stop it from happening, but in the end, I was powerless. They have all the control; Romy and I have none, not as things stand. We are no longer at the manor – our new address is above; it's the best way to get hold of us these days, but rest assured we don't expect to hear from you. It has been an absolute honour to call you a friend all these years. I am sorrier than you'll ever know to lose you. With our love and deepest regret, R&R.*"'

'OK?' Connor said, drawing the word into a question. 'What the heck was that about?'

'Believe it or not,' Clove replied, 'even Theo Crush doesn't know. Here's what he said in his covering message: *"Dear Clover, I am attaching a scanned, handwritten letter from Rudi that you will see is dated September last year. I had forgotten all about it until after you got in touch concerning Romy, so I went in search of it, and I have to say, I am as mystified by it now as I was when I received it."'*

Pushing open the French doors to step outside, Cristy said, 'But he must have contacted Rudi to ask what he meant.'

'You'd think,' Clove agreed, 'but I haven't been able to get hold of Mr Crush yet. When I do, I'll try to get him to talk on the phone so I can record what he says, just in case it's something we might want to use.'

'Good call,' Connor responded. 'Have any of the other Facebook friends been in touch again?'

'Not with me, but a couple more have responded to the latest video – nothing significant, more of the same really, although someone replied to the AV post calling him a troll and telling him he should be ashamed of himself. I'll reach out when we're done here, just in case she knows who AV is or why he might have said what he did.'

'Any more from Romy?' Cristy asked.

'No more from her. Interesting, though, that the AV comment didn't seem to bother her, given the kiss emoji.'

'Maybe it's her way of flipping off trolls,' Connor ventured.

'Could be. Anyway, I've gone back a few months on her page to see if he's posted before, or if anyone else has, in a similar vein, but the only stand-out was in April from someone calling him- or herself JayCob saying, *"If something looks too good to be true, that's usually because it is. Same goes for people."'*

'What was that in response to?' Cristy asked.

'Nothing. It was just posted on her page and left there. No follow-up from her or anyone else. And JayCob's proving as untraceable as AV.'

'We definitely need Jacks,' Connor declared. 'Did you get anywhere with Casey Kaplan, by any chance?'

'All I can tell you so far is that it seems a bit of a rare name.'

'OK,' Cristy said. 'Are you going to come with us tomorrow?'

'Sure, but maybe I'll meet you there? I've got a couple of errands to run first thing. I guess you're going to try some door-to-door interviews with the neighbours?'

'We are,' Connor replied, 'and as you're so good at those things they'll be all yours while we go on to Haylesford Manor.'

'I'll give Layla a call now,' Cristy said, 'to find out if she can make it.'

Minutes later, Cristy and Connor were on another conference call, this time with Layla. Her mother had found something melded into a handwritten chapter from *Great Expectations*.

'It begins,' Layla told them, 'with Dickens's actual words, *"It was one of those March days when the sun shines hot and the wind blows cold."* We don't know if that's Romy's way of dating what comes next, but it goes on to say – this is Romy writing now: *"Our friends are still being threatened. It began before we left the manor, and it continues. The intimidation is ruthless and could so easily destroy them. I worry about Rudi and how ashamed he feels. He shouldn't; it isn't his fault. I am to blame in every way. Rudi won't hear me say it, but he knows it's true. If only we could turn back the clock, I'd do things very differently. We wouldn't be in this position if I'd taken more care. They're listening all the time; we're sure of it.*

"How many of them are there? We've only seen three,

but maybe there are more. Rudi thinks there must be, but we have no way of knowing. We wonder all the time how much longer they will allow us to stay here in this cottage? Will they force us to move again? Where will be next? Wherever it is, please let us stay together.'"

'Wow,' Connor murmured into the silence when Layla stopped. 'Where do we even start with that?'

'What's your mum saying about it?' Cristy asked.

'I'm here,' Beth told her. 'I'm worried sick, obviously, and as confused as you probably are.'

'She talks about friends being threatened,' Connor said. 'Did anything ever happen to you that could put you amongst them?'

'Johnny and I have been discussing it,' Beth told them, 'and we've got no idea who she could be talking about. No one's ever mentioned anything to us.'

'Do you know someone by the name of Theo Crush?' Cristy asked. 'He lives in Vienna.'

'Yes, we know Theo,' Beth replied. 'Why? Has someone threatened him?'

'I'm not sure,' Cristy told her. 'I'll get Clove to send you a copy of a letter he received from Rudi last summer. It reads like an apology, but Theo Crush's covering email makes it clear that he doesn't understand the letter himself. We're trying to get hold of him to find out what more he can tell us.'

Connor said, 'She says she thinks there are three of them. I guess no idea who she might be referring to?'

'Believe me, I'd have told you if I did,' Beth replied. 'I just can't figure out any of it, and as for the business of them being moved on from the cottage . . . I keep asking myself: is that what's happened? They have been forced out and now they're . . . Somewhere together?'

As her voice faltered with uncertainty and deepening concern, Cristy could tell she'd read the very worst into "somewhere together" and only wished she could think of a way to dismiss the fear. She didn't think that both Rudi and Romy were dead, but on the other hand, she was in no position to rule anything in or out.

'You need to keep reading,' she told Beth, 'see if there's any more, and as soon as we're able to put something together that the police won't be able to dismiss, we'll hand it over to them.'

CHAPTER NINETEEN

It was just after eleven the following morning when Cristy and Connor drove over the cattle-grid into Bellbrook and came to a stop outside Romy's cottage. It was dull and drizzly, with only cloud reflected on the lake's inky water, and a vaporous drift of mist was clinging to the trees.

'No sign of Layla yet,' Connor commented, checking the time.

'Nor anyone else,' Cristy murmured, noting the deserted seeming cottages and converted barns straggled along the shore. A middle-aged man with a dog emerged from a trail at the end of the hamlet and seemed not to notice them as he went in through a gate and disappeared into a large front porch.

Cristy turned to stare across the water to the far bank. She didn't exactly expect to spot someone in a boat, but she tensed as something moved in the trees. A heron flapped out, and she relaxed again.

After a while, she said, 'I keep thinking about the *Great Expectations* thing last night. Any more thoughts on it?'

'Not really.' Connor sighed. 'My head's going back to the early days, you know, when they were in Moscow; not that I'm coming up with a single thread of a connection – would that I were – but I was wondering if it might be a good idea to have a chat with Layla's brother, Barry? He might give us another perspective on the Kaplans, given he seems a bit less in their thrall than the others.'

'Sure. Why not? We'll have to get his details from Layla . . . Ah, a text from Clove.' She read it out. '"*Theo Crush just rang. Apparently, he wrote back to Rudi to ask what letter was about but didn't get a reply. Tried again a few weeks later. Still nothing.*" Well, at least Crush doesn't seem to have disappeared,' Cristy commented. 'I must admit I was beginning to wonder.'

She glanced in the rear-view mirror just as Layla pulled up behind them, and got out of the car to go and greet her.

'How's your mum?' she asked, noticing right away how tired Layla looked, and remembering only too well the anguished nights when her own mother's pain had seemed to consume her. And given Beth's concern for Romy . . .

'She's putting on a brave face like she always does,' Layla replied, giving Connor a smile as he came to join them. 'Actually, I couldn't sleep, then the dog got me up early . . . So, if I'm looking rubbish, it's because that's how I feel.' Layla reached back into the car and produced a greasy bag of pastries and a carton of fresh milk. After handing them to Connor she dug into her bag for the housekeys. 'Have you seen anyone since you got here?' she asked, as she went to push open the gate.

'Not a soul,' Cristy replied, following her inside.

The open-plan room was in darkness and still smelled of old fireplace-ash, with a hint of lemony polish.

Layla went to open the kitchen blinds and French doors as Connor got to work on the coffee, and as fresh air and weak sunlight came in, Cristy took a look round.

'You were the last one here,' she said to Layla. 'Is it how you left it?'

Surveying it, Layla said, 'I guess so, but remember, Nula, Clove and the security guy have been in since.'

Glancing over his shoulder, Connor said, 'We were thinking about having a chat with your brother?'

Layla seemed to tense, but then she shrugged and said,

'OK, why not? He's a bit of a dork at times with some of the things he says, but he's as keen as the rest of us to find Romy.' After sharing his details with both Cristy and Connor, she added, 'I'm going to pop upstairs to check on the portrait. I don't know why it's bothering me that it might have gone, but I need to see for myself that it has – or hasn't.'

As she ran up to the bedrooms, Connor left the coffee to brew and went to join Cristy in front of Rudi's portrait.

'It's eerily alive, isn't it?' she commented quietly. 'I mean, in that it looks as though he's about to move right out of that frame and start speaking to us.'

'I find portraits often come over like that if you look at them long enough,' Connor reflected.

'I wonder who painted this one?' Cristy peered into the corners trying to make out some initials or a signature. 'Maybe it's on the back,' she said, but didn't check – the portrait was too large, and she didn't want it crashing down on them. 'Where are you?' she muttered under her breath, gazing at Rudi again. 'Have you deceived us all? Or did you really die in the bath?'

Connor said, 'And if you didn't, who did?'

They both started and looked up at the heavy crunch of Layla moving or dropping something upstairs, then turned as Nula came bustling into the kitchen.

'I spotted you outside,' the old lady declared. 'I was keeping an eye out. Have you found her?'

Cristy admitted they hadn't.

Nula looked both worried and impatient. 'I thought not.' She sighed, going to plonk a foil-covered plate next to the coffee-maker. 'Thought you might like some of these, and to know that I've talked to all the neighbours since you were last here to find out exactly when they last saw Romy. What a concern this is, especially after poor Quentin got woken up in the night with all that—' Her head snapped up as something

146

heavy hit the floor above them. 'Who's that?' she demanded, appearing ready to go up and fight.

'Layla,' Cristy told her.

'Of course. I saw her car. What's she doing?'

'Just checking around. So you've spoken to the neighbours?'

'That's right – and I've made some cookies, so help yourselves.' Nula tore the cover off the plate, then poured herself a coffee, while saying, 'I've written everything down, but everyone's happy to talk to you themselves. Like I said, we're very worried, especially after all Romy's been through.'

'Do you know of anything else, apart from the shock of Rudi dying?' Connor asked.

Nula's eyes flashed. 'Isn't that enough?'

Quickly stepping in, Cristy said, 'So, did you learn anything interesting from the neighbours?'

Nula reached for one of Layla's pastries, tucking in as she said, 'I'll let you be the judge of that, but I can tell you this: it's still looking like I was the last one to see her here. I expect you'll want to talk to them yourselves though, and with it being a Saturday, most of them are in. I'll come and make the introductions if you like.'

'That's very kind of you,' Cristy smiled, 'but one of our researchers should be along later, Clover . . .'

'Yes, yes, I met her when she came a few days ago. Lovely girl. So she'll be recording us, will she? I must say, everyone's going to be quite disappointed not to meet you. We're big followers of *Hindsight* in our little hamlet.'

'Nula! I thought I heard your voice,' Layla declared, coming down the stairs. 'How are you?'

'Look at you!' Nula scolded. 'What's all that in your hair?'

Putting a hand up to check, Layla grimaced and pulled away a cobweb. 'No sign of it,' she told Cristy and Connor.

'What are you looking for?' Nula demanded. 'Maybe I can help.'

'Romy's portrait,' Layla reminded her.

'Ah yes. I could have told you it wasn't there – I searched for it myself, you know. Do you have a coffee? No? Then I'll pour you one.'

As she turned to the kitchen, Layla looked at Cristy, clearly trying to alert her to something without drawing Nula's attention.

Realizing what was needed, Cristy said to Nula, 'I can take over there while you go and tell your neighbours that Connor and I will be happy to say hello before we leave.'

Appearing delighted, Nula immediately took off to share the good news, and as soon as the door closed behind her, Layla said, 'I've just found something . . . I didn't want to bring it down while Nula was here, but you need to see it.'

As Layla ran back up the stairs, Cristy went to add milk to the coffee Nula had poured, while Connor helped himself to a cookie.

'Here!' Layla declared, slightly breathless from the quick sprint up and down the stairs. She was holding out a large, padded envelope, crumpled, cobwebbed and slightly torn. 'I moved an old chest of drawers to see if the painting was behind it,' she said, as Cristy took it, 'and this fell to the floor.'

Cristy opened up the package and reached inside, feeling around. Her heart jolted as she realized what her hand was closing on.

'Jesus! A gun!' Connor declared, as she pulled it out. 'What the hell . . . ?'

Cristy stared at it, turned it over, and hating the feel of it, quickly put it on the table.

Connor picked it up. 'Is it loaded?' he asked. He spun the barrel, found no bullets and put it down again.

'I don't understand,' Layla said shakily. 'Why on earth would Romy or Rudi have a gun?'

Cristy checked the envelope again, found a smaller one inside and pulled it out. 'Have you looked in here?' she asked.

Layla shook her head.

As Cristy opened it, Connor said, 'You know, it's going to flip Clove right out if it contains a bunch of fake IDs.'

Knowing it would flip her out too, Cristy pulled out the contents, unfolded them and quickly scanned each document in turn. Her eyes focused on the last, then shot to Layla. 'I don't know what to make of this,' she said, 'and I'm not sure you will either.'

CHAPTER TWENTY

They were seated at the table now, below Rudi's portrait, the smaller envelope's contents spread out between them, the gun back inside the larger one.

'I've got so many questions I hardly know where to begin,' Layla groaned, pushing her hands through her hair and looking more tired than ever.

Clove, who'd arrived a few minutes ago, said, 'Should we record a description of what we're looking at?'

Connor nodded and gestured for her to go ahead.

Taking out her device, she kicked things off herself.

CLOVE: 'What we have here is a bunch of certificates. Rudi's and Romy's births, their marriage, Rudi's death, showing that he drowned on Thursday 21st March 2024 . . . No middle names.'

Layla's anguished eyes went to Cristy.

CLOVE: 'There's also a short-form birth certificate for a Casey Callaghan, born 17th February 1992 in Matlock, Derbyshire. So she'd be what, now? Thirty-two?'

CONNOR: 'The right sort of age to be Rudi's daughter? With Callaghan being her mother's name?'

CLOVE: 'And now she's a Kaplan? Presuming she's the

owner of the baggage receipt, and I guess she has to be. Unusual first name, and too much of a coincidence otherwise.'

CLOVE: 'Weird that it was all wrapped up with their certificates. Not to mention secreted away with a *gun*, for God's sake.'

Everyone sat with that for a while.

LAYLA: 'Do you think she was blackmailing them in some way? But why would Rudi give up his home to hide the fact he has a daughter? If that's who she is. Romy would never have left him for having an affair, especially over thirty years ago.'

CRISTY: 'And it still doesn't explain why they needed a gun, or why her birth certificate is with theirs.'

Everyone started at the sound of a sharp rap on the kitchen window. Nula was beckoning them outside.

'The neighbours await,' Clove remarked, ending the recording. 'Is there anything in particular you want me to cover? I've made notes, obvs, just . . .'

'Ask if anyone knows Casey Callaghan or Kaplan,' Cristy instructed. 'And describe the blue-eyed woman who went into the giftshop and the townhouse in Portugal, in case anyone has spotted someone like that coming and going.'

'On it,' Clove assured her. 'Big question now: what are you going to do with the gun?'

Having already considered it, Cristy said, 'As none of us has a licence, it'll have to stay here?' She made it a question for Layla.

'I agree,' Layla said, 'but we can take the certificates with us.'

'Of course.'

151

As they began folding them back into the envelope, Clove said, 'Are you coming to do the meet and greet now, or do you want to wait until I'm done?'

'You could be here all day,' Connor pointed out, 'so we'll do it now.'

After Clove had left, Cristy picked up the envelope containing the gun. 'I guess we should take it back upstairs?'

'I'll do it,' Layla offered. 'I know where I found it, and we don't want Nula stumbling across it when she's looking around. Not that she has any reason to search for anything now, but best to be safe.'

She was back a couple of minutes later, dusting herself down and taking out her phone, which was ringing. Seeing who it was, she looked at Cristy. 'My brother,' she announced. 'I can always call him back, but, if you want to talk to him . . .'

Cristy turned to Connor.

'No time like the present,' he said. 'We can always call him again if we need to.'

Clicking on, Layla said, 'Hi, Baz, how are you?'

His response wasn't audible, so Connor signalled for her to switch to speaker.

Doing so, she said, 'Yeah, I'm OK too, I think. I'm with Cristy and Connor at Romy's cottage – we've found a couple of things that are pretty weird and worrying.'

'Like what?' he asked, sounding intrigued.

Ignoring the question, she said, 'They'd like to have a chat if you've got time? I think they probably want to record it?'

Cristy nodded.

Barry said, 'Sure. I was about to head to the gym, but hey, let's go for it, although not sure how helpful I can be. You know much more than I do about everything.'

With a humourless laugh, Layla said, 'Which is like next to nothing as it turns out. OK, you're already on speaker, and

152

Connor's just getting set up . . . Do you mind if I make this a video call?'

BARRY: 'Sure. Not looking my best, so don't hold it against me.'

A moment later he appeared on her phone screen, clear-eyed and clean-shaven, so not looking bad at all.

CRISTY: 'Hi, Barry. Thanks for agreeing to this. I know it's short notice, and I'd like to have been better prepared, but as you happened to call now . . . We can always talk again if we need to.'

BARRY: 'No problem. Happy to do whatever.'

CONNOR: 'Hi, Barry, Connor here, Cristy's co-producer. She'll probably do most of the talking from our end, but if you can begin by introducing yourself and telling us how you're connected to Rudi and Romy.'

BARRY: 'OK, so . . . I'm Barry Cates, younger brother of Layla, and my connection to the Kaplans is basically the same as hers. We've known them since forever; they've always been more like family than close friends, although I guess in some people's books, the latter is better. They're great people, really cool, took us on loads of holidays when we were kids – and later, actually. They had some pretty wild friends, I remember, and amazing parties . . . I'm sure Lay's told you all this already, so stop me if I'm going over old ground.'

CRISTY: 'It's good to hear you talking about them too, but I'm keen to ask about something that came up between you and Layla when I was at your parents' house.'

153

BARRY: 'Let me guess, it was me calling them dodgy – which, for the record, I'm sure I only ever said once . . !'

LAYLA: 'Once that I heard, which is why you can't deny it!'

BARRY: 'Why would I even want to? They *were* dodgy – or I guess eccentric's a better word, and everyone knows about his time in Moscow. OK, it was a long time ago, and just because they were there, doesn't actually mean anything, but it was me, not you, Layla, who Rudi told he was a spy!'

LAYLA: 'The only weird thing about that is that you believed it!'

BARRY: 'I was twelve, so why wouldn't I? Plus, he had guns!'

Cristy's and Connor's eyes met.

LAYLA: 'For God's sake, they weren't real!'

BARRY: 'How do you know? He didn't show them to you!'

LAYLA: 'He had tons of props for all the plays they put on – you know that!'

BARRY: 'These were different. They weren't in the usual storeroom; they were in a safe. I guess they were valuable collector's items, that sort of thing, but I'm telling you, they were real!'

CRISTY: 'We've just found a gun, here at the cottage, presumably belonging to Rudi or Romy

BARRY: 'No shit! Jeez, they kept a gun there? How random is that? What type of gun?'

CONNOR: 'It's a revolver, and actually it could be a prop.'

BARRY: 'Still strange though, wouldn't you say? So maybe now you can't blame me for thinking there's more to them than the rest of my family wants to see. I mean, who else do we know keeps a gun? Real or otherwise. And actually, thinking of them still being involved in some sort of intelligence swap has never been a stretch for me.'

LAYLA: 'Because you spend your life disappearing down conspiracy theory rabbit holes.'

Barry turned away from the camera, apparently distracted by something or someone at his end. Cristy and Connor watched and waited, not able to tell if he was talking to someone or if he was listening as someone else spoke, only certain that something had snagged his attention and wasn't letting go in a hurry.

In the end, Barry turned back and appeared slightly rattled as he continued.

BARRY: 'Sorry, thought my flatmate was out, but seems not. Anyway, nothing to do with this, so where were we? Oh, that's right, the old conspiracy theory chestnut. You're so predictable, Layla – should definitely have seen that coming. But what the hell – this isn't supposed to be about me, is it? I thought we were discussing Rudi and Romy, and do you know what? I wouldn't think worse of them if they did have something shady going on, and if you've found a gun . . .'

LAYLA: 'Talk about me being predictable . . .'

CONNOR: 'OK, let's move this on. Barry, can you tell us about the last time you saw the Kaplans?'

BARRY: 'Sure, it would have been at Rudi's funeral that I last saw Romy. No, actually, I saw her once after that, at my parents' place. She was in bits. Really upsetting to see, especially for Mum. I guess it's why Romy stopped coming as often; she didn't want to stress Mum any more than was necessary when Mum's health was – is – so . . . you know.'

CONNOR: 'And Rudi? When did you last see him?'

BARRY: 'I can't be certain about that. Could have been at Romy's birthday party last May – if I went.'

LAYLA: 'We all did. You, me, Mum and Dad.'

BARRY: 'Then that would have been the last time. I was mainly in touch with him by phone or email . . . He'd give me advice now and then on stuff I was doing, or he'd ask me how things were going with my job. He always showed an interest – that's the kind of guy he was. Oh, I remember at the party, he talked to me about some crypto thing. He wanted to know if I knew anything about it. I told him I didn't, and he should probably stay away from it unless he had someone he trusted to advise him.'

CRISTY: 'Do you know if he took it any further?'

BARRY: 'No, but it seems pretty likely given how things started to go downhill for him after that.'

CRISTY: 'Layla, did you know about his interest in cryptocurrency?'

LAYLA: 'First I've heard of it, but it's not the sort of thing Rudi would discuss with me.'

BARRY: 'I'm pretty sure Dad knows. Actually, he does, because I remember telling him myself so he could maybe give Rudi a steer in the right direction – i.e., away from it.'

CONNOR: 'Do you happen to know who approached Rudi about the crypto investment?'

BARRY: 'Not a clue, and I'm not saying it happened – it's just the coincidence of him losing everything that makes it look like it probably did.'

CRISTY: 'Did you see anything of him around the time they left the manor?'

BARRY: 'I don't think anyone did, not even Mum. They kind of kept the move to themselves, and the first most of us knew about them being where you are now was when Mum got the change of address.'

LAYLA: 'We found Rudi's death certificate just now, but there's still no proof the body was definitely his.'

BARRY: 'Are you serious? Why are you doing this, Layla? You know how much it upsets Mum, and all you've got to go on is a reflection in some sunglasses . . .'

LAYLA: 'And the fact no one else saw the body, apart from Romy.'

BARRY: 'Jesus, if she says it was him, then it was him. Why would she make it up? Cristy, tell me you're not supporting this, please.'

CRISTY: 'We're checking ID protocols with the coroner, but for what it's worth, I agree: it most probably was him who drowned in the bath.'

BARRY: 'I'll look forward to hearing you've had it confirmed. Meanwhile, the question we all should be asking is: what the heck has happened to Romy? Why would she just take off and not tell anyone where she's going or when she'll be back? You've got to agree, there's something pretty fishy about it, especially now you've found a gun. Do you have any theories yet on where she might be?'

CRISTY: 'I'm afraid not, but we are keen to find someone called Casey Callaghan or Kaplan. Does either name mean anything to you?'

BARRY: 'No. Should it? Hang on, Kaplan? Is she some sort of relative?'

LAYLA: 'We've just found a birth certificate in the name of Casey Callaghan, and I told you about the baggage receipt we found in Portugal. The name on that was Casey Kaplan.'

BARRY: 'Hah! So have we uncovered one of Rudi's many dark secrets?'

LAYLA: 'I wish you'd take this more seriously. Anything could have happened to her, and it's like you don't care.'

BARRY: 'I probably don't as much as you do, but she's not my godmother, is she?'

LAYLA: 'What's that got to do with anything? She's still a human being, and I know how much she means to you.'

BARRY: 'Not denying, and I'm fully supportive of you wanting to find her – knock yourself out trying – but if you want my honest opinion, wherever she is, whatever she's doing, she's not getting in touch because she doesn't want to. And if she doesn't want to, well, you've got to think the same as me, surely: is the past catching up with her?'

CHAPTER TWENTY-ONE

An hour later, after meeting the Bellbrook neighbours and even signing a few autographs, Cristy and Connor were heading to Haylesford Manor, with Layla leading the way in her own car.

As soon as Connor had finished on the phone to Jodi, Cristy said, 'If we put aside the notebook entries, and I'm not actually sure how we do that, do you agree with Barry Cates that Romy might not want to be found?' She was mindful of the fact she'd said more or less the same thing to David a few days ago and so needed to explore it further.

'I can certainly see where he's coming from,' Connor concurred, 'but you'd be hard pressed to get Layla or her mother to agree.'

'But if she *doesn't* want to be found, if she has gone into hiding for whatever reason, we have to ask ourselves: are we doing the right thing trying to find her, especially in what will ultimately be quite a public way?'

'That's impossible to answer when we have no idea what's going on in her head, but I guess, if something has happened to her . . .'

'Like what?'

'I've no idea,' Connor replied, 'but if she is out there somewhere, hoping someone will understand her posts are all a front and they're actually a cry for help, the way Beth and Layla think, do we want to be the ones to let her, or them, down?'

Viewed that way, the answer obviously had to be no, especially when they took Romy's notes into consideration. 'Maybe it's time to talk to the police?' Cristy suggested.

'Maybe you're right, particularly now we've found the gun, which might not actually be real. Even if it is they're obviously not using it, are they, given that it's still in the cottage. So, knowing what big fans the police are of cryptic messaging – as in, not fans at all – I reckon that as things stand, they'll just carry on seeing Romy's video posts as proof that she's OK and probably wants to be left alone for a while.'

'And if the videos turn out to be fake – older videos reused?' Cristy asked.

'Well, obviously that would be a game-changer, but we don't know for certain that they are, and are the cops going to try and find out? Not a chance. So, it's down to us, or more specifically Jacks.'

Sighing, Cristy sat quietly for a while, reflecting on what Connor had said, before allowing her thoughts to move back to their chat with Barry. It had raised something for her, if she could only put a finger on what. He'd said something – maybe it was just a throwaway line that even he hadn't realized might have a significance . . . It wasn't Rudi claiming to be a spy when Barry was a child, or the guns he'd kept in a safe . . . It wasn't the crypto investment thing either, although that was certainly interesting.

'It sure is,' Connor agreed, when she brought it up. 'He wouldn't be the first to lose big time to that sort of scam, and looking at when he talked to Barry about it, early summer of last year . . . Seems unlikely he'd have lost everything that quickly, but maybe David will come up with something when he does his thing. In the meantime, we could get Layla to ask her dad what he knows.'

After sending a quick text to Layla, Cristy said, 'You know, I have an increasingly uneasy feeling about the way things are going with this.'

160

'Hah, no arguments from me on that front – stuff is getting weirder by the minute, although nothing to eclipse the accidental drowning that could actually turn out to be murder . . . Anyway, talk to me about the Bellbrook neighbours. Did any of them strike you as . . . particularly interesting?'

Cristy pictured the friendly residents, some local business owners, others retired doctors and teachers, all easily described as upstanding citizens and seeming as keen to be helpful as they were delighted to meet the *Hindsight* team. She slowly shook her head. 'Did anyone stand out for you?'

'I don't think so, but Clove will report back when she's finished interviewing them. Ah, Layla's indicating left up ahead, so we leave this road at last.'

For the next twenty or more minutes, they wound through endless, narrow country lanes and picture-book villages, across vast swathes of farmland and over meandering streams and rivers, until finally they reached a leafy lay-by seemingly in the middle of nowhere.

'Any thoughts on where we actually are?' Cristy asked, as they pulled in behind Layla, who was already getting out of her car.

'I'm guessing still Gloucestershire,' Connor ventured, 'and I'd say the fancy-looking gates across the road are why we've stopped.'

Stepping out into the dank summer air, scented with tangy rural smells and damp earth, Cristy stared at the gates. They were tall, with narrowly set rails and some intricately scalloped ironwork at the top. Either side of them, for at least two hundred yards in each direction, high, dense beech hedges and dry-stone walls protected the property grounds, with the occasional old oak soaring skywards and seeming to stand sentry in the way only that sort of tree could, imperious and immovable.

'What's the plan?' she called out, as Layla crossed over the road.

'I'm going to ring the bell, see if they'll let us in,' Layla replied.

'And why not?' Cristy muttered. 'They can only say no.' And checking there was no sign of traffic, she followed.

'Is it a video entry system?' she asked Layla, as she reached her.

'I should say.' Layla smiled and nodded to the CCTV cameras set atop poles just inside the gates. 'I guess they're watching us, and the bell seems to be working, so let's see who answers.'

'What are you going to say if someone does?'

'Still working on my script,' Layla admitted, and together they peered through the gates, down a long, poplar-lined drive, to where the front of a house was only partly visible about a quarter of a mile away. However, it was enough to see that it was classically Georgian in style, with perfectly symmetrical sash windows either side of a grand portico entryway.

'Impressive place,' Cristy remarked.

Layla smiled. 'They couldn't have treasured it more or been more generous in how openly they shared it. I don't recall any cameras in their day. Then again, security was never a big issue for them.'

'Until it was time to hide a gun and a mysterious birth certificate behind a chest of drawers, and get their cottage checked for bugs every two months,' Connor commented, as he joined them. 'Wow! Will you look at this place? I've got the recorder on, so do you want to do the honours, Cris? Your powers of description always outclass mine.'

She was about to respond when an old Jeep rumbled up alongside them and a jovial looking man, of some girth and apparent hunting-habits, clambered out. 'Hello there,' he cried cheerily. 'Peculiar sort of day, innit? Not sure whether it's going to rain or not.'

Stepping forward to shake his hand, Layla said, 'Nice to meet you. I'm Layla Cates. And you are?'

'Bill Butler, at your service. Lost, are you?'

'No, no, my godmother used to live here. Romy Kaplan?'

'Oh, is that right? Godmother, eh? Well, I know Romy. And Rudi. We were really sorry about his passing. Lovely bloke. Lovely people. We were sad to see them go, me and the missus. We're about three miles down the road, Blackberry Farm. Can't miss it.' He turned to stare in through the gates. 'If you're hoping to get inside, I don't think you'll have any luck. The new people are hardly ever there, and as far as I know . . .' He broke off as a black, open-topped Aston Martin appeared at the far end of the drive and began coming towards them.

'Flash git,' Butler muttered under his breath.

'Who is it?' Cristy asked.

'Chap who takes care of the place. Nothing gets past him. Well, it wouldn't, would it – all the cameras they've had put up? You'd think they had bloody royalty in there. Hello, Mr Aalders. Fancy seeing you here,' he said, as the car came to a stop only feet in front of them, and a short-haired, deeply tanned Adonis sprang out of the vehicle.

'Hello there, Bill,' the Adonis said, approaching the gates. 'Is everything all right?' Though his eyes were hidden by dark glasses, he exuded nothing but charm as he looked from Cristy to Layla to Connor and back again.

'I was just explaining,' Layla replied, 'that my godmother used to live here . . .'

'Really? Do you mean Romy Kaplan? Yes, I'm sure you do. How is she? I was very sorry to hear about Rudi. Such an awful thing to happen.'

'So you knew them?' Layla said.

'Not well. We met a few times when they were handing the manor over. I think it was difficult for them, leaving . . . Well, it would be – it's such a beautiful place.'

'Were you involved in the handover?' Cristy asked.

He regarded her quizzically, flicked a quick glance at Connor and said, 'Sorry, I'm not sure . . .'

'Cristy Ward,' she told him, putting a hand through the bars to shake. 'And this is Connor Church.'

'Good to meet you,' Connor said, clearly not meaning it at all.

'Are you filming something?' Aalders asked, clocking the recorder.

Before Connor could respond, Cristy said, 'So were you? Involved in the handover.'

Resummoning his friendliness, Aalders said, 'Not exactly. Slightly above my pay grade, but I do manage the property these days.'

'Must be quite demanding,' Connor commented, 'an estate that size.'

'Oh, it's not so big. So, Romy was your godmother?' he said chattily to Layla.

'That's right. I'm just showing my friends where she used to live. My family and I used to come here a lot before she and Rudi moved out. I don't suppose you've seen her lately, by any chance?'

Apparently startled by the question, he frowned curiously. 'I'd have to say probably not since they moved out. How is she?'

Layla turned to Cristy, clearly stuck for an answer.

'We don't know – she's missing,' Cristy said. Then, 'Would it be possible for us to come in and have a look round? We're making a podcast about her disappearance, and the place she used to live would be good background.'

Aalders looked faintly worried. 'Well, I don't imagine it would be a problem,' he said, 'but I'll have to contact my employers first to ask if it's OK.'

Layla smiled. 'Shall we wait?'

He laughed. 'They're away travelling at the moment, so it might take a while, but if you can let me have your number . . .'

As Layla took his in order to send hers, Cristy said, 'Can I ask who the new owners are?'

164

His tousled head tilted to one side as he considered the request. 'I probably ought not to give out my employers' personal information,' he said, 'but once I've spoken to them, I'm sure they'll be happy to meet you themselves.' He turned back to Layla. 'I'll be in touch soon,' he promised, and after casting a quick look Bill Butler's way, he got back into his expensive car, deftly turned it around and took off back up the drive.

'Full of himself,' the old farmer grunted. 'Lording it around here ever since the Kesingers took over. That's their name, by the way – Michael and Maria Kesinger. South African, I think. Seem decent enough folk. Not that we see much of them; they're more – how shall I put it? – exclusive than Rudi and Romy ever were.'

'Do you know where our friend with the Aston Martin is from?' Connor asked. 'He didn't sound local.'

'Definitely foreign,' Bill Butler stated. 'My wife reckons he's a Yank, but Simon in the pub says he's from Norway. Got a bit of both accents if you ask me. Anyhow, if he hasn't seen Romy since she left the manor, then he must have had a day off the last time she was here.'

Cristy blinked, and Layla said, 'What do you mean?'

He shrugged. 'I saw her myself a few weeks ago, give or take. Plain as day, driving in through these very gates in her little blue Smart. I suppose she struck up some kind of friendship with the Kesingers. It would be just like her. Everyone's friend, was Romy. Rudi too. I saw him coming and going a few times before her, you know.'

Deciding to deal with the surprise later, Cristy said, 'Can you think back to exactly when it was you last saw Romy? You said a few weeks ago, but maybe you can narrow it down a little?'

He lifted his cap to scratch his head and spent the next two minutes chuntering away under his breath, recalling everything and everyone who might help him pinpoint when he'd last seen Romy. Finally he said, 'That's right, my brother-in-law was with me at the time, so it would have been sometime around the early May bank holiday.'

Layla turned to Cristy. 'That's more or less when Nula last saw her.'

Thinking fast, Cristy said, 'Was anyone in the car with her?'

After giving it some thought, he said, 'Yeah, I think there was, now you come to mention it. A young woman. Can't tell you who she was, but hardly my business, is it? None of it is.'

And with a cheery wave, he jumped back into his Jeep and continued on his way.

CHAPTER TWENTY-TWO

It was gone four by the time they got back to the office, tired, sticky and in sore need of a long, cool drink.

'I spoke to Mum and Dad while I was driving,' Layla said, going straight to the fridge as Connor opened the window. 'Mum had no idea Romy had become friendly with the manor's new owners, or that she ever visited the place after she left. Honest to God, Romy is turning out to be such a dark horse I might actually start agreeing with Barry if it goes on like this. As Mum put it, just when you think you know everything about someone, it turns out you know nothing at all, and she's pretty hurt by it.'

Not surprised that an incipient sense of distrust was starting to move in, Cristy said, 'What about your dad? Did you ask him about a crypto investment?'

'Yeah, he said he did bring it up with Rudi, after Barry mentioned it, but Rudi told him it had gone away and he didn't need to worry.'

Taking the glass of water Layla was offering, Cristy sank into her chair and drank deeply before saying, 'We need to get everything written up and entered on the whiteboard. What are you doing?' she asked Connor.

'A search on the Kesingers and Matey with the fuck-off car,' he replied. 'What's his first name?' he asked Layla.

Checking her phone, she said, 'Bram, as in Stoker.'

'Appropriate,' Connor muttered.

'I wonder if he lives on site,' Cristy said. 'I guess he must. Anyway, if Bill Butler saw Rudi going in and out several times after he was supposed to have left, why did Matey say he hadn't seen them since the handover? As estate manager, he must have been aware of at least some of the visits?'

'I didn't trust him from the moment I clapped eyes on him,' Connor asserted, 'although I have to admit I might have had some car-envy going on.'

'No!' Cristy cried in mock shock. 'But you're Superman; you can fly. Bet he can't compete with that.'

'Yeah, funny. Anyway, those cameras would give us all the information we need about the comings and goings, if we could get to them.'

'Is there a way?' Layla asked.

Connor's eyebrows rose. 'Not if we want to stay legal.'

'But if we don't, there's a track that runs alongside the perimeter wall at the back, and a tree that overhangs . . .'

Stopping her, Cristy said, 'And once we're in, what then? You can't seriously think we could get anywhere near the computer that controls the cameras without being seen. So no, we won't be breaking in. We'll just wait to see if he gets in touch to offer you a visit.'

'And if you don't hear from him,' Connor added, 'no reason not to call him.'

Breaking into a smile as Clove came into the room, Cristy said, 'And here comes the real star of the show. Let me get you a drink. I expect you need one after gossiping with the neighbours all afternoon.'

'A couple of vodka shots with a whisky chaser should do it,' Clove responded, dropping her heavy bag on the floor and collapsing into her chair. 'Failing that, I'll take a beer.'

Passing bottles to everyone, Cristy said, 'So, did you learn anything interesting?'

'You mean apart from never to tell anyone my life story unless asked? God, some people, they just don't know when to stop. Anyway, no one's ever heard of Casey Callaghan or Kaplan, or seen anyone who fits the description I gave. Of course, they wanted to know who she was, so I just said we're trying to find out, which is basically the truth.'

Picking up her phone, Cristy said, 'Connor and Layla will fill you in on our very interesting trip to the manor, while I go and reassure my children on our WhatsApp group that I haven't abandoned them and am still completely fascinated by every minute detail of their endlessly chaotic lives.'

Laughing, Connor said, 'I wondered what was going on with your phone as we were driving back. Say hi from me.'

'And me,' Clove added.

After spending the next ten minutes in the meeting room, catching up on Hayley and Aiden's latest news – Hayley was currently in Oslo with her boyfriend, Aiden in discussions with his father about financing a surf trip to South West France – Cristy returned to the office, just as Layla was saying,

'So, are we thinking it was the blue-eyed woman in the car with Romy when Bill Butler saw her driving into the manor?'

'I'd say there's a good chance it was,' Connor concurred.

'So if she is Casey Kaplan or Callaghan . . .'

'Callaghan for ease?' Cristy suggested.

'OK, if she is Casey Callaghan . . .' Layla sat back and threw out her hands in frustration. 'We still don't have the first idea who she actually is.'

'I'm guessing you still haven't found out anything about her?' Cristy asked Connor.

'I've been on it since we got back,' he replied, 'but as far as the internet goes, she doesn't seem to exist.'

'Which could mean neither Casey, nor Callaghan, nor Kaplan is her real name,' Clove offered.

'In which case, we should check if the birth certificate is authentic,' Cristy said. 'And let's not forget' – she turned to the whiteboard – 'that according to the baggage label, she was in Portugal on 6th June , the day before Romy posted one of her videos. And she was either still there, or went back, on 12th June, when Maria, the cleaner, saw her, which was after we believe the portrait was taken from the cottage.'

After a few moments of mental checking, Connor said, 'Having all these movements and sightings is great, but what are they actually adding up to?'

Cristy shrugged. 'That Casey Callaghan knows Romy, has travelled with her, passes messages to her, possibly collects clothes from the cottage for her, visits the manor with her . . . In other words, Romy knows exactly who she is and for whatever reason, she seems never to have introduced her to her closest friends or neighbours. I'm afraid I can't give you any more than that right now, but what I can suggest is that we go home and take a break, come back on Monday to discuss whether or not we're going to upload a podcast on Tuesday.'

'Are you thinking of not?' Layla asked worriedly.

Unwilling to admit that was exactly what she was thinking, Cristy said, 'Before we make a decision, we need to be certain of what we do and don't want to reveal at this stage. Number one to hold back on, I would say, is the chance that Rudi is still alive. The press will leap all over something like that, and it'll just complicate things even further. The next thing to consider is whether or not we actually believe Romy wants to be found.' She raised a hand as Layla started to object. 'I'm not saying we should give up the search,' she said. 'I'm as keen as you are now to find out where she is, but maybe before we go public, you should talk it through with your parents again to make sure they're still fully on board.'

'They will be,' Layla told her confidently. 'After what they've already found in Romy's notebook, there's no way they'll want to stop now.'

'OK, but talk to them anyway and be really straight with

them, because if it turns out Rudi didn't die in the bath, then he and Romy could be facing some very serious charges if and when we catch up with them. This isn't me trying to help them avoid justice; it's me asking you to make sure your mother is fully aware of where this could end and what it could actually mean for her – and for you.'

CHAPTER TWENTY-THREE

The whole team, including the Quinns, Iz and Jacks, gathered at nine-thirty on Monday morning. First on the agenda was another ambiguous extract from Romy's notebook, which Beth had found inserted into some lines from Elizabeth Barrett Browning's poem, *Aurora Leigh*.

As Layla read it aloud, Connor recorded it.

LAYLA: 'It starts "*. . . I who have written much in prose and verse / For other's uses, will write now for mine . . .*

"'*It is 17th March, and Beth and I have just spent a beautiful day quietly soaking up the sun, reading, remembering, laughing and sometimes crying. She tells me she won't die, and I believe her because I have to. Life would be as unbearable without her as it would without Rudi. I don't want to think about either.*

"'*I dreamt of her last night, and in the dream, I told her everything, but even as I spoke the words, I could feel them turning to ash in my mouth, and I saw her starting to fade.*

"'*I can't ask her to share this with me. Rudi thinks I will while we're here in Portugal, but he's wrong. How is he managing without me? Has there been any more contact? Please don't let anyone hurt him. He doesn't deserve it. He's done everything they ask, but I'm afraid he might have some crazy idea of taking matters into his own hands."'*

As soon as Connor stopped recording, Layla said, 'Mum is more certain than ever that Romy needs help, wherever she is, so she wants us to keep going.'

Cristy nodded solemnly, still inwardly debating how to view what they'd just heard. 'And your dad agrees?' she asked.

'Definitely. He also said, in light of what might or might not have happened to Rudi, can we try not to involve the police yet?'

Cristy looked around at the others and felt the intensity of their anticipation as if it were some sort of pressure. In addition to this extract and Layla's father's request, they were readying themselves for the start of a new series, with no idea yet whether it would remain in their control after the first Call to Arms. The police would surely take an interest if they became aware of these extracts – or would they? She guessed only time and an upload would tell.

'OK, I think we need to take a deeper look into the positioning of the extracts,' she said. 'Is it in any way relevant? Does the book or poem or text around it contain anything else we should be looking at?'

'Obscure,' Clove commented, 'but agreed – definitely worth a look, so leave it with me.'

'Thanks, and now, before we go any further, we should welcome Jacks back from his Peruvian adventure. It's great to see you, my friend, and please know how much you were missed.'

'Goes without saying.' He grinned and affected a small bow to each of his small audience. His spring-onion top hair had grown in the past month, no longer shooting up like he'd plugged himself in. Instead, it was tamed into a knot at the nape of his neck, while his boyish face had acquired a faint shadow-beard.

The new look suited him, Cristy thought, as did the purple poncho and ceramic beads.

'We're hoping,' Connor told him, 'that you've got something to share with us from Romy's laptop?'

Jacks grimaced. 'Well, the good news is, I got into it,' he replied. 'The password, by the way, is LaylaBethMe3.'

Surprised and clearly touched, Layla said, 'How on earth did you manage to get to that?'

'I have a certain sort of brain,' he informed her. 'Anyway, the bad news: it's been restored to factory settings. So, no emails, no accounts, no contacts, no internet history, nada, nil, nix, naught – apart from the password. Obvs, this strongly suggests there was once something on it that someone, possibly Romy herself, didn't want anyone to see.'

'But if she was behind the reset,' Meena said, 'surely it would have been easier just to take the laptop with her when she left or get rid of it somewhere. So surely someone else reset it?'

'You'd think so,' Jacks agreed, 'but there's still the issue of the password. A factory reset wipes them all, so it must have been added *after* the reset. It's interesting, because it definitely seems to be Romy's. Anyway, I've arranged to take it to my old prof at UWE to see if . . .'

'UWE?' Iz broke in, confused.

'University of the West of England,' he clarified. 'The prof is right up there with the best in his field, so lucky he can fit me in on Wednesday. Hopefully, I'll have more to offer after that. Meanwhile, I've been getting stuck into other stuff like her social media and trying to get some intel on her phone. I saw a note,' he said to Layla, 'that you were trying to speak to someone at Vodafone?'

'That's right,' she confirmed, 'but so far data protection won't allow them to give anything up.'

'Mm.' Jacks grunted. 'Going to be a hard one, but I'll stay on it.'

'Well, I think we're all feeling more optimistic now you're back on board, Jacks,' Cristy said, 'so we'll leave that with you and crack on with the plans for tomorrow's upload. The intro is already recorded. Connor and I did it a couple of weeks ago. Of course, things have changed since, but some of it remains usable – we'll play it for you later – in the meantime, to precis, we've flagged that this is a special episode asking for help with a missing person. There's also mention of a potential murder, but we're going to park that unless we hear from the coroner's office . . .'

'We have!' Clove jumped in, fingers straight to the keyboard. 'Turned up early this morning . . . I'll share it when I find it, but basically it says all protocols were followed, blah-di-blah, blah-di-blah, so they haven't actually answered the question.'

'Which was?' Harry prompted.

'Was Romy's identification of Rudi's body sufficient for them to accept he really was Rudolph Kaplan?' Cristy provided. 'In other words, are any further checks carried out after the one given by the next of kin?'

'Typical bureaucratic reply,' Connor commented. 'Or we've hit on an anomaly and they don't want to admit it. We'll take it up again if it turns out to be necessary. Meantime, jury's still out on whether he did or did not drown in the bath, but I still don't think we can make a thing of it until we know more.'

'OK,' Cristy said, 'as it won't form part of the first upload, let's stay focused on what we *are* going to share. Which is, that the last time anyone saw Romy was six weeks ago at her home in Bellbrook. We've decided not to mention Bill

Butler spotting her driving into Haylesford Manor around the same time; we're still hoping to get in there, and if they think we're trying to accuse them of something, the doors might not be thrown open.'

'So do you think she's in there?' Meena asked doubtfully.

'We have no idea,' Cristy replied, 'but we know she's been in Portugal since the last sighting here, so frankly, she could be anywhere.'

Connor said, 'This upload will include the interviews with Romy's neighbour, Nula Higgins, also the one with Beth Cates, Layla's mother, and with Layla herself.'

'What about the giftshop owner?' Clove interjected.

'It's there,' Connor assured her, 'along with Quentin the neighbour. We're also running snippets of our trip to Portugal?' He looked at Jacks expectantly, but Jacks's head was down whatever rabbit hole he was now in, so Connor continued. 'There's nothing to say Romy's still in the Lagos area, but no harm in getting listeners to keep a look out if they're in the Algarve. We'll be directing everyone to our website, as usual, and to our social media, where Romy's photograph is already featuring.'

'We've also decided to talk about the baggage receipt,' Cristy added, 'just the discovery – not who we then learned it belonged to. Actually, why don't we play what we've put together so far, so we can get some feedback?'

Calling up the file, Connor hit play and put his feet up to listen along with everyone else.

It was a fairly straightforward pod, lasting no more than thirty minutes, and ending with some words that made everyone turn to him and Cristy in surprise.

CONNOR: 'So, join us again soon to find out more about a missing portrait, a curious letter from Rudi Kaplan to an old friend in Vienna, a mysterious birth certificate, a gun, and how it all relates to our search for Romy Kaplan.'

CRISTY: 'We also hope to share more about the mystery surrounding her husband's sudden death – was it really him, or did someone else die in his place? Perhaps he's still out there somewhere, maybe listening to this.'

As the playback stopped, Cristy smiled. 'We'll be editing out the last bit,' she assured them all, 'but the questions do need to be asked, in spite of – or maybe because of – the coroner's evasive response.'

'I've got goosebumps,' Iz confessed. 'I already can't wait to find out what happens next.'

Appreciating the feedback, Cristy said, 'There's a lot still to do to get things ready for tomorrow, so unless anyone has questions . . . ?'

'I do,' Harry said, putting up a hand. 'Do you seriously suspect them of being involved in some kind of covert op, possibly state-run, because that's how it's coming across to me.'

Cristy handed that one to Connor.

'Given what we know so far, it's a definite possibility,' he replied.

Harry's face darkened with concern. 'You realize, if you're right, you could find yourselves upsetting people you probably ought not to mess with?'

'Bring it on,' Iz and Clove declared, in unison.

Harry wasn't amused. 'You know the Kaplans best,' he said to Layla. 'What do you think?'

'All I can say,' Layla replied, 'is that my mother has known Romy most of her life. She's always been an open book, and I don't believe she could be deceitful if she tried.'

'And yet . . .' Jacks put in.

Everyone looked at him.

He shrugged, as if to say, *Here we are.*

Having to concede his point, Layla simply looked lost.

'What do you know about the manor's new owners?' Meena asked Cristy.

'So far, only name and nationality,' Cristy told her. 'I believe you're on it, Jacks.'

'Only got started last night,' he replied, 'so will report back as soon as I have more.'

'And don't forget to include Matey of small dick and flash car,' Connor reminded him.

'They're talking about you, Dad,' Aiden declared.

As everyone laughed, Cristy turned to find her son and his father standing in the doorway, Aiden looking extremely pleased with himself in spite of the cuff he'd just received from Matthew.

'Can't hang around, I'm afraid,' Matthew said. 'I'm just dropping him off. I'll catch you later.' And with a quick wave to everyone, he left.

'If you're staying, you can sit,' Cristy told Aiden, 'but we're in the middle of a meeting, so try not to be you.' Turning back to the others, she said, 'Where were we?'

Aiden said, 'Matey with the small—'

'I'm not talking to you,' Cristy cut in.

Laughing, Harry said, 'Have you thought about what you're going to do if Romy suddenly decides to show up again and the mystery's over?'

'It'll still be extremely interesting to hear where she's been and why she hasn't made any direct contact,' Cristy replied. 'Although obviously we don't know if she'll want to share. Connor, do you remember the programme we did on GCHQ? It has to have been about seven or eight years ago . . . Who was the guy we interviewed? He was incredibly helpful and offered up quite an interesting perspective on various methods of intelligence gathering.'

Iz said, 'GCHQ – Government Communication Headquarters?'

'Correct,' Connor told her, 'and I should have the guy's name in my contacts somewhere. Why, you think he's worth talking to?'

'Maybe,' she replied. 'Let's see what comes back after tomorrow's drop first.'

A few minutes later, after Harry and Meena had gone and the others were getting stuck into their various tasks, Cristy said to Aiden, 'Are you here for the day? If so, you can make yourself useful . . .'

'Just stopped by to pick up some keys,' he told her. 'I'm staying at yours this week, remember? And I've lost mine.'

'Again! For God's sake, Aiden. Funny how you never seem to lose your phone.'

'Surgically attached. Anyway, Dad's dropped my stuff in the meeting room, so I'd be grateful if you could bring it home with you later.'

'You're presuming I have my car.'

'It's outside. Oh, and while we're on the subject, can I use it for my driving lessons as soon as I'm seventeen? Or would you rather get me one of my own?'

'Nice try,' she said archly, 'but not going to happen. Now, if I give you my door keys, I want you to go straight to get them copied and bring them back here before you go home.'

'Cool. Oh, and the bloke you interviewed at GCHQ? Henry Godfrey.'

She blinked as Connor looked up, clearly as surprised as she was. 'How can you remember that?' she asked. 'You'd only have been about nine when we made that programme.'

'He came to our school to give a talk last year. Great bloke. We were all ready to sign up as the next James Bond after. Actually, still sounds like a blinder. I hear Cambridge is the place to start, if you want to get into that business, right?

179

Let's put it on my list for when we start scoping out unis. I can see myself as a bit of a Jason Bourne, can't you?'

Cristy laughed. 'More like Johnny English. Now, on your way, we've got a lot to do here – and don't forget to bring my keys back.'

CHAPTER TWENTY-FOUR

It was much later in the day, with the first upload still only half-edited and decisions still being made on what to include, that Jacks surfaced from one of his deeper dives to murmur, 'This is interesting.'

Cristy and Connor both looked up.

Jacks's head remained down.

'Hey!' Connor prompted.

Jacks looked up, surprised, then apparently realizing he'd spoken aloud, he said, 'Oh, sorry, geeky stuff . . . Just doing a bit of cross-referencing, but has anyone noticed Romy's post on her Insta page?'

'You're kidding,' Clove cried, grabbing her phone. 'I thought that account was dormant.'

'Not any more,' Jacks responded, and using his own phone, he flicked the posted images onto their screens.

'Not a reel this time,' Cristy murmured, as she began studying the latest posts, 'just a happy-looking tourist taking in the sights of . . . Lucerne?'

'That's what it says,' Jacks confirmed. 'Don't know the place personally.'

'I've only been once,' Cristy said, focusing on each shot in turn.

The first was of Romy in stripey dungarees and baseball cap, standing on the iconic Chapel Bridge, pointing up with one hand and down with the other, presumably bringing attention to the tiled roof above and hanging baskets below. In the second, she was in jeans and T-shirt on a hillside with a stunning view of the lake in the background.

The third showed her laughing delightedly as she rode a cable car up a mountainside, and in the fourth, she was leaning against the landmark water tower with flowers in her hair and blowing a kiss to camera. '"*A perfect day out with loved ones,*"' Cristy read aloud.

She looked at Layla, who was staring at the images, clearly as bewildered as everyone else.

'Lucerne's in Switzerland, right?' Clove asked. 'Just to be clear.'

Cristy nodded.

'So definitely no longer in Portugal.'

'When did she post it?' Connor asked Jacks.

Checking, he said, 'Half an hour ago.'

'Any comments yet?'

'Two,' Clove replied. 'One from SophieBReiner saying, "*Having the best time in one of our favourite places.*" The other's from JakeReiner saying, "*So happy to be here with Romy, making new memories.*"'

Cristy's eyes returned to Layla.

'I've never heard of them,' Layla told her, 'but I'll check with Mum.'

'Their profiles are set to private,' Clove said, 'but I'll see what I can find out about them. Not to tread on your toes, Jacks, but guessing you're pretty stuck into the Haylesford Manor crowd?'

'Go for it,' he told her, and returned to his own mission.

Cristy's phone rang, and seeing it was David, she decided to take a break and go outside while they spoke.

'How are you?' she asked, as she sank into a chair under the copper beech.

'*Savner dig,*' he replied.

182

She laughed. 'Impressive. Going to tell me what it means?'

'I think, hope, I'm missing you. However, the guys around here aren't always to be trusted, so I might have just propositioned you.'

'Well, I'm cool with that. Are you having a good time?'

'I guess, but I'll call again later for a proper catch up. I'm ringing now because I've just had some news you'll want to hear.'

Immediately alert, she put a finger to her other ear to block out the noise from a nearby construction site.

'Rudi Kaplan,' he said. 'According to my source, his net worth is estimated at around fifteen million . . .'

'Hang on, how far back are you going?'

'This is current.'

She blinked. 'I don't understand. Are you saying he's still a wealthy man?'

'Correct.'

'But how can . . . ? I mean, apart from everything else, he died three months ago.'

'I'm just telling you what I have.'

Cristy was trying to take this in. 'So why did he and Romy move out of Haylesford Manor?'

'Good question.'

'And who are the Kesingers?'

'I've no idea. Who *are* the Kesingers?'

Realizing she hadn't mentioned them before, she said, 'They're living at the manor now, or so we were told. But let me get this straight: Rudi didn't lose everything back in 2023?'

'Not according to my guy – who, by the way, had never heard anything about Rudi dying in a bath four months ago.'

'But it was in the news. I've seen the stories myself . . .'

'Doesn't mean everyone else heard it, especially if it was only run locally. I realize there's a whole can of worms opening up here, but what I can tell you is that Rudi is either still very much with us, or someone else is running the show and making it look like him.'

Stunned, Cristy said, 'Is that even possible?'

'Of course, if it's the way you want to play things.'

'So are you saying . . . Actually, what are you saying?'

'That people can get very creative where money's concerned.'

Sighing, she said, 'I'm not sure that helps.'

'OK, if he didn't die four months ago, then something pretty damned serious must have happened to make them fake it . . . Well, you know that, but whatever it was, it hasn't cost Rudi, or Romy, their fortune.'

'But it has cost someone their life?' she muttered. Then clocking the way he'd inserted, *or Romy*, she said, 'Are you suggesting Romy could be running . . . ?' She was thinking too fast again. What was she trying to say? 'Is it possible Romy has taken control of the estate . . . ? No, no, that doesn't make any sense – she'd surely still be living there if it was true.'

Maybe she is living there.

'Wives have been known to do far worse than a little mariticide to get their hands on the reins,' he reminded her dryly.

Would Romy do that? Was she actually capable? Not the Romy she'd been hearing about, but how reliable were the sources? How well did they really know her?

Speaking the rest of her thoughts aloud, Cristy said, 'So, this might not be about espionage? It could be about fraud – and murder, if Rudi *is* dead. Actually, even if he isn't, because *someone* died . . .'

'All I can tell you is that he's still playing the markets, investing in his preferred funds, backing various start-ups, but I'll stay on it if you like.'

'Yes, please do. Anything about cryptocurrency?'

'It hasn't come up.'

'OK.' There was a lot to take in here - if only she knew where to begin. 'And what would be really good to know from your guy is if anyone in his world has actually *seen* Rudi in the past four months, because no one in ours seems to have, apart from the reflection in Romy's glasses.'

*

'I've just spoken to Dad,' Layla announced when Cristy returned to the office. 'He remembers the Reiners, who posted on Romy's Insta pics. They're old friends from Atlanta, Georgia, who've travelled a lot with Rudi and Romy over the years. He has their email address, presuming it's not out of date.'

'OK,' Cristy responded. 'Send it over to Clove so she can get in touch.' Her head was still spinning with what she'd just learned from David. Should she tell Layla that Rudi's estate was still intact, that someone – possibly him or Romy – was running it, in spite of having left the manor? She had to, of course. Why was she even holding back?

'You're looking worried,' Connor told her. 'Everything OK?'

'I'm not sure it is,' she replied. 'David's just told me something about Rudi's estate . . .' As she explained, careful to keep any suspicions of Romy's part in the apparent deception to a minimum, she could see how baffled and even fearful Layla was becoming. In the end, she said, 'David's still talking to people, and obviously we'll redouble our efforts to get hold of Rudi's lawyers, but that's where we're at right now.'

Clearly still struggling with it, Layla said, 'Are you going to use any of it in tomorrow's upload?'

'I don't think we can. In fact, the way it's going, it's becoming increasingly likely we'll have to hand things over to the police, but we won't do that until you've told your parents what I've just told you.'

'I don't want to do it over the phone,' Layla said, starting to pack up, 'so I'll head off now and see you tomorrow.'

CHAPTER TWENTY-FIVE

True to her word, Layla was back the next morning, arriving soon after everyone else and looking as though she'd had a pretty bad night.

'Dad didn't want me to tell Mum,' she said, as Cristy passed her a coffee. 'He thinks all this is taking too much of a toll already, so being asked to see Romy in this horrible light . . . I must admit, it's shaken me up. A lot.'

'How did your dad react when you told him?' Connor wanted to know.

'He was shocked, obviously, but in the end, he said he'd rather not think ill of either of them, so he's just hoping there's a good explanation for everything.'

Understanding how torn Johnny Cates must be feeling, trying to protect his wife, while worrying about his friends' duplicity – betrayal even - Cristy decided to let it drop. It would have to be dealt with later, and probably not by her.

'OK, Jacks,' she said, 'are you ready to share anything about the Kesingers? Why do I get the feeling they don't actually exist?'

'Looking pretty real so far,' he told her, 'but still a way to go. If you're asking me to read it out, you might want to record for future use.'

'Let's do it,' Connor agreed, and after setting up the nearest device, he gave Jacks the cue to begin.

JACKS: 'OK, Michael Robert Kesinger. Born 1979,

Cape Town, South Africa. There's a whole load of stuff about his parents: father started Kezmer Mining, etc., etc. . . . . IOW, a pretty minted family. Michael educated in the UK, Harrow and LSE, graduated in Business and Modern Languages. For twenty-something years, he worked between Cape Town and City of London, set up a hedge fund, made a pile, then moved to New York and did the same there. He now has himself down as a retired financial strategist. At the age of forty-five. Lucky him.

'Moving on to the wife, Maria Kesinger, nee Bachman. Born 1980 in Appenzell, Switzerland, educated International School of Zug and Luzern, graduated Sorbonne in Paris 2002 with a degree in Fine Art. Ran a gallery in London from '98 to 2010, was a director at Sotheby's from 2010 to 2015. She's also listed as retired and resident in the Caymans.'

CONNOR: 'Is that where he's resident?'

JACKS: 'He is, but they have properties all over: Barbados, Melbourne, Singapore, St-Jean-Cap-Ferrat, Zurich, and . . . dah, dah, Haylesford Manor in Gloucestershire.'

CRISTY: 'So he *does* own the manor?'

JACKS: 'Actual ownership of properties like that is always hard to establish. Shell companies set up for tax avoidance, keeping everything opaque – you get the picture, or don't in fact, but as I said, still a way to go. It's even possible they're just renting the place off the actual buyer. Who knows?'

CONNOR: 'OK, anything else on Maria Kesinger?'

JACKS: 'Only that she's mentored a few artists over the years who've gone on to achieve some success. I

188

mention it because we know that Rudi and Romy did something similar.'

LAYLA: 'They gave encouragement and support to just about everyone.'

CONNOR: 'OK, so let's get to our friend with the flash car.'

JACKS: 'Aka Bram Aalders, born 1993, Amersfoort, Netherlands. Family moved to Colorado, US, in 1999. Young Bram schooled at Culver Academy, Indiana; graduated MIT Boston, 2013. He seems to have drifted for a couple of years, but comes back on radar in 2015 as part of a tech start-up, Analytics Anon, based in New York, specializing in creative tech solutions, it says here. It folded in 2021, and Bram took up his current post as property estate manager of Haylesford Manor in 2023. His partner, Lisa McIlvoy, works there too as "admin co-ordinator".'

CRISTY: 'Do you have a visual for her? Actually for all of them?'

JACKS: 'Sure do. Coming to a printer near you any time . . . now. For the whiteboard, once you're done with them. Anyway, back to Matey Bram: it's my hunch, Connor, that the decent set of wheels belongs to the Kesingers, for his use when they're not around.'

Clearly preferring the assumption to someone of Aalders's insufferable smugness being able to afford such a vehicle, Connor saluted Jacks with his coffee as he said, 'Any more, or shall I stop recording?'

'That's it for now. Basic profiles, and you can see from the printouts what they look like. Loads more shots of them, particularly the Kesingers, hobnobbing around the world

189

with the top-toff set . . . I've been trying to spot Rudi and Romy amongst them, but no sign so far. It's the kind of circles they moved in though, isn't it?' he asked Layla.

She nodded. 'Sometimes, yes.'

Cristy was studying the close-up of Lisa McIlvoy, who didn't have short fair hair, at least not in this shot. This young woman's was coppery and styled in a long, wavy bob. However, her face, small and freckled, was strikingly enlivened by cobalt-blue eyes. 'This has to be her,' she stated. 'Casey Callaghan, or whatever her actual name is.'

'Just what I was thinking,' Connor said. 'The hair doesn't match, but that's easy to change. Shame she's not smiling – a gap in the front teeth could seal it.'

'See if you can find any more shots of her,' Cristy said to Jacks, and setting this one aside, she moved on to the one of Bram Aalders. Seeing him here, handsome, immaculately groomed and undeniably full of himself, reminded her of how insouciantly he'd claimed not have seen Romy since she'd left the manor.

'I'm trying to find some sort of background connection between the Kesingers and the Kaplans,' Clove said, 'apart from both women being patrons of the arts.'

'We have all the connection we need with Haylesford Manor,' Connor pointed out.

Clearly troubled, Layla said, 'Do you think there's a chance Romy's actually in there?'

'According to her Insta page, she's in Lucerne,' Cristy reminded her.

'Do you think one of us should pop over there to check it out?' Clove asked hopefully.

'Before you go packing your bags,' Jacks piped up, 'let's make sure these shots are for real. As you know, it's not difficult to create false content these days, but not always easy to tell. Don't worry – the prof and his students will be all over it by Wednesday.'

'So you're thinking the videos she's posted could also be fake?' Cristy asked.

'Sure am, but still working on it.'

'What does it even mean if they are?' Layla asked.

Connor said, 'That she's either deliberately misleading everyone . . .'

'Or,' Jacks came in, 'someone is creating content to make it look as though she's out and about when actually she's . . . Well, that's the point, isn't it? We need to find out where she is, and if you want my advice, amigos, start bracing yourselves, because IMHO, this has all the hallmarks of being PDD – pretty damn dark.'

'As does this,' Layla said soberly. She was staring at the screen of her laptop, face pale and expression drawn. 'Dad's just sent it,' she said, realizing everyone was looking at her. 'Another extract from Romy's notebook. It starts with Robert Browning's "Home Thoughts, from Abroad" – we all know the opening line . . .'

'Hang on,' Connor interrupted, 'before you start reading, let's record it.'

As soon as he gave the signal, Layla returned to her father's email.

LAYLA: '"Oh to be in England / Now that April's there, / And whoever wakes in England . . ."'

She broke off and looked up. 'Do you want me to read the whole of the first verse? Romy's words come in towards the end.'

Cristy said, 'Go straight to it, and Clove can study the verse.'

LAYLA: '"I have been thinking about Beth a lot today, her love of April and Robert Browning's poem. It's April now, and I am here in this cottage, thinking of Italy –

it's where Browning was when he wrote the poem. We spent many holidays there, Rudi and I . . . How I wish I was there now, sharing precious memories with him, making new ones.

'"When will we be together again?

'"I spoke to Beth earlier; she didn't want to tell me, but I know the cancer has come back. I could hear it in her voice; I can even feel it in my bones. Beth, my darling, you don't deserve this. You have so many reasons to live, so please, fight it. Don't let it win!

'"I want, with all my heart, to be there for you, to help you through the darkest hours, but with everything that's happening here . . . Do you feel I'm betraying you? Are you angry and hurt that I am proving myself worthless at this critical time? Are you excusing me by telling yourself I'm grieving? I am, of course, desperately. I know how incapable you are of thinking the worst of those you love. I would forgive you if you did think the worst of me, Beth, but would you be able to forgive me if I told you the truth?"'

When Connor ended the recording, quiet followed, as though they'd all fallen into a slump of confusion and sadness.

Cristy roused them by passing over the emotional impact of the words straight to the practical meaning. 'April is after Rudi is supposed to have drowned,' she said, 'but I don't think this makes things any clearer about whether he did or didn't, although it veers more towards the fact that he did. She talks about the desire to make new memories, but obviously we all wish that about people we've lost. She also wonders when she and Rudi will be together again, then goes on to say she's grieving.'

'What's concerning me the most,' Layla said, 'and I know it'll be the same for Mum, is how worried she seems that Mum wouldn't be able to forgive her if she knew the truth.'

Turning to Clove, Cristy said, 'Have you found any relevance yet to the text she's using to surround her writing?'

Clove shook her head. 'Sorry, nothing, unless there's a bigger picture I'm just not seeing.'

'OK, let's not allow it to become a distraction,' Connor advised. 'Right now, we need to refocus on what's going into the next episode, and I'm guessing this won't?'

'My parents are still keen for us not to use anything from the notebook yet,' Layla told him. 'They want to know more about what they're leading to, just in case . . . Well, just in case, I suppose.'

Understanding Layla's reluctance to spell out her gravest concerns, Cristy said, 'Please make them understand that we can only hold back for so long, because the last thing we need is to find ourselves implicated in some sort of conspiracy to cover up a crime.'

CHAPTER TWENTY-SIX

The morning after the Call to Arms upload, Cristy was barely out of bed when Layla called in a panic.

'It came last night,' she cried. 'Mum's phone was off, and she was—'

'Stop! Stop,' Cristy cried, trying to slow her down. 'Take a breath, and start again.'

'Sorry,' Layla gasped. 'Sorry, it was a bit of a shock, that's all . . . Mum's had her phone off, you see. She needed to rest, but she turned it back on a few minutes ago, and there was a message from Romy.'

Cristy's insides tensed. 'Go on,' she prompted.

'It was definitely her – we're sure of it – and she's asking us – you – not to post anything about her. It was before the pod went live, and now it's too late. It's already out there, and Mum's really worried about what might happen.'

'I need to hear it,' Cristy said. 'Can you forward it?'

'It's a voicemail. I don't know how to do that.'

'OK, just play it and hold your phone close enough for me to hear.'

As Layla sorted things out her end, Cristy activated her own phone to record.

Moments later, the voicemail was playing.

ROMY: 'Beth, my darling, you have to do something for me. I'm told that Cristy Ward is going to post a podcast asking if anyone's seen me. Please, darling, you must stop her from doing that. I'm all right, really. There's nothing for you to worry about, but if you don't make her stop, I'm afraid of what will happen. Things are such a very long way from what they might seem to you. Trust me on this, if you can. Love you, my darling, darling friend. I'll call again soon.'

*

'What the fuck?!' Connor exclaimed, as Cristy ended the playback. They were at the office now, everyone having been summoned early by Cristy's text alert. 'Do we think it's genuine?'

'Mum does,' Layla hastily told him. 'She knows Romy better than anyone, and she's absolutely certain of it. Plus, it came from Romy's number.'

'I guess your mum tried calling back,' Cristy said.

'Several times. She's left messages too, asking her to stop talking in riddles and to please call again.'

'Do you have your mum's phone there?' Jacks asked.

Layla held it up.

'Try ringing the number again,' he instructed. 'It'll be interesting to see if it's a UK or international ring tone.'

Layla quickly pressed redial: the call went straight to voicemail: no ring tone.

Still focused on the message, Clove said, 'So what's she afraid of?'

'"Things are such a very long way from what they might seem to you,"' Connor quoted. 'What the hell does that even mean?'

'What I'd like to know,' Cristy said, 'is how she knew we were going to upload last night. Have you transcribed the message yet?' she asked Clove.

'Done,' Clove assured her.

'OK – what does she say right at the beginning?'

Reading aloud, Clove repeated the words: '" . . . you have to do something for me. I'm told that Cristy Ward is going to post a podcast asking if . . ."' She stopped when Cristy raised a hand.

'It's not certain she knew exactly when we were going to post,' Cristy said, 'but the fact that she knew it was about to happen and says she was told . . . Who would have told her?'

As the others shook their heads, trying to think, Connor said, 'My money's on Matey Bram. I reckon he either sussed who we were or he knew anyway and made out he didn't.'

'One of the hazards of being famous,' Jacks quipped.

'If it was him,' Cristy said, 'then it'll mean he knows a lot more about Romy than her name and old address. I guess he hasn't contacted you, Layla?'

Layla was already shaking her head as she checked her phone.

'Then maybe pop him a text to find out if he's heard back from his employers.'

'My money's on us never being let in there,' Connor declared, 'but let's try not to be negative.'

Sighing, Cristy said, 'Well, there's clearly something strange going on regarding the manor, but what isn't clear – as if anything is – is if Romy is a willing party to it.'

'She sounded pretty troubled in her message,' Clove pointed out.

'By her conscience?' Cristy countered. 'Or because someone was forcing her to make the call? She could also be a very good actor.'

'It wasn't an act,' Layla came in strongly. 'You know what she's written in her notebook, so you can't not be aware of how afraid she was when she wrote those things into *The Woman in White* and *Jane Eyre*. And how worried she is about Mum and upset about not being with her.'

'But she never says why she isn't,' Connor pointed out.

Unable to argue with that, Layla closed her eyes despondently.

Jacks said, 'Sorry, I have to go. Seeing the prof at ten and he doesn't like late. Just leaving you with this: if we're buying into her being upset when she left the voicemail on Beth's phone, then what's it telling us about the social media posts where she's anything but?'

After he'd gone, Layla said, 'Jacks obviously doesn't think Romy made those videos, but if she didn't . . . Except it's *her* – you saw them yourselves – so has someone forced her into making them? Is that what he's saying?'

'We need to see what he comes back with,' Cristy advised. 'He's obviously picked up on something; he just wants clarification or maybe verification before he shares it with us.'

After a beat, Clove said, 'So what happens now?'

'I guess,' Connor replied, looking at Cristy, 'we carry on as if the voicemail never happened?'

Wide-eyed, Layla cried, 'Are you serious? How can we just ignore what she said?'

'Sorry, but the pod's out there now.' He grimaced. 'There's no way of pulling it back, so we either sit around waiting to see what happens or we continue trying to find out where she is.'

'What about talking to the police?' Layla asked. 'I know Mum and Dad are reluctant, but after this call . . . It's really shaken Mum up.'

Cristy nodded. 'As it was your mother who received the call,' she said, 'it'll probably be best to start with whoever you dealt with when you first reported Romy missing.'

When Layla looked doubtful, Connor said, 'We could be looking at a confusion of jurisdictions with Beth being in one and Romy the other – God knows which one she's in right now. So how about we contact John George? He could be up for giving some guidance on this?'

'Who's he?' Layla asked.

'A detective with Avon and Somerset,' Cristy replied. 'Connor and I consulted him quite a lot during our TV days. So sure, if he's still with the force, let's try him first. Clove, do you want to do that? Tell him who you are and offer to send him a recording of the pod, and the voicemail. Meanwhile, I'm going to reach out to Henry Godfrey at GCHQ, see if *he* thinks there's anything we should know about Rudi and Romy.'

'So we're back to some sort of intelligence op?' Clove asked, perking up.

'Exploring all avenues,' Cristy responded. 'Did you find any contact details for Godfrey?' she asked Connor.

'I should let Dad know what's happening,' Layla said, returning to her phone and leaving the room.

Cristy said to Clove, 'I don't suppose you've heard back from the Reiners yet? The friends who are supposedly with Romy in Lucerne?'

Clove shook her head and held up a hand as she said into the phone, 'Oh, hi, it's Clover St Jean here, from the *Hindsight* team. I'm trying to get hold of DC John George . . .'

Leaving her to it, Cristy picked up Godfrey's email address from Connor, sent a quick message asking if they could be in touch about Rudi and Romy Kaplan, FO employees circa 1980s, and she was about to get started on an update for Harry and Meena when Layla returned.

'Dad says you should do whatever you think best,' she said bleakly, 'and he will help all he can.'

Touched by the stoic support, Cristy said, 'Incidentally, do you know if your mum has found any contact details for Romy's old housekeeper yet?'

'She hasn't mentioned it, but I think I'll go home now to see how she is. I'll ask her then.'

'OK,' Clove said, putting the phone down just as Layla left, 'John George is no longer a DC. He's a DCS – that was me

198

told – but a friendly sidekick listened to everything I had to say and assured me someone will get back to us in the next twenty-four hours.'

*

It was nearing the end of the day when Cristy received a reply from Henry Godfrey at GCHQ, saying he'd looked into the Kaplans and had found no record of them post-1996.

'He hopes that's helpful,' she said, looking up from her screen.

'Given the source,' Connor said, 'we could be forgiven for thinking that was a brush off.'

Cristy had to agree.

Clove groaned. 'So actually we're none the wiser?'

Wheeling his chair back from the desk and treating himself to a luxurious stretch, Connor said, 'Has anyone heard from Jacks yet?'

'Right on cue,' Clove told him. 'He's just texted saying he'll be here first thing in the morning and has plenty to share.'

'Great.' Connor yawned. 'Hey you,' he said, as Aiden ambled in the door.

'Hey, gang,' Aiden responded, going to embrace his mother. 'I brought this,' he said, holding up her wallet. 'Thought you might need it.'

Startled, she said, 'I didn't even realize I'd left it behind. Thanks. And feel free to hang out here if you've got nothing else to do. We can walk home together when I'm done.'

Shrugging, he said, 'That's kind of the main reason I dropped in. Dad's got tickets for some gig, and I'm hoping you'll take my place?'

Cristy was about to protest when Connor said, 'Go for it. We could all do with a few hours' downtime.'

'Apparently, it's one of your favourite bands,' Aiden told his mother.

199

'Which one?' she asked, certain she'd know if Springsteen or Stevie Nicks were in town.

'The Dinosaurs. He said you danced to one of their tunes the first night you met.'

'I've never heard of them,' she retorted, 'and for the record, we didn't dance to anything the night we met.'

'I see. Straight to horizontal, was it?' he countered. 'That's what I love about my dad – he's got all the moves.'

CHAPTER TWENTY-SEVEN

'He's not wrong, is he?' Matthew laughed when Cristy repeated Aiden's comment about his moves. 'I mean, there was a time when you'd jump me just for the way I walked in the door.'

Arching an eyebrow, she said, 'In your dreams,' although she had to concede they had been pretty much all over one another back in the day. For a lot of their marriage, actually – until he'd cheated on her with a younger woman and turned her life upside-down and himself into a cliché.

They'd arrived at this pub in Redland a few minutes ago, where a young blues band was due to appear once the prolonged set-up was complete, and she was actually starting to feel glad she'd come. Connor was right: a step back from trying to figure out what they could be missing, and what their next steps should be, was far more likely to result in clearer heads and new ideas than remaining obsessively focused so they couldn't see the wood for the trees.

'Thanks for coming,' Matthew said, raising his glass.

Smiling, she tapped it with her own and took a sip, all the time thinking she'd actually rather be having some downtime at home, talking to David on Facetime or to Hayley, who she hadn't spoken to for a few days. Realizing how hurt Matthew would be if he could read her mind, she smiled again and briefly dropped her head onto his shoulder. 'How do you know about this band?' she asked, finding the familiar scent

201

of him a little more pleasing these days than she had for a while.

'We featured them on the programme a couple of weeks ago,' he replied. 'Going places, they say. We were lucky to get tickets.'

Eyeing him knowingly, she said, 'You never really did expect Aiden to come with you, did you?'

He cocked an eyebrow and sipped his drink. 'I thought you might need . . .'

'Need what?' she asked when he stopped.

He shrugged. 'Nothing. Just glad you came.'

Shaking her head fondly, she watched the stagehands running around and wondered if she should ask him about Marley and the baby. It wasn't something she wanted to get into, but it seemed mean not to show an interest when his wife and son and the bizarre situation they were in clearly mattered a lot to him.

Just as she started to speak, he said, 'So do we buy Aiden a car for his birthday?'

Having expected the issue to come up at some point, she replied, 'Maybe let him learn to drive first?'

'In his own car?'

'If you want to get him one.'

'I thought it was something we could do between us, now *Hindsight's* doing so well.'

A gift from his parents – how together that would make them seem. 'I don't mind contributing,' she said, 'but what about this summer of surfing he's planning?'

'It's still under discussion, but the guys he's hoping to go with are not entirely without a few brain cells. I would say unlike him, but he's smart enough when he wants to be. I've said he needs to be back in time for his results mid-August. Maybe we should hold off on the car until then.'

They turned to the stage as a young lad in a sharp blue suit and jaunty trilby hat stepped up to the mic, and said,

'Sorry folks, having a few tech issues, but we'll be right with you.'

Pointing to her near empty wine glass, Matthew said, 'Another?'

'I have to drive,' she reminded him, 'so a sparkling water will be fine.'

While waiting for him to return, Cristy checked her messages just in case one of the team had made some kind of useful breakthrough or had some thoughts to run past her, but it seemed they were all taking the evening off. So she sent a quick WhatsApp to Aiden, thanking him for setting her up on a date with his father (followed by an upside-down face emoji) and another to David asking how late she could call.

'Here we go,' Matthew said, setting down their drinks and shifting his stool closer to the table. 'Cheers.'

'Cheers,' she echoed, wishing the band would just get on with it now.

'Are you OK?' he asked.

Surprised by the concern in his voice, she said, 'Sure. I didn't miss you while you were at the bar, if that's what you were thinking.'

He smiled. 'It wasn't actually. I was just hoping I called it right tonight and being out is cheering you up.'

She frowned. 'What are you talking about? Why would I need cheering up?'

His eyes filled with what looked like despair. 'Aiden didn't show you, did he?' he groaned.

'Show me what?'

Reaching into his jacket, Matthew pulled out his phone, scrolled to a recent message and passed it to her.

Seeing the image of David with Laurent on a sailboat, presumably somewhere off the coast of Denmark, she said, 'And?'

'Keep going,' he told her.

She swiped the screen, and her heart turned over. The next

three shots had clearly been taken on the same boat at the same time, but these included Laurent's mother, Juliette, who was apparently also on this "boys-only trip" to Skagen. God, she was a beautiful woman, and didn't they seem to be having so much fun?

Swallowing dryly, Cristy said, 'Where did you get these?'

'Laurent sent them to Aiden,' he replied. 'He's apparently loving being on holiday with his parents.'

Her head was spinning as she passed the phone back.

'I'm sorry,' Matthew said quietly.

'No, you're not,' she snapped.

Several tense moments passed, until she got to her feet. 'Enjoy the band,' she said tightly, and left.

'Cristy! Wait! Wait!' he called, running down the street after her.

'Don't touch me,' she growled, snatching her arm free as he tried to take it. 'You enjoyed that, didn't you? You think, just because your life is fucked up, mine should be too.'

'That's not true. I'm sorry – I swear it. I thought Aiden had shown you the pictures.'

'Well, he didn't, and it's not really the point, is it?' She was beyond furious. 'You must have known I wouldn't want to discuss it with you, besides which, David is free to go on holiday with whomsoever he pleases—'

'But not to lie about it—'

'—and you are free to go fuck yourself and leave me alone.' She was at her car now, fumbling for the keys.

Standing against the driver's door, he said, 'He doesn't deserve you, and you know it.'

'One more word,' she seethed. 'Now move out of the way.'

'Let me come with you.'

'Just go! I don't want to look at you any more, or hear anything else you have to say.'

Matthew stood aside, allowing her to open the car door,

then looked down at her as she got behind the wheel. 'I don't blame you for being angry,' he said, 'I would be, too, in your shoes . . .'

'Go away, Matthew,' she raged, and grabbed for the door. 'Just go away and *leave me alone*.'

By the time she'd reached the flat, she'd decided not to ring David right away to find out what the hell was going on. He hadn't responded to her text earlier, nor had he tried to call, so he was obviously somewhere with Juliette and Laurent, and the last thing she wanted was to get into some kind of scene while his ex was nearby. He knew very well how she felt about his relationship with Juliette, which was presumably why he hadn't told her she was going to be with them in Denmark – but lying to her, making out the trip was something it wasn't . . . that was going too far. She couldn't forgive that. In fact, she wasn't even going to try.

'Hey, Mum, you're back early. Band no good?'

Cristy started when Aiden came out of his room, then glared at him as if he was in some way responsible for how she was feeling.

'Oh shit,' he muttered. 'Dad showed you the photos.'

'When did you get them?' she asked, going to pour herself a drink.

'Yesterday. I kind of knew they weren't a good thing, but hey, listen, they're probably not the way they seem . . .'

Cristy went to cup a hand around his face, looked deep into his eyes, and said, 'Nice try.'

Pressing a kiss to his forehead, she took herself and her wine off to bed.

CHAPTER TWENTY-EIGHT

'Cristy, for God's sake, I didn't know she was coming,' David cried when they spoke the next morning, while Cristy speed-walked to work and wondered why she'd allowed herself to get into this now.

She was already halfway to the office, navigating a path along the harbourside through cyclists, joggers, dog-walkers and other commuters. God, it seemed to get busier every day! Still, at least the sun was shining at last, throwing dazzling puddles of light onto the water and probably brightening everyone's mood but hers.

'She just turned up,' he told her, 'so what was I supposed to do? She's his mother; he was thrilled to see her—'

'How long's she been there?' she interrupted.

'I don't know – two, three days? And before you ask, no, she's not staying on the boat with us—'

'Actually, it's none of my business where she's staying.'

'Well, you're sure as hell acting as if it is.'

Stung, almost to a halt, she said, 'We haven't actually made any kind of official commitment to one another, so if you want—'

'For God's sake! Do I go off like this every time Matthew shows up on your doorstep? Do you think I like how much time you guys seem to spend together? I'm here, hanging out with friends. She turned up on me. I had no idea she was coming . . . Cristy, come on – you can't stay mad about this.

We've both got pasts. We have to accept that, and anyway, she's not even here any more.'

Pleased to hear that, Cristy slowed her pace a little. She wasn't quite ready to be fully mollified but maybe she was getting there. 'You should have told me,' she stated, feeling as childish as that sounded.

'You're right, I should have, but I didn't, probably because I was afraid you'd go off like this. Anyway, how did you find out?'

'Laurent sent photos to Aiden, who shared them with Matthew, who took great pleasure in showing them to me last night.'

Groaning, he said, 'I'm sorry. Definitely not a great way . . . Hang on, you were with Matthew last night? Do I need to be worried about that?'

Realizing he was baiting her, Cristy slowed almost to a stop and said, 'Maybe let's get off the subject now?'

'Sure, just as long as I'm forgiven and you understand how much you mean to me.'

As pleased with that as she was no doubt supposed to be, she said, 'Same here. And I'm sorry too. I guess my stubborn old insecurities still haven't quite gone away.'

'I know, and it's why I didn't want you to hear about it, in case you read more into it than was there. Which you did, big time, but now you know you were wrong, and we're good, yes?'

'We are,' she confirmed with a smile. 'I'll do better next time.'

With a laugh, he said, 'As will I. So, how come you were with Matthew last night? Actually, don't bother answering that – just tell me what's on your agenda today.'

Turning into the cobbled street that led to the studios, she said, 'Given the way things have been going, I'm fascinated to find out. I just hope we're doing the right thing trying to track down a woman who might very well *not* want to be found. Which reminds me – have you found anyone who's actually *seen* Rudi Kaplan in the last few months?'

'Not yet, but I'll stay on it.'

Relieved to have sorted things out with him, and grateful for his help, she said, 'Thanks. I mean it, thank you. Now, I've just arrived at the office, so I should probably ring off. Shall we speak again later?'

'Sure. Call me when you can. If I end up somewhere with no signal, I'll try you when we're back online. Oh, and I'm going to send you a link to a Chris Stapleton number – see what you think.'

Curious and wishing there was time to follow it up now, Cristy ended the call and went straight to the coffee machine.

'Morning, team,' she declared cheerily. 'Trust we're all ready to seize the day.'

'Sounds like someone benefited from a night off,' Connor commented dryly.

'Looking good,' Layla told her.

'How's your mum?' Cristy asked.

Layla grimaced. 'Kind of the same.'

'I'm guessing no more messages from Romy, maybe expressing disappointment that we went ahead with the pod? Or advising us not to continue?'

Layla shook her head. 'And no more strange entries in the notebook. To be honest, Mum's worn out by it all, but no way will she give up. She's still reading in spite of Romy's handwriting being so small and difficult to make out in places, and Dad's having another go at trying to find Inge's full name.'

'The housekeeper/PA?' Connor clarified.

Layla nodded. 'She's surely got to know something, given she was around almost until they left the manor. Maybe she'll hear the podcast and get in touch?'

'There's always a chance,' Cristy agreed. 'I take it your mum's keeping her phone on all the time now?'

208

'Of course, and Dad has it while she's sleeping.'

Cristy nodded and went to turn on her computer.

'No news overnight,' Clove said, 'apart from a few more friends responding to Romy's posts, a couple of possible sightings in Lagos, and lots of advice on how to proceed from the know-nothings. Oh yes, and a text from Nula Higgins asking if there's anything else the Bellbrook neighbours can do.'

'I was thinking we could ask them to stake out Haylesford Manor,' Connor quipped, 'check on comings and goings, you know, but I don't suppose they're the best suited individuals for a covert op.'

Wryly, Cristy said, 'I wouldn't underestimate Nula, if I were you. I reckon she could achieve anything she set her mind to.'

'Apart from finding Romy,' Layla pointed out.

Cristy smiled sadly. 'OK, so where's Jacks?' she asked, looking around. 'I'm ready to hang on his every word.'

'Apparently something "major" came up,' Clove told her, 'so he's back at UWE with the prof and will be in touch def before end of day.'

'Great,' Cristy muttered. 'And where exactly are you going?'

Clove was putting on her coat. 'DCS John George is sending someone to talk to us,' Clove explained. 'I'm treating them to a coffee at the River Station.'

'And I'm going with,' Layla added.

Minutes later, Connor took off to one of the studios to check out music and sound effects, so seizing the moment, Cristy quickly opened the link David had sent to a YouTube video. She wasn't surprised to be taken to a Chris Stapleton song – he'd already told her to expect it – but the title, the lyrics and the beautifully performed duet with Dua Lipa just about melted her heart. 'Think I'm in Love with You.' They'd never said those words to one another before.

For several minutes, she simply sat, listening, imagining him somewhere on his boat, thick fair hair blowing in the wind, strong muscles flexing as he took the helm or hauled sails, the way he laughed, his eyes penetrating and knowing as he looked at her, the feel of his body wrapping around hers, the smell and taste of him . . .

'Knock, knock.'

Starting, Cristy looked up to find a woman standing at the door, but not just any woman. It was one of her oldest and dearest friends, whose exquisite aquamarine eyes and inky dark curls were as familiar to her as they were beloved and missed.

'Andee Lawrence!' she cried, leaping to her feet and wrapping the other woman in a bruising embrace. They were the same height, even had a similar look, although Cristy was fair-haired and less olive-skinned. They fit, in just about every way, and always had.

'What on earth are you doing here?' she asked. 'It's so good to see you. It's been too long. How are you?'

Laughing, Andee pulled back to get a better look at her, and apparently happy with what she saw, declared, 'As gorgeous as ever.'

'Look who's talking.' Cristy laughed. 'Have you just decided not to do the ageing thing?'

Clearly amused, Andee said, 'We're both going to be fifty far sooner than I'm ready to admit, but luckily it doesn't seem to be slowing either of us down. I'm sorry I haven't been in touch for an age . . .'

'I'm just as bad. What matters is that you're here now. How long are you staying?'

'This is just a flying visit, I'm afraid. Mum's having tests at the BRI today, so I need to get back to her.'

'Oh God, nothing serious I hope.'

'Fingers crossed not. She sends her love, by the way, and we'd both love it if you came to visit when you have time.

Bring David, if you think he'd like to meet us. I know Graeme would get a real kick out of meeting him.'

Laughing, Cristy said, 'I'm sure the feeling will be mutual, but at least stay and have a coffee with me now.'

'I can't, honestly. I need to be there in case they finish with Mum early, so let me tell you why I've called in, apart from to lay eyes on you. I listened to your latest pod on the drive up and you mentioned a missing portrait?'

Blinking in surprise, Cristy said, 'That's right, we did.'

Andee smiled. 'Well, there might be nothing to this, but just in case . . . There's a couple who live a few miles from me, on Exmoor – it could be worth you talking to them. They have quite an interesting story to tell about one of their parents' portraits.'

Cristy's eyebrows shot up. Since Andee was an ex-detective who now spent a lot of time helping people in her community with police issues, Cristy was more than ready to listen. 'Are you going to give me any more than that?' she pressed.

'I'd rather they told you themselves, as I don't know the entire story. They're cruising the Fjords right now, but I'm sure they're picking up emails, so I'll check they're happy to talk to you. I'm sure they will be. Then you can decide for yourself if what happened to the parents has any bearing on what might be going on with Rudi and Romy Kaplan.'

*

'Andee Lawrence was here!' Connor cried in delighted surprise. 'Why didn't you come get me?'

'She couldn't stay long,' Cristy replied. 'Anyway, turns out she heard the latest pod and it reminded her of something, so she's going to put us in touch with a couple who apparently have an "interesting" story to tell about their parents' portraits.'

Clove's jaw dropped. 'What?' she exclaimed. 'Definitely didn't see that coming.'

'What kind of story?' Connor urged.

'She wants them to tell it, but we both know she wouldn't have brought it to us if she didn't think it might be relevant.'

As Connor went to enter Andee Lawrence's details on the whiteboard, Cristy asked Clove, 'So how did it go with the police officer?'

'It didn't,' Clove responded. 'She just assured us someone will get back to us in due course.'

Cristy was as dismayed by the prevarication as Clove clearly was, although not altogether surprised. 'Well, I guess we won't hold our breath. How about the Raynors? Anything from them?'

'Reiners,' Clove corrected. 'Nothing yet, so whether they're still in Lucerne with Romy, or were ever there . . . Ah! Here's Jacks at last. Hey, Einstein!' she exclaimed, accepting his video call.

'Is everyone there?' he asked, looking faintly wild-eyed and mussy-haired. 'This needs to be a team meeting.'

'We're all here,' Cristy assured him, as she and Connor joined via their own screens. Layla came to look over Cristy's shoulder, and Cristy said, 'Ready to hang on your every word.'

Jacks glanced away from the camera as someone in the background spoke to him. He nodded, then returned to them, saying, 'I'm going to play you something now, an audio message that was sent to you, Cristy, earlier today. You won't have seen it come in, because we got there first. It's a total mindfuck, so better prepare yourself.'

CHAPTER TWENTY-NINE

Minutes later, Cristy was staring at her screen, completely lost for words. If she hadn't just heard the recording with her own ears, she'd never have believed it.

'Where the fuck did it come from?' Connor exploded.

'We don't know yet,' Jacks replied. 'We intercepted it on its way to the *Hindsight* email account.'

'But it's obviously a fake,' Clove protested.

Finding her voice, Cristy said, 'Play it again.'

Moments later, the audio waveform was back on their screens.

CRISTY: 'Hi guys, Cristy Ward here. Welcome to *Hindsight*. It's been quite a roller-coaster ride since last week when we introduced you to Romy Kaplan's mysterious disappearance. So many of you have been in touch to share sightings, details of old friendships with Romy and her husband Rudi, thoughts on where Romy might be now and why she would leave her Gloucestershire home without letting anyone know where she was going.

'It certainly sparked a lot of speculation, not to mention imagination, and the outpouring of love for Romy has touched us deeply. I can tell you it's touched her too. In fact, she was moved to tears when she read some of your messages.

213

'Yes, I'm delighted to say we've found Romy – or perhaps I should say, she found us, at her home in a Gloucestershire hamlet when she returned, quite unexpectedly, three days ago

'She hadn't realized until then that her need to get away for a while had caused so much concern, and of course she was deeply sorry for not responding to her friends' lovely comments under the reels and photos she'd shared during her short absence. Here she is, in her own words.'

ROMY: 'My goodness, if I'd only known . . . How silly and horribly negligent of me not to check who was reading my little posts. My only intention was to make sure no one was worried, that you all knew I was fine and even enjoying being alone for a while. As you probably saw, I took a few trips down memory lane to places Rudi and I visited with some of you, so you were always there in my heart, and you still are.

'I'm so very sorry for all the fuss I've caused and for the confusion that has, I hope, now been put to rest. I'm leaving my home again for a short time to go and stay with friends while all this settles down, and I apologize wholeheartedly to my dear neighbours for any intrusion and inconvenience they've had to suffer as a result of my thoughtlessness. I hope, in the fullness of time, to make it up to them.'

CRISTY: 'So, mystery solved. Romy is fine, and everyone's concern for her safety, while genuine and heartfelt, turns out to have been misplaced. Actually, I have to admit it was nothing short of alarmist on our part, and for that, I sincerely apologize. Perhaps this has taught us a very valuable lesson – that we need to do our research more thoroughly before jumping to conclusions.

'Thank you again for engaging with us. Of course, there is no longer a series to bring you concerning this, but rest assured, we'll be back in the autumn with a whole new case to uncover and hopefully resolve.'

As the recording stopped and the screen went dark, Cristy, still stunned, said, 'It sounds exactly like me.'

'And like Romy,' Layla added.

'I could go into the tech detail of how it was created,' Jacks said, 'but basically, because of *Hindsight,* there's a massive sample of your voice readily available to anyone who wants to use it. Anyway, that's hardly relevant right now. What is, is the fact that almost everything you've seen online to date is just as fake. The reels, the images, some of the friends' responses . . . If you go far enough back in Romy's social media, you'll see that in some instances, old videos and photos have provided some of the source material . . .'

'I did go back,' Clove protested.

'I'm talking years,' Jacks told her, 'and the way it's been used . . .'

'Are you saying that *nothing* we have is real?' Connor demanded incredulously.

'Not much,' Jacks confirmed. 'The recent message on Beth's phone is probably legit, and it's possible a couple of other things are too, but the appropriation of all her accounts, email, phone, social media, is apparent once you know what you're looking for. We're guessing the same goes for her bank, but without those details, it's not possible to check.'

'So what are you saying?' Layla demanded, clearly horrified. 'That someone has taken everything from her and . . . Oh my God, what the hell have they done with her? We have to find her,' she urged Cristy.

Agreeing, Cristy said to Jacks, 'Do you have something you can send to the police that proves all these posts are fake?'

He turned from camera again as someone spoke to him. A moment later, his former professor, Jared Grinner, who with his long hair and rimless specs could be Jacks's Asian uncle, if such a thing were possible, appeared on the screen.

'When Jacks says her accounts have been appropriated,' he said, 'I'm afraid we can't, at this point, be certain that she herself hasn't played a part in making it seem that way . . .'

'You mean she's falsifying herself!' Layla cried, aghast. 'Don't you realize how crazy that sounds?'

Calmly, he said, 'I understand that to you it seems very unlikely, but maybe there is a motive, a reason that you aren't aware of—'

'I can assure you—'

'It's not me you have to assure; it's the police, and as we have no way of knowing who is actually behind these deepfakes, only that they *are* fake, it simply isn't possible to be certain it's happening without her permission, or even under her instruction.'

Tears shone in Layla's eyes as she said, 'You obviously don't know her like I do, but . . .'

'We can, of course, forward everything we have to the relevant authority, and we're willing to do so. I simply want you to be aware that what we've uncovered is not definitive proof that she's being forced to act against her will, or has had her entire identity and her home stolen.'

Stepping in, Cristy said, 'Maybe you can let us see exactly what you'd forward to the police so we're better informed ourselves?'

'It's pretty high-tech stuff,' Jacks replied, 'which I'll be happy to interpret, but essentially, all you're really going to see is what we've done to get to where we are. I know this is wild – sorry, Layla – but I have to put it out there: it's pretty likely that all these recent posts and messages are a smokescreen to cover something . . . deeper?'

As Layla visibly reeled, Cristy said, 'I don't see how doing something like this gives cover. It's actually drawing more attention to her disappearance.'

'Which isn't a disappearance at all,' Grinner reminded her, 'not if you look at it from a police perspective. True, we can realign that perspective, and we will try, but what I'd be just as concerned about right now, if I were you, is the fake podcast. As far as we know, it hasn't been posted yet . . .'

'No, it hasn't,' Jacks confirmed, 'but you do need to read the message that came with it.'

A moment later, it was on all their screens, and Clove read it aloud:

'*"Dear Cristy and Connor,*

'*"Please listen to the audio file attached to this email. You might, of course, want to use your own words, but here you have mine, and I trust you will now make it clear that your search for me is at an end. I'm very sorry for all the trouble you've been put to, and I deeply regret any professional embarrassment this might cause you. However, I'm sure your listeners will be glad to know I am safe and well, as will Beth and Layla and all my wonderful friends and neighbours. I wish I could be there in person to show you and them that I am completely unharmed and in good spirits, but sadly that's not possible at this time.*

'*"I hope to hear this next podcast in the coming days. I believe Tuesday is your usual drop day, but would you mind terribly if I asked you to post sooner, perhaps by the weekend? If it hasn't happened by Monday, I'm afraid I'll have no choice but to upload it myself. Yours with affection, Romy Kaplan."'*

As Clove stopped reading, all eyes went to Cristy.

'What the fuck?' Connor muttered. 'Who the hell is behind this? It can't be her, but even if it is, she can't be doing it alone.'

'She almost certainly isn't,' Grinner agreed. 'However, this recording is clearly meant to demonstrate exactly what kind of chaos and confusion can be created for you if you don't do as requested.'

'So it's blackmail?' Connor stated.

'I'm never going to believe Romy is a part of this,' Layla insisted. 'And if she really wants us to stop looking for her, why doesn't she just come home so we can see with our own eyes that she's "safe and well"?'

'Precisely,' Cristy responded. 'And no way are we going to upload this nonsense. In fact, I'll tell you exactly what we're going to do.'

CHAPTER THIRTY

It was Saturday evening, and the entire team was gathered, including Iz, who'd spent the past thirty-six hours organizing media alerts for this unscheduled drop. Harry and Meena had brought one of the company's lawyers, Charles Goodman, with them, and Professor Jared Grinner was in the process of joining via video link.

Though alert, Cristy was sickeningly aware of how invaded she felt, how helpless even, knowing that her actual voice had been stolen and used against her in this way. She'd had nightmares about it since Thursday, dark and deeply disturbing, indefinable and yet so trenchantly, unshakably real. It could be just the beginning. What was to stop them from taking her image next and using her like a puppet to perform however they wanted?

It was a truly despicable form of identity theft, an egregious violation of her person that, strangely, felt every bit as horrific as a physical assault.

By now, everyone had listened to the fake podcast and to the already-recorded response to it that Cristy and Connor had created. Both were about to be uploaded to all their usual channels. There would be no surprises in this room. However, there was a strong hope that DCS John George, whom Connor had contacted earlier, would listen as promised and be in touch right after.

'OK, are we ready?' Cristy asked, looking around at the

intense, almost belligerent faces. Their precious podcast was under attack, and they weren't going to take it sitting down.

'Hit it,' Clove instructed. 'And fuck them, whoever they are. Sorry, I don't mean Romy,' she quickly added to Layla, 'although if it turns out she's—'

'Let's not go there again,' Cristy stepped in. 'Go ahead, Jacks, let it roll.'

As the standard intro began to play, announcing sponsors and thanking contributors, Jodi, Connor's wife, moved quietly amongst them, refilling wine glasses and offering nibbles. Then the main body of the podcast was underway:

CRISTY: 'Hi everyone, and welcome to this special edition of *Hindsight*. Those of you who follow us live are no doubt intrigued to know why we're coming to you three days before our usual drop and I'm sure, when you hear the reason, you're going to be as blown away by what's happened as we are.

'On Thursday evening, we received an audio file from Romy Kaplan's email account. Whether or not it was sent by Romy herself, we can't be certain, but it does contain her voice, and . . . wait for this, it also contains mine. We're going to play it for you in a moment, but first, I want to warn you that you'll hear me saying things I've never actually said. That's right! It will sound exactly like me, but *they are not my words*. We've added a distortion to the sound in the fake-recording in order to distinguish it from this, the real podcast, that you're hearing now.'

CONNOR: 'To be clear, and to keep it simple, someone, somewhere, has used artificial intelligence to create a *Hindsight* podcast in which Cristy is telling you that the search for Romy Kaplan is over. It is not.

'You will also hear Romy's voice assuring you that she is safe and well. We have no evidence of that.'

CRISTY: 'Connor and I will talk to you again when the deepfake finishes. You'll know it's real because my voice will be as you're hearing it now.'

Everyone was silent as the counterfeit pod began to play, this time with a grainy sort of echo added to Cristy's voice, making it sound as though she was in a large, empty room, with a faint hiss of static underlying the words. Romy's contribution remained as received.

After it finished playing, there was a short pause before Cristy and Connor picked up again.

CONNOR: 'Many of you will be aware of the case of OpenAI copying the voice of a Hollywood actor to promote their product – well, that's more or less what's happened here: the use of an AI-generated voice to emulate Cristy's with the aim of shutting down our podcast.'

CRISTY: 'Leaving all the legal ramifications of that aside for the moment, we can certainly take from it that someone, somewhere, wants us to stop looking for Romy.

'Maybe now is the time to reveal that the videos posted on her social media accounts over recent weeks are also fake, as are the images and some of the friend responses. Since she disappeared on, or around, 7th May, there has, in fact, been only one voicemail from her that our experts have deemed genuine. In it, she is asking her best friend to stop us from posting about her. She says, and I quote, that she is "afraid of what will happen" if we don't.'

CONNOR: 'Unfortunately, the message didn't reach us until after our first pod went live, so now we're left to wonder: is she afraid of what will happen to her or to us at *Hindsight*?

'It could be that the digitally manipulated podcast you just heard is the start of a much bigger attempted tech-takedown of our series. Or, we have to ask ourselves: has something already happened to Romy that we don't yet know about?'

CRISTY: 'Of course, the police should get involved in this case now, and we have invited them to do so. We're hoping, once this message hits the airwaves, someone will be in touch.'

CONNOR: 'A final word to whomever sent us the fake podcast: until we lay eyes on Romy Kaplan and see for ourselves that she's safe and well, our search continues.'

As Jacks faded out the closing credits, Cristy looked around the room, her eyes finally landing on Charles Goodman, whose legal advice they'd followed while putting this answering podcast together. He was in his sixties, with silver hair and a short, dark beard, and, it being a Saturday evening, was casually dressed.

'Good job,' he told them. 'It remains to be seen what effect it will have, but at the risk of repeating myself, bringing a lawsuit against someone whose identity and whereabouts are unknown is virtually impossible.'

'Meaning,' Harry said tightly, 'that there's no obvious way of shutting them down and preventing another fake pod.'

'Which in itself makes it a case for the police,' Meena pointed out.

Cristy's phone vibrated, but it was Matthew, not DCS John George, so she let the call go to voicemail.

Apparently reading her mind, Connor said, 'There's a good chance George hasn't actually heard it yet, in spite of promises to listen right away.'

'I guess you realize,' Harry said, 'that if the police do take this over, that'll be the end of the search as far as *Hindsight* is concerned?'

'Whatever happens,' Cristy said, 'Romy's safety has to come first, and at some point, we'll surely be able to tell the real story. Whatever that might be.'

'You'll be shut down completely if it does have something to do with the intelligence services,' he warned.

Aware of that, and annoyed by it, Cristy looked at her screen as Jared Grinner said, 'There are two things I'd be focusing on right now, if I were you. First, what kind of reaction are you going to get from the fake podcasters by calling them out? And second, how are you going to stop them actually posting anything, using your voice, to deny or contradict everything you recently claimed?'

There was a moment's silence as they took this in, until Iz suddenly said, 'I'll contact the various channels to give them the heads-up, so they'll know not to accept anything from *Hindsight* unless it comes with a certain code, or phone call, or whatever system we set up.'

Jared nodded, seeming to approve, but he added, 'If they're as good as they seem, they'll have ways around that, but definitely go ahead with it. There just needs to be another protection in place. Can I make a suggestion?'

'Of course,' Cristy and Connor said in unison.

'That someone else voices your podcasts at least for the next couple of weeks – someone whose voice is not quite so readily available online. That's if you're going to continue posting. Do you plan to?'

Cristy looked at Connor and said, 'I guess a lot depends on the reaction to this latest one, but until we hear from someone, anyone, there's no reason not to carry on putting together another episode, even if it does have more questions than answers. Sometimes that's not a bad thing, gets everyone engaged.'

'OK, good,' Jared responded. 'If the counterfeiters don't have knowledge of who you're going to use from one pod to the next, they won't be able to replicate.'

'But Cristy and Connor are *Hindsight*,' Iz protested. 'They're the reason the sponsors are on board . . . Except, once the public knows we're being subjected to some sort of deepfake attempted coup that could involve deep-state espionage and sinister blackmail, the numbers will go through the roof.'

'Along with our credibility, if we put it like that,' Connor muttered.

Layla suddenly stood up, her eyes brimming, as she said, 'Do you mind if I go now? I'm finding this all quite hard to take when the police apparently can't even be bothered to call, and when, as far as I'm concerned, the focus here shouldn't be on trying to save your podcast. It should only be on finding Romy and making sure no more harm comes to her!'

'We don't know that any has yet?' Meena pointed out gently.

'If you think using her voice in that recording doesn't count as harm,' Layla shot back angrily, 'then you and I have a very different understanding of the word.' Her eyes were still burning as she turned to Cristy. 'Mum's found more extracts from her notebooks, if you're interested in seeing them.'

'Of course we are,' Cristy hastily assured her. 'Do you have them there?'

Layla took a breath, a clear effort to calm herself, then sitting back down she called up the link on her laptop. 'Just like the others,' she said, 'they're secreted inside literary texts. Apparently, one is from *The Mill on the Floss* and the other Percy Shelley's "The Cloud".' To Clove, she said, 'Still no sense of whether or not the classic texts are relevant.' She attached the link to a group email and pressed send.

As everyone opened it, Cristy said, 'How would you feel about reading it aloud for us and having Connor record?'

Layla shrugged. 'No idea what it says yet, but why not?'

After quickly scanning the words while Connor set up, Cristy said, 'OK, don't worry about the surrounding text, just go with what Romy herself has written.'

LAYLA: 'So, this is the first: *"I have never considered myself a bad person, someone deserving of harshness and scorn. I've made mistakes, of course, and I'm sure I've hurt people along the way – unintentionally, this can just happen. I find it easier not to consider the wisdom of my choices, and I try not to judge others, although that isn't always easy. Sometimes, things have to be done for the greater good. How pompous that sounds, but it's true. Rudi taught me that a long time ago – sacrifices often have to be made to protect the innocent."'*

Layla paused but didn't look up before continuing.

LAYLA: 'This is the second: *"I was thinking of Beth again today, remembering, reliving our time on Venice Beach in California. We got tattoos on our ankles, tiny dragonflies, and Layla, aged three, had one done in henna.*

'"Boy did she kick off when hers faded and ours didn't.

'"I wonder why that memory was so vivid in my mind today? There are so many from over the years; I'm going to search out more and allow them to keep me company as I continue this wait. Along with all my reading of poetry and favourite books, they might help me to breathe and stay calm.

'"How much longer will it be?

'"What will happen in the end? Will there even be an end?"'

'There's also a line from Emily Dickinson,' Layla told them. 'Mum included it because apparently Romy wrote it out at least half a dozen times.'

LAYLA: *'"The Truth must dazzle gradually / Or every man be blind."'*

Layla looked up, and as Connor ended the recording, Cristy took in all the puzzled faces.

'OK, thoughts on where we go with any of that?' Connor challenged, clearly with no real hope of an insightful answer.

'Staying with the Emily Dickinson,' Cristy replied, 'it means that some truths, at least, have to be revealed carefully, gradually, or maybe they won't be believed or accepted.'

Connor blinked. 'Well, I don't think anyone can claim that this is coming at us in a rush,' he said sardonically. 'Quite the reverse, in fact, so now I'm asking myself: what kind of manipulation is this?'

CHAPTER THIRTY-ONE

It was Tuesday morning, and although their inboxes had been busy over the past few days with all kinds of comments and not particularly helpful feedback from listeners, they still hadn't heard from the police. This in spite of repeatedly leaving messages for someone to call them back.

'I don't get it,' Connor growled in frustration. 'John George or *someone* in a position to act has got to have heard Saturday's pod by now, so what the hell is this wall of silence all about?'

'He's been told to steer clear,' Clove declared decisively. 'Someone from on high has given instructions not to touch it.'

Deciding not to engage with that, Cristy said, 'We can call them out again at the end of tonight's drop. In the meantime, we need to focus on what we're going to include in it.'

'I say we put everything out there,' Connor responded rashly. 'The fact the Kaplans worked for the Foreign Office at a very shady time in our country's history, that he was expelled from Moscow in some sort of creepy spy-sweep, that it's possible they continued to engage with the intelligence services over the following decades . . .'

'Hang on, just noting it all down,' Clove said, hammering at her keyboard.

'Should we go all out now on the possibility of it not being Rudi who died in the bath?' Jacks asked.

Cristy paused at that. 'David hasn't been able to find anyone who's actually seen him in the last few months,' she said, 'so let's leave it for now. However, we should include the fact that they were having their cottage regularly checked by a security company.'

'Sherman interviews,' Clove muttered as she typed. 'What about the missing portrait?'

'I'll drop Andee Lawrence a quick email to find out what's happening her end,' Cristy replied, getting to it. 'Until we hear back, I'm not sure there's any point in bringing it up today.'

'What about the letter from Rudi to his mate, Theo Crush, in Vienna?' Jacks asked. 'Kind of weird, so could be worth mentioning?'

'Go for it,' Connor instructed.

'The Reiners have come back to me,' Clove said. 'They're travelling in the Far East at the moment, haven't been to Lucerne since 2018, when they were, in fact there, with Rudi and Romy. So looking like their Insta accounts were cloned.'

'Find a place for it,' Connor told her. 'There's also the mysterious birth certificate belonging to someone called Casey Callaghan, who might also be the Casey Kaplan of the baggage receipt, who could also be the woman at the giftshop days before Romy disappeared. Not to forget being seen in Romy's car going into the manor.'

'She could also be,' Jacks reminded them, 'Lisa McIlvoy, partner of Bram Aalders, estate manager at Haylesford—'

'If we mention Aalders now,' Cristy interrupted, 'we're unlikely ever to get in there, but maybe see if you can magic up some contact details for the Kesingers. It could be worth trying to approach them direct for an interview about the manor?'

For the next few hours, they all remained so focused on putting a script together, editing interviews and selecting relevant statements, that they barely noticed the time passing.

They only paused to check again and again, if an email or some other kind of message had come through from the police.

However, the silence continued.

'OK,' Connor said, finally pushing back from his computer, eyes slightly wild, hair on end, 'time for you guys, Jacks and Clove, to record the opening. Don't worry if you screw up first time around – easy enough to do again. Have you got the script in front of you?'

Giving him the thumbs-up, Clove and Jacks leaned into their mics.

CLOVE: Hi, and welcome to *Hindsight.* I'm Clover St. Jean.'

JACKS: 'And I'm Jackson Caine. As many of you will already know, thanks to our unscheduled drop at the weekend, our podcast is under siege from a malign force. So Clove and I, as the team's senior researchers, are bringing you this episode on behalf of Cristy and Connor.'

CLOVE: 'We should just quickly add that, for those who'd prefer to hear it in Cristy's and Connor's voices, we will be posting their version onto our website straight after this one has dropped.'

JACKS: 'OK, before we go any further into the AI invasion of our airspace, we're going to share all that we've uncovered so far in this case. Stand by – you're in for some surprises.'

'OK, that's great,' Connor said, hitting pause. 'We'll cut to the pre-edited package here, which runs for just over twenty, then we'll add the close. Are you ready to record? Script all lined up?'

'Right here,' Jacks assured him.

CLOVE: 'It's now the afternoon of Tuesday 25th June, and we still haven't received a response from the fraudsters to our unscheduled drop on Saturday alerting you to their handiwork. We thought we might have by now.'

JACKS: 'Incidentally, for those of you who've been asking how someone was able to use Cristy's voice the way they did, and how the fake posts were detected, we've decided, with our lawyers, that while your interest could be genuine, we don't want to turn our podcasts into some sort of instruction manual for crazies with an agenda. So, I'm afraid there will be only the most basic of detail posted to our website.'

CLOVE: 'Before we go, we have to point out that our efforts to involve the police in our investigations have so far been met by silence. There are many things we could read into that, but rather than give rise to wild speculation, we'll throw our invitation out there again: if anyone in law enforcement would like to contact us, we are more than ready to share everything we've discovered surrounding the bizarre and troubling disappearance of a woman whose recent social media videos are fake and whose current whereabouts remain unknown.'

JACKS: 'Join us next time for . . .'

Hitting stop, Connor said, 'You can add the music and effects in the studio.' To Cristy he said, 'It was the right call not to mention John George by name. He wouldn't appreciate it.'

'We need to contact Sherman Securities,' Clove put in, 'just to let them know that the interviews are featuring in this episode.'

Remembering Mr Ripped, Cristy said dryly, 'I'll leave you with it.'

Her phone rang, and she checked it, hoping it would be someone from the police by now. It was Matthew so she connected quickly to tell him she'd call back.

'You need to,' he told her. 'I've been trying you for days.'

'Sorry, but things have gone a bit crazy here, literally, and we're in the middle of a recording.'

'Any word from Layla today?' Connor asked, once she'd ended the call.

'She wanted to spend the day with her mum,' Cristy replied. 'I think she'll be here later. OK, you guys, time to go put it all together.'

After Clove and Jacks had gone, Cristy sat back in her chair and said to Connor, 'Are you starting to think what I'm starting to think?'

'Give me a clue,' he prompted.

'Well, someone in John George's world must have heard the pod by now so—'

The sound of someone clearing his throat made Cristy turn around, and she gave a laugh of surprise. It was the man himself, standing in the doorway, all five foot nine of him, with shining bald head and ironic brown eyes.

'See what happens when you speak of the devil,' he chuckled.

Laughing, Connor got to his feet to go and shake hands. 'Long time no see,' he said, slapping George's shoulder. 'How are things?'

'Interesting,' George said wryly. 'Always interesting.'

Going to greet him too, Cristy said, 'Glad to see your promotion hasn't put an end to house visits.'

He grinned. 'Never too grand for you guys.'

'Good to hear. So, now you're going to tell us what the heck is going on? Something clearly is or you'd have been in touch sooner.'

Checking the time, he said, 'One of my colleagues should be here in a few. Is there somewhere more private we can talk?'

'There's the meeting room across the hall,' Cristy suggested, noticing two grey-suited men standing back in the shadows close to the front door. *Detectives? Close protection?*

As George glanced over his shoulder, one of the men went to push open the meeting-room door, and after treating the space to a once over, he gave George a nod. 'Don't you usually deliver a podcast on Tuesdays?' George asked Cristy and Connor.

'We do,' Cristy confirmed, 'but we can always postpone today's if you have something to . . . add?'

'I'm afraid you might need to cancel that drop, but we'd like to listen to it, if it's ready?'

'It's being put together as we speak,' Connor told him.

George nodded and started over to the meeting room. 'Oh, you should probably invite the rest of your team to join us,' he said, glancing back. 'It'll save you having to explain everything after.'

CHAPTER THIRTY-TWO

By the time George's colleague, Detective Inspector Katherine Weeks, turned up with a two-man support team of her own, everyone, including Harry and Meena, was seated around the meeting room's conference table, various drinks and notepads to hand. The new arrival was a short, wiry woman in her mid-to-late forties, with such a severe set to her lean features and rough cut to her short brown hair that it might have been hard to warm to her, were it not for the easy tone of her voice and the keen intelligence in her pale-grey eyes.

The back-ups, whoever they were, had remained out in the hall.

As Connor played the latest podcast from his laptop, the only movement came from DI Weeks, making notes and tilting her head as she listened. Occasionally she leaned into John George to mutter something quietly. For his part, George simply tapped a finger on the table as he took it all in.

When the recording finally finished, all eyes went to him. He thanked them and got right into why he and DI Weeks were there. 'Katherine is one of my officers currently seconded to a cross-agency operation between the UK Financial Intelligence Unit and the National Cyber Security Centre. If you're not already aware of the former, it's a division of the National Crime Agency focused on organized crime and terrorist finance.'

Feeling a chill go through her, Cristy glanced around and saw that it was the same for the others.

'Don't let that alarm you,' George went on lightly, 'I'm simply letting you know that there is an ongoing investigation into a certain sort of fraudulent activity that it appears you, as a team, have stumbled into.'

Clearing his throat, Connor said, 'I'm sorry, but I can't get past organized crime and terrorist finance and how the hell it could connect to someone like Romy Kaplan.'

Nodding his understanding, George gestured for Katherine Weeks to take over.

'Try not to get hung up on labels,' she advised. 'The UKFIU covers a wide range of financial illegalities. Yes, many are related to mafia-style gangs and terrorist cells. However, there are plenty of other types of aggressors in play today, no less nefarious in their fraudulent activities, in some ways every bit as abhorrent. I'll point you to a CrowdStrike report after this that could be useful, but to paraphrase the foreword of that report: generative AI has lowered the barrier of entry for minor-skilled adversaries, making it easier to launch more sophisticated attacks, even on protected systems.'

'CrowdStrike?' Connor prompted.

'You can google it,' she told him, 'but essentially, it's a cybersecurity company that provides attack response services.'

After allowing a moment for that to sink in, Weeks continued. 'On a more relatable level, are you familiar with the term "mate crime"?'

Cristy frowned and nodded. 'It's when someone befriends a vulnerable person and basically steals all their money.'

'Correct. They choose their targets carefully, gain their trust and ultimately clean out their bank accounts before taking off into the sunset. Or not taking off, as happens in some cases, but we'll come on to that. In this digital age, we're dealing with a much more sophisticated method of appropriation, resulting in equally if not more devastating consequences for victims. It can begin in the time-honoured fashion of befriending and building trust, but today's targets, while they're still selected for their perceived susceptibility and monetary value, become the unwitting subjects of identity-based attacks that circumvent multifactor authentication.'

Cristy decided to let Jacks explain later in simpler language, knowing he would have a far greater understanding of what was being said than the rest of them.

'Having already established that deepfake technologies are a key tool in most cybercrime these days,' Weeks continued, 'let's focus for a moment on how you, as a team, have been targeted. You dealt well with the fake podcast. In fact, you have it to thank for bringing the Kaplans to our attention. We've looked into them since, and it seems highly probable that they've fallen victim to the kind of exploitation consistent with what I've already outlined – which, for your purposes, could be described as a high-tech take on mate crime.'

Clove asked, 'Is it like cuckooing?'

Weeks rocked a hand back and forth. 'Similar, in that a "malign force", to quote from your podcast, appears to have taken over the Kaplan's home, as generally happens in cuckooing. In this case, however, it's possible that many other aspects of their lives are also being exploited. This can range from bank accounts to social media, from investment portfolios to entire identities. In some cases, it can happen so fast and so thoroughly, that by the time the victim realizes what's happening, it's already too late.

'That being said, some do try to fight back, and as your own investigations will have shown you over the years, there is no end to the lengths some people will go in order to try to save themselves, their families, their fortunes or their friends from predators.'

Cristy was thinking of Layla and her parents, and how upset and bewildered they were going to be to hear all this.

'People like the Kaplans,' Weeks was saying, 'are, in many ways, the perfect prey for this type of scam – and make no mistake, that's exactly what this is: a scam. Even companies and banks have been compromised by similar attacks, but while they generally have robust security in place to block the malware, private individuals often don't. I'm afraid it's not possible to say how the Kaplans might have come to these scammers' attention, but it appears they have.'

'So basically,' Clove said dismally, 'they're not Russian agents?'

Weeks blinked.

'It was just a theory,' Clove explained. 'Given their history with the FO, expulsion from Moscow, all the hobnobbing, then sudden disappearance . . . OK, embarrassing myself now, so going to stop.'

With a smile, Weeks said, 'Theories are always worth exploring, even the more outlandish ones, so don't be embarrassed. However, what seems to have happened to the Kaplans fits with the known MO of a certain sort of predatory network that's been under scrutiny for some time now.'

'This is starting to sound *way* bigger than we imagined,' Connor interjected worriedly.

'It is,' Weeks confirmed, 'and yet it isn't. We think that whoever's targeted the Kaplans is more likely to be a copy-cat operator than someone from the core organization. Dozens of imitators have sprung up all over the world, small groups of tech savvy keyboarders, in some cases single players with digital expertise, all interacting via dark web message boards, gaining and sharing new methodology or names and profiles of potential victims.

'Whether the Kaplans came to attention this way isn't possible to say. What's likely is that a rogue player in the financial world knew enough about them to put them up as subjects of interest. Please keep in mind that we have no proof of them being targeted this way; it's simply that your investigations have thrown up many similarities to others we are conducting in various parts of the world.'

'What I don't understand,' Meena put in, 'is why they didn't report what was happening to them?'

'It's a good question,' Weeks told her. 'Some do report it as soon as they realize it's happening, while others are simply too afraid of what will happen to them and those they care about if they don't go along with what's being demanded. Email and social media accounts are seized to make it look as though they are sending messages to their own contacts threatening or accusing them in ways that could, if made public, ruin entire lives and reputations.'

Cristy immediately thought of the letter from Rudi to his friend Theo Crush, apologizing for something Crush apparently knew nothing about.

When she cited the example, Weeks said, 'It's quite likely that Rudi believed some kind of accusation had already been made against this friend. Maybe it was a threat that could have shamed the man and ended his career.'

Sickened to think of such malicious coercion, Cristy said, 'We know that the Kaplans cared very much about their friends, so I guess that's why they've never said anything?'

Weeks nodded slowly. 'It's been known,' she said, 'for victims to try to get back what they lost by working with, or for, their tormentors to direct them to other potential victims.'

Cristy's mind immediately flashed to Romy driving into Haylesford Manor with Casey Callaghan in the car.

Clove said, 'Are you saying they become scammers themselves?'

Taking the question, George said, 'It's not likely they'd have the tech know-how, but they could give details of promising targets. In the case of Rudi Kaplan, that would be difficult with him being dead, but . . .'

'We're actually not entirely convinced that he is,' Connor told him.

George's eyebrows rose with interest, but before he could

respond, the door opened and one of the back-up team came to speak in Katherine Viner's ear. She nodded, the man went away, and George said to Connor, 'Why are you querying Rudi Kaplan's death?'

'Well, apart from Romy's reluctance to have the drowning investigated,' Connor replied, 'we think he could have been in Portugal with her recently—'

'We know that was a regenerated video now,' Jacks reminded him. 'So there's no proof Romy was in Portugal at all.'

'Of course,' Connor muttered, 'but there seems to be this anomaly where ID-ing a dead body is concerned. It could be that if the next of kin says it's them, then no further checks are made. No one else who knew Rudi saw his body before it was taken away and cremated, apart from Romy.'

Frowning, George said, 'Have you contacted the coroner?'

'Of course. Just got some generic brush off about all correct protocols being followed.'

'OK, I'll have someone look into it,' George promised. 'In the meantime, Kate, let's move this on to the real reason you're here.'

'Sure.' DI Weeks took a moment to look around the table. 'I don't know if I've given you too much or too little information so far – I mean in a tech sense – but please bear in mind there are aspects of our investigations I can't share. However, I am prepared to give you sight of some documentation that illustrates how, on a basic level, the assets of people like Rudi Kaplan are seized and cloned. And how, in some cases, the targets themselves are made to disappear behind a wall of cleverly constructed digital imagery. It will provide a rather different take on organized crime to the one you're more familiar with, but make no mistake, that's what this is.

'Focusing back on Romy Kaplan. I realize your aim is to find her, while ours is to root out members of the online predatory gangs operating in this country and beyond.

Unfortunately, the gangs themselves are controlled by remote operators, mostly located in the Far East or Russia. The kingpins are known to some as the Hydra – meaning that as soon as one head is removed, another grows in its place. Others refer to them as Simulacra, which, if you're familiar with *The Matrix*, you'll know basically means the replacement of reality with representation.'

Shuddering at the sheer scale and opacity of it all, Cristy almost missed the next words.

'. . . what is most relevant to us,' Weeks was saying, 'or more particularly to you, is that we are prepared to lend you some help with your investigations.'

Clove practically leapt out of her chair with excitement, and only just managed not to cheer.

'Help in what way?' Cristy asked warily.

Before Weeks could reply, Harry said, 'If you're hoping to use these guys as decoys of some sort, then I, for one, will want some sort of risk assessment.'

Apparently unfazed by the directness, Weeks said, 'Rest assured, we're not in the business of putting members of the public into dangerous situations.'

'Really?' Clove asked, seeming almost disappointed. 'But what about Rudi and the fact he might have been murdered? And we're not actually a hundred percent that Romy's still alive.'

Cristy could only feel relieved that Layla wasn't there to hear those words.

All eyes were on Weeks as, appearing unruffled by two excellent points, she said, 'Before we go any further, I'd like to ask if there's anything you haven't shared on the podcast, including the episode we've just listened to, that might be useful for me to know.'

Cristy threw a quick glance at Connor as she said, 'A portrait of Romy has disappeared from her home, but we're not sure yet where that might fit in.'

Weeks frowned. 'OK, get back to me on it if you find it does. Anyway, picking up for a moment on the birth certificate and baggage receipt, you're probably aware that faking ID won't be difficult for the kind of people we're dealing with, so it's doubtful this person is even called Casey, never mind Callaghan or Kaplan.' She checked her notes. 'You mentioned a Lisa McIlvoy?'

Jacks said, 'Partner of Bram Aalders, estate manager at Haylesford Manor. We don't have anything on her yet, but she kind of fits the description of the woman the cleaner saw in Portugal and the giftshop owner saw in Gloucestershire – and possibly of the passenger in Romy's car when she was last seen driving into the manor.'

'When exactly was that?' George asked.

'Around the time of Romy's disappearance,' Cristy replied. 'As far as we know, Romy and Rudi moved out of the manor back in September 2023, and not even her best friend was aware of her staying in touch with the new owners. Except we're not actually sure now that they do own the place. It's possible they could be renting.'

'Do you know who they are?' Weeks asked.

'A couple called Kesinger, from South Africa, we're told.'

'They bear out,' Jacks informed them. 'We've gone deep into it, and no reason to think they're not real. Proper hotshots, proper minted.'

'Apparently not in residence at the moment,' Connor put in. 'The place is being run by the aforementioned estate manager, who we rubbed up against when we went to do some background on Romy.'

'Did you go inside?' George wanted to know.

'Not even past the gates,' Connor told him.

There was a pause, before Weeks said, 'It doesn't surprise me that the Kesingers are real, and I'd say there's a good chance they'll be renting the property. It's another example of how some of these people work. They let out high-end

240

residences, estates even, for vast sums and bank the gains. In some cases, they've been known to give themselves cover by acting as housekeepers or estate managers . . .'

'I knew it!' Connor cried, slapping the table. 'I told you, Cris, it was written all over him. Dodgy as fuck!'

'Have you checked him out?' Weeks asked Jacks.

'Everything appears for real so far,' Jacks replied, seeming to share Connor's disappointment in that. 'But some gaps in his history could be worth digging into.'

'If his profile has been generated by AI,' Connor protested, 'how are you ever going to know if it's real?'

'There are markers, when you know what you're looking for,' Jacks told him.

Connor said to George, 'Are you at least going to go and check the place out?'

Weeks glanced at her colleague, then said, 'We'd never get a warrant at this stage, and knocking on the door won't achieve anything, because if this estate manager is a malign operator and there's something to be found inside, he'll refuse to let us in, then disappear before you can even say magistrate.'

Cristy said, 'Layla has his number, so maybe we do have a way in. She's waiting for a call back from him.'

'Layla is Romy's goddaughter?' George asked. 'The one interviewed on the podcast?'

Cristy nodded. 'We asked if we could go in and have a look round to do some background on Romy. He's supposed to be clearing it with the Kesingers, so it's possible he'll call back with an invitation.'

'If he's even asked them,' Connor pointed out. 'I'll lay money we never hear from him.'

'Maybe not,' Cristy responded, 'but we've already talked about contacting the Kesingers directly . . . Have you managed to get anywhere with that yet, Jacks?'

'Barely got started, but confident I'll come up with something.'

241

'If they are renting the place,' Cristy said to Weeks, 'or even if they own it, it'll be interesting to find out if they're willing to let Layla take a trip down memory lane.'

Weeks was looking interested. 'It's certainly worth a shot,' she responded, glancing at George and receiving a nod.

'If Layla does manage to get in,' Cristy said, 'then what is she supposed to be looking for? I mean, apart from Romy, and do we really think she's in there?'

'Whether she is or isn't,' Connor protested, 'you can't seriously be thinking of letting Layla do it on her own.'

'No, of course not. We'll go with her.' Turning to George, Cristy said, 'It's perfectly normal for podcasters to check out the places someone used to live. We do it all the time. To refuse us entry – well, that would tell us something in itself, wouldn't it?'

George merely looked at Weeks, whose expression was inscrutable as she thought. In the end, she said, 'These guys are not as incapable of making mistakes as they like to think. Producing a fake podcast proves it, in this case – certainly not a smart move, which those behind it surely understand by now. So, if they are inside the Kaplans' old home . . . I'll have a couple of my team scope out the surrounding area, see if they can get some idea of comings and goings.'

'If I might be so bold,' Meena put in, 'I think, if this "tour" of the manor is going to happen, we need to revisit the question of risk.'

'There's always risk in covert ops,' Clove informed her.

'This is hardly that.' Cristy laughed. 'We'll be going in as ourselves, doing what we do—'

'Knowing what you know,' Meena argued. 'It's covert, and therefore it could be risky.'

George said, 'If there is anything to hide inside, it won't be anywhere in evidence when these guys go in. They'll have had enough time to make certain of it.'

'So, to repeat, if we do manage to get in, what exactly should we be looking for?' Cristy asked.

'Without having been in there,' Weeks replied, 'I guess, anything that doesn't feel right about the place. It could be that Layla will have a better sense, given her prior knowledge, but basically, watch the body language of whoever shows you around, keep an eye out for anyone else, and clock anything that seems as though it doesn't belong. In other words, use your instincts.'

'And at the same time record everything quite openly,' Cristy declared. 'A doddle.'

'But you won't be able to use it,' George reminded her.

'For now,' she conceded.

Eyeing her meaningfully, he said, 'I need to make it clear that you are under no obligation to try this. In fact, if you want to step away from the case now, you can put out an announcement saying you've handed all your findings to the relevant authorities and will continue to help in any way you can but there will be no more podcasts relating to this search.'

'Which of course would be the sensible thing to do,' Meena declared.

'Bugger that!' Clove exclaimed.

Choking back a laugh, Cristy said, 'I think the next step is to bring Layla into this so she can prepare herself for the visit, if the Kesingers give the go head.'

'A big if,' Connor retorted. To Weeks, he said, 'What if Romy is there?'

She shook her head. 'I'd be very surprised if she is, given it'll be known in advance that you're coming.'

'Just to be clear,' Clove said. 'Are we seeing Romy as villain or victim here?'

Weeks pondered it. 'I'd be more inclined towards the latter,' she replied, 'but it wouldn't be wise to rule out the former.'

George said ruminatively, 'Going back to the possibility of Rudi Kaplan not being dead. It lends a whole other dimension to this, because as you'll already have worked out, someone has to have died for a body to have been taken away and cremated.'

'Have any other victims died as a result of being scammed like this?' Clove asked.

'There have been suicides,' Weeks admitted, 'but actual murder . . . Not that I know of.'

Cristy said, 'There was a horrible case of mate crime about fifteen years ago. Obviously, it wasn't at this level – I guess the technology wasn't there then – but I'll never forget Gemma Hayter.'

'Ah yes,' George said quietly, 'that was one of the first of its sort to gain public attention.'

'You can look it up,' Cristy told Clove, 'but basically, she was the victim of so-called mate crime, and what they put her through, the cruelty and torture before they killed her . . . It was absolutely horrendous – and heartbreaking.'

George nodded soberly.

Connor said, 'So how many victims are there, would you say, in this country?'

Weeks took a breath. 'Bearing in mind that not every case is reported, it's not possible to put an accurate figure on it. However, we as a team, have dozens under review, ranging from your everyday scam staging quick sweeps of bank accounts, to the kind of full immersion into duplicate identity that we could be seeing here.'

Cristy said to Clove, 'Please, whatever you do, don't mention the Gemma Hayter case to Layla.'

CHAPTER THIRTY-THREE

The following morning, Cristy and Connor took Layla to the Harbourside Kitchen to talk her through what they'd learned from Katherine Weeks the day before and why they'd cancelled last night's drop. It was a bleak, rainy day with no sign of the sun breaking through or of it feeling like summer any time soon, which was why they were inside, grouped around a table next to a steamy window and protected from the unseasonal chill.

As Layla listened, her distress visibly deepened, although she said very little, only nodding occasionally or seeming about to protest before apparently deciding not to.

By the time Connor finished explaining that they were going to push harder for a 'memory-lane' tour of the manor, she'd turned to stare through her own reflection in the rain-spattered window, seeming to have become lost in a world of her own. Cristy couldn't help wondering if the mention of mate crime had triggered Gemma Hayter for her, although Layla would have been a young teen at the time, so would she really remember it? Besides, wasn't it enough to imagine her beloved godmother being psychologically terrorized and financially ruined by someone she'd presumably started out trusting, without adding the fear of her being ruthlessly tortured?

And what about Rudi? They still had no idea what might have happened to him.

Speaking at last, Layla said, 'Do *you* believe Romy might

be helping these people now? Working with them, betraying others, to try to save herself?'

Cristy regarded her helplessly. 'Without knowing the circumstances she's in,' she said, 'what sort of hold they might have over her . . .'

'She'd do anything to protect the people she loves,' Layla interrupted, 'so turning them into victims too . . . She'd never do that.' To Connor, she said, 'Do we know for certain that Bram Aalders is one of this group?'

'No, we don't,' Connor admitted, 'but it's looking likely. This Casey or Lisa woman too.'

Layla nodded slowly. After a moment, she said, 'Mum and I read something last night, written by Romy, about the artist who did her and Rudi's portraits. It's on my phone . . .' Calling it up, she read aloud:

'"I moved my portrait upstairs today. It felt like a terrible wrench taking it away from Rudi's side. It was almost physical, but I simply couldn't bear to look at it any more. It isn't me. No matter the similarity, I am not who the artist was seeing when she painted it.

'"Oh, that artist, that artist, how she haunts me. I could tell by the faraway look in her eyes as she worked, the wistfulness and depth of feeling that seemed to come over her at times, that she was engaged elsewhere. It was as if she was seeing, even channelling somebody else. She didn't speak of the woman who maybe resembled me; she hardly spoke at all, but I saw tears on her cheeks once or twice, and Rudi said he'd noticed them too.

'"She did a much better job of his portrait. She was happier around him than she was around me. Everyone was happier around Rudi. He didn't only make my world a better place; he did it for everyone without even trying. I miss him so much; sometimes it's too hard to think about him, to remember the love that bound us so tightly together, and yet it's almost impossible to think of anything else.

246

'"*Was I wrong to move the portrait? It's creating a sense of separation now that I'm finding bewildering and very upsetting. If I close my eyes, I can almost feel the joy of the hours we sat together, watching each other and laughing as the artist captured us in ways we had no understanding of at the time. Oh my, the trust we put in her, the way we welcomed her into our home . . . If only we'd known what it was all going to lead to.*"'

As Layla looked up, Cristy could feel her heart rate increasing. 'So it was a woman who painted them,' she said, not sure why she'd presumed it was a man. 'And clearly the portraits were a part of winning their confidence.'

'Is there anything else?' Connor asked.

Layla shook her head. 'It's followed by some verses from *Beowulf*, apparently one of Rudi's favourites.'

'Let's send what you've just read to Katherine Weeks,' Cristy said. 'It's possible this artist, whoever she is – I'm thinking the blue-eyed woman – has used her skills to "capture" other victims already known to the police. It's also highly possible that the people Andee Lawrence is putting us in touch with will be able to identify who did their portraits.' She checked her phone to find that a WhatsApp had come in from Jacks.

Are you still at the Kitchen?

Yes.

On my way.

'More coffee?' Connor offered.

Seeming not to have heard, Layla said, 'Actually, I have some other news. Not as major or shattering as yours, or as obscure as Romy's notebook, but Mum and Dad have managed to make contact with Inge Trevors, Rudi and Romy's old housekeeper? She's in Vancouver, where she's been since they had to let her go. Mum says she was really upset to hear about what's going on, and she's happy to talk to you whenever you're ready. Don't worry about the time difference.'

'That's great,' Connor declared. 'At last, someone who might shed light on what went on at the manor before the Kaplans left. She might even be able to ID the artist as well. I'll have Clove set things up.'

Cristy said, 'Are we dismissing the possibility that Inge Trevors might be involved in some way?'

Connor considered it. 'Who knows who the fuck is involved at this stage,' he grumbled, 'but I get the impression Inge was trusted by the Kaplans?' He was looking at Layla.

'I'm afraid they trusted everyone,' Layla responded. 'So I'm not sure what to tell you about Inge.'

Minutes later, Jacks plonked himself down at the table, raindrops spotting his glasses and coating his jacket. 'We're in!' he declared, opening up his phone and scrolling. 'I emailed Maria Kesinger last night, on behalf of you guys, and here's the voicemail she left this morning.'

MARIA KESINGER: 'Hello, Cristy and Connor – I hope you don't mind me using your first names. I'm afraid I haven't heard your podcasts, but I shall certainly be listening out from now on. Regarding a visit to Haylesford Manor: I shall contact the estate manager right away to assure him you are very welcome. His name is Bram Aalders. I'll email his contact details. I only wish I could be there in person to take Layla around and hear her stories about the times she's spent there over the years. My husband and I would like to visit the place more often, but you know how life gets in the way.

'You have this number now, so please feel free to call if I can be of any further help. Enjoy the tour, and don't forget to let us know when we can expect the podcast.'

As the message ended, Cristy high-fived Connor. 'So how do we want to play this now?' she asked.

Coming to a quick decision, he said, 'If we haven't heard from Bram Aalders by the end of the day – hard to see how he's going to avoid it if Maria tells him to be in touch...'

'You realize she more or less confirmed he hadn't even been in touch about it?' Cristy put in.

'Exactly. So I say we contact him with a date and time for our visit. In the meantime, forward that voicemail to Katherine Weeks,' he said to Jacks. 'Who are you calling?' he asked Cristy.

'Andee Lawrence,' she replied. A message arrived before she'd finished dialling, and seeing it was from David, she read it, briefly smiled and returned to her call. 'Voicemail,' she told the others once she'd connected to Andee's number. 'Hey, it's Cristy. How's it going with your portrait guys? We're really keen to speak to them.'

Andee rang back half an hour later. 'They're leaving the cruise ship today,' she told them, 'so should be home late this evening – and they're very happy to talk to you. I'll text their names and contact details, but they've asked if you could delay until tomorrow. They have to settle his father back into his flat before they can deal with anything else.'

CHAPTER THIRTY-FOUR

'You only *think*?' Cristy murmured, gazing into David's eyes as they lay, face-to-face, in the afterglow of their snatched hours together.

He frowned curiously.

'Chris Stapleton's song,' she reminded him.

'Ah.' He broke into a smile. '"Think I'm in Love with You".' Putting his mouth to hers he murmured, 'No doubt,' and drawing her in closer, he kissed her deeply.

He'd been waiting when she'd arrived home an hour ago, having made an unscheduled stop on his way back to Guernsey, and since Aiden had taken Laurent over to Millennium Square, they'd wasted no time in ending up where they were now.

'I miss you,' he told her, smoothing her hair behind her ear. 'When we're not together, things don't feel . . . quite right.'

'I know,' she whispered, 'but doesn't the time apart make being together even more special?'

He considered it, and said, 'You could have a point. What just happened felt pretty special, that's for sure.'

Smiling, she kissed him again, then aware that the boys could return at any moment, she reluctantly rolled onto her back and made herself sit up. Immediately, she started to laugh. The trail of hastily discarded clothes leading to the bed told its own story, as did the tangle of sheets and duvet around their limbs. More interesting, though, was the potent masculinity of his naked body, so strong and tanned beside her own.

She could probably never get enough of looking at him.

Twenty minutes later, after quick showers and a tidy up, David opened a bottle of wine and carried it out to the garden, where she was drying rain off the table and chairs. A sudden burst of evening sunshine was causing steam to rise from the patio stones, while the flowers and leaves appeared impossibly bright.

'Aiden just messaged to say they're grabbing a pizza with a couple of his mates,' she told him, as he filled two glasses.

With no small irony, David said, 'Good of him to let us know after we got up. I had the same message from Laurent.' He tapped his drink to hers. 'To beautiful you, who I seem to love and admire more with each passing day.' He frowned. 'Or would that be after each mind-blowing . . . event?'

Kicking him, Cristy laughed and said, 'You need to work on your lines. They start off well, but the finish . . . ?'

Laughing too, he said, 'There are some pretty good rejoinders to that, but I'll spare you, just tell me you love me too, and then why don't you bring me up to speed with everything?'

Tilting her head, she said, 'How about I do it the other way round and save the best for last?'

He thought about it, apparently decided he didn't mind the suggestion, and raised his glass again in a gesture for her to continue.

They'd almost finished the bottle by the time she'd talked him through the past twenty-four hours, from John George and Katherine Weeks turning up at the office, to the new understanding of what could be happening to Romy, and just how freaked out she'd felt about having her voice stolen by the fake podcasters.

'It's like some weird out of body experience,' she said with a shiver. 'It feels like you have another existence that you have no way of controlling, which I suppose is what it is. You've been cloned, used to do things you'd never normally do, so God only knows how it feels to find yourself in a porn film. Or how it feels to be Romy, if they've taken her over the way we think they have.'

'So,' he said, frowning thoughtfully, 'a division of the NCA is now on board for the pod?'

She grimaced. 'I'm not sure they'd see it like that, but, eventually, we could have an amazing series on our hands, some of it coming from the very heart of a covert op.'

'Impressive. But your next move is to get inside Haylesford Manor?'

'Or to identify the artist Romy wrote about. Actually, both are a priority. Layla and Connor are messaging Bram Aalders this evening to let him know that we'll be at the gates by three o'clock on Friday afternoon. In the meantime, we're recording a couple of interviews tomorrow that Katherine Weeks is keen to listen in to.'

'Does Katherine Weeks know about anyone else who's been "taken in" by a portrait artist?'

'She doesn't, but it's being looked into in case it's come up elsewhere. At the moment, our best shot at identifying the artist is through Andee Lawrence's people, who we're interviewing at five tomorrow. Ordinarily, we'd go to their home, but they're on Exmoor and our second interview of the day is set for seven, so we'd never make it back in time.'

'And the second is with?'

'Rudi and Romy's old housekeeper, who's now in Vancouver. Clove has offered to go to Canada in person, which, as I told her, is extremely generous of her, but we don't need to put her to all that trouble just yet.'

David laughed, then noticing their empty glasses said, 'Shall I open another bottle?'

'Why not? And I should make us something to eat . . .'.

She frowned as the doorbell sounded. 'Oh God, don't tell me Aiden's lost his keys again,' she groaned, getting up. 'All right, all right, I'm coming.'

Going to the entry phone, she said, 'You don't have to keep ringing . . .'

'Cristy, please let me in,' Matthew said urgently. 'I have to talk to you.'

Surprised and already concerned, she released the door, and glanced at David as he went to take more wine from the fridge. 'Matthew,' she told him. 'Sorry, but he's been trying to talk to me for days . . .'

'It's OK. Always happy to see your ex. I'll get another glass.'

Moments later, Matthew was in the room, looking as dishevelled and distraught as he'd sounded and hardly able to stand still. 'What on earth's the matter?' she asked, feeling a rush of unease as she put a hand on his arm to steady him.

'Sorry,' he said, reaching out to shake David's hand. 'I didn't realize you were here. I don't want to interrupt . . .'

'It's not a problem,' David assured him. 'You're not looking great, if you don't mind me saying.'

Noticing the wine, Matthew said, 'I'll take one of those if I can.'

As David poured, Cristy asked, 'Is it Marley? The baby?'

'No, they're fine. Well, she wants a divorce, but that's not what this is about. I mean, it is, but . . . Oh Christ, I don't know how this has happened . . .'

'Sit down,' Cristy said, leading him to the dining table and pressing him into a chair. 'Take a breath,' she instructed.

Doing as he was told, Matthew thanked David for the wine, took a mouthful and said, 'Sorry. I didn't mean to barge in. I just had to talk to someone.'

'Maybe I should leave you guys alone,' David suggested.

'No, stay,' Matthew insisted. 'You might as well hear it – the whole effing world will know soon enough.' And to

Cristy's horror, he started to cry. 'I'm sorry,' he sobbed, as she knelt in front of him, 'it's just so fucking overwhelming.'

'Shush,' she soothed, taking his hands in hers. 'It's going to be all right. Whatever it is, we'll sort it out.'

He gave a dry, bitter laugh. 'Those used to be my lines when you were upset,' he reminded her, 'but let me tell you, it's never going to be all right, not if any of this gets out.'

Going to sit next to him, David put a firm hand on his shoulder and said, 'Just tell us what it is. We can't help until you do.'

Matthew nodded, dashed a hand through his hair and looked for a moment as though he might cry again. Instead, he swallowed hard and said, 'I first knew about it at the weekend. I got a call at home from Malinda in HR. She wanted to give me a heads-up, she said . . .' He closed his eyes tightly, took a breath and tried again. 'Apparently, they've had complaints about me from a couple – that's what she said – "a couple of" female members of staff. They're saying I . . . that I've harassed them, sexually. One's even claimed I . . . you know . . . forced her to go all the way.' His eyes, so like their son's, came to Cristy's, bloodshot, frightened and utterly devastated. 'You know me better than anyone,' he cried wretchedly. 'You know I'd never do something like that.'

'But who's saying it?' she demanded. 'Did Malinda give you any names?'

'She doesn't have to, apparently. They have the right to remain anonymous. I got called in by the MD on Monday to discuss it, and I just found out earlier that I've been . . . *suspended*.'

Cristy quickly wrapped him in her arms and looked at David as she said, 'We need to speak to a lawyer?'

David nodded, as Matthew said, 'I thought of that, but I know just about everyone in town, and I don't want them thinking this of me. Anyway, I shouldn't need a fucking lawyer when I haven't done anything wrong.'

Because she had to, Cristy said gently, 'Has something happened with someone that they might have misunderstood?'

'No!' he shouted. 'I swear, I haven't laid a finger on anyone. I'm not stupid – I know what crossing the line is, and I make sure I never go anywhere near it. I don't even give anyone a compliment these days, I'm so afraid it'll be taken the wrong way. I swear, the allegations are false, but if I don't know who's saying these things, I've got no way of defending myself.' The horror of it clearly intensified as he said, 'What the hell am I going to tell the children? Thank God Aiden's off to France tomorrow and Hayley's in Oslo with Hugo.'

'Just think,' Cristy urged again. 'Is there someone who might have a grudge against you for some reason? Someone you might have upset without meaning to? Have you passed someone over for a promotion? Criticized someone's research?'

'There isn't anyone,' he growled. 'I've got a great relationship with all the women I work with . . . Or I thought I did until *this* fucking shitshow.'

Carefully, David said, 'Do you know if it's someone who works at the company now? Could these . . . complaints be historical, and for some reason they're only just being brought to attention?'

Matthew regarded him helplessly. 'I swear to God, mate, I've never laid a hand on anyone in that way. Cristy, tell him. You know I wouldn't.'

'I know,' she said softly, 'and I'm really sorry this is happening. If you like, I'll try to have a chat with Malinda, see what I can find out. Maybe if we're able to pin it to some dates we'll have a better idea of who it could be.'

'Whoever it is, they're lying,' he growled. 'I just don't understand why someone would want to do this to me. OK, I can be a prick at times, we all can . . . Well, except you, I suppose, David.'

David laughed. 'I have my moments, but what matters

now is that you try to get yourself together, because I think Aiden's just got back.'

Closing his eyes in despair, Matthew said, 'I'll go out to the garden, pretend I'm on a call. Don't, for God's sake, tell him anything.'

'Of course not,' Cristy assured him, 'just go.'

It wasn't until much later, after Aiden and Laurent had disappeared into Aiden's room to play on the Xbox, that Cristy was able to say to Matthew, 'This is probably going to sound crazy, but the people we're up against in the case I'm working on, the fraudsters . . . It's the way they operate . . . I can't explain it all now, but there's a chance that what's happening to you is some kind of warning to me that if I don't back off our investigation, this is what will happen to the people around me. They tried shutting us down with the fake pod, remember? It didn't work, so this could be them showing me what they'll do to my family and friends if I don't start paying attention.'

Matthew stared at her in disbelief, glanced at David and back to her. 'I'm not sure I followed any of that,' he said, 'but I should have known it would be all about you.'

It was a familiar tease, one that usually made her smile, but this time neither of them did. 'For your sake, I hope I'm right,' she muttered, not adding, *because the alternative would mean the accusations have come from real female colleagues and I have no idea how any of us will handle that.*

CHAPTER THIRTY-FIVE

When Cristy arrived at the office the following morning, she found Connor white-faced, unshaven, and clearly furious.

'Jodi had an email last night from social services,' he growled at her. 'They want to come and talk to her about the baby. Apparently, they've had reports of her going out and leaving Aurora alone in the house.'

Horrified, Cristy cried, 'Why the hell didn't you call me?'

'I was trying to deal with Jodi, and I knew David was there. It wasn't until I got over the shock myself that I guessed what it really was, so . . . I got in touch with Jacks.'

'I did the same . . .'

'What?'

'We'll come back to it. Where is Jacks?'

'At UWE with the prof. He was pretty sure the email was fake, but he's getting it confirmed.'

'Of course it's fake,' Cristy declared angrily. 'We've already been warned that this is what they do. I think they've gone after Matthew as well.'

Connor listened in appalled silence as she told him about the sexual harassment complaints Malinda, their old HR director, had received, swearing under his breath and looking about ready to throw a punch.

'I know it's you,' he growled, glaring at Aalders's headshot on the whiteboard. 'And I'm coming for you! Picking on my wife is your biggest mistake.'

'Where's Jodi now?' Cristy asked, going to pour them both a coffee.

'At her mother's.' Firing up again, Connor cried, 'You know, the trouble with this kind of stuff is if anything gets out, it never goes away. There'll always be someone who believes it, no matter how fake it is.'

Cristy knew this was exactly what Matthew feared and they both had a point, because it was true: those kinds of slurs were virtually impossible to shake once they were made. 'Listen,' she said, 'if you want us to back off and let Katherine Weeks take it from here—'

'The hell are we doing that,' he raged. 'No way is that bastard getting away with it. We just have to make sure nothing ever goes any further than it already has – as if that's not fucking far enough.' He looked around the room and threw out his hands in fury and despair. 'Should we be discussing him here?' he cried. 'Is he listening to us? Are you listening?' he shouted. 'You fucking asshole!'

Coming to a stop in the doorway, Layla regarded him cautiously.

'Shall I go away and come back . . . ?'

'No, no, come in,' Cristy told her. 'I'm afraid we've been getting a taste of what Romy and Rudi must have experienced with the threats to their friends.'

Confused, Layla said, 'What do you mean?'

When Cristy told her, she almost started to cry. 'Oh my God! I'm so sorry. I had no idea something like this would happen when I came to you. Poor Jodi – is she OK?' she asked Connor. 'And Matthew? He must be devastated.'

'Jodi's coping,' Connor told her, 'but I can tell you, it shook her up big time.'

'Matthew's flying to Guernsey with David later today,' Cristy informed them. 'He needs to get away, so that's what they've decided.'

Connor gave a laugh. 'Did you just say Matthew's going to Guernsey with David?' he asked.

'I know, crazy, isn't it?' she said. 'But they actually seem to like each other. Aiden calls it a budding bromance, and I don't suppose I can argue with that. Of course, Aiden now wants to go with them instead of surfing in France, so I left them trying to change his ticket.'

Going to Iz's desk in the corner, where she usually sat when Iz wasn't around, Layla said, 'Did you contact Bram Aalders about turning up at the manor tomorrow?'

'Done,' Connor barked. 'No reply, natch, but we're going anyway. Maria Kesinger's message gave us all the permission we need.'

'It's Jacks!' Cristy declared when both her and Connor's phones signalled an incoming text. '*"Jodi's email def not sent by Social Services. Matthew's case more complicated as complaints not accessible. Prof suggests you contact HR at his company, explain situation and request further info."*'

As soon as she'd finished reading, Connor got on the phone to Jodi. Cristy could only wish she was able to do the same for Matthew. Being told that his situation was "more complicated" would only increase his stress levels, and God knew it wasn't doing much for hers. Almost certainly the email complaints were fake, but the HR investigation very much wasn't given that Matthew had spoken directly to Melinda and he'd already been put on suspension.

She looked up as he came into the office with David, her heart flooding with a potent mix of emotions.

'Thought we'd stop off on the way to the airport,' David said, coming to drop a kiss on her forehead. 'Aiden's going to join us for a few days, then he'll catch up with his mates in Biarritz. Hey, Connor. How're things?'

'Better than ten minutes ago,' Connor responded. 'You look all in,' he told Matthew.

'Not the best of times,' Matthew admitted, and went to embrace Layla. 'How are you?' he asked.

'I'm OK,' she replied, looking searchingly into his eyes.

With a brief smile, he turned to introduce her to David, then said to Cristy, 'Any news?'

'Nothing definitive,' she hedged. 'I'll let you know as soon as I receive confirmation it's what we think it is. Where's Aiden now?'

'He was in the car with Laurent, but . . .'

'Hey, gang,' Aiden said, coming in the door. 'Just wanted to say bye, Mum. And try not to worry about me.'

'Too late for that,' she said dryly, as he hugged her. 'It goes with being your mother. Did you remember to pack everything? I left a list this morning . . .'

'All done. We're just popping up to Dad's for my diving gear.'

'Hi, Laurent,' Connor said to the skinny, dark-haired boy who'd followed Aiden into the room. He was so like his beautiful French mother, with David's cobalt-blue eyes and captivating smile. 'How you doing? Do you remember me?'

'Course,' Laurent assured him. 'You were at ours last Christmas, with Jodi and the baby. You had those really cool hiking boots.'

Winking, Connor said, 'I'm known for my style.'

'Bit like you, Dad,' Aiden teased.

As Matthew pulled him into a playful headlock, Cristy opened her arms for Laurent to come and give her a hug, which he did willingly and affectionately. She'd developed a very real fondness for the boy over the months she'd known him, and she only wished there were more opportunities to get to know him better.

'Take care of them all while they're in Guernsey,' she instructed, 'and don't let Aiden lead you into any trouble.'

Laurent grinned, clearly up for it whatever it might be.

Cristy walked outside with them and waited for the others

to get into the car before saying softly to David, 'Thanks for doing this. It's beyond the call, but it would drive Matthew mad if he had to stay here kicking his heels all weekend.'

'It's a pretty bad time for Marley to start talking about divorce,' David commented, turning from the car so Matthew wouldn't hear.

Groaning, Cristy said, 'Has he mentioned it this morning?'

'Only to say what I just did, that the timing could have been better. Anyway, he'll have us to distract him for a few days, and my mother to talk to if he feels the need.' He leaned in to kiss her on the mouth.

'Come on, Dad, or we'll miss the plane,' Laurent grumbled from the back seat.

'Speak later,' David murmured, and got into the passenger seat as Matthew started the engine.

As they drove away, Cristy couldn't help noticing how Matthew avoided looking at her, and knowing how deeply he was hurting on so many fronts tore painfully at her heart. He obviously felt as though his whole life was falling apart, and right now, it very well could be.

Going back inside, she found herself just in time to hear Katherine Weeks on a speaker call with Connor and Layla, saying, '. . . we should be able to release more later, but essentially, early access to Romy's phone and bank records are showing a pattern of movements you should find quite interesting.'

*

'OK, the first stand-out here,' Connor stated, scrutinizing Romy's phone log, 'is that she was in Portugal on 6th June. The same date as on Casey Kaplan's luggage tag. So they must have been there together?'

'Or Casey Kaplan had Romy's phone,' Jacks pointed out. 'Same goes for Lucerne when the images were uploaded to

261

Insta. That was on 21st June. Lots of calls on that day to a UK mobile.'

'On it,' Clove declared, pressing in the number. 'Automated voicemail,' she told them moments later. 'There's another UK mobile here . . .' Trying that one, she was soon shaking her head again. 'Same. Straight to voicemail. No personalized message.'

Layla said, 'The only transactions on this particular bank account are direct debits and standing orders, apart from one cash withdrawal of £500 on 12th June.'

'Does it give a location?' Jacks asked.

'No. Just an amount.'

'What's the balance on the account?' Cristy asked.

Layla checked. 'Wow, it was just over £14,000 in April; it's now down to just under £300, thanks to an automated payment made to American Express on 14th June.'

'We need to get hold of that credit card statement,' Cristy declared. She was still studying her screen. 'There's a note here from Katherine Weeks . . . They've tracked the phone's location on 17th and 18th June to the area that includes Haylesford Manor.'

As Layla gasped, Clove said, 'That was Monday and Tuesday last week. Two days after we were there.'

Turning to check the whiteboard, Cristy said, 'It's when she left the message for your mother, Layla.'

Wide-eyed, Layla said, 'So what does that mean?'

'That her phone was active and at the manor as recently as last week,' Connor replied, 'and it looks like she used it herself.'

'I'm going ask Katherine Weeks if anyone's staking the place out yet,' Cristy said, opening up a fresh email. 'Are you recording all this, Connor?' she asked, noticing a red light at the corner of her screen.

'Brilliant stuff,' he pointed out, 'should we ever get to use it.'

Smiling, Cristy quickly messaged Weeks.

A reply came thirty minutes later: *No movements in or out of the manor during past twenty-four hours, but two or three people thought to be inside. No phone or online activity.*

'Aalders must know he's being watched,' Connor declared. 'And the cowardly bastard still hasn't got back to me about tomorrow.'

'Spells of radio-silence could be a part of their MO,' Jacks suggested.

'Or they're waiting for someone?' Clove mused.

Noticing the time, Cristy said, 'We need to set up for the interview with Andee's people. Names again, Clove?'

'The Patricks,' Clove provided. 'Tania and Evan. The portraits were of Tania's parents, as opposed to Evan's.'

'And we're not talking to the parents themselves because?' Connor prompted.

'Both deceased.' Clove glanced awkwardly at Layla, as she added, quietly, 'A joint suicide, apparently.'

CHAPTER THIRTY-SIX

By ten the following morning, they'd edited both Tania Patrick's interview about her parents' experience of a young artist named Lisa McIlvoy, and Inge Trevors' recollections of how enamoured Romy and Rudi had been by the young woman.

Katherine Weeks had both recordings, and the combined edit was lined up for Harry and Meena to view. The first to appear on screen was Inge Trevors, a ruddy-cheeked fair-haired woman in her early sixties.

INGE: 'Actually, I remember Romy wasn't so thrilled with her portrait when it was finished. Have you seen it? Perhaps it is a little harsh around the mouth, and it doesn't altogether reflect the warmth in Romy's eyes, but you only have to look at the one of Rudi to see that Lisa's a talented young lady.'

CRISTY: 'Did you get to know her at all?'

INGE: 'No, not really. She was quite shy, kept mostly to herself when she wasn't in the studio or walking around the grounds. She always looked rather lost to me.'

CRISTY: 'It sounds like she stayed at the manor while she was doing the portraits?'

INGE: 'Yes, she did. She had a room on the top floor –

very nice room, I might say, and a private bathroom, of course.'

CRISTY: 'Do you remember how they came to commission her?'

INGE: 'Mm, I wouldn't want to swear to this, but I think she was introduced to them at Romy's birthday party last May. She was brought along by someone who wanted to recommend her. I'm sure that's what Romy told me.'

CRISTY: 'Did she say who the someone was?'

INGE: 'If she did, I'm afraid I can't remember.'

CRISTY: 'Can you describe Lisa McIlvoy for us?'

INGE: 'Well, as I said, she was quite shy, not very comfortable in her own skin – you know the type. A little nervy, always keen to please. I guess I'd put her in her early thirties; short blonde hair and very blue eyes. Beautiful eyes. She reminded me of an actress whose name has slipped my mind for the moment. I think she might have been Scottish. The accent wasn't strong. Just a hint of it, you know.'

Pausing the playback, Cristy said to Harry and Meena, 'We're going straight to an excerpt from Tania Patrick's interview now.'

A portly woman with an abundance of dark curls and a solemn, pale face filled the screen.

TANIA: 'My parents fell for Lisa almost from the get-go, and to be honest, it wasn't hard to see why. She had a gentle, kind of unassuming way with her, and was always interested in anything you had to say. We liked her a lot on the couple of occasions we met her, didn't we?'

EVAN: 'Yes, we did. And she was great with our children. We were keen for her to do their portraits when she'd finished Don and Allison's, but she said she was all booked up for the next year, and after she left, no one knew how to get hold of her. She didn't even have a website.'

CRISTY: 'Did you find that strange?'

TANIA: 'Yes, we did. She'd got along so well with Mum and Dad, and she seemed so pleased when we toasted the unveiling of the portraits with champagne. Then suddenly she was gone. It wasn't until later, looking back, that we realized that was when everything started going wrong for my parents.'

CRISTY: 'In what way?'

TANIA: 'Well, you know, they'd never really tell us what was happening; they'd just say they'd hit a bit of a rough patch, financially . . . Most of their worth was tied up in the house so we suggested equity release when we realized things were getting difficult, but Dad insisted on selling up. It was heartbreaking for them. They'd lived in that big old pile – Dad inherited it from his grandfather – for all of their married lives.'

CRISTY: 'Do you know who bought it from them?'

TANIA: 'A family from the Midlands – the Mercers or Mellers. I think they're still there.'

CRISTY: 'Where did your parents go after they left?'

TANIA: 'To a small flat in Porlock.'

Pausing the recording again, Cristy said, 'We're switching back to Inge now so you can see the similarity in the stories.'

266

INGE: 'Romy and Rudi missed Lisa a lot after she'd gone. I think they'd got used to having her around and enjoyed her company.'

CRISTY: 'How long was she actually at the manor?'

INGE: 'A month, I'd say. I was away for some of the time, here in Vancouver, visiting my father, but she was still there when I got back at the end of June, putting the finishing touches to Romy's portrait.'

CRISTY: 'And that's when she left?'

INGE: 'Yes. Maybe the first week of July – I can't be certain about dates.'

CRISTY: 'Did she stay in touch after she'd gone?'

INGE: 'No, and I could tell they found that quite surprising and upsetting when they'd come to care for her so much. But then Romy would say, "Ah well, she's young, she has a life to lead." I thought for a while that Rudi had taken it particularly hard, because he started to fall into a bit of a depression, which wasn't like him at all. Of course, I realized soon enough that it had much more to do with his financial situation than it did with Lisa.'

CRISTY: 'Did he ever talk about those difficulties?'

INGE: 'Not specifically, no, but I got the impression he'd made some bad investments and ended up losing everything, or it's possible they simply ran out of money. They were incredibly generous, you see, and I have to be honest: there were some who took shameless advantage of them. They didn't see it, or maybe they didn't care, thinking there was always plenty more where that came from.'

CRISTY: 'But there wasn't?'

INGE: 'In the end, no. You could see it just about broke Romy's heart when she told me they had to let me go. They were moving out of the manor, she said, and it would either be sold or rented to help them make a new start. They gave me my fare to Vancouver and a small sum to help cover other expenses, and I always remember her saying, "I hope you don't end up thinking badly of us, Inge." As if I ever would.'

Meena held up a hand for Cristy to stop again. 'Were these two events with Tania Patricks' parents and the Kaplans happening around the same time?'

Cristy reached for a pen. 'We need to make that clearer,' she said, noting it down. 'Tania's parents' misfortune began at the end of 2021 – they died in March of 2023, so before Rudi and Romy were introduced to Lisa. This makes Don and Allison earlier victims, and as yet, we haven't found a connection between them and the Kaplans – apart from Lisa McIlvoy, of course.'

'The timing,' Connor put in, 'is actually less significant than the parallels, which is why we've edited it this way.'

'What I want to know,' Harry said, 'is how having a portrait painted led to what happened to them.'

'It was all about luring them in,' Cristy replied, 'winning their trust. A classic kind of confidence trick.'

Connor pressed play again, and they continued to listen.

TANIA: 'Mum and Dad had always been quite sociable people, but after they moved into the Porlock flat, they started shunning contact with their friends, and they hardly ever went out. I could tell they weren't eating enough, because they both lost weight and Dad's health was really deteriorating. He kept saying he was seeing the doctor, but we found out later that it wasn't true. No doctor had seen either him or Mum at all since they'd moved.

'It was about a week before they died that she told me she'd reached out to the Samaritans for help. It really scared me to hear that. I had no idea things had got so bad. I tried to make her tell me why she'd felt the need to call them, and what she said really chilled me.'

'You can't stop there,' Meena protested, as the recording suddenly cut off.

'It's the possible end of an episode,' Connor explained, and a moment later, the interview began again.

TANIA: 'She told me that Lisa had taken everything. I didn't understand what she meant. How had Lisa, a portrait artist, taken anything, never mind everything? She said it didn't matter now, that she and Dad had been very naïve, and she was sorry that there wouldn't be anything for us and the children when they'd gone. Six days later, Evan found them . . .'

There was a muffled pause as Tania blew her nose and Evan did his best to comfort her.

CRISTY: 'We can stop.'

TANIA: 'No, no, it's just hard to talk about sometimes, but I want to do it. People should know that this kind of thing could happen to them – to anyone. The way lives and homes can be taken over by scammers, the cruelty of it. . . They know what they're doing, some of them even look their victims in the eye, but they don't care. It's as if the people they're hurting aren't even human. . . Sorry, I'm getting worked up again.'

CRISTY: 'It's OK. It's perfectly understandable.'

TANIA: 'Thank you. I just - Maybe, if my parents had left a note, we'd have a better understanding of why they did it.'

CRISTY: 'How did they die?'

TANIA: 'Large doses of paracetamol.'

EVAN: 'We wondered afterwards if they'd been forced to take it, but there was no evidence of that, so we had no choice but to accept it was suicide.'

CRISTY: 'Were you ever aware of Lisa coming back into their lives after the portraits were done?'

TANIA: 'No, but she could have without us knowing.'

EVAN: 'If she did "take everything", she couldn't have acted alone. We're sure of it, but we have no way of proving anything.'

CRISTY: 'Where are the portraits now?'

TANIA: 'Mum told me they'd made a bonfire of them before they moved.'

There was a moment of solemn silence in the office before Cristy spoke again.

'Back to Inge now,' she announced. 'There will be drop-ins from me and Connor to signal the changes; we just haven't got round to recording them yet.'

INGE: 'I believe Rudi and Romy hung onto their portraits, but I can't say for certain. They didn't keep in touch with me after I left. I contacted them often, and it upset me a lot not to hear back. It wasn't like them to just cut someone off, and it wasn't as if anything had

270

gone wrong between us. I always liked to think we were close.

'Still, they'd obviously hit hard times, and there's never any knowing how that sort of thing will change someone. So, I let it go after a while, telling myself that they'd be in touch again when they felt ready. I . . . I should have tried harder to find out how they were.'

CRISTY: 'I don't think you can blame yourself for anything.'

INGE: 'Maybe not, but since I got the call from your researcher to set this up, I've been thinking about them such a lot; of course I have . . . Something that might be of interest to you is that before I left, I remember Romy telling me one day to change my passwords, because she was afraid someone had hacked into her and Rudi's computers. I asked who'd do such a thing and she said it might have been a friend of Lisa's. I was shocked by this; I'd never heard them utter a negative word about her before, but Romy put a finger to her lips and wouldn't talk about it any more.'

Stopping the audio again, Cristy said, 'So we're still assuming that Lisa McIlvoy and Casey Callaghan-Kaplan are one and the same person – it's possible neither name is real, because Jacks can't find anything about Lisa McIlvoy online. What's clear is that she used her talent as a portrait painter to get close to people whilst in their homes.'

'And meanwhile,' Connor continued, 'Lisa's friend, as referred to in Inge's interview, was working away in the background, using all the personal information she was feeding him – or her – to create some very convincing duplicate identities. Obviously, thanks to the increasing sophistication of AI, it's no longer necessary to go to such elaborate lengths to set up this sort of a scam . . . To paraphrase the CrowdStrike

271

report Weeks sent us: adversaries can authenticate systems or user accounts with stolen credentials obtained by information stealers. Stealers are basically Trojan viruses sent into a system to gather personal or sensitive data. It says here that they can also socially engineer a victim, and if that doesn't send shivers down your spine, then nothing will.'

'Jesus,' Meena muttered, glancing at Harry. 'Are any of us safe?'

'No,' Jacks told her. 'Scammers are getting more sophisticated by the day, and if big banks, telecommunication companies and government websites can be infiltrated – and they are, regularly – what hope the rest of us? Having said that, our net worth isn't at a level that would get us much interest. I guess, one of the upsides of being an average joe – at least as far as this sort of fraud goes. There are still plenty out there targeting the little man using very similar techniques and the poorer you are the more devastating it can be.'

'I hate myself already for even thinking this,' Cristy said, 'but the far more personal approach of someone moving into your home could have a stronger resonance with listeners than the faceless invasion of viruses and scammers.'

'Actually, something else I'd like to know,' Meena said, 'is why Romy's portrait was removed from the cottage but not Rudi's. Don't you find that weird?'

'Very,' Cristy agreed.

'Oh my God!' Layla suddenly cried when her phone rang. 'It's Bram Aalders. Shall I take it?'

'Of course,' Cristy urged. 'Stay quiet everyone. Layla, put it on speaker.'

CHAPTER THIRTY-SEVEN

'Hey, Bram, how are you?' Layla said, glancing at the others as she held the phone out so they could hear the call.

'Sorry I'm only just getting back to you,' Aalders said, his voice smooth, faintly accented and very friendly. 'It's been a hectic time, but I've finally heard from Mrs Kesinger, and she's keen for you to take a trip down memory lane.'

Layla's eyes went to Connor as he began to scribble a note. 'That's wonderful,' she said.

'She's only sorry she can't be at the manor herself when you come,' Aalders continued, 'but we have instructions to make you very welcome tomorrow.'

Layla's eyebrows rose questioningly as she looked at Cristy. 'Please thank her on my behalf,' she said. 'Did you ask about my friends who you met the other day?'

Cristy gave her a thumbs-up.

'Yes, yes, of course,' he said. 'If they're with you now and listening, she is happy for them to come too. She is excited that Haylesford Manor might feature in one of their podcasts. Incidentally, you mentioned when you were last here that your godmother was missing. Has there been any news of her?'

Cristy shook her head and Layla said, 'I'm afraid not. We're really worried now. It's been more than seven weeks.'

'That is most alarming. Are the police helping you to look for her?'

Again, Cristy shook her head.

'Not yet,' Layla replied. 'We're hoping they might come on board if we haven't found her soon. It's very odd for her to disappear like this.'

'Yes, indeed. I can understand why you're worried, but I am sure no harm has come to her.'

Cristy's cynicism showed as Layla said, 'I hope you're right.' She paused, caught Connor mouthing 'time' and said, 'So when would be it be convenient for us to come to the manor?'

'Would tomorrow afternoon work for you?'

Cristy held up three fingers and Layla said, 'Perfect. We'll aim for three, if that's OK. Shall we go to the gates where we saw you last time?'

'Yes, yes. Ring on the entry phone, and you will be allowed through. I'm very sorry that I won't be around myself, but I intend to connect via video link to make sure your visit is as pleasant as you hope. I shall enjoy listening to your stories of old times, and I know Mrs Kesinger will too when the podcast comes out.'

'Thank you, but can you tell me who'll be there to let us in? Just so we have a name.'

'Of course. It will be my wife, Amy.'

Once Aalders had rang off, Connor screwed up the note he'd written. 'He's obviously chosen to ignore the fact that we were going to land on him this afternoon, but that's fine. We'll go with his plan.'

'Jacks,' Cristy said. 'I don't recall you mentioning a wife when you ran a check on him.'

'Because there wasn't one,' he replied, 'only female mentioned was his "partner" Lisa McIlvoy, but I'll check again.'

Layla shuddered. 'I'm not sure how I feel about going into Haylesford Manor now, apart from . . . nervous?'

Knowing what she meant, Cristy said, 'I'll let Weeks

know what's happening so she can alert the people she has watching the place. Presuming they're still there.'

Clove said miserably, 'You're going to go without me, aren't you?'

Laughing, Cristy said, 'As I don't want to risk you abseiling in over a wall and setting off the alarms, you'd better join us. You can help create a distraction if we need one.'

'I'll base myself here,' Jacks said. 'Plenty more digging to do, and it'll be easier with no interruptions.'

'Are you planning on dropping an episode next Tuesday?' Meena wondered. 'Asking for Iz.'

Knowing her answer probably wasn't going to go down well, Cristy said, 'I'm not sure we can commit at this stage . . .'

'But the promos are already going out,' Meena protested. 'You can't do this to the sponsors . . .'

'They can't be a priority right now,' Cristy interrupted. 'I'm sorry – I know it'll be embarrassing, maybe even costly, but you and the sponsors have to understand that we're not fully in control any more. A lot's going to depend on this visit to the manor, and what Weeks is and isn't willing for us to share. Even the interviews with Inge Trevors and the Patricks could be too hot for exposure right now, given the mention of Lisa McIlvoy.'

'Who could be Amy Aalders?' Clove piped up.

'AKA Casey Kaplan,' Cristy added. 'What is it?' she asked Connor, sensing that something was bothering him.

Shaking his head, he said, 'We're obviously not going to find anything when we get to the manor; they'll already have made sure of that, so I have to wonder what actually is the point in going?'

Harry said, 'If you think you're walking into some kind of trap . . . Is that what you think?'

Connor shrugged. 'Hard to imagine, but I'm not keen on the idea of Matey Bram phoning it in. Are you?' he asked Cristy.

'I'm not sure what to make of that,' she replied, and

avoiding both Harry's and Meena's eyes, she added, 'but, look at it this way: you'll have me, Layla and Clove to protect you, so what can possibly go wrong?'

*

'And what did Connor have to say to that?' David laughed when Cristy caught up with him later.

'He threw something at me and got on with drafting the next pod, even though we're still not sure when we can go live again. Probably no time soon, given Weeks's feedback from the recent interviews. Apparently, she's hoping to make some arrests out of this.'

'At the manor? While you're there?'

'No. Our job is just to get Matey Bram's wife to give us a guided tour while we record and hopefully take some video and photos to pass on to Weeks. Now, tell me how things are over there? I hope you aren't regretting inviting them already . . .'

'Not a bit. And actually, there's some news you'll really want to hear. Matthew will give you the details himself when he wakes up – he's crashed out on the sofa now, I guess from exhaustion and relief. He got a call from his company about half an hour ago, the MD I think, and it turns out it was all a scam. Apparently someone from HR contacted the women in question and they confirmed that they hadn't sent the emails. Given the time, it seems like whoever was behind it must be related to your lot.'

'Jesus,' Cristy muttered, baffled and appalled, but most of all relieved that the horror of it seemed to be going away so quickly, and with relatively little harm done. 'No wonder he's passed out,' she sighed. 'It clearly terrified the life out of him.'

'With good reason – it could have been career-ending for him if it had got out, guilty or not.'

Knowing how true that was, she said, 'Well, I'm sure, once he's had time to take it all in, he'll have something to say about the knee-jerk reaction of his suspension. I know I would.'

'Indeed,' David agreed. 'It wasn't well handled, that's for sure, but apparently it's already been lifted.'

'Does Aiden know anything about it yet?' she asked.

'Not unless Matthew's told him, and I shouldn't think he has. I guess you realize what's going on with Aiden, don't you? Why he wanted to come here?'

'I think I do, but give me your take on it.'

'He sensed something was up with his dad and decided to stick around to keep an eye on him. Once he's satisfied things are OK, he'll head off to join his mates.'

Sighing, she said, 'You read that right. They're very close, those two. I'm just surprised Aiden hasn't asked outright what's going on. It's not like him to hold back.'

'He knows about Marley wanting a divorce, so I think he's putting it down to that and maybe losing his baby son.'

'Mm, makes sense. They all bonded with Bear when he was here for two months, him, Matthew and Hayley. I guess I fell for the little fellow too – and so did you.'

'Not denying it. He's cute.'

She smiled, and after a beat she said, 'You know, I'm not sure I like being here on my own while you're all over there.'

'Well, you know what to do.'

'Believe me, I'd be on the next flight if we hadn't arranged to go to the manor tomorrow, but I can't miss it.'

'No, I guess not,' he sighed, 'I just wish I didn't have such an uneasy feeling about it.'

'Will you stop,' she chided. 'You're as bad as Connor. Nothing's going to happen that we intrepid investigative reporters can't handle – just you wait and see.'

'OK, well, Rosie's waiting for me to take her to rehearsals, so I'll have to ring off, but don't think,' he added wryly, 'that I've forgotten you have something in particular you want to say to me. It doesn't have to be now – just know that I'm still waiting. And call me as soon as you're out of there tomorrow; I'll want to know that you're safe.'

CHAPTER THIRTY-EIGHT

The following day, as they headed north into Gloucestershire, Connor driving with Cristy beside him and Clove and Layla in the back, Layla said, 'Mum found another of Romy's diary-style entries this morning. I can read it out to you if you like. Or I can precis. This one's actually dated – 3rd May, so the week before she disappeared.'

Feeling an unexpected swell of tension, Cristy said, 'Give us the whole thing.'

Layla opened her phone, and after finding the right place, began to read aloud. '"*Lisa brought me a note today. I was at the shop, enjoying a few hours of calm and normalcy when in she popped, and I felt darkness encircling me. I'll have to do what they say. I've learned it's best not to argue. For her sake, as well as my own.*

'"*I'm afraid I've made the mistake of emailing Layla, again, asking for Cristy Ward's details. I should have remembered that all my messages go straight to him, incoming and outgoing. Rudi will be disappointed in me for forgetting. 'You don't help yourself, Romy,' I can hear him saying. 'Remember, dear one, they have control of everything, and in every way that matters, they are you. They have your home, your money, your emails, your phone, your voice, even your image.'*

'"*That is what Rudi would say, and as I hear him in my mind, I can feel his tears rolling down my cheeks and all*

279

the way through the cracks in my heart. I know I should never have let things get this far; I just didn't know what to do to stop it, and I still don't. I can't allow other people to be hurt, destroyed by what is happening, just to save myself."'

Layla's voice quavered, and she looked up, her eyes too blurred by her own tears to carry on for the moment. As the others sat quietly, Cristy reached from the front seat to squeeze Layla's hand, while Clove passed her a tissue.

'There's so much I want to say,' Layla whispered brokenly. 'I just . . . It's all so awful, and I'm terrified to think of where she might be now. What they might have done to her.'

Wishing she had some words of reassurance, Cristy said, 'Hopefully we'll find something out today.'

Layla nodded, and after a moment she took a breath and went back to reading from the notebook. 'Same day, 3ʳᵈ May,' she said. '"*Lisa will come for me soon, and together we will go to the manor. I've no idea if we'll stay there. Maybe I'll be able to come back to the cottage once I've promised to behave. Funny how attached I've become to this place now – I'm lucky to have it, and I try not to feel resentful of how they've stolen my home. It will only make things worse.*

'"*I wonder how Beth is. I think about her all the time, while trying not to think about her at all. I miss her terribly, and I'm sure she misses me. What would happen if I told her about Rudi?*

'"*I can never tell her about Rudi.*"'

Layla lowered her phone and turned to stare out at the descending mist. It was as though the world outside was turning as opaque as their purpose.

'Do we think that means—' Clove began, but Cristy shook her head to cut her off. Layla was clearly in no state to hear their theories right now.

After a while Layla said, 'Maybe we should have started

the notebook at the end, given this is the last entry, but even if we had, we still wouldn't know where she is.'

✻

An hour later, they pulled up outside the manor, and Cristy got out of the car to go and announce their arrival. Before she could press the bell, the gates started to sweep slowly open, telling her the cameras must be watching.

'OK, recording,' Connor announced, as she returned to the car.

Cristy picked up a mic and began to take in their surroundings.

CRISTY: 'So, here we are on a foggy Saturday afternoon in June, entering the gates of Haylesford Manor to head along what we know is a splendid tree-lined drive. We just can't see much of it right now. It's C.S. Lewis eerie, being shrouded in mist like this, as though we're being drawn into the heart of the unknown.'

CONNOR: 'Which we kind of are, of course. Apart from Layla, who's obviously been here before. Anyway, we've been told that Amy Aalders, wife of Bram, the estate manager, will be at the house to meet us, and he, apparently, is going to connect by video link. Weird, huh? But hey ho!'

CRISTY: 'We're catching glimpses of the grounds as we go: large, sweeping lawns either side of the drive, beautiful wildflowers clustered around tree roots . . .'

LAYLA: 'There's a lot you can't see from here – a knot garden, fountains, an orchard . . . An orangery . . .'

CRISTY: 'Wow, will you look at that! The fog has parted right in front of us, and there is the manor in all its glory.

281

It's actually made my heart turn over it's so lovely. We'll be posting video and photos, obviously, so you can see for yourselves that there's something truly magical about this place, in spite of all the windows being shuttered and wisteria no longer in flower.'

CONNOR: 'It's definitely not as big as I was expecting, although pretty big – creamy white, three storeys, with four tall windows each side of a colonnaded entrance – I think it's called a portico – a black tiled roof, half a dozen chimneys . . . It's the kind of gaffe most of us only get to dream about.'

CRISTY: 'So poetic. How does it feel being back here, Layla?'

LAYLA: 'I guess kind of surreal with the fog swirling around it. And it seems – I don't know – sad, but maybe that's because Romy isn't running out to meet us.'

CONNOR: 'Ah, but it looks as though someone's coming. The door's just opened.'

As they crunched to a stop in the turning circle, Cristy got out of the car, expecting Amy Aalders to emerge from the house to greet them, or at the very least to wave them in, but no one appeared.

Coming to join her, Clove said, 'Did you see anyone?'

'No,' Cristy replied, still watching the door. 'Hello!' she called out. 'We're here!'

Silence.

Clove said, 'Maybe Amy's having trouble connecting to Bram? But why would that stop her from coming outside?'

'Someone has to have opened the door and the gates,' Connor pointed out.

'OK, getting spooked,' Clove muttered.

Cristy looked around, checking to see if someone might be

282

approaching through the mist, but there were no movements, no sounds, not even an animal or bird – just complete and utter stillness.

'I say we go in,' Connor declared, and shouldering the recorder, he switched it on and headed for the door.

Cristy followed him.

CRISTY: 'Strange things are happening here at the manor. It seems like no one's at home, and yet someone obviously is. Just wondering why they haven't come out to meet us.'

CONNOR: 'Hello! Is anyone here?'

As his voice echoed around the entrance hall, the others stepped in behind him.

CLOVE: 'Wow, will you look at this place! Those stairs, and the fireplace, and the ceiling!'

Cristy looked up to where a cracked and peeling fresco of frolicking cherubs and winged angels was creating an illusion of floating art.

LAYLA: 'I remember when they first restored that, quite a long time ago. They always took such pride in it, but judging by the cobwebs, no one's been up there in a while.'

CRISTY: 'Do we know when the Kesingers were last here?'

No one answered, so she called out again, 'Hello?' Her voice resonated around the silent mezzanine, which was as full of closed doors as the entrance hall.

'OK, not liking this,' Clove muttered.

Layla shouted, 'Romy! Are you here? It's me, Layla.'

Not a sound. Nothing apart from the sharp creak of an old chest nearby that made them all jump.

After a while, Clove said, 'So what do we do?'

'I guess,' Cristy replied, still listening hard, 'we carry on with what we came here for, to take a look around?'

'And maybe at some point, Matey Bram's wife will show herself,' Connor commented, 'or Matey himself might decide to turn up.'

'Shall I try his number?' Layla suggested.

Cristy gestured for her to go ahead, and they waited as the call went straight to voicemail. Layla said, 'Hi, Layla here, we're at the manor, but no sign of your wife. Do you want to ring me back when you get this?'

Cristy turned to Connor as he said, 'It's not as if we broke in, and the Kesingers gave their permission, so I say we get on with it?'

Cristy nodded her agreement. 'OK, why don't you start us off, Layla? Tell us about this entrance hall and the memories it evokes.'

As Layla began, sounding uncertain, nervous even, Cristy assessed the paintings on the walls and climbing the stairs: some abstract, others traditional, several Pre-Raphaelite, a couple of Degas ballerinas (surely not originals), and half a dozen portraits of no one she recognized.

Layla was still speaking, her voice gaining confidence now, and out of nowhere, Cristy became aware of the scent of something flowery and light, so pleasing it actually made her heart lift. She glanced around, in search of the source, while already suspecting she wouldn't find it. This happened to her sometimes: she'd catch the gentle drift of a fragrance that invariably made her think of her mother and even wonder if she was close.

Interesting that it should come to her now, in this house that, as far as she knew, her mother had never visited. But she didn't have to be anywhere her mother had known to get a sense of her being nearby, and now she'd like to know what, if anything, she was meant to take from this?

She inhaled again, but the scent had gone, and Layla was still talking . . .

LAYLA: '. . . most of the paintings were done by friends of Rudi and Romy. "In the style of" or "influenced by" or total originals. I wasn't expecting to see them still here . . . Do you want me to describe them?'

CRISTY: 'Let's come back to it, and maybe when we do, you can share some memories with us of times you've spent here. For now, why don't we start opening some doors?'

Layla grimaced, clearly unwilling to go first.

Understanding her reluctance, given the strangeness of having no host – or none they could see (were they being watched?) – Cristy pointed to a set of double doors. 'What's in there?' she asked.

'It used to be Rudi's music room,' Layla replied.

Going to it, Cristy ignored the prickling of unease that came over her and pushed down one of the handles. The right-hand door opened, and a shaft of light from the hall fell into the darkened room. She gulped when a shadow appeared; it took a moment to realize it was her own.

The others laughed, and Connor went to unbolt some shutters, while Layla exclaimed in surprise to find that nothing seemed to have changed. She was clearly eager to share stories of events that had taken place here, concerts and recitals, piano practices and trombone solos – one of Rudi's favourite instruments. There had apparently been a lot of dancing and laughter in this room, parties spilling out onto the terrace beyond, while various entertainers entranced everyone with illusions and charm.

For the next half an hour, they moved from one room to the next, each one as full of memories as it was empty of people. Connor continued to record while Cristy only half-listened. She wanted to know what the hell was really going on. Why wasn't anyone here? Had Bram Aalders and his missus just deserted the place? Were they somewhere upstairs or outside, watching and waiting to strike out in some terrible way? Surely to God they weren't planning to set fire to the place with the *Hindsight* team trapped inside? That was too extreme, unsettling even to think.

Maybe Weeks's officers had made some arrests and forgotten to tell them. But even if they had, it still didn't answer who'd opened the front door.

'I sent a couple of guys up there to be on hand in case you needed them,' Weeks said when Cristy got through to her. 'You haven't seen them?'

'No,' Cristy replied, thinking it would have been nice if someone had told her before now, 'but it's so foggy out there it's hard to see anything. Where are they?'

'I'll find out and get back to you.'

Everyone was heading upstairs now so, keeping her misgivings to herself, Cristy followed.

LAYLA: '. . . and sliding down these banisters was so much fun when we were small. It used to feel as though we were flying. And you should have seen some of the staged grand entrances . . . No one ever really took them seriously; they just overacted the parts of nobility and knobheads, as my brother used to call them, to see who cracked up first. It was almost always Romy – she never could keep a straight face about anything.'

While Layla continued describing all the colourful and significant occasions she'd been a part of, leading them from one grand bedroom to the next, Cristy kept trying to get a

286

sense of why she was feeling so on edge when nothing so far, apart from their lack of host, appeared unusual or out of place. She glanced at Clove and saw that she wasn't alone in her unease. It was as if they were treading carefully without actually doing so, or counting down to something with no idea of how many numbers were left to go.

There was something forlorn and lonely about the place. An odd thing to think about a house, except they *did* have characters – everyone knew that. And Cristy was in no doubt this one had absorbed all the love and appreciation that had once been lavished on it. It was still here, a quiet and yet powerful force held invisibly within its walls, shadowed, in these moments, by a disturbing air of malevolence that might only be in her mind.

As Layla took them into an exquisite Japanese-style sitting room adjacent to the master bedroom, her voice began to fracture with emotion.

LAYLA: 'A friend from Tokyo . . . designed and decorated this parlour specially for Romy. She . . . loved it so much. She and my mother used to shut themselves in here for hours having their private chats. We'd hear them laughing . . . Of course, a lot of wine was consumed, and sometimes they'd laugh so hard that we'd all laugh too, even though we had no idea what was so funny . . . Sorry, I keep crying . . .'

Leaving them to it, Cristy backed quietly out onto the landing and made her way to a door she'd already spotted further along the mezzanine. Apart from the brass ballerina's shoe on the front she couldn't say what was drawing her to it, but something was. She put an ear to the wood panels to listen. No sound from within. Should she knock or call out before entering?

She pressed down on the handle. It wouldn't move. She

reached up to the ledge over the doorframe, and sure enough, she located a key. She inserted it into the lock and felt her heart skip as it turned with ease.

She pushed the door gently, and as it swung open, she realized right away that there were no shutters to block out the light. She hesitated, half-expecting someone to speak, to beckon her in or ask what she was doing there, but nothing happened, so she pushed the door wider and stepped inside.

The entire space was filled with easels, presumably holding paintings – every one of them was covered by a dustsheet. All sorts of other artist's paraphernalia was scattered about the place, from brushes and palettes to chalks, oils and acrylics, empty frames and huge, dog-eared sketchpads. Central to it all was a large table laden with various sized wooden canvas stretchers, and across the wall opposite the door was a giant mirror with a slim horizontal ballet barre attached.

And there it was again – the gentle drift of a fragrance so sweet and flowery that it could only have come from a fresh bloom, even though there were none in the room.

She walked to the table, trying to get a sense of what her mother might be wanting to convey, if it was indeed her mother – most would think her crazy for believing it. She even wondered it herself at times, but only after the scent had gone. It was still with her, and it almost never stayed this long.

She looked up at the mirror, caught her own reflection and then, behind her, the reflection of someone standing there, watching—

She swung round, gasping, too shocked to scream. 'Oh my God,' she choked. 'What the hell . . . ?'

CHAPTER THIRTY-NINE

Cristy looked up from the chair she'd sunk into, still dizzied by the sudden rush of horror that had unsteadied her. Her heart continued to pound, and she was actually shaking, in spite of now realizing that what had seemed to loom up behind her was a portrait. She'd thought it was Romy herself.

'WTF?' she muttered, pushing a hand through her hair.

Getting to her feet, she went to stand in front of the painting, searching the features, assessing its likeness to photos she'd seen. It didn't take long to understand why Romy hadn't considered it flattering. It was like her – there was no doubt about that: same hair, same shape to the face; even the graceful neck was Romy's – but the individual features seemed flatter, somehow, less defined, and there was an unsettling sort of deadness to her eyes.

Hearing the others on the landing, she called them in.

The instant Layla saw the portrait, she clapped her hands to her mouth. 'Oh my God!' she cried. 'What on earth is it doing here?'

'Apart from giving me the fright of my life?' Cristy responded dryly. 'I have no idea.'

Clove began tilting her head from side to side to get different angles on it. 'It's like her, but not,' she decided.

'I'm going to suggest we don't touch it,' Connor said, as Layla put out a hand. 'Forensics,' he explained when she looked at him curiously. 'You never know.'

'What's under the dustsheets?' Clove asked, taking in the covered easels standing like ghosts around the room.

'There's only one way to find out,' Cristy said, and went to expose the closest.

It turned out to be the portrait of a man in his seventies, grey-haired, sharp-featured and brown-eyed. No one they recognized, so Cristy moved on.

The next was of another man, around eighty, smiley and bearded.

Layla's phone rang.

Cristy turned, expecting it to be Aalders.

'Dad,' Layla told her, and went out onto the landing to take the call.

Clove and Connor set about removing more dustsheets. 'Ah ha! The man himself!' Clove declared, revealing an impressive likeness of Bram Aalders.

'I'm going to guess,' Connor said, standing back to consider a young woman in her early thirties, with short fair hair and electric blue eyes, 'that this one here is a self-portrait?'

Joining him to look, Cristy said, 'Is there a name on it?'

After checking both front and back, Connor shook his head.

'No names on any of the others either,' Clove confirmed.

Moving on to the last easel Cristy tore off the covering, and it took only a moment for her to turn cold to the core. 'Jesus Christ!' she muttered, unable to turn away from the sudden catastrophic meaning of this painting.

'What is it?' Connor demanded going to look.

Cristy grabbed the dustsheet and threw it back over the canvas. 'For God's sake, don't let Layla see it,' she warned.

'What is it?' Clove repeated.

Cristy shook her head and turned her towards the door. 'We're done here for today,' she said. 'Time to start heading back.'

*

The car was quiet during the return journey to Bristol, as if they'd been stunned into silence, which they had, apart from Layla, who still had no idea what had been uncovered in the studio, or why they'd left so abruptly. She was clearly in a world of her own after the call from her father, and Cristy couldn't help wondering if there had been some difficult news concerning her mother. She'd have asked if Layla's eyes were open, but they remained closed all the way to the office.

As soon as Connor drove into the car park, Layla said, 'I'm going to head straight home, if you don't mind.'

'Of course,' Cristy assured her. 'Is everything OK?'

Layla nodded and swallowed. 'I guess being at the manor kind of . . .' She shrugged, seeming not to know what else to say. 'I'll call tomorrow.' And climbing out of the car, she went straight to her own.

'So what's going on?' Clove demanded, as soon as they were in the office.

Cristy took out her phone. 'First,' she said, 'I need to tell you that I had a text from Katherine Weeks on the way back. Apparently, her surveillance guys found Romy's Smart car in one of the garages at the manor.'

'No shit,' Clove murmured. 'When was that?'

'While we were there. They must have been checking the outbuildings . . . Anyway, they also spotted an Aston Martin leaving the estate via a back gate minutes after we arrived.'

Clove's eyes widened.

Connor said, 'So they let us in and then scarpered? Did anyone follow?'

'Weeks didn't say, but with all the fog . . . They're inside the manor now, checking to make sure Romy isn't there somewhere. I directed Weeks to the studio, so they'll see what we saw and—'

'Excuse me,' Clove interrupted. 'I didn't see anything, apart from Romy's portrait, which was definitely weird. So what was the painting you covered up again?'

Cristy's phone rang. Glancing at it, she saw it was Matthew and said to Connor, 'You can take over from here. I'll be right back.'

Going to the meeting room, she clicked onto the call and closed the door behind her. 'Hi,' she said, 'Are you OK?'

'Fine,' Matthew responded. 'David told you the news?'

'He did – a great relief, and I'm really sorry you had to go through that.'

'Yeah, well, definitely not the best time of my life. Funny how you start doubting yourself even when you know you did nothing wrong.'

Knowing that happened, she said, 'Let's discuss it when you're back. Tell me now, did Aiden get off all right earlier?'

'He should be landing any time now. I guess he texted to let you know he was leaving here?'

'He did. So how long will you stay in Guernsey?'

Dryly, Matthew said, 'I've been made so welcome I wouldn't mind staying, but before I go back to work, I've negotiated some time off to fly to LA. I want to try and sort something out with Marley.'

'That's good,' Cristy agreed. At least it would get him away from the trauma he'd just suffered, although spending time with his young wife probably wasn't going to do much to cheer him up. 'So how are things between you and Marley at the moment?' she asked.

'She still wants a divorce so we can both move on with our lives.'

'And is it what you want?'

Sighing, he said, 'Sure. I mean, the marriage is dead – there's no point trying to pretend otherwise – but I don't want to lose access to my son.'

'No, of course not, and you won't. You just need to find yourself a good lawyer to make sure you retain some kind of custody.'

'I've already made a couple of calls. I just wish . . .'

'What do you wish?' she prompted when he didn't go on.

There was another pause before he said huskily, 'That I hadn't totally fucked up my life by leaving you. That's what I wish.' And as he started to break down, he ended the call.

Finding herself swamped by emotion, Cristy held off returning to the office. She needed a moment to assimilate and reset. She hated to think of him hurting so badly and to hear how lonely he sounded. In a way, it was as if his pain was hers, and she guessed with them having been so close for so many years, it was likely to stay that way for a very long time.

True, she'd hated him when he'd first betrayed her, almost six years ago, and she'd continued to hate him for a long time after, but there was no satisfaction to be gained from knowing how deeply he regretted it. There was only the sadness of all they'd lost and would never, no matter how hard he wished it, regain.

She blinked back tears and looked up when the door opened.

'We have an unexpected visitor you're definitely going to want to see,' Connor told her.

CHAPTER FORTY

Cristy's eyes widened with shock when she walked into the hallway, where a young woman was waiting, almost hiding herself in the shadows, but not quite. There was no doubting who she was; she fit the descriptions they'd heard perfectly: blonde, slight and very definitely blue-eyed. And her nerviness was as apparent as the small gap in her front teeth when she attempted a smile.

'I – I'm Lisa McIlvoy,' she said quietly, her voice burred by the hint of an accent. 'I need to talk to you—'

'Where's Romy?' Cristy asked.

'She's . . .' The younger woman's breath caught in her throat. 'She's safe. She—'

'Where is she?' Cristy repeated.

'Right now, I – I'm not exactly sure, but I can take you to her.'

Cristy frowned and watched McIlvoy glance over her shoulder, as if expecting someone to come in behind her. 'How can you take me to her if you don't know where she is?' Cristy demanded.

'Not now,' McIlvoy replied. 'Later. Will you meet me?' Her eyes were wide, beseeching and very definitely frightened. 'I've been gone too long already. I have to get back . . . Please. I know you want to help Romy . . . I can bring her to meet you – just say you'll come. Please.'

'Come where?' Connor wanted to know.

294

McIlvoy's eyes flicked to his and back to Cristy. For whatever reason, she seemed lost for words. She could only take breaths, short and shallow as she wrung her hands and glanced over her shoulder again.

'Are you expecting someone?' Cristy asked, looking past her, out to the car park. There was no one there.

McIlvoy's eyes went down as she shook her head. 'I should go,' she said. 'Please say you'll meet me later. I can get into Romy's cottage without anyone seeing . . .' At the sound of voices outside, she spun round, suddenly so tense that Cristy thought she might scream. It turned out to be people passing along the cobbled lane beyond the car park.

'Who are you so afraid of?' Cristy asked, injecting a note of gentleness into her voice in the hope of calming her.

Again, McIlvoy shook her head, almost as if trying to clear a thought. 'I swear, I don't mean you any harm,' she said. 'Just say you'll come. Ten o'clock this evening? At the cottage, and please don't tell Layla.'

As Cristy's eyed widened, Connor said, 'Why not?'

'Will you meet me?' McIlvoy pressed, still looking at Cristy.

'Why not say whatever you have to say now, here?' Connor demanded.

'I can't – there isn't time.' Her eyes remained on Cristy, as if she, and only she, could understand.

'How do I know I can trust you?' Cristy asked.

'I'm not sure how to answer that. I don't have anything to offer to prove it – just please be there . . .'

She turned suddenly and started for the door. Connor shouted, 'Stop!' and Cristy tried to grab her. She wrenched herself free, and as a trio of technicians bustled in from outside, McIlvoy darted around them and was out of the car park before Cristy or Connor could get to the alley.

'Which way did she go?' Connor cried, as they looked both ways, towards the harbourside and up to the Cumberland

Road, but McIlvoy had vanished. 'What the hell?' he growled. 'How could she get away that fast? And why come here to ask to meet us? Why not just pick up the phone?'

Exactly what Cristy was thinking. Still scanning their surroundings, she said, 'Maybe because phones can be bugged?'

'OK, but she just got us in person – no bugs here, especially not outside – so why does it have to be later at Romy's cottage, and not now, here?'

'I've no idea.' Cristy started back inside. 'She implied she'd bring Romy,' she said, 'but why on earth would we believe her?'

'And what the hell was that about not telling Layla?'

Cristy had no answer for that either, although it was sending her mind to places she'd rather it didn't.

'She looked scared witless,' he continued, as they entered the office. 'Maybe it was an act. Anyway, someone must have been waiting for her out there for her to have got away so fast.'

'In which case they'd have been up on the main road,' Cristy observed. 'Or, she just disappeared into the crowds on the harbour. Regardless, there's only one way to make sense of anything . . .' She checked the time, and seeing they still had a couple of hours in hand, she called Weeks's number. 'Katherine! It's Cristy,' she said to the voicemail. 'We've just had a surprise visit from Lisa McIlvoy. Please ring me back.'

Minutes later, Weeks was on the line, and almost as soon as Cristy finished telling her about the requested meeting, the detective said, 'OK, you did the right thing to bring me into this when there's no way of knowing what she's actually planning. Or if what she's saying about Romy being safe is true. So this is what we're going to do.'

*

Over the next two hours, there was a lot of back and forth with Weeks and her team, as Cristy and Connor received and noted instructions, occasionally queried them and made their own suggestions. It wasn't until they were in the car, heading for Gloucestershire, that they were able to reflect again on why McIlvoy had asked them not to tell Layla. Under Weeks's instructions, they hadn't, but they'd still like to know what the heck it was about.

'I've got a shitload of stuff going round in my head,' Connor confessed, 'and I'm not sure I'm liking any of it.'

'Same here,' Cristy admitted.

'Do you want to try some of yours out on me?'

'I would if I could articulate it. It's just left me with a really bad feeling. Have you spoken to Layla at all since? I mean, about anything else?'

'No, and I'm guessing you haven't either?'

Cristy shook her head and continued to search the gathering dusk, making sure they didn't miss the turning to Bellbrook. 'Weeks and her team should be there by now,' she commented, as they entered a dip just before the signpost.

'Jeez, was that a bat?' he cried, ducking as it hit the windscreen. 'Shit, it was.'

Cristy watched it flutter into the trees and felt the darkening shadows of night closing in on them as they approached the hamlet. Everything was so still, no sign of another living soul. It was starting to feel beyond eerie, and not even the knowledge that Weeks and her team were already out there somewhere made it better.

'Christ!' she gasped suddenly, as a figure loomed out of the darkened hedgerows to step into the road.

'No, Weeks,' Connor responded drolly.

They were twenty or so metres before the cattle-grid, hidden from the cottage but not from the lake, where the water was so black and silent it seemed like a void.

Cristy's nerves sharpened as Weeks came to open the car

door. 'Is everything OK?' Cristy asked, keeping her voice low. This hadn't been part of the plan, for Weeks to greet them on arrival.

Weeks glanced briefly over her shoulder. 'Not panning out quite the way we expected,' she said, 'but nothing to worry about.'

She moved away as a black-clad figure appeared from nowhere to speak to her.

Unable to hear them, Cristy turned to Connor. 'Are you OK?' she asked before he could.

He smiled. 'I'm fine, but I'm not the one who has to go in there.'

Staring straight ahead again, she said, 'Why do I have a feeling that Lisa won't be there? It's going to be Bram Aalders, isn't it?'

Connor didn't argue.

'Question is, how dangerous is he?'

'He's a scammer, not a killer.'

Cristy's heart thudded a beat. 'Rudi,' she reminded him. 'And who knows what Bram will do if he thinks he's about to be taken down.'

'Weeks is here. And her guys will all be armed – certain of it.'

Not much reassurance in that; if anything, it made things worse.

'Are you sure you want to go through with it?' he asked.

She was and wasn't. If it did turn out to be some sort of trap, the hell did she want to get caught in the crossfire . . . But it was why Weeks and her team had purposefully got here early: not only to set up visual and audible surveillance, but to plant themselves close by and out of sight, ready to act at a split second's notice.

Catching the detective signalling her to come forward, she swallowed her nerves and got out of the car.

'We've got everything covered,' Weeks told her, 'so no

need for a wire . . .' She broke off, pressing a finger to one ear as a message came through. 'Great. Good!' To Cristy, she said, 'Something kicking off a few miles from here.'

'To do with this?' Cristy asked.

Weeks was already heading for the cottage.

After casting a glance back to Connor, Cristy followed.

'Yeah, do it,' Weeks was saying, as they reached the front door, apparently still speaking to the person in her ear. Turning to Cristy, she said, 'We'll be right outside, hanging on every word,' and pushing the door open, she gestured for Cristy to go ahead.

Feeling suddenly rushed and unprepared, Cristy started to protest, but Weeks was already turning away.

Telling herself she could do this, Cristy took a steadying breath and stepped into the kitchen.

Immediately and confusingly, she caught the faintest drift of the familiar fragrance she treasured so dearly. Her mother, there . . . and then gone. A warning, or a reassurance?

Then she heard a male voice singing softly: Leonard Cohen's 'Hallelujah'.

She looked around, hardly breathing, so tense she'd stopped moving. Her heart contracted with shock as a shadowy figure got up from the sofa.

It was bizarrely like seeing a ghost come to life. The woman she'd begun to know so well and yet still didn't know at all was right here in front of her, and for a fleeting moment, she felt unsteadied, as if she'd lost contact with her senses.

'Hello, my dear,' Romy said, coming forward to take both her hands.

CHAPTER FORTY-ONE

This was the first time Cristy had heard Romy's actual voice, and she was aware that the fake recordings still seemed to be skewing her perception, making her suspicious when there was no need to be. That was what fakery did, she realized: distort and disrupt belief in certainty even when it couldn't be denied.

'Rudi and I are big fans,' Romy told her. 'He'd be so happy to see you. Thank you for coming.'

Still trying to ground herself, Cristy tried not to squeeze the delicate fingers too hard in hers. 'It's good to meet you,' she said. 'I admit there were times when I feared I wouldn't.'

Romy showed no surprise at the comment, simply gave a small nod of understanding. 'Rudi wanted to ask for your help,' she told her. 'I emailed Layla . . .' She shook her head slowly. 'Gosh, it seems such a long time ago now . . .'

Cristy watched her, still absorbing the fact that she was actually here, that Weeks must have known it but had been too distracted to tell her. She thought of Lisa McIlvoy, her nervousness and the way she'd suddenly fled. Where was she now?

Did it matter?

'Will you have a drink with me?' Romy asked. 'There's some very good brandy, one of Rudi's favourites.'

'I'd like that,' Cristy said, feeling she'd probably never needed one more. 'Thank you.'

Romy directed her to a sofa, and Cristy noticed that a decanter and two glasses had already been set on the coffee table. 'I hoped you'd say yes,' Romy said and sat down to pour.

When they both had a generous shot each, Romy raised hers and said, 'Thank you again for coming, and for trying to help Layla. It was comforting to hear that she and Beth had you to lean on.' She glanced up, and Cristy followed her eyes to a camera indiscreetly positioned in front of the hearth, angled in a way to capture them both.

'I told Detective Inspector Weeks that I don't mind this being recorded,' Romy said, and added in a faintly distracted way, 'she was quite surprised earlier, when she found me here instead of Lisa.' She turned back to Cristy. 'Don't worry. We guessed you'd inform the police, and it's fine; they have to be involved. Lisa understood that. I'm afraid they might already have arrested her.'

As Cristy struggled again to understand, even to know what to say, she took another gulp of her drink. It seemed a lot had happened in the last hour that she sorely needed to catch up on.

'We had a nice little chat, the detective and I,' Romy said, 'but by the time I've finished telling you everything – she's very happy for me to do that, by the way – you'll understand why you won't be able to use the recording for a podcast.'

Cristy simply looked at her, not thinking about *Hindsight* now, only of how disorientatingly compromised her sense of reality still seemed.

Romy's eyes drifted, and as she touched a hand to her head, Cristy said, 'Are you OK?'

Romy nodded. 'Just tired and desperate for all this to end.' Her smile was so faint that it wasn't a smile at all. 'The only way it can,' she said, 'is for something truly awful to happen, and there's been so much already . . .' Her eyes went to Rudi's portrait, then closed as if it hurt simply to look at him. 'Layla has always been so special to me,' she said. 'And Beth, of course.'

Cristy heard herself saying, 'You mean the world to them too.'

Romy nodded, blinked and took a sip of her drink. 'Rudi will want some of this when he gets here,' she said.

When he gets here?

'Of course he won't be coming, but I like to pretend sometimes that none of this has happened, that I'm just waking up from a bad dream.'

Understanding, even without knowing the full story, Cristy said gently, 'Will it help if I tell you that I think I know how you met Lisa McIlvoy?'

Romy's eyes came to hers, seeming both puzzled and hopeful, as if Cristy might somehow have the power to change it all simply by knowing.

'It was Barry who introduced you, wasn't it?' Cristy said. 'Beth's son, Layla's brother.'

Romy's face was so pale, so ghostly even, it was as if she might fade away. 'How do you know?' she asked hoarsely.

'I've had my suspicions for a couple of weeks – when we interviewed him, he knew that Casey Callaghan was female, before being told. It could have been a lucky guess or assumption, but then we found his painting at the manor.'

Romy turned to look at her husband's portrait again. 'You're right,' she said. 'Barry introduced us to her at one of our parties, just over a year ago, but I want you to know that she isn't to blame. She's . . . I guess you could say that she's a victim of all this too.'

'In what way?'

Instead of answering, Romy leaned forward to top up her drink, although she'd barely touched what was already in her glass. 'I've had a lot of time to think about this,' she said, putting the decanter down again, 'and I see now, in a way I didn't before, that it all comes down to neglect in the end. For Lisa, and for Barry.'

When she didn't continue, Cristy said gently, 'Tell me.'

'Yes, yes, I will. I've written it all down – it might make more sense on the page when I had so much more time to think before putting it into words – but I will tell you now. That way, the police will have a full statement in my own hand and in a video recording. I'm sorry that you won't be able to use it, but I think, by the time I've finished, you will understand why.'

Fairly certain that she already understood – at least some of it – Cristy said, 'I won't be doing anything to make things any harder for you.'

Romy's eyes came gratefully to hers, and as they filled with tears, she took a tissue from her sleeve and dabbed them.

'As far – as far as I know,' she began haltingly, 'Barry met Bram Aalders online. It's what Lisa told me, and I've no reason to doubt it. Anyway, it hardly matters how they met; it's what they did that counts. I still don't understand the methods they used, how they were able to manipulate and clone our accounts . . . I'm simply not well-versed enough in these things. I only know that we didn't fully realize what was going on until it was too late.

'Even then, we had no idea that Barry was involved, or Lisa, and we'd never met Bram, so we couldn't have known it was him who'd taken control of our . . . our lives. All we knew was that things were happening we simply didn't understand. Instructions were being given to brokers that Rudi hadn't provided himself, but they conformed to his normal activity, so no alarms were raised at the broker's end. Funds were transferred out of our accounts to others that had been set up in our names but that we had no access to.

'It was all very organized, but for us terribly confusing. We could see details of transfers being made to Rudi Kaplan, but we couldn't find out how to get into the new accounts.

Every time Rudi contacted someone to ask for advice or information, he was assured everything was happening according to his specific requests, and proof was provided. He was made to feel as if he was losing his mind, and I have to admit, we thought for a while that he might be.

'I wish I could say it all came clear a few weeks after Lisa left, when she turned up out of the blue one day with Bram Aalders. Even when he told us, quite openly, that he'd changed all our passwords and taken control of everything, we still didn't fully realize the extent of his reach or the kind of power he had over us. That only came when we tried to contact the police and every call we made went straight to Aalders. He'd taken over our phones as well as our computers. We realized we had to go to the authorities in person, but when we went to the car, we found him barring the way. He didn't turn violent, not then . . .' She pressed a hand to her mouth, gave a fast, shallow breath and pushed herself on.

'Rudi tried so hard to stand up to him, but we soon realized we were trapped in our own home. Bram Aalders was quite openly running our emails, our social media accounts, our credit cards, Rudi's entire portfolio – he was even paying our taxes to make sure no alarms were raised on that front. It was – is – a very complex operation that I still don't fully understand, and I doubt I ever will, but we felt sure that a much bigger organization had to be involved, some truly awful predators that we couldn't see or even name. We only knew that Aalders was a part of it. To them – to him – we were, I suppose, like a gift that kept on giving. And as long as they were operating in our names, using our accounts and businesses to generate funds for their own purposes, it was necessary for them to control our every move.

'I sometimes think it would have been easier if they'd taken everything and just disappeared, but that's not what happened. Maybe it would have eventually – I mean, they couldn't go on using us like that forever, could they? No, it was more likely, Rudi and I kept telling ourselves, that they'd find someone else to prey on and we'd finally be left alone. A lot poorer probably, but at least we'd have our lives back. How naïve we were – how ignorant of the way things worked, at least in their world.

'Have I already told you that there were devices all over the manor picking up our conversations, so that Aalders would know if we were planning some sort of escape? Of course, we kept trying to send texts and iMessages to our friends and Rudi's financial advisers, but everything was set up to go straight to Aalders. He even showed us emails he'd sent on our behalf, responding to friends, turning down invitations due to diary conflicts, or just keeping in touch. He played us recordings of Rudi leaving instructions for his brokers. It sounded so like Rudi that even *I* wouldn't have known it wasn't him if they'd been played to me any other way.

'It was a terrible and terrifying time. Hearing and seeing ourselves in some sort of parallel existence – you can't imagine what it's like. Aalders seemed to have no conscience about what he was doing, and we started to feel as though we were being buried alive, submerged in something so awful it might actually erase us altogether so only our replicated selves existed.

'You might think that was bad enough, but then things got even worse. So bad in fact that I truly thought one, or both of us, might have some kind of breakdown.'

Long minutes ticked quietly by as Romy gazed into an abyss of memory. Cristy's heart ached when she thought of the kind of nightmare Romy had experienced, one nobody in a normal world could even imagine, much less be prepared for or know how to deal with.

'It was Barry – our Barry – who told us we had to leave the manor,' she eventually said, clearing the hoarseness from her throat. 'We hadn't seen him since the party when he'd introduced Lisa in the May. It was September by now, and I

305

remember how pleased and hopeful we were when he turned up that day. Neither of us imagined he knew anything about Lisa's other side, or indeed about Bram Aalders; we felt sure he'd find a way to help us as soon as he found out.

'But then we realized what he was saying . . . We could hardly believe it. It was so shocking, so terrible that I had to cover my ears.' She did this now, as if the words were echoing through them again. 'He told us that if we didn't follow the instructions laid out for us by Bram Aalders . . .' She caught her breath. 'He explained how easy it would be for Aalders to make up accusations against our friends that could devastate their lives – and everything would look as though it was coming from us. We had absolutely no understanding of the technology involved, but we knew it was possible because we'd seen enough already to know what harm could be done.'

Cristy realized that Rudi's letter apologizing to Theo Crush must have been a part of the deceit, that the threats made against Crush – whatever they were – had probably never actually been sent, only shown to Rudi. She could only feel sickened by the cruelty involved. How many more letters and threats like it had there been? How tormented and stricken poor Rudi must have felt to have his innate kindness and respect for others used against him in such an evil way.

Romy was still speaking. 'This was when we woke up to the fact that Barry – the boy we'd known since his birth – was a part of this terrible thing. *He* had led Bram Aalders to our door. Of course, I threatened to tell his parents what he was doing, but he told me – *he told me* – that I'd do everything in my power to protect his mother while she was in such a vulnerable state. He was right, of course. How could I tell her that her precious son was a fraudster, a cheat, someone who'd got caught up in some dreadful scheme to terrorize and impersonate people he'd known all his life? What parent would want to know that about their child?

'Now, with the benefit of hindsight, I can see in a way I couldn't at the time, that even he probably didn't know the extent to which he was being used, manipulated, taken for a fool even – but he came to know later; I'm sure of that.

'Anyway, we ended up agreeing to leave our home. They were going to rent the place out, we were told, and take the proceeds. We thought, once we were out of the manor, it would be much easier to contact the police. Unfortunately, that didn't turn out to be the case. They couldn't risk us exposing them, so the threats to create chaos and hardship for our friends continued . . . We saw letters claiming to have proof that Rudi was an embezzler and that I had stolen from charities . . . Goodness, the things they made up about us . . .'

'Was Barry involved in these letters?' Cristy asked.

Romy swallowed dryly. 'I think so. Of course, I didn't want to believe it, I still don't, but he's a very mixed up and misguided soul . . .'

Cristy pictured the redheaded young man with navy eyes and scruffy beard, his easy insouciance and willingness to talk to them, the convincing front that hadn't betrayed even a hint of his part in Romy's disappearance. She realized now that all the information he'd gained about their investigation had come from Layla, or from her.

He'd known how she and Connor were thinking virtually every step of the way, how much they'd uncovered, who they were intending to speak to next, even where they were planning to go. Everything, right up to when they'd contacted the police. So this was why Lisa McIlvoy had instructed them to say nothing to Layla.

Romy was gazing at Rudi's portrait again, as if, Cristy thought, she was taking energy or even guidance from the man himself.

'Once we came to this cottage,' she said, 'we didn't see them often, hardly at all in fact, but we knew we were being monitored. We could feel their presence like they were ghouls in the shadows. Of course, there were opportunities for us to raise the alarm, but we needed to be certain that when we did, no one was going to get hurt or ruined in whatever chaos followed. We still hadn't suffered any physical harm, but the threat of it, our certainty of it, was always there.

'Lisa acted as a kind of go-between when it was necessary. She entered through the back so as not to be seen, and it soon became clear that she was almost as upset as we were about what was happening. She was racked with guilt for having got close to us in order to provide Aalders with an account of our day-to-day routines, of who our closest friends were – obviously, they already knew about Beth and Johnny from Barry – and to provide a general picture on how tech-savvy we were – which of course, we weren't at all. She hated herself for what she'd done, and was continuing to do, but that monster, Aalders, has such a hold over her . . .

'He bullies and abuses her in ways most of us wouldn't stand for, but as we know, some women – and she's one of them, I'm afraid – find it very hard to break free of their tormentors. She's trying now . . . It was her idea to come to see you earlier . . . She'd have rung, but she was too afraid her calls were being listened to, so she risked driving all the way to Bristol. She couldn't be away for long without having to explain where she'd been; that's why she wouldn't, couldn't, talk to you then.

'To be honest, I didn't think she'd have the courage to go through with it, but thankfully she did. Another very mixed up and damaged soul . . . Talented, certainly, and in a way quite attached to me now, but she's tragically vulnerable and very easily manipulated by the Bram Aalders of this world.

'Anyway, from the moment she returned from seeing you, I was afraid she might end up telling him what she'd done. Mercifully, she didn't, and you had the good sense to involve Detective Weeks. A necessary step in case Lisa *had* told Aalders and he was waiting when you got here.'

Thankful it hadn't gone that way, Cristy said, 'So how did you get here this evening?'

'Lisa brought me, dropped me at the top of the hill behind and drove off again. I'd hoped to convince her to stay, but she wouldn't. So I walked down through the trees and was met by one of Detective Weeks's team in the garden. It was quite startling at first, but of course a big relief when I realized who he was.'

Imagining the scene – a burly stranger stepping out of the shadows, maybe even holding a firearm – Cristy almost felt her own heart contract. 'And what about Barry?' she asked. 'Where is he now?'

Romy took a breath and let it out slowly. 'I haven't seen him for a while, so I'm afraid I don't know for certain where he is.'

Cristy nodded, and decided his location might not be important for the moment. 'Do you have any idea why he did this to you?' she asked. 'I mean, apart from the money.' It seemed so much more spiteful, even vengeful, than that.

'I'm afraid the why,' Romy said shakily, 'is yet another heartbreaking aspect of it all. Goodness, there are so many, but oh dear, oh dear, the complexities of the human mind, the tricks it plays on us, the things we tell ourselves, believe of others . . . I have no proof, of course, that his misdeeds have backfired on him horribly, but I'm fairly certain they have.'

'Meaning?'

Her hand shook a little as she lifted it to her head and let it drop again. 'As I mentioned earlier, I think he's almost certainly realized by now that he's a victim too, but it's too late to go back. He's unable to escape these predators out of fear of what they might do to him, or us, or his mother. I'm not sure who I'm trying to keep safe any more: him or Beth. Actually, it's both of course, because when all is said and done, I can't allow any harm to come to him, even though you might think he deserves it.'

She leaned forward, picked up her brandy and, after taking a sip said, 'Let me tell you a little something about Barry. It might help to explain things, or at least to cast a new light on them for you.'

Intrigued to hear more, and hoping that the police outside had allowed Connor to listen in, Cristy waited for her to go on.

'He was never an easy boy to understand,' Romy began, glancing down at her clenched hands as though not quite comfortable with what she was saying, while determined to do it. 'Beth will tell you herself that he always had a . . . problematic way with him. He was often destructive as a child, could fly into a rage at the drop of a hat, and he never made friends easily, which was hard to watch when you could see that all he really wanted was to be included. The trouble was: he had to win, to be the best, to make everyone else feel small . . . He was vindictive and derisive of others – not all the time, but it was there, lurking in the background, ready to flare up at the slightest provocation, or what he perceived as a provocation.

'I don't know what made him like that, but he did seem to get better as he got older. His confidence seemed to grow, and he could be sweet and charming when he chose to be . . . He was always clever, perhaps not top of his class, but close, and he did well at uni. That was when the change for the better became more noticeable. He'd left home, of course, was living his own life, had girlfriends, was taking part in sports and other group activities.

'After graduating, he got a good job – at least, he had one for a while, but then . . . Well, I don't know exactly when or how he became involved in internet scams, but I believe it started out quite small time until he connected with Bram Aalders. Lisa told me quite recently that he'd told her he'd wanted to make more in order to pay for his mother's treatment. He had taken it upon himself to make sure she had the best doctors in the world and was included in any trials that might help improve or cure her condition. And actually, I believe that probably was his motive. At least in part.

'Of course, he knew that Rudi and I would willingly pay for everything if it came to it, but that would mean we'd get the credit for making her well again. What mattered to him – because on some level it's always mattered – was that he was looked up to, admired, seen as the great champion, the hero.'

She paused reflectively, as though still assessing the conclusions and whether or not they were correct. 'Looking back on it, as I have over these last few weeks,' she continued, 'I can see how conflicted he was even when he delivered us to Bram Aalders like lambs to the slaughter. I could tell he wanted to impress Aalders, that he was in awe of him and perhaps even then a little fearful of the "foreigners" who were driving things. That's what Lisa called them, but I have no idea who they are or where they might be.

'Anyway, I made the mistake of telling Barry one day that he was being used, that no matter what he thought or what he was being told, he was never going to get away with what he was doing. None of them were. He came back at me so viciously . . . It just seemed to burst out of him, how I knew nothing about anything, that I only ever saw what I wanted to see, I was blind to what evil and cruel people Rudi and I were, and how we deserved everything we had coming to us. He accused me of so much, going all the way back to his childhood, when he said I'd always treated Layla as my favourite . . .

'I couldn't deny it; she *was* my favourite. Not that I didn't care for him, because I did. The trouble was I did so much with Layla . . . She loved to dance, just like me. She was never happier than when we put on plays or concerts at the manor. During the times we travelled, she was so excited by everything we did, whether it was sightseeing or sailing, skiing, exploring places her mother and I had visited as teens.

'Of course, Barry was regularly invited to join us, and sometimes he came, but he always seemed happier to be with the men. I don't remember him ever complaining about feeling left out, and I just know Beth would have mentioned it if he had. She'd have wanted to put it right as much as I would, but now, mostly thanks to all this, I can see that the resentment, the hatred in him towards me and Rudi, has been building for years.'

Her watery, distressed eyes came to Cristy's. 'So, this is how he's punished us – me –for loving Layla as if she were my own and for neglecting him. I swear it wasn't intentional on my part, but that's hardly the point, is it, when he's perceived it that way and been so dreadfully hurt by it.'

Wondering how Romy could even begin to mitigate on behalf of someone who'd caused her so much heartache and harm, Cristy said, 'I take it Beth still knows nothing about what he's done?'

'No, no, and as far as I'm concerned, she never will. Considering how weak she is now, it would kill her, I'm sure of it, and that is why I say you can't use any of this in a podcast. I just want you to know the truth and why it matters so much to me that Beth doesn't suffer for her son's actions.'

Cristy was uncertain how that would be got around once he'd been arrested, and he surely would be when they found him. She watched Romy get up and go to the piano, where an old-fashioned tape deck had finished playing a while ago. She took out a cassette, turned it over, and the music began again. It was only when she turned to Rudi's portrait and gazed at it with such love and sadness that Cristy realized it was him singing, this time it was a jazz rendition of 'My Girl'.

'He had a beautiful voice,' Romy said softly, as she sat down again. 'He used to sing to me all the time, and we danced . . . Not so much in recent times, but I have so many memories to cherish.'

'What exactly happened to him?' Cristy asked gently.

Romy swallowed hard and turned back to the painting. 'I still don't know,' she replied hoarsely. 'I try to tell myself it was an accident, because the alternative, that someone came here and . . . did that to him . . .'

'Why would they?'

Her gaze returned to Cristy. 'They knew we'd considered coming to you for help. We thought we were so careful, not discussing it indoors, but then I emailed Layla, asking for your details . . . How stupid of me. How could I have forgotten that they were seeing everything? And blocking it, of course. I realized my mistake as soon as we were confronted with it.

'We were reminded of how much they could hurt the people we know if we tried to alert anyone to what was happening to us. They – Aalders – made physical threats as well, not only against us, but also against Barry. I don't know if Barry was aware of that, but obviously we couldn't allow any harm to come to him, in spite of what he'd done. Beth had only just completed a horrible bout of chemo. I couldn't put her through any more, at least not before she got the all clear, and we still had no idea if that would even come. So, when she and I went to Portugal to celebrate the end of her last treatment, I didn't tell her anything. I just worried about Rudi instead, being here all alone, and when he stopped answering the phone . . . I was terrified they'd hurt him in some way, so Beth and I ended up flying back early and . . .' She broke off and held her breath as she pressed a hand to her eyes.

'So you really don't know if his death was an accident or not?' Cristy gently prompted.

Romy shook her head. 'I asked Lisa, but she doesn't know either. Or she says she doesn't. I think what might have happened . . .' She took a breath. 'It's possible Rudi used my time away to try and square up to Aalders, to make a few threats of his own . . . We had an old prop gun that we'd brought with us from the manor. Silly really, but we thought it might offer some sort of protection if we ever needed it . . . I found it next to the bath when I found Rudi and without thinking, I quickly hid it. I suppose I wasn't sure what would be construed from it, and everything was happening so fast . . .

'Of course, it hadn't been fired because it wasn't real, but if Rudi had tried to threaten Aalders . . . I still don't know if that was what happened . . . Maybe Rudi just took the gun into the bathroom with him after he returned from his swim, and Aalders . . . Maybe Aalders didn't mean to kill him, just frighten him . . .' She inhaled shakily. 'I suppose it doesn't matter now what he intended . . . Rudi drowned, and there's nothing I can do to change it. All I can do is try to carry on protecting Beth and Johnny from the awful truth of what their son has done to me.'

Cristy let the silence run for a while, bound in the horror of what might have happened that day . . . A struggle? The fear that had made Rudi take the gun into the bathroom with him. Shock and terror when – if – Aalders had turned up.

Or had Rudi simply drunk too much and drowned?

She was taken by surprise when, out of the blue, Romy said, 'When you spoke to Beth, did she tell you that we knew your mother?'

Cristy's voice was soft as she said, 'Yes, she did.'

Romy nodded. 'And I expect she said something about serendipity as well?'

Cristy smiled.

'It's what this feels like,' Romy told her. 'Your mother, Helen, was there for me once, during the most terrible time. She gave me advice on how to distract myself from the worst of it . . . I've followed the advice for years.'

'We found your notebook,' Cristy told her when she didn't continue.

Romy's eyes came to hers.

'We thought – when we came across your own words

in some of the writings, we thought they might be clues, something to lead us to where you were.'

Romy seemed puzzled by that, then, apparently understanding she said, 'I'm sorry. If I'd realized . . . I didn't imagine anyone ever reading . . . They were just thoughts that came to me as I wrote – you know how they do sometimes, when they overwhelm everything else?' Her gaze drifted again. 'Dear Helen,' she whispered almost to herself. 'All these years later, her advice still holds good for me, most of the time, and now, it's as if she's sent you, her daughter, to help me out of the darkness again.' Her eyes were full of feeling as they came back to Cristy. 'You're so very like her, my dear. So like her I can almost believe she is right here with us.'

CHAPTER FORTY-TWO

It was past eleven o'clock when Katherine Weeks came quietly into the room to join them. They were shrouded in night shadow by now, only two small lamps lit each side of the hearth, while Rudi's beautiful voice continued to serenade them hauntingly, movingly from the cassette player.

During the past hour, after talking about Cristy's mother and what a lasting impression she'd made on thirteen-year-old Romy, Romy had gone on to explain much of what had happened to her since the terrible day when Rudi had died. She'd spoken softly, mostly coherently, although once in a while, the horror and trauma of her ordeal slowed her down and almost swallowed her words completely.

Cristy had mostly listened, occasionally guiding her to the many still unanswered questions, all of which continued to be captured by Weeks's recording devices. None of it was usable for *Hindsight,* but maybe they could put it into their own words, explain something of Romy's ordeal since leaving the cottage, how she'd fought the confusion and fear by filling page after page of another one of her notebooks with lyrics from her favourite songs.

'I have that notebook with me now,' she told Cristy, as Weeks came in. 'It kept my mind active and my heart strong to think of Rudi singing the words. Broken but strong, if such a thing is possible.'

They turned to Weeks as she said, 'Maybe it's time to finish for the night?'

Cristy looked at Romy. It was hard to tell with so little light, but she surely had to be exhausted by now.

Showing little sign of that, even if she felt it, Romy set aside her empty glass and got to her feet.

'I thought you'd like to know that three arrests have been made,' Weeks told them, as Cristy stood too. 'Bram Aalders, Lisa McIlvoy and Barry Cates.'

Romy's eyes closed as she put a hand to her head, taking a moment to deal with what Cristy could only presume was a profound conflict of emotions. Surely only relief over Aalders? As for McIlvoy, how complicated those feelings must be in light of the peculiar bond that had apparently developed between her and Romy during the past two months of Romy's captivity. And heaven only knew what she felt about her best friend's son, although there had to be a sense of relief on some level to know that they'd found him, presumably unharmed.

Finally, seeming more resolute than anxious, Romy said to Cristy, 'Beth is very sick, isn't she?' Before Cristy could even think how to answer that, Romy said, 'I'm sorry – I shouldn't have asked so bluntly, not when I already know. I can feel it, here.' She touched a hand to her heart.

Cristy could only feel moved by how much they clearly meant to one another. This was the connection that had allowed Beth to know that Romy needed help.

Addressing Weeks, Romy said, 'Is there any way to stop Barry Cates's mother finding out about all this? She doesn't deserve to die with it on her conscience, and that's what will happen if she's told. She will blame herself, as surely as I have.'

'You don't know if she's going to die,' Weeks pointed out.

'I do,' Romy told her, 'and she is.'

Cristy's throat tightened as Romy turned back to her. 'I

need to see her before she goes,' she said. 'She'll want to know I'm safe. I can at least give her that.'

Cristy didn't argue, nor did she point out the complications that were likely to arise when she tried to explain where she'd been and why. 'Do you want to go now?' she asked.

'Tomorrow,' Romy answered. 'You'll be needing to get home, and I will probably deal with everything better if I've managed to get some sleep.'

As they moved to the door, Cristy said, 'Will you stay here tonight?'

Romy nodded. 'Silly, I know, after everything that's happened, but I feel closer to Rudi here, probably because he's right there watching me.'

'In spite of what having your portraits done eventually led to?' Cristy couldn't help asking.

'Yes, in spite of that. Lisa isn't a bad person at heart; I'm certain of that. She's just weak and frightened . . . If you knew her . . . Well, you don't, and maybe you never will, but she's been through a great deal in her short life – the kind of things most of us wouldn't survive. Or that would turn us into victims, the way it did her. But, like I said, she brought me here tonight, so I guess we can say she did the right thing in the end.'

Having to agree with that, Cristy asked, 'Do you think Aalders would have let you go eventually?'

'I really don't know the answer to that, although Lisa told me that he started making plans to move on right after you and Layla turned up at the gates to the manor the first time and he realized who you were. Quite how he intended to deal with me . . . Well, thankfully, we'll never find out.'

Turning to hug her, Cristy said, 'I understand now why Beth and Layla love you so much, and I'm proud to know that my mother was there for you all those years ago when you lost yours.'

Romy hugged her back. 'I'll call Johnny and Layla tonight

to let them know I'll be there in the morning,' she said. 'Will you come?'

Surprised, Cristy said, 'Do you want me to?'

'Yes, I do. It seems right, somehow. Not to record it, just to . . . be there for us, if you don't mind.'

Deeply touched by this, Cristy said, 'I don't mind at all. In fact, I'll be happy to come and pick you up.'

'It's rather out of your way . . .'

'Doesn't matter. I'll be here by nine unless you want to make it any later.'

'Nine will be fine.'

Gazing into her lovely eyes, Cristy put a hand tenderly to her face. 'Are you sure you're going to be all right here on your own tonight?'

'I'm sure. And if I'm not . . . well, I expect Nula will be happy to come to keep me company.'

CHAPTER FORTY-THREE

After agreeing with Katherine Weeks on the way out that they'd catch up in the morning, Cristy walked to Connor's car to find him dozing in the driver's seat.

Coming fully awake as she opened the passenger door, he said, 'Hey. Are you OK?'

As she got in, she let go an enormous sigh, as though expelling some of the pent-up, emotion-filled tension that had built in her over the past two hours. 'Fine,' she assured him. 'Have you called Jodi? She must be wondering where you are.'

'She's good. Sends love.' He allowed a few moments to pass, watching her closely, clearly keen to do or say the right thing, while having no idea what that might be.

'Did you listen to any of it?' she asked, reaching for her seatbelt as he started the engine.

'The first hour or so,' he confirmed. 'Then Nula showed up and I was sent to distract her.'

'How far did you get?'

'To when Romy talked about your mother. That was kind of moving – must have meant a lot to you.'

Cristy smiled as she nodded. Yes, it really had, but she wasn't keen to discuss it right now, even if she could find the right words, and she wasn't sure she could. 'So there's still quite a bit to fill you in on?' she said. 'I guess you heard they've made some arrests?'

'I did. Apparently all three of them were found in some farmhouse near the Wiltshire border. Turns out one of the officers who was at the manor yesterday clocked the Aston's number plate on its way out. ANPR picked it up on the Cirencester ring road, and it was tracked from there.'

She nodded thoughtfully and reached down to pick up his workbag. 'Let's record a chat between us now,' she said, 'while the part you didn't hear is still fresh in my mind.'

'Good idea, if you're up to it. I guess there's no chance the police will give us access to their recording?'

'They might not be able to for legal reasons, but we can always try further down the line. Meanwhile, we'll have this.'

When everything was ready, they began.

CRISTY: 'OK, I'll start with where Romy has been since she left the cottage.'

CONNOR: 'It was going to be my first question.'

CRISTY: 'Well, mostly, she was at the manor. With the Kesingers hardly using the place, Aalders kind of took it over and moved her out when his so-called employers came to stay. For those short spells she was, to quote her, "in a large, musty-smelling place in the countryside", which I'm going to guess was the farmhouse where the arrests happened.'

CONNOR: 'Any idea *why* they held her? I mean, she and Rudi had been at the cottage for several months by the time he died, and they left her there after that, right up until the May bank holiday. So what happened to make them take her then?'

CRISTY: 'Apparently, she reached out to Layla again, asking how to contact us. In her confusion, and I guess grief, she forgot that it was what had got them into trouble the first time they'd tried. All their emails were being intercepted and read. So holding her at the manor was to stop her from trying again. Heaven only knows what they were expecting to do with her in the long term. Maybe we don't want to dwell too much on that, but I'd say it's quite possible all her money's gone by now.'

There was a thoughtful silence as they sat with that, both of them aware of how much of it might still exist in cloned accounts and investments, although the greater likelihood was that it had been moved on to untraceable sources by now. Cristy dreaded to think what might have happened to Romy if she and Connor hadn't got involved. The scammers had probably only kept her alive for so long because another death, so soon after Rudi's, would have set off all sorts of alarms. So by making it look as though she was alive and well, they'd avoided suspicion. What they hadn't reckoned with was the bond that connected Romy with her best friend.

CONNOR: 'I wonder what Romy thought we could do, if she had got hold of us?'

CRISTY: 'Expose the scammers in the way we ultimately are? You know, I think her faith in me has a lot to do with the faith she once had in my mother.'

CONNOR: 'From everything I heard, I'd agree with that. And let's face it: you have helped her.'

CRISTY: 'We all have, in our own ways, including Lisa.'

CONNOR: 'Well, I could take some issue with the last, but let's leave it for another time. Did she say how she felt about the arrests? Actually, I guess she realizes that now Barry's in custody, Beth will inevitably find out what he's done.'

CRISTY: 'I think she's taking that one step at a time. But

let's go back to why they moved her out of the cottage. Did you hear what she said about the note she was passed in the giftshop?'

CONNOR: 'No.'

CRISTY: 'It was Lisa who delivered it – no surprise there – and it was telling her to come to the manor to discuss how things were going to change. She said it frightened her a lot when she first read it, but then she started to hope that maybe they were going to leave her alone at last, and all she had to do was swear never to tell. So, she went, ready to promise anything just to get them out of her life, but that wasn't how it worked out. They kept her there, and every now and again, Lisa was sent to the cottage to get more clothes or anything else she needed.

'She didn't know her laptop had been restored to factory settings until I told her, but she assumes it was Lisa who did it. Lisa and Aalders knew *all* of the passwords, of course – so I guess Lisa must have added it after the reset to delay anyone finding out that the computer had been wiped.

'Incidentally, you got that they knew our every move because Layla was discussing most things with Barry?'

CONNOR: 'I did. So, talk me through Portugal. Did Romy actually ever go back after the time she spent there with Beth in March?'

CRISTY: 'No, it was Lisa who went later, using a fake ID – Casey Kaplan – in order to plant the luggage label. Romy could only guess, but she feels certain it was meant to send us off down blind alleys chasing someone who didn't exist, wasting our time, tying us up in knots. However, she also thinks it's possible Lisa was going to leave us a note when she went into the townhouse, letting us know where to find her, but lost her nerve at the last minute.'

CONNOR: 'Bravo, Lisa. Let's give her a medal. And the birth certificate?'

CRISTY: 'Same as the baggage receipt. They created a fake and got Lisa to go to the cottage to put it with the Kaplans' personal papers in order to fire us off in meaningless directions again. That's what she was doing the night Quentin, the neighbour, heard someone moving around, searching through everything; she was looking for the real certificates. And while she was there, she took Romy's portrait.'

CONNOR: 'Why?'

CRISTY: 'The answer to that is almost as pathetic as it's bizarre. Apparently, Romy reminds Lisa of her mother – or she wished Romy was her mother; I couldn't quite get to the bottom of that. Anyway, the portrait was a mix of them both, and Lisa wanted it. So she took it, assuming no one would notice, and hung it in Romy's studio at the manor, which, as we know, she'd turned into her artist's workroom.

'There's no doubt a connection of sorts has formed between Romy and Lisa during the past couple of months.'

CONNOR: 'I think they call it Stockholm syndrome?'

CRISTY: 'Mm, you could be right about that. Apparently, Lisa's mother never really wanted her, kept putting her into foster care or palming her off on people she barely knew. It's possible she even tried to sell her once to get money for drugs. She allowed all sorts of horrible things to happen to her, and like so many abused and neglected kids, she spent most of her childhood trying to please her mother so she'd keep her and be kind to her. It never worked.

'Lisa was – still is – desperate to be loved, and that's how Bram Aalders was able to take advantage of her. It's my guess that Romy treated her with more tenderness and understanding than she's ever had in her life. It'll be why Lisa tried to help her, first by letting her make the call to Beth, then by asking me to meet her.'

CONNOR: 'OK, makes sense, but if you ask me, Lisa never tried hard enough. I mean, it couldn't have been that difficult to contact someone to let them know where Romy was.'

CRISTY: 'It's easy to see it that way when you're coming at it from our perspective, but apparently Lisa is terrified of Aalders and the people behind him. The "foreigners", she calls them, apparently. I'm not sure that gives Weeks and her team much to work with, considering it's something they already know . . . Anyway, I'm sure they cut loose a while ago, leaving Aalders to sort out the mess he'd created here, and we all know how well that's gone.'

CONNOR: 'So what did Aalders actually intend to do with Romy before he took off himself?'

CRISTY: 'I've no idea, but I guess we can assume Lisa expected it to be bad, which is why she was finally able to get her act together and stop him.'

CONNOR: 'But she was arrested with him, so seems she still hadn't managed to tear herself away?'

CRISTY: 'Tragic, isn't it?'

CONNOR: 'I guess that's one way of putting it. Going back to the "foreigners". The big takeaway from it is that we all need to feel terrified of them being out there in the multiverse, injecting their bloody malware into our lives. Is anyone safe? Is there any way of stopping them? How far can they go?'

Sobered and silenced by the questions, Cristy let her head fall back and closed her eyes. It was too late, and she was too tired to get into the horrors of what could be coming down the line thanks to the malign use of AI. All she knew was that this one case probably barely registered on the scale of what was already possible, never mind what could happen in the future.

It was a while before she registered that Connor was asking how Romy had been when she'd left.

CRISTY: 'Exhausted, I think, but clearly relieved it's over. Now, her only concern is for Beth. She's certain she's close to the end.'

CONNOR: 'I'm afraid she's right. Layla called when you were in there. They think it's imminent, and they were desperate to know if there was any news, so I hope I did the right thing, I told her that Romy's safe.'

CRISTY: 'It's good that you did. Romy will probably have called them herself by now. Did Layla say anything about Barry?'

CONNOR: 'Only that they were trying to get hold of him.'

Sighing, Cristy let her head fall back again and turned off the recorder. 'Romy's determined that Beth never finds out what he's done,' she said, 'and it sounds as though she's going to get her way. I just can't bear to think of how difficult it's all going to be for her now, having lost her husband and her best friend within a few months of one another – the awful, unimaginable grief while trying to recover from the trauma of everything else.'

Connor didn't respond; there was nothing he could say to in any way ameliorate the truth of that.

'She seems so alone,' Cristy murmured, still picturing Romy when she'd left. 'The way you are when the most special people in your life are no longer there. Nothing, no one, can fill that space, and Layla will have her dad to consider.'

Connor cast her a knowing glance. 'It sounds to me,' he said, 'as though Romy might have you?'

Cristy nodded. 'I admit I'd like to be there for her, and I will be tomorrow when I take her to see Beth.'

CHAPTER FORTY-FOUR

The next morning, unsure of what the rest of the day might bring, Cristy phoned Weeks from the car while driving to collect Romy. It turned out that the DI had little more to report than the fact that Romy's abductors – that was what she called them – had spent the night in cells and were currently 'lawyering up', ready to be interviewed later in the day.

Next, she rang Hayley, who was still in Oslo and apparently not up yet; then she tried Aiden, who, given his failure to answer, was no doubt crashed out on a beach somewhere after a boozy night. She tried Matthew, and again it went to voicemail, so she left a message explaining she might not be able to take calls later, but that she'd try him as soon as she could.

Fortunately, David picked up on the third ring, so she spent the rest of the drive updating him on what had happened last night, until eventually they returned to the subject of Matthew.

'He's flying back to Bristol later,' David told her, 'and he's booked himself a flight to LA at the end of the week. He's already set up meetings with a couple of lawyers: one to give future custody advice, the other for the divorce – if it goes ahead. I guess we'll know more after he's seen Marley.'

'Well, at least the worst of his nightmares is over,' Cristy commented, slowing up to cross the cattle-grid into Bellbrook. The morning calm of the place made the activities of last night seem as though they'd happened in another world, at another time, maybe even in a dream. 'I'm here now,' she said, pulling up outside the cottage, 'so I'll have to go. Shall we speak later?'

'Counting on it,' he said. 'Oh, by the way, did I tell you I love you?'

Smiling, she said, 'It's OK, I haven't forgotten,' and after ending the call, she turned off the engine just as Romy came out carrying a flask of coffee, two mugs and a small picnic basket. Apparently, she was ready to go.

*

It was a little before ten-thirty by the time they pulled up outside the Cates's rambling old house in Pensford. Romy had dozed for parts of the journey – at least, her eyes had been closed – but now and again she'd talked, seeming to want to share what was on her mind, as if saying the words out loud was the only way she could unlock their hold on her.

'I miss him so much,' she'd said at one point, 'so very much that sometimes it's like I've filled right up with it and there's no room for anything else. Do you know that feeling when you can't even breathe, you're so full of love or happiness or longing or grief? All the years we spent together . . . More than forty. We shared so much: happy times and sad, wonderful and absolutely terrible, but mostly good. I'm still finding it hard to make myself accept it's over, that I'll never see him again, at least not in this life. That's how it's going to be for Johnny when Beth goes. Coming to terms with loss is maybe even harder than the loss itself. That's why I have to be there for him, and all this with Barry . . . It might, in a way, feel as though he's lost his son too.'

'Does Johnny know about the arrest yet?' Cristy asked.

'Yes. The police had already contacted him before I rang last night. Poor man was so confused; he could hardly make

329

head or tail of what was happening. Anyway, we agreed that there was no reason for Beth to know anything yet – not at all if we can help it, although of course she's going to wonder why Barry isn't there when everyone else is.'

'Do you know how Layla's taken it about her brother?'

Sighing sadly, Romy said, 'I didn't speak to her for long, but she's angry, shocked, upset – everything you'd expect.'

Knowing it was probably still taking its time to sink in, Cristy said, 'But mostly she was relieved that you're all right?'

'Yes, she was that too.'

They drove on quietly for a while, each with their own thoughts as they sped along the M4 towards Bristol, until Romy said, 'There's a lot to sort out now with the banks and everything. I don't expect it'll be as easy for me to regain control of my accounts as it was for Bram Aalders to take them over in the first place. That's an irony, isn't it?'

Cristy glanced at Romy, wondering if she was even capable of bitterness; she certainly didn't sound as though she was being troubled by such a corrosive feeling. She was, however, terribly sad; there was no mistaking that, and if she had a selfish bone in her body, it certainly wasn't activating now.

Romy said, 'I keep thinking about Lisa. Poor thing is probably terrified. Do you know if she's been charged with anything yet?'

'I haven't heard,' Cristy replied, 'but I'll be sure to let you know when I do.'

'Good. Thank you.' Then, 'Perhaps I should help to find her a lawyer? I know plenty, so yes, that's what I'll do. She doesn't have anyone else, and she needs someone on her side. We all do in times of difficulty.'

'What about you?' Cristy asked gently. 'Who's going to be there for you?'

'I shall be fine. As long as I keep busy . . . I've been thinking, actually, that I ought to do more to help women like Lisa. You know, those who suffer at the hands of abusive men, or in some cases, their parents. I can donate money, of course, when – if – I have some again, and I'm afraid I might not. Gosh, that's a shocking prospect, isn't it?

'Anyway, if there is anything left, I wonder if we can convert a couple of the outbuildings in the grounds at the manor into some sort of refuge? A safe space for abused women and their children. I know those sorts of places already exist, but that's no reason not to build more. I believe Rudi would approve of the idea. And I know Beth will, when I tell her. Of course, she'll want to be involved. If she was going to get better, I'd love to do it with her, but maybe Layla will be interested. She's very good with people, just like her mother, but of course, she has her own life to lead in Dubai. I wonder when she'll go back. Probably not right away. She won't want to leave her father to deal with everything on his own. I'll be doing my best to help him, of course . . .

'I'll tell Beth that when we get there. She'll want to know I'm on the case, taking care of things. I won't be gloomy about anything – she won't enjoy that – so I've been collecting up memories to share with her, ones that'll make us both laugh. We've laughed a lot in our lives, and cried, but mostly we've tried to have fun and do the right thing and be there for one another. That's why it means so much to me that I can be there for her now.'

Understanding how close Romy was to the edge, how hard she was trying to talk herself away from it, Cristy reached out for her hand and gave it a comforting squeeze. She wasn't surprised when Romy clung to it; it probably felt like a lifeline, which was what Cristy had intended.

They were still holding hands right up until Cristy turned off the engine and Layla came running out to tear open the car door and wrap Romy in her arms.

Glad to have a moment to collect herself, Cristy watched as they held one another so tightly it seemed they might never let go. They wept and laughed, touched one another's faces as if to make sure they were really there, and hugged again.

'I'm so glad you're safe,' Layla kept saying, over and over. 'We were so worried, and now we're so sorry . . .'

'Shush, stop that,' Romy chided. 'You have nothing to be sorry for. Nothing is your fault, do you hear me? Nothing. What matters now is that you put all your heart into caring for your parents, and I am here to help you.'

Not sure how much more she could take of this remarkable woman without breaking down herself, Cristy got out of the car and watched as Johnny came to greet Romy. She shouldn't be here, not really. She wasn't a part of this family, and yet the welcome Layla and Johnny gave her almost made her feel that she was.

'Beth is very keen to see you,' Johnny told her, as they went into the house. 'You know that we aren't telling her—'

'Don't worry, I won't mention it,' Cristy assured him. Then, 'How is she this morning?'

'Better, I think,' he replied, but his eyes didn't match the words. He clearly knew in his heart that there weren't going to be many more mornings; what mattered now was making each one count.

Romy went into the bedroom first with Layla, while Cristy helped Johnny to make coffee. As he seemed not to want to talk about his son, she didn't mention him either, until eventually he said, 'We're telling Beth that he's too upset to come, that he can't face it.'

Unable to imagine how Beth felt about that Cristy said, 'Have you spoken to him yourself?'

'Only briefly. He wanted me to recommend a lawyer, so I did. I suppose there'll be a lot of conversations between us in the future, but right now, I'm not sure I know what to say to him.'

Understanding that, Cristy said, 'Have you been told anything about possible charges?'

'No, not yet, although I believe they might come later today or tomorrow'. He glanced away awkwardly, showing how difficult it was for him to talk about this. 'Apparently, things could go better for him if he's prepared to help bring down those who were behind it. Including this Aalders fellow.'

'Does he actually know who the others are?'

'He says not, but maybe he's just too afraid to name them. Regardless, he still has a great deal to answer for, and right now I'm not sure what to do if he's let out on bail. I don't want him here, upsetting his mother, but at the same time, he's her son. She wants to see him.'

Cristy put a comforting hand on his arm, aware of how torn he must feel between the need to protect his wife and whatever fatherly concerns he presumably still felt for his son. Perhaps there was guilt too, for the role he might have played in turning Barry into someone who could behave the way he had.

They both looked up as Layla came into the kitchen, teary-eyed and clearly struggling not to cry any more. 'Mum would like you to go in now,' she said to Cristy. 'She wants to thank you for finding Romy.'

To Cristy's surprise and relief, the room Layla took her to was filled with sunlight, and the slight figure on the bed, though clearly frail and only able to breathe with assistance, still had a faint sparkle in her eyes and enough strength to summon part of a smile.

'Come closer,' she croaked, reaching for Cristy's hand. 'That's it – sit there, on the bed where I can see you better. Isn't she lovely, Romy? So like Helen. Do you remember Helen?'

'Of course I remember Helen. How could I ever forget? Our first big crush, until we discovered Davy Jones.'

Beth made a noise like a laugh, and her jaundiced eyes fluttered closed. 'Thank you for believing me, Cristy,' she said softly. 'You kept going when others probably wouldn't have.'

Knowing she didn't need to hear how close Cristy had come to giving up herself, at least at the start, she simply said, 'I'm glad I did keep going.'

Beth was quiet after that, her breath shallow, her eyes still closed and remaining closed as Romy began to speak.

It was a few moments before Cristy realized Romy was sharing memories of her and Beth's past at school: first loves, crazy adventures they'd been warned against but plunged themselves into anyway. She talked about their weddings, Beth's terrible food-poisoning on honeymoon, a time in Moscow when they'd all got very drunk and Rudi had pretended to be James Bond. They'd found it even more hilarious when he'd been expelled from the Embassy a few weeks later. She talked them all the way through the years, from Beth's children's births, to their many holidays together, to Rudi and Johnny's fascination with UFOs and their own short-lived obsession with all things psychic and metaphysical.

Though Beth didn't say anything herself, it was clear she was listening and from time to time, she managed a smile. At one point, a tear trickled from the corner of her eye and Romy leaned forward to dab it away.

Cristy was so moved by their inner-strength, not only for being able to share these end-of-life moments so stoically and even joyfully in a way, but in how ready they seemed to accept the inevitable, as if fighting would only make it worse. Beth wanted to go quietly, peacefully, and she could do that with Romy, Layla and Johnny around her.

It was time now for Cristy to leave.

CHAPTER FORTY-FIVE

ONE MONTH LATER

CONNOR: 'Hey and welcome to *Hindsight*. In case you've been wondering about the radio silence these past few weeks – we know you have, thanks to all your messages; please keep them coming – we're about to explain.'

CRISTY: 'As you know, the stories we bring you inevitably continue to play out long after the series is over, and this one, I'm afraid, is no different. It's called life, I guess, and the fact is that it just keeps going, and any best guesses as to how things might turn out often prove to be wrong. However, in this double-length episode, we are going to bring you an exclusive update on where we are now regarding the strange and deeply unsettling case of what happened to Romy Kaplan.

CONNOR: 'You'll have been hearing about it in the news, of course, but there is so much more to tell that you'll only hear here.'

As Connor paused the playback to make a note, Cristy allowed herself a moment to inhale the fragrant fresh air of their surroundings, while enjoying the heady contrast of the outdoors to the more familiar confines of the studio and busyness of the harbourside. This glorious place was, in its own quietly resplendent way, like paradise. The old stone terrace, home to a large mosaic-topped table where they were seated, was sheltered beneath a vine and jasmine covered gazebo. A freshly cut lawn sloped languorously away from them, flanked on one side by an intricate and colourful knot garden, on the other by a high, carefully tended laurel hedge. At the centre of it all, a duck and lily pond glinted and rippled beneath the tangled overhang of a weeping willow. Beyond, the horizon was currently hazed by wispy remnants of a late morning summer mist. It was heavenly, hypnotic; the Cotswolds at its finest.

Connor resumed the playback.

CRISTY: 'We're at Haylesford Manor today, Romy's true home, where she is now once again in residence. More to come on that later. Quite unlike our last visit here, all the doors and windows are wide open as if to welcome in the world ...'

CONNOR: 'Or to let out the ghosts that have no place here.'

CRISTY: 'In a minute, you'll be hearing from Romy herself. For now, we're going to play a recap of her story, including some police recordings, to bring everyone up to date.'

Connor hit pause again and adjusted his headset to release one ear, while Cristy glanced over her shoulder to see Romy emerging through the French doors of the music room, where dusty bands of sunlight were streaming over the instruments and lighting the shadows. She was carrying a large coffee pot in one hand, a small notebook in the other, and with her recently highlighted fair hair caught up in a jaunty bun, and her violet eyes seeming to twinkle, she looked, Cristy noted

336

with tenderness, the happiest sad person she'd ever seen. How was she able to put up such a convincing front, when inside she was still so horribly bruised and broken?

'Layla's right behind me with mugs and biscuits,' Romy said, as Cristy and Connor made room for refreshments amongst their clutter of laptops and script pads. 'I heard your introduction.' She grimaced. 'You're not going to make me sit through the recap, are you?'

Cristy laughed. 'Of course not. It'll be edited in later. Today is all about you and whatever you want to share with us a month on from your release.'

Romy's eyebrows rose. 'That's what we're calling it, is it?' she asked, seeming both perplexed and entertained. 'Yes, well, I suppose that's what it was. A release and a relief to finally bring it all to an end, at least the abduction part of it. Have you recorded anything about Beth yet?'

'We have something for you to listen to,' Connor told her. 'If you or Layla want any changes, just say and we'll redo it. Would you like us to play it back now?'

'While we drink our coffee?' Romy mused. 'I suppose so. Maybe we should ask Layla.'

'Ask me what?' Layla said, coming along the terrace with a large, fully laden wooden tray.

Going to take the burden, Connor repeated the suggestion, adding, 'But if you'd rather wait . . . ?'

'No, let's do it now,' Layla insisted. 'I'm keen to hear it. You didn't make it too long, I hope. We don't want to all end up in tears. I think we've shed enough for a while.'

Cristy smiled as Romy said, 'There'll be plenty more, I'm sure, but no shame in that. Will you do the honours, sweetheart?'

As Layla poured and Cristy passed around the cookies, Connor called up the link on his laptop, ready to play.

'Oh, I need to tell you,' Romy said, settling into a thickly padded chair opposite Cristy, 'Johnny rang just now and

337

asked me to send his apologies; he won't be able to join us today, after all. Barry's lawyer called last night, so that's where they are this morning.'

Knowing they'd get onto the detail of all that during the next couple of hours, Cristy said, 'Will Lisa be here at some point?'

Romy wrinkled her nose uncertainly. 'She says she'll join us, so let's wait and see.'

'My brother is still too ashamed to face you,' Layla informed them tartly. 'So don't let's count on him turning up at any time to do the decent thing and explain himself.'

'You're being too harsh,' Romy scolded. 'His lawyer is probably advising him not to go on the record with anything at this stage, and the same goes for Lisa, so I'm not sure how much she'll tell us if she does come along. But don't worry; I have full permission to speak on her behalf if you think it'll help.'

Cristy was still amazed by the bond that had formed between Romy and McIlvoy, while mindful of Connor's suspicion of Stockholm syndrome, one shared by Weeks and her team. She said to Connor, 'I think, after you've played the piece about Beth, we should go on to the other pre-recordings that Romy and Layla haven't heard yet.'

'Agreed,' he said, and after hitting a few keys on his laptop to line everything up, he checked everyone was ready. As the playback began, Cristy watched Romy's hand reaching for Layla's. She could almost feel their connection, the love that was going to help them through the grief and heartache they would share for a long time to come.

CONNOR: 'As I'm sure you'll remember, the first we knew about Romy Kaplan was when her goddaughter Layla came to alert us to the fact that she was missing. Layla's biggest fear at that time wasn't only for Romy; it was also for her mother, Beth, Romy's lifelong best

338

friend. Beth was dying and desperate to know Romy was safe before it was too late.'

CRISTY: 'The two women were as close as any sisters I've ever met, perhaps even closer. Beth knew in her heart that Romy hadn't just gone off without telling anyone. She *knew* something was wrong because she sensed it. She could hear and see beyond the videos we now know were fake to a reality she couldn't explain, only feel.

'In much the same way, after we found Romy, she *knew* that Beth didn't have much longer to live because Romy sensed it.

'Beth passed three weeks ago, with Romy at her side. Of course, the rest of Beth's family was also there, but in those final few days, Romy spent many hours talking to Beth, reliving with her all the good times they'd shared and promising to take care of everyone after she'd gone.'

CONNOR: 'Romy didn't divulge to Beth the most painful part of the truth of what had happened to her during her time at the cottage and afterwards, when she was held captive by Beth's own son, amongst others . . . It meant everything to Romy that Beth was never troubled by it, and in the end, she got her wish.'

CRISTY: 'Romy Kaplan is a remarkable woman by anyone's standards, and when you consider what she's endured this past year at the hands of truly malignant operators, and how she's coping now, your opinion of her can only grow.

'Every one of us here at *Hindsight* has developed a very real affection for her, not to mention a great admiration and respect. It's our hope that we'll always be in touch.'

As the playback stopped, Romy laughed at her own tears and seemed almost startled when Layla drew her into an encompassing embrace.

'I don't know about you,' Layla said, teary-eyed too, 'but I don't want to change a word of that.'

Using a napkin to dab her eyes, Romy said to Cristy, 'I think you're being a little too . . . kind about me, but I'm very happy to know I have your affection.'

Cristy smiled and thought fleetingly of her mother, who'd cared so much for this lovely woman when she was still a child. She wondered if Helen and Beth were together somewhere now, maybe even looking down on this. Of course, it was fanciful to think that way, but there was no doubt a swift glance up to the perfect blue sky made it seem possible.

'Before we line up any more playbacks . . .' Connor began, consulting his notes. He stopped, seeming uncertain for a moment, and looked over at Cristy.

Realizing what he'd probably just bumped up against, she decided to take it on herself and, turning to Romy, said, 'We have a couple of quite sensitive questions for you; the first and most important is concerning Rudi.'

Romy swallowed and nodded, her eyes going down as she reached for her coffee without picking it up. 'I think I know what's coming,' she said softly, 'and my answer – I have given it some thought, I promise – is that I don't have any objection to you saying there is some ambiguity around the way he died. I just don't want you to get into any trouble, legally, for mentioning it.'

Layla said, 'It's already out there that the police have reopened the investigation. Is there any more to add?'

'Not much,' Cristy admitted, 'but we could confirm that Bram Aalders is the focus of the new enquiries.'

Romy nodded slowly again. 'Well, it's good that Barry and Lisa aren't being treated as suspects,' she said, 'because I certainly don't think either of them had a hand in it. As for

Bram Aalders . . . It's hard to see how the police are going to prove anything with no witnesses and no body to examine. I'm afraid it's quite possible that no one will ever be held accountable for what happened to my dear husband.'

'At the risk of sounding vengeful,' Connor said, 'I don't have a problem with putting it out there that Aalders might very well get away with murder. At least the slur will be on him, that way.'

As Romy's eyes fluttered closed, Cristy sensed how hard this was for her, and said, 'Perhaps let's not get into anything like that at this stage. Leave the detectives to do their job, and if anything changes before we post this episode, we can always revisit.'

Apparently happy with that, Romy said, 'Have you recorded anything yet about the charges they're facing? Maybe we could listen to that?'

'Of course,' Connor agreed, 'coming right up.'

As he searched for it, Layla refreshed the coffees and popped back inside for a jug of iced water and glasses. Cristy knew she was here most of the time now and apparently had no immediate plans to return to Dubai, if she had any at all.

'OK, I'm going to run it from the top,' Connor said, 'so bear with. It definitely gets to the charges; we just need some background first.'

As the playback began, pulling in everyone's attention, Cristy tuned into the backing track of birdsong and bee hums and watched a trio of butterflies flitting and settling amongst a bed of lavender. A robin came to perch on the balustrades in front of them, its tiny head tilting from side to side as though it was listening. She immediately thought of Rudi and could see from the look in Romy's eyes that she was thinking the same – when a robin appears, a loved one is near.

CONNOR: '. . . So we're going tell you how our search for Romy led us into working with a team of special

341

investigators from the cyber section of the National Crime Agency.'

CRISTY: 'No, we didn't see that coming either when we started out on the series, but when we discovered that Romy's image and social media posts had either been digitally generated, or old ones had been repurposed to create an artificial pattern of activity, the police finally took note. The aim of these false posts was to mislead or reassure Romy's friends and loved ones that she was alive and well and there was no need to worry.'

CONNOR: 'You could say she, and all her accounts, had been cloned, so she now existed in two parallel worlds: one her reality, the other a virtual one that she had absolutely no control over.'

CRISTY: 'Romy herself will be sharing some details of her ordeal – the police are allowing us to use some of her recorded statements, which include the little she knows about the amorphous network of foreign internet scammers who basically masterminded the takeover of her life.'

CONNOR: 'The only known faces from this network – at least known to us; the police aren't sharing any information on the wider investigation at this stage – belong to Bram Aalders, Lisa McIlvoy and Barry Cates. You've probably already heard about them in the news. If you haven't, you can find headshots and bios of all three on our website, plus details of the crimes they've now been charged with. These include identity fraud, grand larceny, false representation, and false imprisonment. It's highly possible more charges will follow. We will, of course be keeping a close eye on things as they unfold.'

CRISTY: 'To quote one of our consulting lawyers: "these scammers and the pyramid-style scheme they're a part of have broken laws that aren't even on the statute books yet – something that needs rectifying without delay."'

CONNOR: 'OK, a bit of an oxymoron there, but he's right in so far as the capabilities of generative AI are growing so fast that the whole world is struggling to keep up with it.

'So, is this a cautionary tale for our times? You bet your life it is.'

Cristy's eyes moved to Romy as she shifted slightly in her chair. It wasn't possible to tell what she was thinking, only that she appeared to have eye contact with the robin as she listened.

CONNOR: 'We know that artificial intelligence is vastly improving our lives in ways most of us couldn't even have imagined a few years ago, but it's also making us so much more vulnerable to all manner of malign influences. Most of us have seen or heard about the way today's technology can put an innocent person into exploitative photographs and videos, but some of you might not be aware of how it can trick your family and friends into believing they're having actual conversations with you.'

CRISTY: 'Even some developers find the use of their inventions terrifying and are issuing warnings about how AI, if unchecked or regulated, could quite literally take over the world.'

CONNOR: 'All that is for another pod. For this one, we're going to focus on how it was used against Rudi and Romy, and how any one of us could be a similar target at any time.'

Noticing that Romy was starting to seem uncomfortable, Cristy raised a hand for Connor to stop.

'Is everything OK?' she asked gently.

Romy attempted a smile. 'Yes, I . . . Well, I suppose it's hearing it phrased that way . . . Of course, I don't imagine everyone is as gullible as me and Rudi . . .'

'You weren't gullible!' Layla protested. 'You were tricked and deceived in ways no one in a normal world could have foreseen. And let's not forget that you allowed a lot of it to continue to try and protect Mum. Which you did in the end, but honestly, she probably could have coped a lot better with the truth than you think.'

'Well, I wasn't prepared to take that risk,' Romy told her. 'We all know what happens to the messenger, and she meant too much to me to lose her. Or to hurt her. I just felt sure Rudi and I would work it out somehow. He did too, and I think we would have if . . . if things hadn't gone the way they did.'

Pulling her into a hug, Layla said softly, 'I know, and I'm sure you would have. I'm just sorry we didn't realize what was happening long before you lost him.'

'You have nothing to apologize for,' Romy said hoarsely. 'I'm just being a little emotional. I'll be fine.' To Cristy, she said, 'If there's more, I'd like to hear it.'

Cristy gave Connor the nod, and she noticed Romy's eyes return to the robin as the playback started again.

CRISTY: 'According to our tech expert, Professor Jared Grinner of the University of the West of England, what happened to the Kaplans wasn't even a particularly sophisticated fraud in tech terms. It's probably easy to see it that way if you're from his world, but from a victim's perspective, it can be absolutely devastating. Rudi isn't the only one we know of who lost his life in what could be related circumstances; there are others whose family you'll hear from much later in the episode.'

CONNOR: 'Professor Grinner will talk us through *how* the Kaplans' lives were seized in the way they were. He will not, however, be providing a masterclass in how to scam decent people out of just about everything.'

CRISTY: 'It would obviously be totally irresponsible to go into the detail of what they did; we just want to make you aware of how easy it can be these days for someone with the relevant know-how to take over your world in the way Bram Aalders took over Romy's, as the puppet of his invisible masters.'

CONNOR: 'Given the courts' current backlog, it could be many months before Aalders, McIlvoy and Cates are in front of a judge to account for their crimes.'

CRISTY: 'However, we're told that all three intend to plead guilty when the time comes. This means there will be no trial, which makes our podcast all the more relevant for the information we can bring you. For now, the offenders are out on bail with conditions that include daily attendance at a local police station and no internet use.'

CONNOR: 'We're not certain of Bram Aalders's whereabouts, only that he's with his family somewhere in London, and none of them are giving interviews. Barry Cates is staying with his father in Somerset and also blocking interviews. Lisa McIlvoy . . . Well, you might be surprised to hear where she is.'

As the recording ended, all eyes went to Romy. She seemed lost in her own thoughts, until eventually she said, 'Would you like me to talk about her now?'

'Only if you want to,' Cristy replied.

Romy gave it a moment and nodded.

Connor quickly reached into his workbag and brought out a small case of lapel mics to pin on everyone present – not an easy job in summer, when there were no thick jumpers or sturdy collars to support the devices. However, the scalloped neckline of Romy's cream-coloured T-shirt held firm, as did the wide shoulder strap of Cristy's pale-blue shift dress and Layla's bright-yellow tank top. Connor's black and beige polo shirt wasn't a problem at all, and there was always the table mic as back-up.

'OK,' he said, sitting down again. 'If everyone's ready . . .'

Romy rose to her feet, and Cristy turned to see who she was holding her hands out to. Although it wasn't a complete surprise to find Lisa McIlvoy standing on the threshold of the music room, it had caught her slightly unaware.

'You were listening,' Romy said, encouraging her to come forward.

Lisa didn't deny it, only said to Layla, 'I can make more coffee if you like.'

'No, no, please sit here,' Romy insisted, indicating the chair the other side of her. 'If we're going to talk about you, you should at least hear what we have to say.'

Lisa almost smiled at that, and Cristy noticed there was a slightly healthier hue to her complexion and hair than the last time she'd seen her. The weeks since her arrest had treated her far more kindly than she deserved, at least in Cristy's opinion, although she'd be the first to admit she was no Romy.

Passing Lisa a coffee, Layla said, 'Is Therese still here?'

'She's just left,' Lisa replied, her Scottish burr seeming more pronounced this morning, 'but she'll be back to see Romy later.'

This was the art therapist Romy had engaged to help both her and Lisa to work through their recent traumas, and Cristy could only reflect on how typical it was of Romy that she was playing to Lisa's strengths by steering them both along a path that she would be comfortable with.

'How are things going on the therapy front?' she asked, looking from one to the other.

Romy turned to Lisa, eyes shining with fondness. 'I think we're making progress, don't you?' she said.

Lisa rolled her eyes. 'There's so much hard stuff to deal with, but she seems kind of happy with you. Not sure about me, but I guess it takes time to transition from being a total basket case to a fully functioning normal.'

'Well, that's one way of phrasing it.' Romy laughed. 'But she tells me that you're showing a lot of bravery in the way you're expressing things that happened in the past through your art.'

Blushing slightly, Lisa said to Cristy, 'I still can't quite believe this woman next to me is for real, and I've spent so much time with her now. I mean, when did *you* ever meet anyone like it?'

Smiling, Cristy said, 'I must admit she's pretty unique.'

'As are we all in our own ways,' Romy told them knowingly. 'Now, shall we continue?'

Aware that Connor was already recording, Cristy said, 'We're on it, so let's just keep going. You're staying here at the manor, Lisa – is that right?'

Seeming embarrassed again, Lisa said, 'I know, weird, isn't it . . . ?'

'She didn't have anywhere else to go when they gave her bail,' Romy interrupted, 'and she'd already set up a studio here, so it made sense for her to come back. She's very talented, you know, and needs encouraging.'

Cutting in, Connor said, 'Can we ask what happened to the portraits we saw upstairs in the studio? Are they still there?'

Lisa looked pinched and miserable, a brief outward show

of the tangled and debilitating emotions she was struggling with, the chaos of unholy horrors she'd both witnessed and been a part of that were clearly still haunting her. At least it meant she had a conscience; that was one thing in her favour.

Answering the question, Romy said, 'They've gone. The police took them.'

'Were they of potential new targets?' Connor asked bluntly.

Lisa's eyes stayed down. 'Yes,' she answered quietly, 'they were, but the subjects have been informed, and it's been established that no harm has come to them.'

'Unlike the couple you targeted on Exmoor?' Connor pressed.

Lisa's eyes filled with anguish and protest as she looked at him. 'I didn't know what had happened to them until you put it in a podcast,' she cried. 'After I left . . . I didn't have any more contact with them. Bram wouldn't allow it, and I felt so bad about what he was doing—'

'So why didn't you stop him?' Connor cut in forcefully.

Lisa flinched and regarded him helplessly, apparently having no excuse or explanation for her failure.

Romy said, 'She was afraid to stand up to Aalders, and please remember that this is the kind of thing she's addressing with her therapist, so I don't think it's a good idea to bully her now. If you don't mind.'

Connor's eyes went to Cristy, and seeing how much further he'd like to dig into this, she decided it was time to take over. 'Perhaps you can tell us why there was one of Barry?' she said to Lisa. 'Was he supposed to be a target?'

Lisa shook her head. 'No, no. He asked me to do it. I think it was supposed to be a gift for his mother.'

Under her breath, Layla muttered, 'Deluded.'

Romy said, 'Our plan, with the lawyer, is to present Lisa to the judge as someone who's showing genuine remorse – which she most definitely feels – and who's receiving professional help to overcome her very difficult start in life. By the time we go to court, we're certain she'll be ready to move forward as a more rounded and responsible citizen. Plus, she will have a job and somewhere to live. That will certainly count for a lot.'

'A job?' Connor queried.

Romy looked surprised. 'As a portraitist,' she reminded him, as if no ill-use of this talent had ever been made or would ever be held against Lisa in the future. Cristy almost smiled. Romy's disingenuousness, or blank refusal to accept obvious obstacles of any kind was as remarkable as the woman herself.

'And you know about our other project?' Romy continued. 'It's still early days, of course, but Lisa's helping with that. As is Layla, and Johnny's going to join us when things are more settled with Barry.'

'You're talking about your plans to set up a refuge for abused women?' Cristy asked, aware of a car arriving at the front of the house.

'That's right. We've already had a meeting with an architect to discuss converting some of the outbuildings here, and we're hoping to meet one of the town planners next week. And in case your listeners are wondering about where the money's coming from . . . Actually, they'll probably be more interested to hear how much was stolen . . . Well, it seems some of it might still exist in the cloned accounts and investments, although the greater likelihood is that it's all long gone by now.'

Although Romy seemed saddened by that, and even bizarrely mystified, what struck Cristy the most was that she was able to talk about it with no hint of bitterness or anger.

'What upsets me about it,' Romy continued, gazing at the robin now, 'is that it belonged to Rudi. No one had the right to take it from him, and I still don't understand why anyone would when he was always so generous.'

Having to accept that Romy's mindset wasn't quite the same as most other people's, Cristy watched the robin go to perch on the back of an empty chair. 'But you haven't been left destitute?'

'No, I don't think so,' Romy replied, 'but maybe. There's still a lot to be sorted out. At least the house is still in my name.'

Cristy's eyes moved to Lisa, who was also watching the robin.

'I didn't know anything for certain,' Lisa said, 'but Bram was definitely planning to move on in the next week or so, and his usual MO when that happened was "to clean out and clear off", as he put it. That meant leaving nothing behind.'

'I can't actually access any of my accounts at the moment,' Romy admitted, 'but friends are being very generous in helping to tide me over, and of course, I'm getting a lot of very welcome advice and support from your wonderful David. He's so knowledgeable, isn't he? And very patient. I'm sure he must want to shake me until I rattle at times.'

Cristy smiled. 'He has his good points,' she said dryly, knowing that David, like everyone else, had fallen under Romy's spell.

She turned to where he'd come to stand in the doorway, leaning against the frame, arms folded as he listened to their chat. His look of amusement confirmed what she'd suspected, that he hadn't realized she knew he was there.

'Will you have a coffee?' Romy invited, going to greet him.

'I'll get another mug,' Layla said, springing up.

'No, don't let me interrupt,' he protested. 'I can sort myself out. We'll talk later,' he said to Romy. 'Just a couple of things for you to sign.'

Satisfied with that, Romy returned to the table as David dropped a quick kiss on Cristy's forehead, saluted Connor and went off to the kitchen.

Layla was the first to resume the chat. 'Can you tell us if

Barry was involved in setting up the final sting, if we can call it that?' she asked Lisa.

Lisa's colour rose, and for a fleeting moment, Cristy actually felt sorry for her. It couldn't be easy sitting here being interrogated by those she'd wronged, so she surely deserved some credit for facing it.

'I can only tell you that Barry was mostly keeping out of the way by then,' Lisa said, 'so I don't think he was involved.'

'Which doesn't explain why he didn't tell us where to find Romy,' Layla said coldly.

'He was almost as scared of Bram as I was,' Lisa told her, 'but you're right: he could have raised the alarm sooner. We both could. In my case, I was afraid of what he might do to Romy before I could get her free. In Barry's . . . Well, I guess he should speak for himself.'

'Not much chance of that,' Layla snorted sourly, 'but I can tell you, it would have been all about saving his own skin. He knew he was going to be locked up for the part he played in it all, and he just couldn't face it. Plus, I guess it was still making him rich.'

'His accounts have been frozen,' Cristy pointed out, 'and I imagine there's a chance his willingness to work with the police, plus his therapy sessions, will present well to the judge to help reduce his sentence.'

'Which could be,' Connor said, needing to get it in for the record, 'a hefty seven year stretch as things stand. Could be ten for Aalders.'

'As far as I'm concerned,' Layla stated, 'it's no more than either of them deserves. Much less in fact, especially in Aalders's case. In my opinion, he should be going down for life. Barry too, for what he did . . .'

'Layla,' Romy chided.

'I mean it,' Layla told her. 'Poor boy didn't get enough attention when he was younger, wasn't made to feel special enough, so thought it would be a good idea to make himself look big by stealing your and Rudi's money to help pay for Mum's treatment. What the actual fuck?'

Having very little sympathy for Barry herself, but not wanting to dwell on him any longer, Cristy said, 'I guess what really matters now is that Romy has been able to return to her home. Are you still in touch with the Kesingers?' she asked Romy.

'Now and again,' Romy replied, refilling her glass with water. 'Apparently, they're pursuing a case of their own to try and get back the three-quarters of a million they paid in rent since they took the place on. Can you imagine charging them such a sum?'

'Can you imagine being able to pay it?' Connor muttered.

Romy smiled, and both she and Cristy watched as the robin finally flew off.

'OK, anything we haven't covered yet?' Connor asked, checking his script.

Cristy glanced at Romy's notebook on the table. 'Is there something you'd like to share with us?' she asked.

Seeming surprised, Romy put a hand on it and said, 'No, no – I just like to keep it with me. That's all. Sorry, have I misled you again?'

Cristy smiled and said to Connor, 'Maybe play the closing link?'

Quickly calling it up on his laptop, he hit play and sat back in his chair to listen along with everyone else.

CONNOR: 'Before we go, we've been given clearance from the police to share some information that could well be related to this case. No confirmation of that yet, but apparently, in the last few days, hundreds of arrests have been made in Nigeria at an office block on the outskirts of the capital, where it's believed a very well-organized gang of online scammers were operating. It's likely Bram Aalders was working with them – remotely, of course. Most of those arrested are presumed to have been recruited for their computer skills. Unfortunately, the dark forces behind them – thought to be from China and the Philippines – remain at large.'

He paused the recording to see if anyone had anything to say about the news, but for the moment, it seemed they were all still taking it in, and maybe thinking, as Cristy was, of Weeks's warning that the taking down of gangs was one thing but dealing with the 'dark forces' another altogether. They were Hydra-like. Remove one head and another would spring up to replace it.

'We need Hercules and his nephew,' Romy said, proving that she was indeed thinking along the same lines as Cristy. 'But at least these arrests are going to save someone, that's what's important.'

'Maybe hundreds, even thousands,' Layla added hopefully.

Deciding not to mention the fortunes that had probably already been lost to these people, and the lives ruined, Cristy signalled for Connor to let the tape run.

CONNOR: 'That's it for this truly chilling episode of *Hindsight*, detailing how artificial intelligence can be – and is being – used by an ever-growing number of malign players to come for you and yours.

'We'd like to thank . . .'

Frowning, Cristy held up a hand for him to stop. 'Does that sound sinister enough?' she asked. 'It needs to really hit home just how vulnerable we all are to what's coming down the line. It might have been your delivery,' she told him. 'It needs more emphasis on *you* and *yours*.'

Connor tried it out, played it back and nodded in agreement. 'I think I scared myself there,' he said, only half-jokingly. 'It's true, though: we really do need to hammer it home, because we never think these things will happen to us. All the really bad stuff is what happens to somebody else.'

'Unless you're Romy,' Layla reminded him grimly.

Realizing his mistake, he quickly offered an apology.

Cristy watched Lisa bow her head, and she wondered if she was as overcome with shame as she appeared. She wanted to believe it, and in Lisa's favour, she was at least still here listening and, even to a degree, taking part.

Romy said cheerily, 'I hope you, Connor and David are still planning to stay for lunch, Cristy. Layla and I have prepared some cold plates and salads. There's plenty to go round.'

'Sounds perfect.' Cristy smiled, spotting David carrying a coffee over to the balustrades while talking to someone on his mobile. To her amusement, the robin reappeared to join him.

'And will the others be coming?' Romy asked, starting to clear the table. 'Clove and Jacks?'

'They should be here any minute,' Cristy assured her.

She inhaled deeply and closed her eyes, finding she needed a moment to release herself from the encompassing demands of the podcast, the pressures of telling Romy's story in a way to both resonate and inform. She had spent so much time with it over the past few weeks, had immersed herself almost exclusively in the horror and sadness of it, not to mention the threats everyone with a computer and smartphone was facing that she knew she'd been neglecting her own world. But it was OK; Matthew was back at work, and the children were where they were supposed to be, so she had no need to worry about them – at least not today.

Becoming aware of the continuing birdsong, the distant sound of a farm machine, the squeal and clang of a nearby kissing gate as a gardener came in from the next field, she opened her eyes again. No one had left the table; they were discussing the various soundbites Connor had begun to play back, their favourite so far being the part when he'd announced that this was a cautionary tale for our times.

Deciding to leave them to it, she wandered across the terrace to join David. The robin was still there, its tiny head tilted to one side as it watched her come.

'Hey,' David said, putting his phone away as she reached him.

Enjoying the intimacy of his tone, and the way his eyes seemed to shut out everyone but her, she said, 'Romy's right about your patience.'

He nodded, clearly agreeing – and it took only a moment for her to realize he wasn't thinking about Romy.

She smiled. 'You know I do, don't you?'

'Do what?' he countered.

'Love you.'

He frowned, as if assessing. 'Could do better,' he told her.

Wanting to laugh, while wishing they were completely alone, Cristy said, 'OK, David Gaudion, I love you.'

He raised a hand to her face, and as his mouth came to hers, Connor called from the table, 'FYI, we're still recording.'

Everyone laughed, and Cristy turned to treat them to a meaningful look, while David pulled her back against him and wrapped her in his arms.

'I'll take it,' he shouted over her shoulder, as the robin hopped along the balustrade. 'I can always use it to remind her any time she forgets.'

Acknowledgements

It's always a great pleasure to thank those who were involved in helping to bring a book together and considering the huge, yet subtle complexities of Romy's story, I have one person to thank above all others. Professor Larry Bull of the School of Computing and Creative Technologies at the University of the West of England. Larry let me loose in a world completely unknown to me, urging me to understand that these days, thanks to Artificial Intelligence, virtually anything is possible. The sophistication and infiltration of scams into our lives has become increasingly horrific and is all too often undetectable until it's too late. What happened to Rudi and Romy in this story, with their identities not only being stolen, but cloned, is apparently not difficult to pull off, and could actually prove a whole lot worse than I was able to imagine. So, a cautionary tale for us all to stay vigilant or we could end up meeting ourselves in places we've never been, doing things we'd never dream of!

I'd also like to thank Denise and Mike Hastie for sharing their long experience of the Algarve with me. A highly treasured few days with my dearest friends, researching, exploring, swimming, surfing, eating and drinking. Nothing not to love there! (I lied about the surfing!)

Huge thanks and much love to my crack publishing team at HarperCollins, and to my fantastic agent, Luigi Bonomi, for making the painful bits easy and the pleasurable bits cause for celebration with dizzying regularity. It's an honour and a joy to work with you guys – maybe this is a good opportunity to apologize for the times frustration gets the better of me and I am not operating as my best self!

Last, but never least, my love and thanks to James Garrett who's always there for me and somehow manages to navigate the unnavigable seas of living with an author.

**Don't miss the next gripping thriller in
the Cristy Ward series...**

Who Can You Trust?

Twenty years ago, Nicole's twins disappeared without a trace.

No bodies. No witnesses.

Despite her pleas of innocence, Nicole was convicted.
Now she's confessed and she's out.

But for true crime podcast host Cristy Ward,
the story doesn't add up.

Having worked on the case as a young reporter,
Cristy can't help but wonder whether Nicole is
the villain everyone believes her to be.

Why did Nicole confess after so many years . . . and
is the truth still out there, waiting to be found?